BLOW UP THE ASHES

AMERICAN MAYHEM, VOL. 2

GUERNICA WORLD EDITIONS 73

BLOW UP THE ASHES

AMERICAN MAYHEM, VOL. 2

PERRY GLASSER

GUERNICA
World
EDITIONS

TORONTO—CHICAGO—BUFFALO—LANCASTER (U.K.)
2023

This is a work of fiction. Names, characters, places and incidents
are products of the author's imagination
and are used fictitiously. Any resemblance to actual persons,
living or dead, is coincidental. Time and geography
are distorted for the sake of the fiction. References
to historical figures should in no way be understood
to be accurate representations of the facts of those people's lives.

Guernica Editions Founder: Antonio D'Alfonso
Michael Mirolla, general editor
Scott Walker, editor
Cover design: Allen Jomoc, Jr.
Interior design: Jill Ronsley, suneditwrite.com

Guernica Editions Inc.
287 Templemead Drive, Hamilton (ON), Canada L8W 2W4
2250 Military Road, Tonawanda, N.Y. 14150-6000 U.S.A.
www.guernicaeditions.com

Distributors:
Independent Publishers Group (IPG)
600 North Pulaski Road, Chicago IL 60624
University of Toronto Press Distribution (UTP)
5201 Dufferin Street, Toronto (ON), Canada M3H 5T8

First edition.
Printed in Canada.

Legal Deposit—Third Quarter
Library of Congress Catalog Card Number: 2023936020
Library and Archives Canada Cataloguing in Publication
Title: Blow up the ashes : American mayhem. Vol. 2 / Perry Glasser.
Names: Glasser, Perry, author.
Series: Guernica world editions (Series) ; 73.
Description: First edition. | Series statement: Guernica world editions ; 73
Identifiers: Canadiana (print) 20230220444 | Canadiana (ebook)
20230220452 | ISBN 9781771838580 (softcover) | ISBN 9781771838597 (EPUB)
Classification: LCC PS3557.L335 B56 2023 | DDC 813/.54—dc23

for
the Moofky–Boofky Mob
with gratitude to Sam, Crowbah, Ketch, Bro, and Kels

Plants that cannot bloom by day
Must flower in the night
—Jack Traylor w/The Jefferson Airplane

Buckles Sinclair, in search of a revolution, crossed the one nation, under God, indivisible, with liberty and justice for all, on a stolen BMW motorcycle named Lilith.

In the same nation, Pierre Doucet shook out his rain-soaked umbrella and found KJ Sinclair working as a bored clerk in a bookstore.

And this was also the one nation under God, indivisible where, had she not been mounting tornadoes, wise Grandma Dot surely would have pointed out that Pierre Doucet's story required complete telling. As she—Grandma—fervently believed, no narrative of a life properly begins with birth.

We are who we are because of those who came before.

1926

HIS LIPS SO CLOSE HIS breath tickled her ear, the sailor shouted, "That cat plays hotter than Beiderbecke!"

"What's a Beiderbecke?"

"Not what. Who. Bix. Bix Beiderbecke, sister. Just the hottest cornet ever was and ever will be."

"Oh. Him. Sure. Bix."

Kolinda Doucet was unsure how she had arrived on the sailor's lap.

The room spun, a new feeling that was mostly good when it was not outright bad. Her sailor smelled of tobacco, beer, stale sweat, and good times. A dark wet oval on the belly of her cotton blue shift clung to her like a second skin. When she pinched and tugged a bit of her neckline, the material peeled away. She pursed her lips to blow down her own chest, but that left her no cooler. The sudden view down of her chest was not lost on her sailor, so she tugged at the shift a second time, holding it away from herself long enough that he got himself a good look.

Her sailor was a real-life Navy pilot, the genuine article. His warm hand was on her bare knee. When his hand inched up her thigh, she pushed it away, gentle-like, and he must have been raised proper because he did not try that again right off, but took his time, the hand creeping under her blue shift like a cat hunting in tall grass. When she firmly gripped his wrist, he respectfully did not force the issue, though his fingers continued to knead her thigh like bread dough. That had no offense to it; it felt dreamy.

1

Irene, the mother-loving little chickenshit, would want to know every detail, so Kolinda tried to commit every sensation to memory, a hopeless task. Too much was happening too fast. Beer was turning her memory into warm shit. That very afternoon in the clearing in the woods where they smoked Irene's stolen Xanthia's, they'd plotted their escapade, pledging no excuses and no backing down. They'd compare notes in the morning, but get laid that very night. Then, free as birds, they'd say farewell to Pensacola.

But the plan had already gone awry; here was Kolinda with a sailor's hand trilling up her skirt, but Irene was nowhere to be seen.

Earlier, Kolinda had shimmied into the blue cotton shift she kept for special occasions, though there were never no special occasions ever since her Daddy blew his fool brains out, and there had been pitiful few before that. The shift was not much more than a cotton slip that had once belonged to her older sister. Kolinda had tiptoed down the upstairs hall to the window that opened easy because the sash weight rope had rotted through. When the window fell shut it would sound loud as the Final Trump, so she left a piece of broken broom handle jammed in the sill for her return. She stepped through one leg at a time, and then skittered across several feet of tar-roof shingles to shinny down the drainpipe. On the ground, Kolinda checked herself for splinters, rubbed her hands clean of rust with spit, and set out to walk the perimeter of the airbase to find herself a Navy pilot, the only kind of man worth giving herself to.

At the worst part of the abandoned airbase road, one side hugged a mile strip of piney woods. Uncaring trees loomed skyward; weeds struggled to grow higher than men through crumbling concrete. Voices in the rustling weeds called to her, 'linda, 'linda, 'linda. On the road's other side, the ground was carpeted by sparking souls come down from Heaven now trapped as moonbeams in green shards of glass, all that was left of barrack windows shattered by rock-hurling boys who planned to be the next Walter Johnson. Softer than the voices of the dead whispering to her from the weeds was the distant rumble of waves that surged and retreated and surged again to fall on an unseen pebbly shore, the endless groans of drowned men died before their time. Where the drained swamp crept back to reclaim what it would always own and could never really lose, the air smelled of brackish water and rot gone mushy white. Mosquitoes had pestered her neck and legs; cold ghostly fingers clutched her bare arms for the dead envied the living.

Kolinda ran full out, her eyes squeezed shut lest she recognize a spirit among the dead. When she stopped, she spit three times to her left to appease the dead pilots forever barred from Paradise. They'd burned alive in crashed biplanes made of balsa wood and canvas, cast down for drawing too near Heaven, and so would forever walk the earth and hover in the wind of this world having died without Confession. The half-moon, a crescent like a rudderless boat, sailed amid stars on a sea of shredding clouds over the earth.

At their little clearing, she gasped, "Irene?" then waited while bugs made supper of her blood. Her hands had gone to her knees while the stitch in her side eased. An owl fluttered, the sound of its wings first halting and then quickening her heart. Her breath slowed.

Naturally, the bony milk-eyed bitch never showed up. She should have known the skank would leave Kolinda on her own.

At that moment, Kolinda could have chosen to return home. She'd have been free to lord it over Irene on any other day. She could have created an elaborate tale about how she'd dazzled servicemen and musicians and had become the toast of the Navy, the belle of the ball. She could boast about a dozen wavy-haired sailors and blue-eyed pilots mad for her, how she spurned them all until she settled on a shy, soft-spoken pilot fair as Gary Cooper in *Wings*. She could have told any lie at all. But Kolinda saw no reason to postpone the good times awaiting her beyond Pensacola just because her bony-ass girlfriend proved gutless.

So she'd pushed herself beyond the grasp of the spirits two hundred yards further down the dark road to a place with some light where the aromas of cayenne, oil, and ether displaced the smell of death. Ether, injected by big hypodermic needles through cork stoppers, added a powerful kick to ersatz beer. Stronger, local hooch was coaxed from corn mash in copper kettles in the hill country to the north, the quality of a community's white lightning being a point of local pride. With food coloring, tea, maybe a dash of shellac, coal tar, or benzene, once a label was pasted on a bottle, moonshine transformed into scotch, rye, whiskey, or bourbon. Gin began life as turpentine in bathtubs before anyone added juniper, while rum, the genuine article, was not home brew but came ashore carried by speedboats from far off Cuba, a place where all they did was burn sugarcane, dance the rumba, roll cigars, smoke maryjane, and bless the stupid *Americanos* for making them rich.

F'true, Kolinda smelled the no-name juke-joint before she stepped 'round a bend to where her future beckoned with a crooked come-hither finger shaped by Dixieland music. She drew a deep breath at the cyclone fence, kicked at the unlocked gate, and wondered if she should have worn her one pair of good shoes to appear a little less country even though she was hardly bound for church. Barefoot would do. Unless she stepped on a pine cone, the ground never hurt her none. Then Kolinda summoned all the courage a sixteen-year-old girl required to thread her way among cars scattered this way and that over dark gravel. If gravel did not hurt her feet, nothing would.

The bouncer set on the tall stool at the door wore a crimson shirt, a camel-colored vest, and the fanciest brown buckled shoes Kolinda ever hoped to see. Wiry chest hair peeped from below his unbuttoned collar. His smile gleamed with one incisor filled by solid gold. He looked Kolinda up and down, shrugged, and informed her that if he learned she was whoring and failed to fork over his fifty percent, he'd have her ass in every way an ass could be had. "Those jugs ain't old enough to sag, so I expect you'll make plenty. Don't you forget good ol' Gus looking out for your interests at the door. Every mouse gets the same deal from good ol' Gus. Fifty percent, and not one red cent less." His arm backhanded the door open. He never took his eyes off her. The *fonchock* patted her behind as he allowed her to pass, but she pretended to like it.

She stepped into a cauldron of heat; music crashed over her like a hurricane surf. Tabasco and maryjane tickled her nose. Her eyes watered. The room held a half-dozen picnic tables scattered this way and that on the hard dirt floor, the wood bench seats worn slick by a thousand backsides. Three or four people sat hip to hip on each bench, more if the girls sat on the men's laps, which mostly they did. An entire table could tip if they did not keep the weight even. When a man beckoned to her, she sat beside him just as heaps of people toppled to the dirt floor and on each other. The ensuing hilarity was general. As the crowd drunkenly tried to stand, every part of Kolinda's body worth groping was groped. It only made her laugh harder. Over it all, the Dixieland music never, ever stopped.

Someone closed his big hand on Kolinda's small wrist, and she found herself in a clear space on the dirt floor. She was swung this way and that, passing from the arms of one sailor to another. There was nothing mean in it. She was dancing, was all. They gave Kolinda beer in stoppered Coke bottles. Her molars closed on a cork, yanked it free, and she spit the cork to the ground, an act that somehow won her all manner of applause. Her bare feet never hardly touched the dirt, the floor being covered by crumbling cork.

How she knew how to dance was a mystery, but she must have been good at it because it was an hour before they let her sit long enough to catch her breath. She did a jitterbug, the Black Bottom, and a Charleston, sailors tossing her from one hip to the other, the music stirring her bones, her blue shift riding above her hips. When Kolinda sailed through the air doing a Lindy Hop, everyone peered up her dress to see her bare legs, but nobody thought that a scandal. She wished she owned heels with straps that twined halfway up her calves, but mostly the women who had stylish shoes kicked them off to go as barefoot as she. At least she wore underwear, and that could not be said of every girl who danced as fiercely as Kolinda did.

It was a revelation. To dance you did not need to know how to dance. Like all the best things in life, you just did it.

She perched on the lap of her serviceman who admired Bix. He was arguing good-naturedly with his friends, and that alone seemed remarkable, the talk of grown men being wholly unknown to her. These handsome clear-eyed Navy men in khaki knew and cared for the great issues far from shitty Pensacola. It was Opening Day, whatever that meant, so they passionately debated whether Ruth was better than Hornsby, and whether the Senators would repeat over the Yankees. Her sailor placed his soft khaki cap smelling of sweat and lavender pomade on Kolinda's head where it slipped over her eyes. When she tipped his hat back off her face, she smiled, wondering if her uneven teeth were all right.

They clinked their green Coca-Cola bottles of foaming beer. There were glasses to be had, too, and a zinc bucket sloshing full of ice cold suds. All a body needed to do was dip her glass and drain it. Kolinda never had to pay. She was more welcome than a movie star. Her tiny damp hand and fingers explored the sailor's hard chest and shoulders through his shirt, and when he stroked her back and pulled her close to put his tongue in her ear, *frissons* spread the length of her neck and arms.

"You like that?" he whispered.

She nuzzled his neck and thought she might mount him right there; when she felt him go hard she realized she was sitting in a puddle of her own creation.

They went for fresh air, walking into the hot night. Sweat ran off her as if her skin had sprung a leak. Nothing could take the heat from her face, and damn! but her sailor was handsome, brown-eyed, blond and wavy-haired with a lop-sided smile, she saw in the late moonlight. When she asked if he'd been to France, he said he expected to see France any day now.

"I'm a Kansas boy, but I joined after the war to see a whole mess of places. Can't keep this boy down on the farm."

"What's it like to fly?"

"Well, I guess there's nothing better," he said. His hand was on her breast and her nipple rose to meet his palm. He boasted that he soared among the clouds about every day. "I expect I'll be the first pilot to cross the Atlantic to see Paris. There's a prize, you know. A big prize. This is 1926. It's the new age! I 'spect I'll fly around the world if they make a plane good enough. Someone has to be first, right? I am just the guy to do it."

They sat on a weathered rail fence far from any light, the throbbing Dixieland a distant heartbeat. The crescent moon went from silver to red as it sank to the other side of the world. Her sailor asked about her, really asked as if he was really interested and her opinions mattered. She told him a pack of lies about her family and their money. "My Daddy owns the nickelodeon in town. I had to sneak out because they don't approve of me having a good time."

The truth was that her father, a Cajun shrimper from outside Dulac, down Louisiana way, had given up that good bayou life near water for the life of a storekeeper. He'd thought to settle in New Orleans, but Kolinda's mother, his good wife, would not tolerate that sinkhole of depravity. Instead, while the war raged on, Rennie Doucet took his chance to make his fortune by selling his share of a boat to raise the down payment on a Pensacola general store complete with its inventory of buttons, tools, hardware, and bolts of linen and gingham. He expected his fortune would grow with the expansion of the nation's first Naval air station right there in Pensacola.

But then peace broke out. It was ruinous.

The first Naval air station was dismantled piece by piece. Kolinda was eleven the Saturday evening Daddy quietly worked his tallies for the week, locked the register, retreated to the store's back room, sat on the warped wooden floor with his back against the door where the *gros couillion* closed his lips around the business end of a Remington deer rifle. An eyeball somehow exploded from his head to land intact in his lap. Ever since, Kolinda's mother had taken in laundry and stitched dresses for the most disgusting people in all of the Florida panhandle. Once you have gazed into a hifalutin lady's drawers, it is impossible to ever again think of her as high and mighty.

Kolinda's head flew loop-de-loops, as much from the alcohol as her pilot's gentle hand roaming over her, lingering here, pressing there, moving to another place between her knees until she felt sure every inch of her would burst into a torch right there on the fence. Clouds shredded, stars twinkled. Her sailor-pilot described the perils of an Immelmann Turn as his fingertips traced that maneuver on the bare skin at the back of her neck.

"I expect I'll be a movie star," she said, trying to slow things down, turning her head just the same as Louise Brooks, the pouting black-haired actress who ruined men for sport.

He pointed to the brightest star and said: "Like that one?" But she did not laugh because her eyes closed when his lips nibbled at the back her neck.

"Maybe I am shooting a little high," she murmured, grasped his wrist, and pulled his hand to the upper limit of her thigh. Her eyes closed. The world spun faster. She squirmed.

Her pilot's other hand parted the buttons on the front of her dress, and he said he did not think Kolinda aimed too high. He kissed her bare chest. "I've been in the sky," he said, "and I never seen no star pretty as you."

Frissons rippled through her smooth as midnight swells on a lake with neither breeze nor moon.

She led him twenty yards farther down the road to deeper shadows. With her back against an old palm tree she lifted her dress. She could not recall where she had lost her cotton pants. Far off, bottles clinked and faint jazz thumped and throbbed. The air was as hot and wet as she; her sailor's hands on her became less gentle and more urgent; his kisses to her throat drove her wild. She tugged his belt loose. When his trousers fell, he held her knee so she could stand on one leg. She gripped him as he entered her. Their damp thighs slipped and slapped. She bit his lip.

Five days later, without ever seeing Kolinda again, her sailor shipped out for the New Hampshire Portsmouth Naval Shipyard. No flier, he was a seaman first class, talented with gasoline engines. The closest he ever came to soaring in any airplane was to set the timing on the pistons that spun a biplane prop. He bragged to his mates about the green-eyed girl whose name he did not know but who was so dumb she thought he was a pilot.

"A pilot?"

"Well, I flew her, didn't I?"

Kolinda for a time was a regular at the no-name roadhouse, but since she was never with no other pilot nor sailor, when she missed two periods and could not keep breakfast down, having seen her mother through four pregnancies, she knew what was what. The Doucet Luck meant no luck at all. Drop her drawers just oncet, and fast as Fertile Myrtle she made a baby.

She douched with Coca-Cola and spent hours jumping up and down, but her nipples darkened and her ass spread. That baby was going nowheres.

She made the additional mistake of telling Irene she was pregnant. The milk-eyed bitch had it in her pea-sized brain to lord it over Kolinda. "That's what happens to loose girls," Irene said.

"You was supposed to do it that same night!" Kolinda said, but Irene's lips grew thin with unforgiving moral superiority. She avoided Kolinda as if pregnancy was a contagion. To guard her reputation and elevate her own popularity, Irene blabbed Kolinda's secret to anyone who would listen, which was most everyone. Someone else's troubles are always a welcome distraction. The milk-eyed bitch and her big mouth remained as unpopular as ever, but Kolinda's news made Kolinda the object of rolled eyes, whispered giggles, unkind remarks, and offers from acne-ridden boys who pestered Kolinda to accommodate them based on the irrefutable logic that since she no longer had nothing to lose, why not?

In time, a school committee came to the Doucet parlor to explain to Kolinda's mother that her daughter was now unwelcome in the town school and would be for at least the considerable time of lying in after her child's birth. Their logic also was irrefutable: "We can't allow the boys to be distracted."

After the school committee made its way down the gray un-
painted porch stairs of the old farmhouse the Doucets were
hardly able to afford, Mrs. Doucet slapped Kolinda's cheek. Then
her mother went to her bedroom and shut her door. She did not
emerge for a day. Rolling a cigarette while she was alone in the
woods, feeling gas bubble up in her belly and an itch that must
have been a hemorrhoid, Kolinda allowed herself one good cry, the
last tears of her life, as she relinquished her dirt common dreams.
Louise Brooks? Mary Pickford? She was a barefoot country round
heels who spread her legs for a Navy pilot whose name neither she
nor her child would ever know, though she'd always remember the
worthless prick's sad eyes.

The shame Kolinda brought down on the Doucets was worse
than the shame brought by her older brother, Andre, the convict.
Andre was doing time in the county lockup for driving a bootlegger's truck, ever since he explained to a magistrate that he'd been
told he loaded molasses that somehow along the road had soured
into beer, a miracle of chemistry. After Daddy blew his head off,
Andre remained the only Doucet male in the Doucet household, so
the judge took pity. He was sent to county for illegally operating a
motor vehicle in Escambia County, not for being no bootlegger, a
federal offense. In truth, Andre did his six months in county instead
of a federal pen because no one gave a rat's ass about no boy who
violated the Volstead Act.

Kolinda waddled over to her brother to sit beside him in the
sun on a bench in the jailyard. County was not what no one would
call hard time. Andre's smile was big as ever. She had smuggled him
some cigarettes. He offered to send a friend to find the father of her
baby and mete out justice with a baseball bat. "He needs to do the
right thing, 'linda."

She confessed she had no idea where her pilot was except he
might be living the high life in gay Paree.

"Damn, 'linda, how did you get into this mess?"

"I guess I did it the usual way."

Andre thought a bit. "I could get you drunk and then take care of it. I'll be out soon." Taking care of it meant he might punch 'linda in the belly until she bled, and though the pain would mean little to her, she dismissed the idea out-of-hand. She also dismissed out-of-hand his suggestion to pay a visit to a certain cabin in the woods occupied by a Root Lady. Andre's friends swore the Root Lady cast all manner of spells that would get a girl out of trouble sure as the tea she brewed from tree bark and special mushrooms. The tea had to be followed by a knitting needle probe, but while it was true that some girls left the Root Lady with poisoned blood, Andre believed that poisoned blood was a risk worth taking.

"It ain't your blood, now, is it?" 'linda said. Though none of the Doucets had seen the inside of a church since they buried what was left of headless Daddy, Kolinda feared the certain pains of Hell awaiting those who defied God to scrape a woman's innards bare of life. Besides, her baby was her last and only friend.

She left her brother to walk slowly over hard ground and yard dust to the bus that stopped across the way from the jail gate. If that bus could not rattle her baby loose, nothing could. The tiny life within her clung hard. On the ride home, 'linda whispered promises to her determined child. If Jesus wanted him, she would reluctantly give her baby up, but otherwise she would hold him forever. She was certain she carried a boy. When on the bus her baby kicked at her hand, 'linda knew a pact had been sealed. Her boy was going nowhere but out into the world in his own sweet time.

That same week Andre was out and made a beeline to either Detroit or to Blazes, two places that in Kolinda's mind were pretty much the same places. One day her only ally in the family was there, the next all that remained was 'linda, her mother, and her gaggle of sisters.

On a drizzly day in late December, 'linda felt the first contractions. It did not matter what the calendar said, her boy was on a schedule all his own. She never knew which of her sisters went for their mother, but she was helped to the big bed in her mother's room in which every member of the Doucet family for four generations had come into the world. Nineteen hours later, New Year's Day of 1927, her baby was born with his mother's near-black hair, his father's eyes brown as bitter chocolate, ten fingers and ten toes, and a name borrowed from his Cajun grandparents still on the bayou.

Kolinda looked down at Petit Pierre not an hour old, breathed his sweet breath, peeled back his tight cotton swaddling, and peered through his eyes into his unsullied soul. She thanked the Good Lord he'd been born no girl, but then wept. Her mother and sisters smugly believed she wept with guilt, but that was untrue. Kolinda wept some for the all the trouble that surely would pursue her tiny *beau gamin* all the days of his life, but wept most at her certainty that she would never again produce anything quite so perfect.

1931–1942

SIX MEMBERS OF THE PARISH League of Decency stood in harsh sun to make their third and final appeal to save the soul of the unbaptized fatherless dark-eyed boy whose Papist mother might have lain with a nigger. Despite the heat and sun, the members of the League wore black.

The League was uneasy. The collapse of the stock market and the great Mississippi flood of 1927 were surely visitations of God, the signs of His displeasure at their failure to cast out the sinners among them. How or why the Lord wanted 250 souls drowned in Mississippi for sins in Florida's Escambia County would forever remain part of the Unknowable Plan, but the ways of the Lord were mysterious. Buoyed by righteousness, they once again had returned to the Doucet porch, this time prepared to offer Kolinda a bus ticket to anywhere. "And cash money you can carry. All we want is the boy to have a proper baptism so he can be raised proper at the League-sponsored orphanage."

Kolinda said not a word as she gently closed the door on them.

Earlier that week, Kolinda's sisters had blubbered to Mrs. Doucet that the reason no decent eligible men ever came calling was that every man within fifty miles expected a Doucet girl would spread easier than marmalade on hot toast, depravity being a well-known hereditary contagion. To her credit, Mrs. Doucet turned a deaf ear to her four youngest daughters, but that did not hold Kolinda safe from her sisters' dagger-sharp eyes and punishing sneers. They liked the baby boy well enough, but his aunts did nothing to keep their resentment of their sister a secret, whispering how the princess was still stupid enough to be waiting for her pilot prince to return to her. On meaner days, they danced and sang:

> *Come Josephine in my flying machine*
> *Going up she goes, up she goes*
> *Balance yourself like a bird on a beam*
> *In the air she goes, there she goes*

Kolinda searched for but found no forgiveness for them in her heart. Her sisters would never understand the peace that filled her when Petit Pierre took her breast. Neither her sisters nor the League understood that a sin of the flesh could deliver a miracle of the spirit. Kolinda expected she would someday see Hell, but she thanked God regularly for His mercy and the fullness of her life.

But it came time for her to move on. Before sunup on an early spring morning—her sleeping *beau gamin* limp and warm against her close in his sling—after Kolinda took the dollars due fair and square to her from the family flour bag in the pantry, with nary a goodbye she struck out for the two miles to the nearest paved highway.

Her unfamiliar shoes raised blisters, but she never looked back.

She had learned to sew on the Singer her mother had lugged with her from Louisiana. Kolinda liked the machine on account she could work it with Pierre close by her. She was as soothed as the boy by the cadence of the foot pedal, chewing a bit of white thread so she did not sew up the boy's brain. Sewing was considerable easier than having her knuckles and fingers go raw in a washtub of lye soap.

The carpetbag at her feet beside her and Pierre drowsy against her chest and shoulder, she hoped for a passing bus. Any direction would do. As her boy lazily took her nipple, she wondered if she'd be all day at the roadside swatting skeeters big as quarters.

Then her luck changed. A Buick driven by a dry goods salesman stopped to tell her he was on the long trip from Jacksonville to

Tupelo, every inch of the trip his exclusive territory. He considered himself a lucky man: a job, free to move about, and the loan of a company car.

"That's quite the coincidence," she said to be agreeable. "I am Mississippi bound, too. Waiting on the bus."

He was bald, with a furrowed scalp, and had a small harelip beneath his mustache. "You're in for an awful wait," he said. "No bus to Mississippi will pass here for two days coming."

So Kolinda and Pierre got in. Their whole time together, that good man required nothing of her, though Kolinda was ashamed to admit she had been prepared to do whatever she needed to do. It was good to know not every man wanted to do her dirt. Petit Pierre slept peacefully on the towel the salesman considerately spread on the back seat of that big fine car. His samples rattled in the exterior trunk while the salesman spoke softly for fear of waking the boy. Maybe he was reassuring only himself, but mostly he bragged how dry goods would sustain a working man no matter how bad the 'conomy might get. "In hard times poor people mend and patch and make clothes instead of store-bought. I've loaded up on cloth and thread." Kolinda remarked she knew the ways of a Singer, and the salesman said he believed that as long as she stayed clear of the communists in the mills, and as long as she'd be sure to tell any union agitator that she was a true American, she would never starve. "The Singer Sewing Machine has done more for women than any bunch of pea-brained suffragettes ever will," he said, but smiled at her.

They bounced along dusty rutted roads, Pierre sleeping through most of the trip, the first and last time Kolinda ever hitchhiked. The driver never asked why a boy of four was still at her breast, nor did he stare. The simple fact was that breast milk was free, and giving her breast to the *petit gamin* left them both peaceful.

In Tupelo, the salesman helped her with her carpetbag, into a Rexall where he bought Petit Pierre a ginger beer with ice and thanked Kolinda for her company. Then he motored off beneath a sun that seemed a gold coin burning over the roofs of Spring Street. Miraculously, she found a clean room. The landlady would for ten cents each day watch over Pierre and feed him sorghum or a bit of bread spread with molasses, and on some days a glass of milk. Then, an even greater sign from God, before her money ran out, in a land where there was no jobs, she found work stitching at the Tupelo Textile Company.

She had a roof and she could feed herself and her boy; what else was there?

The country skid from bad to worse. The problem, the best Kolinda could understand it, was that stores up north closed because they had too few customers, and they had too few customers on account of how everyone was losing their jobs, workers and customers in the grand scheme of things being the same people just looked at differently. The country dumped Hoover in 1932, but none of Mr. Roosevelt's alphabet programs included help for Tupelo Textiles with its single rust-stained toilet. Kolinda worked her twelve hours in light so dim she like to have gone blind, air so thick she hardly dared to breathe, and noise so loud she was deaf by day's end until she learned the trick of fashioning earplugs from candle wax.

Kolinda did not vote in 1932, but voted for Mr. Roosevelt in 1936. If they would have let her, she'd have voted for him twice. His voice on the radio was the clarion call of hope. Had she lived in Louisiana—a place where the dead were resurrected on Election Day sure as Jesus Christ rose to save us all—she'd have voted for the Kingfish, Huey Long, that champion of the common man, though once they knew Long wanted to share the wealth, they shot him dead right there in the Capitol Building.

Pierre grew faster than pigweed. The boy was never sick, likely because Kolinda continued to give him her breast at least once each day until he was six. They cut her to twenty-five hours, then twenty, but when there was talk of cutting her to fifteen, Kolinda said *fare thee well* to Tupelo. She and her *beau gamin* spent a little time in Pascagoula, where things were no better, then followed a rumor of jobs in Mobile, but that proved even worse. They settled in Biloxi, which was tolerable.

Kolinda survived because her occasional male friends were generous. They joined her behind the muslin curtain she tacked over her bedroom doorway after one caller complained that her boy's stare could turn auger holes through brick. "I know the Evil Eye when I see it," he'd said. Kolinda laughed at that, but no matter how generous he promised to be, she did not permit that man who might hex her boy to come around again, neither.

Finally, like a marble rolling free in a porcelain gravy boat, they settled into Gulfport where Kolinda took up with a shrimper named Charlie. Charlie loaned her enough money to pay for half of an old Singer. She managed four more monthly installments by eating smaller meals and by taking in enough mending that she kept at her machine until there was no light to see, and then she stayed more anyway.

She also stitched Simplicity Patterns that came to her all the way from Michigan. She told no one where her ideas came from, so she soon had a local reputation for original style and quality by attaching a belt here or turning a collar there in ways Simplicity never imagined. She was clever enough to save material by cutting fabric differently than the Simplicity people suggested. The pawnbroker received only one payment late, and then only by two days, so he had no complaints, money in his pocket beating all hollow having a battered sewing machine in his shop window.

Charlie often being at sea, Kolinda and Pierre celebrated the final payment by taking high seats on the rotating stools at the soda fountain at the local Rexall's. They shared a lime rickey with two straws. Pierre's feet dangled in empty space as he spun this way and that, sure the lime rickey was the bestest drink that could ever pass over a tongue, and sure Maman would love him forever.

Kolinda scared up a few paid hours at the Cosmetics counter in the Five & Dime. Still naturally pretty, though she was no Louise Brooks, she had learned the ways of powder, lipstick, rouge, and mascara. The fine ladies at the counter wanted lips like Lillian Gish and to look as perky as Claudette Colbert, even though they was twenty years older. Kolinda told them what they wanted to hear, how they looked just the same as those movie stars, and though most laughed at the patent lie, a few batted their eyes and willed themselves to believe it.

Petit Pierre believed Charlie to be his father until the hot night the shrimper beat on Maman even harder than usual. He split her lip and near broke her jaw. The drunken son-of-a-bitch blamed Kolinda for the flies that pestered him. He believed he was owed an unmolested life having survived Belleau Wood where he stood shoulder-to-shoulder with the doughboys of the Second Division and General "Black Jack" Pershing. After beating Maman bloody, Charlie staggered out into the darkness to piss on the white wall of the abandoned three-room shack Charlie had made his own, his due as a veteran. It had a water pump over the sink and glass in some of the windows. Charlie sang what words to *Lili Marlene* he could remember, mumbled the rest, then he fell asleep face down in a patch of struggling crabgrass and a puddle of his own piss.

Maman's eyes were both blackened, her left eye swollen shut. Her nose bled, but at least it was not broke. "Damned Jax," she said, a bubble of blood forming in the corner of her lip. Her *beau gamin* mutely watched her pain. He could not have said as much, but he knew he would not forever be ten years old and powerless. Maman stemmed the flow of blood by leaning her head over a flowered porcelain basin and pinching the bridge of her nose. She held a folded wet towel to her face. The water in the basin stained a deep pink. "Bringing back beer might have been the right thing for the 'conomy, but if Mr. Roosevelt should drop by Gulfport, I will offer the President my opinion of that peachy-keen notion." She threw her head back, gagged, and leaned forward again to spit a phlegmy clot of thickening crimson mucous into the basin.

The bleeding slowed. Maman chipped ice with an icepick. Petit Pierre silently wondered if the icepick was long enough to go through Charlie's ear and kill him. Maman wrapped a piece of ice the size of Pierre's fist in a towel, and held the dripping ice to her cheek. She needed to appear the next day at the makeup counter at the Five & Dime, not looking as if she'd gone ten rounds with Max

Schmeling, "Unless Maybelline starts a new line to close cuts and cover bruises." She daubed at her wounds. "I just might send them that idea. I might. Boxer Brown and Pugilist Pink. If they listen to your Maman, won't we live the high life then, *cher?*" Her index finger worked her loose teeth one by one until she was satisfied she would not lose any more than the one that lay in the porcelain bowl.

She lifted her *beau gamin* onto her lap. "It's time you knew that Charlie ain't your daddy," she said. "Don't never forget that." She chewed a cold square of wet terrycloth to relieve the ache in her jaw. "Am I still bleeding?" she asked. Pierre held a flickering candle close to Maman's face, electricity not yet being general in Gulfport, though with the TVA it was expected soon enough. Whether it would find its way to Charlie's shack was another matter.

Her left eye had swollen until it could not swell no more. Her ear was crusted with dried blood. "No, Maman. It stopped," Pierre said.

She hugged his slender shoulders and then with two hands held him standing directly before her so they were eye to eye. "All right, then. Now you mind that man like he *was* your daddy, as you do not want to be on the bad side of no drunk quick to use his hands, but you need to know he is not your daddy. You come from better than that." She leaned back. "Now fetch me some iodine. Be quick."

He clambered to the top of the kitchen counter to find the iodine by candlelight. Its poison skull on the label, the iodine stood in the cabinet behind a small bottle of vanilla and a half sack of cornmeal. Petit Pierre wondered how much iodine he might put in Charlie's coffee and whether that would go against Maman's wishes that he mind what Charlie said. "Then who is my daddy?" he asked as he climbed down.

"Why, your daddy flies airplanes, boy!"

"Better than Amelia Earhart?"

She pushed his straight brown hair from his dark eyes. "Now your daddy is a man, ain't he? Stands to reason he flies better than any Amelia Earhart. He would have been with Lindy except there was only the one seat in *The Spirit of St. Louis!*" She winced as Pierre daubed iodine to her wounds. "You just remember your daddy flies airplanes way up high in the sky, but that Charlie is way down below, nothing but a no-account shrimper who likes his damned Jax too much. Do you think any airplane pilot drinks Jax? They drink pink champagne all the day long, easy as you and me drink water."

"We should run away," the boy said, sure they needed no one other than each other.

Maman laughed aloud. "Boy, ain't you heard there's a Depression going on?" She hocked to spit a last gobbet of half-congealed blood into the basin.

Charlie might go shrimping for days, so there was always the chance that Charlie's boat would sink, he'd drown with a crew of other drunks, and then they would sink to Hell. But he always returned. When Charlie was shrimping, Maman and Petit Pierre were happy playing Boo-Ray, the Cajun card game they played for kisses. She allowed Petit Pierre to shuffle and deal most every hand.

Kisses, Maman, and cards were the stuff of Paradise.

One day Maman risked her job by not paying the Five & Dime where she worked for a brand new pack of Bee, the kind of playing cards with the red diamonds on the back. Petit Pierre crinkled the cellophane and first felt the slick feel and first heard the gunshot snap when he bowed the back of a card, pinched it between his thumb and middle finger, and flipped it face up. *Le beau gamin* had long and slender fingers, even for a boy.

Maman revealed the magic in the Cards, whispers of truth from the future that could be heard by those who knew to listen. Petit Pierre asked how such a thing could be. "Powerful forces are at work in the world. Just because they are unseen, don't mean they ain't powerful," Maman whispered. Pierre sat rigid on her lap. By candlelight, he saw all that Maman saw on the array before them. She shuffled, he blew a breath onto the deck, and she slowly turned cards face up.

"*Cher*, great things are coming toward you. You need only have the courage to make a clean start," she would say, no matter in what order the cards came. "The time is not yet, but it will come. The time will come."

That his fortune always seemed the same was solid proof the cards never lied. Maman explained how the King of Hearts, for example, had been disappointed in love, and so the Suicide King held his own sword in his own head. "Most everyone gets disappointed in love," Maman explained, "though only a *couillion* kills himself and leaves his family to face the hard world alone." The Ace of Spades was Death, not to be feared because Death came to everyone. The card simply meant change, most often. Twos meant love; black threes meant trouble, while red threes meant children. Tens promised riches, the ten of diamonds being richest of all.

The biggest secret the cards revealed to Maman was that her *beau gamin* was the Knave of Diamonds, a card that promised a future of good looks and great wealth in service to kings and queens.

Pierre went nowheres without his Bee deck in a back pocket. Though the cards went limp with handling, he enticed schoolboys to bet on high or low at a nickel each draw. When he and the boys grew older, the game became Blackjack, same as in any of the illegal casinos that dotted the Gulf coast.

Pierre could make it seem as if he dealt a fair game, but he did not. The long fingers of those fine hands could persuade most any card to come from the deck whenever he wanted. Cards made themselves known to him through his fingertips. He allowed the boys he liked to win now and again to keep them coming back, but they never suspected Pierre was anything but honest and lucky.

As he grew, Pierre regularly won sufficient money to buy whatever he needed whenever he needed it for himself and the occasional girl who found the Cajun boy with dark hair falling over his brown eyes to be of more than passing interest. He kept his money hid from Charlie in a pickle jar buried in a half foot of pebbly dirt beside a mostly rotten leafless tree. Charlie groused about how the boy had money without never doing a lick of honest work, so if he did not steal it, Charlie might beat Maman for giving her boy money rightly due him.

But Maman was concerned. How did her boy manage to always have money? Could *le beau gamin* have the same blood as his uncle, the long-vanished bootlegger Andre Doucet? She asked, "Tell Maman true, now *cher*. Do you steal?"

He confessed he was unsure if what he did was stealing. It was a game. People gave him money; they had fun; he threatened no one. So he showed her one day and shuffled the deck, then asked Maman to touch the top card and turn it over. It was the Queen of Hearts. Then he shuffled again and allowed her to cut twice. Once again, she turned over the top card, and once again it was the Queen of Hearts. She laughed and asked how her clever boy could do such a thing, so he showed her in slow motion what it was to palm a card, shuffle, allowed her to cut, and with a light pass of his hand drop the palmed Queen perfectly. She asked him to do it again, and though she never took her eyes off his hands, that queen sat atop the deck perfectly square. When she suddenly flipped his hand over, fast as her hand was, his was faster, able to invisibly flip and hide the palmed card behind his fingers.

"Is that stealing, Maman? I call a tune and *pour moi* the cards dance, *non?*"

She smoothed back his hair and kissed his forehead.

Three weeks before his fifteenth birthday, with no fair warning, the Japanese attacked Pearl Harbor, destroying much of the American Pacific fleet. The capsized USS *Arizona* held 1,177 men who survived explosions and gunfire only to drown or suffocate below decks, trapped in total darkness and rising water. Sailors on the nearby USS *Oklahoma* were captive in a dark world gone upside down when the *Oklahoma* went keel up. They pounded wrenches against the interior hull for most of a week before the pitiful noise grew faint and then stopped, their desperate *S.O.S* unanswered. The men who walked on the overturned steel hull wept. Acetylene torches applied day and night could not penetrate the steel.

Like most boys, Pierre was mad to be in the war. What if someone killed Hitler before he had his chance? The Germans planned to make Americans slaves and rape American women. The Japs planned to rape American women and only then murder all Americans. The tough talk at school was about where to shoot Hitler, head, heart, or belly? But general agreement was that Tojo had to be hanged by his balls.

Charlie's fists, boots, and a razor strop had instilled Pierre with plenty of fight. By December 7, 1941, Pierre had grown into an obstreperous boy who could endure a lot while planning his vengeance. His dark skin stretched tautly over his hairless chest and flat gut. His arms looked as if he had invested hours performing pull-ups, but he'd done nothing. He needed to shave but three times in a week, a schedule that would serve him all his life. His lean face and full lips were topped by honey brown eyes that sucked in all the world from under intense eyebrows, but let out nothing. When three boys made the bad decision to bait him about his mother and what they were sure was his nigger blood, which made his mother a nigger-lover, the small wiry Cajun was unafraid. Like jackals who smelled blood, they relentlessly pressed the point until they pursued him from the dusty schoolyard and confronted him behind the fieldhouse. Pierre had no choice. With a leg sweep, Pierre took down the largest of the three before he kicked that boy in the head. The other two had the better sense to come at him at the same time, but one came away with a broken nose and the second near choked on his own broken tooth. Those two ran, which allowed Pierre to return his attention to the first boy who lay curled on his hip holding his knees to his chest. Pierre did not hesitate to kick and break two of the boy's ribs, and might have stove in his head with his heels if the two teachers that came across the scuffle had not struggled to pull him away. They were used to boys who tested each other and then made friends after a punch or two; Pierre was not that sort. They asked that they boys shake hands, but when the bully extended his to do that, Pierre took it in his right hand while the palm of his left broke the boy's nose flat.

Maman was summoned. She was told that Pierre was headed for reform school. "He was alone, three against one. I don't see no other mothers here, though," she said and stood. "Maybe if you did your job, I would not have had to take off time from work." Without waiting to be dismissed, she took Pierre's hand in her own and they left the principal's door open wide behind them.

They were on a bench in the sun sharing a bottle of orange Nehi with two straws, the other boy's blood spattered on Pierre's shirt. She raked his dark hair from his eyes. "You keep your hands to yourself," she said to her boy.

"Unless someone hits me first."

"Right. Unless someone hits you first."

"Or insults you and me."

Maman hesitated, then said: "Sticks and stones may break your bones, but words will never harm you."

Deflated, he slumped on the bench, but agreed, though the lesson was not lost on him. Come to it, he'd keep his hands to himself and break bones with a stick or stone.

Once the war was on, Gulfport girls had eyes only for men in uniforms. They joined pen-pal clubs and wrote letters to GIs they did not know. The older girl who taught Pierre to smoke, Tamara, also taught him a few other things. Tamara's nose was sharp enough to peel a grapefruit, though to be sure with her clothes off that was not the feature that attracted Pierre's eye most. Her skin was soft as fresh-churned butter where it was not charred a rich brown at her neck, wrists, and ankles. Freckles spotted her everywhere, and there was not much she would not try, clothes on or off, offering several experiments of her own, most of which proved satisfactory, a few of which threatened to explode his head open. In dark and close places, Pierre explored the hidden country that was a woman, learning that terrain more through his skin than through his eyes. Like everyone else, Tamara emulated no-nonsense military talk, but added a smirk that suggested the silly war was being conducted for her personal amusement. When Pierre unbuttoned her clothes, she said, *for your eyes only*, when he entered her, with a sharp intake of breath she murmured that Pierre was *on the beam*; and when they were sated and passing a single cigarette between them, Tamara would ask, *we're top secret, right?*

It could not be confused with love, but when one boy within Pierre's hearing was stupid enough to call her an ugly desperate skank, though he could not know that Pierre and Tamara did what they did, Pierre waylaid the disrespectful sumbitch behind the fieldhouse and kicked the snot out of him.

By this time, the school principal knew that summoning Mrs. Doucet was a waste of his time. He interviewed Pierre directly. "What do you have to say for yourself?"

"The prick had it coming," Pierre said and would say no more.

Pierre received a two week suspension, but was not expelled on the condition that at his return he would report for football. He passed a pleasant two weeks reading the town library's novels by Dumas or, in late afternoons, meeting Tamara in ill-lit places in cool shadow. Defending her nonexistent honor advanced Pierre's education on a number of fronts not even General Montgomery could have imagined. On the rare days when Tamara was unavailable, on three separate occasions Pierre hotwired cars, all Fords, by laying a screwdriver across the battery cables. He went for joyrides, teaching himself to drive by never speeding and banging up only one of the cars when he miscalculated how much time he'd need to make it across a railroad track before an oncoming freight train. The train missed him, but he did pile the car onto a crossing signal. The other two cars were abandoned in pristine condition within five miles of where they were taken.

At his return, as directed, Pierre reported to football practice. The coach took one look at Pierre's wiry frame and thought *half-back*, but after three practice sessions of that fool tooting on a shrill whistle and a bunch of slow-witted crackers in the locker room snapping towels at each other's pale behinds, Pierre never again showed up. War surely required team effort, and there were some who believed that boys could learn that on a playing field, but compared to what was happening at Guadalcanal, high school football wasn't worth the shortest hair off Tojo's yellow ass.

Pierre could read and write and think and fight better than anyone he knew. Girls, sports, and school meant little.

Why stay?

By 1942, Pierre was 15 going on 20, wiry, lean, and smooth-muscled, brown eyes that could smolder to black beneath thin brows. Maybe if he had a heavier growth of beard the Marine recruiter in Biloxi could have brought himself to believe the lie about Pierre's age. At least he did not laugh at Pierre as the Army and Navy guys had done.

The recruiter reached into a red metal cooler awash with ice. "Have a Moxie on Uncle Sam, kid." He loosened the bottle cap with his bare thumb and wiped the bottle's mouth with his palm. "Y'all come on back as soon as you need to shave. The Corps will always need wildcats filled with fight." He tossed the bottle to Pierre.

Without breaking eye contact, Pierre caught the bottle with one hand, but though the recruiter was impressed, he was not impressed enough to let Pierre sign on.

New Year's Day 1943, Pierre turned an honest 16, the same age Maman had been the day Pierre came into the world.

"I'm sixteen and you are thirty-two," he said. "It's time for me to go off on my own."

"That's just shit," Maman said. Maman often muttered *merde*, but she used the harsher English when circumstances called for it. Her boy planning to leave to go to war was no surprise, but she did not welcome the idea, neither.

But a week later she surprised herself and her boy by agreeing it might not be the worst idea for him to strike out on his own, so long as he did not deliberately put himself in harm's way. The world had danger enough without some *fonchock* telling Pierre to zig when he needed to zag.

Her heart had been worn down by Charlie. "Your little boy ain't so little. He don't put no food on the table. He needs to pull his own weight," he'd been saying since Pierre was thirteen, and now with the world at war it was true. Nevertheless, handing over her *beau gamin* to fight so the rich could become more rich was too dear a price. Kolinda Doucet worshipped Roosevelt, but it was sure the Jews who ran things fooled the great man on this one. Their claws were deep into his wife was the problem.

To ease Maman's mind, Pierre invented a plan. He would obtain seaman's papers to become a merchant mariner out of New Orleans, a plan that would keep him from harm's way and leave him with a trade at war's end.

It should have been plain to Maman and her *beau gamin* that the plan could never work. Most folks even in Gulfport knew that, by the middle of 1942, U-boat torpedoes were blowing tankers out of the water all over the Gulf of Mexico. Merchant mariners suffered casualty rates higher than any other wartime service, necessary casualties because Louisiana and Texas supplied the best goddam oil in all the world. The fuel that powered Field Marshall Montgomery's tanks from Tunisia to El Alamein, kicking Rommel's Nazi ass every step of the way, came gushing out of American ground.

The newsreels focused on shipping in the North Atlantic where Britain-bound convoys protected by cruisers cut through gray seas; less reported was how the War Department chose to leave the Gulf a turkey shoot. Wide, sluggish, hastily constructed, thin-hulled Liberty Ships maneuvered like floating bathtubs. A Liberty ship might sport a 4-inch deck gun, but firing that at a surfaced U-boat at 1,000 yards was like pointing a cork popgun at an enemy armed with a Howitzer. Aggravating the death rate of merchant mariners were the fools in many American cities slow to realize that total war meant they had to make blackouts the law of the land. Seen through a periscope from deeper water, a tanker underway became a silhouette backlighted by shore lights, as tough to hit as slow-moving tin ducks on tin waves on a tin sea in a carnival shooting gallery.

Wolf-packs lurked at two choke points, the Straits of Florida and off the coast of the Yucatan. To exit the Gulf and deliver that precious fuel to the front, a ship had to sail through one or the other. Maybe there were ten U-boats out there; maybe there were fifty. There was no telling, but didn't the SS *Virginia*, gasoline to the gunwales, sink in flames in the mouth of the Mississippi River? And didn't the SS *Robert E. Lee* go down just twenty-five miles from safe port?

The *Lee*, a tub of a ship serving as a passenger freighter, steamed from Trinidad and was crippled before it made Tampa. Denied entry to that west Florida port, running for her life, the *Lee* steamed north and west for New Orleans with cargo that included 283 seaman who had survived other submarine attacks. But the merciless krauts settled two more fish amidships. The *Lee* broke into two burning halves, each half casting a malevolent red glow onto the underside of night clouds. They managed to launch lifeboats, but in fifteen minutes the *Lee* sank stern first, taking ten crew and fifteen passengers below the black waves that were aflame. The godless Nazis did not hesitate to torpedo tankers sailing under the neutral Mexican flag. They sank ships within sight of Vera Cruz, Port Arthur, Galveston, and Corpus Christi.

When Maman presented Pierre's plan to Charlie, the shrimper said. "That's the ticket. Join the Merchant Marine and leave the real fighting to some other stupid bastard." He so liked Pierre's plan he keyed open a foaming can of Jax and offered Pierre the first swallow.

Now Maman should have known that nothing Charlie ever thought was a good idea ever was. If Charlie pried his bloodshot eyes open and said, "Nice day," the smart money carried an umbrella. Charlie might have been a worthless rummy, and it might be that after days and days and days of bombardment in France at Belleau Wood anyone's hands might shake forever, but it had to be said that he knew some things worth knowing.

He warned Pierre that New Orleans was Satan's playground, though Charlie also speculated aloud that Pierre might enjoy himself among the sodomites. To impress Maman, Charlie offered to teach Pierre a thing or two he'd need to know to speed him on his way. Charlie taught him how to handle himself in a knife fight; Pierre was astounded that the shrimper knew his business. Maybe it was the only business he knew. Kicking the snot out of a football player for Tamara's questionable honor was one thing, but protecting his own ass called for technique far more elegant.

"Thrust up, not down, so your man falls onto your blade. Do not try to push the blade into the man, but vice-versa. Pull him down. Gut-cut a man and he will go down with far less effort than trying to drive a blade through his ribs. Those are bone," he said as if he were revealing a truth few people knew. "Hold a blade's handle loose but firm across your palm, not in a fist. You're not chopping wood, boy. Use your free hand to pull a man onto the blade. He'll be coming toward you, anyway, so you may as well encourage him."

"What if he has a gun?"

"Then kiss your ass fare-thee-well."

Charlie maintained he learned all he knew on the docks long after his time in France, hinting at the demise of the many men who had crossed him. "I gut them sumbitches like tuna." When he delivered the final lesson, Charlie spit in his palm, wiped his spit onto the seat of his overalls, and shook Pierre's hand, pumping the boy's arm as if with effort he could make Pierre spout water. "No hard feelings," he said. "Come back for your mother's sake. Stay the fuck out of the military and if they get you, don't never volunteer."

At the Gulfport bus station, Charlie gave him a five-inch serrated knife in a black leather sheath that Pierre fastened above his ankle. Maman never knew about that, and Pierre wondered where Charlie stole so fine a knife and a hand-stitched leather sheath. Maman pulled at his arm, leaned close to kiss him, and before he boarded slid five dollars into his bedroll in a way Charlie could not see.

Her lips close to her *beau gamin*'s ear she whispered: "Whatever you do, be best at it."

The bus rimmed Pontchartrain in hard rain. The slick black road shown like polished glass, but as Pierre stepped off the bus into the streets of New Orleans, the sun broke through like a promise.

He was in the Crescent City, 16, handsome, and free. What was not possible?

Pierre wandered for the rest of the day. He tore great hunks from a day-old bread he bought for pennies. At every turn, he expected the luck of a boy in a storybook. He'd rescue a rich girl on a runaway horse or push her from the path of a trolley just as her grateful father saw his courage. Pierre's eyes lingered on stylish women before he came to rest on a wooden bench in Woldenberg Park on the bank of a bend of the Mississippi River.

His arms stretched along the bench's spine; his face lifted to the late sun. No one knew his name. No one knew how old he was, or where he came from. He had family he'd never met in the bayou country down by Lafayette, but they did not know he existed, much less that he was practically on their doorstep. He had heard he had aunts around Pensacola, but they would not know him from Adam. No Cajun boy from Gulfport whose baptismal certificate read *Unknown* in the space for *Father* could be easily discovered.

Pierre was free to be anyone he chose to be.

He had two ambitions. First, he'd be louche. He had seen the word in *The Scarlet Pimpernel* when he'd been suspended from school, had looked it up, and made the word his own hallmark of style. What could be more glorious?

Second, he would remain invisible until it suited him to come out of the shadows. That was a simple matter of good sense.

He crossed the French Quarter to the stalls and vendors of the French Market. Their two-wheeled carts were loaded with fish, flowers, butchered meat, tomatoes, celery, onions—if it came out of the ground, walked the earth, or swam in the sea, it could be had in New Orleans. The aromas were overwhelming. No one seemed aware there was a war going on. Pierre splurged a nickel on a cup of milk heavy with thick cream ladled from a barrel by a Creole woman, sat a while more in the dimming afternoon, then by darkness made his way back to what he was already was thinking was *his* bench.

By night, the Quarter teemed with life. The girls became better-looking, their heels a little higher, their hips more loose. Servicemen had more swagger and became more drunk. By the small hours, exhaustion caught Pierre. Though he had never before been in the Crescent City, with his head on his bedroll he thought dreamily he had at last returned home.

When the sun was not high enough to trouble anyone's eyes, a wooden baton rapped the sole of each of his shoes. It hurt. He sat up quickly and regretted it. He was too stiff. When had he wrapped himself in newspaper?

"Where y'at, boy?" The cop's beefy face was inches from his own.

With a war on, more than a few farm boys, bright-eyed and filled with juice, regularly wandered loose in the parish. As a rule, they stayed happily broke and worked at keeping happily drunk in a race to have all the fun that could be had before they were drafted or signed up. A bit of pussy was not too much to hope for, neither, though that, too, like anything else in New Orleans, cost. The cops chose to be kind to white boys, and now that they saw him close they saw that Pierre qualified for their generosity. They warned him that they could not have Pierre doing his business in the bushes, a filthy act that would surely annoy ordinary citizens. They were, therefore, as a matter of sacred duty, obliged to persuade him to move on.

"I'm O'Hara," the cop said and pointed his thumb at his partner. "That sorry excuse for an Irishman is also O'Hara. No relation, thanks be to Jaysus. How old might you be, boy?"

Pierre rubbed the last of his sleep from his eyes. He needed to pee. If he moved too quickly, he was sure he'd shatter like frozen taffy.

"Twenty," he said. "I want to join the Navy before the Army gets me. I hear the food is better."

O'Hara and O'Hara drew closer to look deeply into Pierre's dark eyes. The lie was plausible, but his beardless face betrayed him.

"If you're twenty, I am a pink-assed monkey," O'Hara said, "but if you can fool a recruitment officer, I'll not stand in the way of a patriot ready to serve his country. Kill a mess of krauts. Shoot a battalion of Japs, but before you kill Der Führer, we will have your bony ass off our bench."

They drove him to the YMCA on Dryades and pointed down the street to a Naval recruitment station in a storefront. "The Navy will open soon enough."

Pierre nodded as if a recruitment office was the thing he most wanted.

"Get a haircut. You'll be spending some time here even if you sign up today. There's lice, but more important is that a lad with the bloom of youth in his eyes and hair falling over his ears might give the wrong kind the wrong idea. Now I hope to Jaysus, the Blessed Mother, and all the saints you will not confess to carrying a knife. If you do, then me and O'Hara here will be obliged to relieve you of the weapon. For public safety, you understand. It goes against our better Irish judgment to leave a white boy vulnerable to the kind that find boys with long hair attractive, but we will do out duty and relieve you of any hidden weapons. If you carry a pig-sticker longer than five inches, our duty is clear. So I will not ask you, and you are not going to volunteer any information about whether you have such a blade. Do we understand each other, lad?"

The mean little knife Charlie had given him was exactly five inches, six if you measured it in the black leather sheath strapped under the left leg of his denim pants. The serrated steel was able to cut bait, shuck an oyster, or butcher a man.

In the Y's white tile lavatory, a five-foot porcelain urinal gurgled water like a mountain stream. The frosted window was open a crack, but not enough to vent the strong stink of the room, carbolic and urine. Pierre peed like a racehorse. When he came out to the lobby, O'Hara and O'Hara were gone.

Thirty-five cents would buy him a cell with a cot and a pillow, no linens, a sink down the hall next to a *pissoir* on a residence floor, two shower baths each week but no guarantees of hot water no matter how many nickels he dropped in the water gauge. The coin-operated telephones in the halls on the first and third floors sometimes worked, but they'd appreciate it if Pierre obtained his coins elsewhere, as the Y's desk clerk had better things to do than make change for every Tom, Dick, and Harry ringing up a hooker. The clerk tugged a tuft of greasy hair growing from his right ear as he slid a flat brass key across a glass counter so thick it seemed green. Then the clerk tipped his creaking wooden chair back, turned up his radio, and crossed his ankles on the counter to continue studying a crumpled black-and-white magazine that featured naked large-breasted women with eyes half closed in lust touching themselves.

Pierre carried his bedroll up two flights of stairs and unlocked his door. A thin mattress curled back on itself on the bedspring. The pillow was stained by what he hoped was coffee. The clean sheets smelled of bleach. He had a cigarette-scarred bureau and a service-able wooden chair that rocked on its noticeably short leg. The walls were a sickly blue-green, the corroded window casements covered by chipped paint that might have once been white.

He uncurled the thin mattress and knelt on the iron bed frame to open his narrow window. The window overlooked an alley lined by telephone poles that leaned every which way. The window case-ment was nailed so that the window could not be lifted more than three inches, a precaution to make skipping out on the rent and suicide difficult.

Pierre knelt on the bed to inhale fresh air through the three inches of the open window. The ammonia-stink of cat piss from the alley was overwhelming. Pierre wondered what might happen if O'Hara and O'Hara found him sleeping in the open on that bench a second time. The alley's pavement seemed alive until he figured that what he saw ceaselessly moving were the cats themselves, thick as roaches.

He would not be the first to carve his initials in the window casement, and probably not the last. Doing so made him the new-est member of an invisible fraternity, the nameless guests of the Y who'd passed this way before him. He lay back, but when the ruddy sun rose high enough to come across the nearby rooftops onto his face, Pierre awoke to realize he had fallen into a deep afternoon sleep to make up for his fitful night shivering wrapped in newspaper on his park bench. He had slept through the day, his room door closed but unlocked. Anyone could have come in, anyone at all. His hand trembled. *Stupid, stupid, stupid.* Leaving himself vulnerable was not part of any plan.

He discovered a café where he could sit at a wrought iron sidewalk table with a surface of acid-washed glass. It was a good place to think. His first order of business had to be to protect himself, then stay anonymous for as long as he was able, and finally find his way free of the Y. He could not plan beyond that.

Girls in tartan pleated skirts who could not possibly be whores came and went from a nearby parochial school, The Blessed St. Something-or-Other and Her Immaculate Banjo Quartet. The girls wore starched white shirts, blocky black shoes, and below the swirling hemline of mid-calf tartan wool skirts showed shapely rounded calves that tapered to ankles enclosed by coarse white cotton socks. They were close to his own actual age, a fact that he would need keep a secret for a long time. Coming clean about how old he was would prove to be a lose-lose proposition. On the one hand, if he claimed to be twenty, his not being drafted was suspicious. On the other, if he claimed his true age, someone would want papers to prove he was who he was. Best would be to keep his mouth shut.

He sipped scalding chicory coffee. While he'd been rolling in the dust fighting boys or in dark places in Gulfport unbuttoning Tamara's blouse, sweet girls like these in New Orleans had daintily breakfasted on light toast, orange-cherry marmalade, and fresh fruit cut by uniformed maids who served them on porcelain plates. These girls attended school with no greater fear than being caught by Sister Whatchamacallit with a cigarette. They looked as saucy as all the Andrew sisters put together, more wide-eyed than Judy Garland catching her first sight of Oz, and though looking at them did not make Pierre horny enough to want to collide with a tree, the sight of them giggling their way down the street made him feel good about himself, the world, and his prospects in it.

He'd navigate through his problems.

The aroma of sea and diesel fuel rose from the nearby Mississippi. A scrawny tree cast dappled shadows. He nursed his unsweetened black chicory and beignet while licking powdered sugar that flaked onto a square of wax paper.

Two girls with arms linked at the elbows saw him, laughed aloud, and hurried away, but the taller of the two looked back at him over her shoulder to flash a perfect smile of perfect teeth and sweep a cascade of perfect silken yellow hair behind her perfect ear. She smothered a giggle before she hurried to catch her friend. Wisps of her hair, tendrils of sunshine, fanned a corona around her when she spun to smile at him. He imagined her perfume, maybe tea-rose, a lingering scent he knew from when Maman sold cosmetics at the Five & Dime. Her white short-sleeve blouse had one extra button undone down her chest. The blouse had broad, rounded lapels and initials embroidered in a flowery scarlet script. KJ.

Kathleen Jones? Kristen Johnson? Karen Jackson? Kayleigh Jacoby?

There was no telling. All he knew for sure was The Yellow-Haired Girl Who Looked Back was carefree. That was plenty.

That same day, he carried a Help Wanted poster into a hardware store. A man with a mustache who wore an apron told him he could not have the job. "You don't look trustworthy."

"How do you come to that, podner?"

"Too dark. You got nigger blood."

The man's accent may have been Dutch, if not German. When he turned his back to help a customer, Pierre pocketed a hasp and staple lock kit. Why not? Already nailed as a thief, he may as well help himself to what he needed. Coming back at night to shatter a window would have been overkill for the *gros couillon*. If he were to stay invisible in the big city, Pierre would need to restrain himself in new ways.

Later still, in his room with nothing but a wedge of white cheese and a half loaf of day old bread, he wished he had milk. He drank warm water and stripped to his cotton shorts to lie back on his bed. The yellow-haired girl's wispy hair had floated around her eyes, beckoning like an angel's hands.

She was no fisherman's daughter; no girl like the Yellow-Haired Girl had ever been in Gulfport. He could not imagine her with her clothes off, though he tried. He knew no one with skin so white. He pretended to have a conversation with her, but quickly realized he did not know enough to say to her. What might interest such a girl?

Wood screws were already in the doorframe, so he used a dime as a screwdriver to loosen them, then fastened the stolen hasp and staple lock.

That night they came for him earlier than he expected. Pierre was sleepless on his narrow bed when his brass doorknob turned, squealing, slow and smooth at first, then jerking back and forth violently. There were at least two voices, but Pierre was unable to make out the words. For all Pierre knew, there could have been more, but he was not about to open the door to discover how many. They sprung his door's feeble lock with a knife of their own, and though the doorframe wood cracked and strained, the hasp and staple held. They cursed. The door rattled as if they hoped to shake it open. Someone kicked at the bottom strike plate; the door banged but held. The other said, "Cut that shit out. You break the door, you'll get us thrown the fuck out."

Pierre wiped his perspiring hand on his pillow to better grip his knife's black wood handle, remembering Charlie's lessons. *Palm up, bring the knife to meet your man, pull him down, let his weight set the knife.* They would not have their way with the dark-eyed boy from Gulfport. He consciously forced his fingers to relax. Too tense a grip was as dangerous as no grip at all.

They called to him through the door crack. "Come on, Sweetmeat. Come out and we can dance by the light of the moon."

"We can have a party. You like parties, don't you? I got something here for you I know you are going to like."

People must have heard the racket, but no one cared.

Pierre said nothing. A taunt would only inspire greater determination. In the limpid light from the street, Pierre's wide eyes locked on the twisting glass doorknob.

He struggled to steady his breathing, coldly visualizing the coming fight, something Charlie had never taught him but he had learned on his own. If the door collapsed, he'd have to slash at one and stab at the other. This would happen; then that, he'd kick just so to keep his balance, this high and no higher. It was a good thing that the door was too narrow for them to rush him at the same time, but it meant he could not hesitate if he wanted to grapple with them one at a time. He'd trip and stab the first man through the door as he fell past Pierre. Then Pierre would take care of the second man. Pierre's weight would go from his rear to front leg, adding force to his arm while holding his balance. He'd stand with his left shoulder to the door so he could move on a man with the full force of his right hand. As Charlie had shown him, he'd need to pull on the shoulder of the second man to have him fall forward, using his momentum to put him down. He would twist the blade in the man's soft underbelly so as the knife withdrew it would do more damage coming out than going in. A man might be as good as dead, but until he bled out could still rise long enough to hurt him. That could take a while.

He could think about none of it when the time came. If he thought about it, he'd fail. And if there were three, he could hope to hurt the first two before he'd be face down with a rolled towel in his mouth, his head hauled back tight as a bridle.

But none of that happened.

The two drunken bulls grew weary of their game, their determination short-lived. With one final kick at the rattling door, they were suddenly gone.

He had pissed himself. No shame in that; his body readying for a fight. He rinsed his boxer shorts in the water of his porcelain wash basin, then dragged his one chair close to the window to drape his shorts over its wooden back. He flipped his bare mattress to the dry side, opened his window, then rested his head on the thin cool pillow.

The room filled with cat-stink as he slipped into an exhausted half-sleep, stilling his fear by thinking again of the Yellow-Haired Girl's smile and the silken tendrils of gold that floated about her face, those angel hands that beckoned to him.

Come morning, Pierre paused at the Y's front desk in the shallow lobby. He made a show of bending to withdraw his knife from under his trouser leg. He pretended to clean his fingernails, then expertly threw the knife to the floor inches from his shoe. It stood trapped in the wood, perfectly vertical, vibrating. He threw the knife three times more, each time closer to his foot, each time expertly trapping the quivering knife.

No one at the Y ever bothered him again. It was an interesting lesson, one he'd fall back on the rest of his life: being thought dangerous could be better than being dangerous.

Most every day, Pierre sat for a bit at the table in shade where The Yellow-Haired Girl had walked by, but she never reappeared. Plenty of school girls in tartan skirts came and went from the school, but none gave the dark Cajun boy with hair falling over his eyes a second glance. He tried different hours of the day, but the girl whose initials were KJ was lost to him.

Maybe that was good fortune. The Yellow-Haired Girl might have told him innocent schoolgirl stories, but what might he tell her? "The day I first saw you I avoided being raped by stealing a hasp and lock and putting it on my door with my knife. The next day I made sure people saw my knife so no one would bother me again. See, my mother's drunken shrimper boyfriend gave the knife to me. That pig beats Maman. He knocked out two of her teeth once. Oh, and I need to tell you that I am lying about my age and who I am to avoid being drafted, so tell no one you know me or who I am."

They came from different worlds; he'd need to remember that.

Many days, he read in the Napoleon Library off Magazine. Dust motes drifted through spears of sunlight that leaked past the sides of opaque window shades. He drifted through the peace, fingers tips on the shelves and tables sleek with lemon oil. Books whispered their secrets to him, secrets that incredibly were available to anyone who cared to know them, though few did. He came to love the feel of worn vellum, so like the skin of a woman. He never quite understood the appeal of fiction, though Dickens and his unschooled orphan boys loose in the streets of London somehow caught more truth than any volume burdened by mere facts.

He found colored-boy work spreading clean sawdust or mucking saloon toilets in the Quarter. Once Pierre was known, bartenders might grant him the free lunch, usually pig's knuckles, wieners, cheese and cracker, anything cheap and salted enough that a customer would order a chaser. From time to time, Pierre was allowed to sink a tin dipper into a foaming chilled zinc beer bucket.

One morning, air all thick with jacaranda and jasmine, after Pierre mucked out two saloons in the Quarter, he sat in front of a patisserie on Ursulines. For a dime, he could sit for as long as he wished over a beignet while he sipped chicory through two cubes of sugar on his tongue. Across the street in a puddle of shade, a man in a shabby mustard-brown zoot suit, a red shirt, and a tie bright as marigolds ran a card game on the rough pine board he'd placed across two orange crates.

The game was 3-Card Monte. Brace two red aces from finger to thumb and a third the Ace of Spades, toss the cards facedown with enough dexterity to deceive the eye and wager the marks can't find the black ace. When Pierre had taken money from Gulfport boys, he never believed the game could yield as much as it did from soldiers and sailors.

The operator on Ursulines needed to shave and his hair was matted, greasy as if he'd been on a bender and was still too unsteady to emerge into sobriety. His hands quavered. His stained loose trousers were held up by a length of clothesline that passed through the belt loops and over his shoulder. The watch chain looped on his left was at least a yard long, the zoot-suit fashion of a decade ago. Had the chain been real gold, it might have been worth more than the fluttering money held under small stones and bits of shattered concrete.

But Pierre saw that the shakes left the operator's hands at the moment he released the cards. They fell to the plank like plummeting birds of prey. *Find black Mariah. Find black Mariah. Find black Mariah. Black Mariah is the girl you need to win. Find black Mariah.* When a seaman in a faded denim shirt, his shirttail out, flipped the Ace of Spades face up three times running, he turned to smile at the crowd as if to brag at how easy it was to take money from the old drunk. He walked off with six dollars. Then three sailors in dress whites elbowed each other aside, eager to take their turn with the unsteady old fool unaware his best days were behind him. They lost a few dollars and then lost interest, off to spend their money on girls.

Pierre watched for a long while. He knew what to look for, and so he saw more than most. Palsied hands or not, the man was a skilled cheat. He palmed cards and performed seamless quick drops. His biggest single score was a ten bet by a half-drunk Marine whose arms circled the waists of two women. He played a long while with one whore at his left and one at his right pressed tightly against him. They urged the gyrene to keep playing so all three of them could have an even better party, though he'd need more money to pay for that. "Have you heard? There's a war going on?" the one with darker hair on his right said, exposed her throat as she threw back her head, and laughed. "A girl has to make a living!" They nibbled at his ears and nipped at his neck. The woman in red platform heels on his left casually stroked the front of his trousers.

"Bad luck, soldier," the operator in the threadbare zoot-suit said. "Play again? By the look of 'em, your girlfriends love a good time."

The Marine varied his bet from five dollars to one and back again to five, and his luck seemed to turn. He doubled and redoubled his bet, money ebbed forward and back, but over time it went in only one direction. Pierre could keep careful accounts in his head. When the Marine tapped out, he'd dropped thirty-three dollars, a small fortune for a soldier who could have been copping feels at the USO for a dime-a-dance.

The whores vanished, the crowd dispersed, the dealer broke down his orange crate setup and disappeared. They left the busted marine standing with his hands deep in his empty pockets, until he realized he was not getting laid that day by either one, much less by two. He broke a rueful smile. What was money to a man headed for the deserts of North Africa?

Pierre swallowed the last of his chicory. The operator must have brass balls. Cheating soldiers drunk or sober was risky business.

Pierre made his way across Royal through milling crowds to make his rounds. What saloon needed help now? Who might need help tomorrow?

It was an accident that he spied the man with the marigold tie and scarlet shirt on a high stool in dim light in the shadows at the end of a long zinc bar. The whiskey quaver in his hands was vanished with the mustard zoot-suit jacket, though the scarlet shirt remained. Instead of worn clothesline, black braces made of silk held his slacks up. He sported what might have been a sapphire pinky ring, the stone big as a cat's eye. He had shaved.

The bartender poured Pierre a short round and asked for no money. The place reeked of vinegar, sweat, cheap perfume, fry oil, salt, and peppers so sharp they made a man's eyes tear. The two tarts who'd hung on the Marine emerged from the Ladies Room, their curly hair freshly pinned like Betty Grable's. Neither wore actual stockings, but with eyebrow pencil had drawn seams on the backs of their legs. They pretended to fuss with their nonexistent stockings as the game operator withdrew a tight roll of bills held by a thick rubber-band from his trouser pocket. The women never sat. They still wore blue and red, but both had thickly applied fresh crimson lipstick so thick it flaked.

The dealer peeled each of them a five. "Can you spare it, Eddie?" the one in blue said. "The jarhead was a pain in the ass."

"Goddam octopus," her girlfriend said. "The bruises on my titties have bruises." She made folding a stick of Black Jack Licorice into her mouth seem erotic as she opened her mother-of-pearl compact mirror, powdered her nose that needed no powdering, and mouthed a cocktail napkin to smooth her lipstick. She never stopped chewing her gum. "What do you think, Eddie? A bonus?

The mark wanted a threesome, but after you busted him he wanted it on credit. Can you beat that? I had a husband once, before the louse took off, and I would not fuck *him* on credit!"

"Can I get that threesome?" Eddie asked.

"We don't fuck dog shit, Dog-Shit. Besides, the world knows you prefer corn holing country boys."

Eddie grinned and gave them each one more dollar. "I just love it when you talk dirty to me."

The whore's head tipped way back to laugh aloud and expose her white throat the same way she had when they were hustling the Marine. Strands of her hair came loose and fell. She had a wine-stain birthmark under her left ear that disappeared from sight down her dress collar.

"Hey, Eddie," the woman in blue said, "f'true, now. You know people who know people. Can you get me a line on some decent stockings? I am crap at tracing a fake seam on my leg."

"And at the parlor they get three simoleons to draw them," her friend said. "Can you beat that?"

Nylon and silk went into parachutes as part of the war effort. Eddie's silk braces and hand-painted tie were probably contraband or pre-war, so maybe he really knew people.

Eddie gestured that the first woman lean close; he whispered something in her ear before she threw her head back to laugh again. "I miss nylons," she said, "but not that bad." She patted his freshly shaved cheek. Then the two hiked their skirts to straighten non-existent seams before wobbling on unsteady heels into the milling crowd swelling on Bourbon Street.

The swabbie in blue denim who'd first made the game look easy joined Eddie next. He said, "Podner," and straddled a stool beside the dealer who peeled off another fiver for him. Eddie ordered a crawfish boil, a Po' Boy with extra remoulade, and two foaming drafts of Falstaff, the only beer Pierre ever drank that tasted so bad he spit it out. The fake sailor wiped his hands on his denims as the two stared blankly at each other in the bar's antique speckled back-glass mirror.

So Pierre saw how it was. He liked New Orleans, and now he liked his chances that much more.

He stole a small mirror from the same hardware store that had refused him a job, and then sat on his bed to practice manipulating cards. He watched his own hands. Caught cheating by a boy in Gulfport, Pierre could expect a scrape and a blooded nose, but caught cheating by men trained to kill called for a different order of know-how. Maman had urged him to be the best at whatever he did. Maman was wise.

With more balls than brains, he found his own orange crates at the French Market, breaking the thin rough wood against his knee to the lengths he needed. His first day out, he cleared $7.25, not a bad haul since he worked with no partner, no shills, and was on a shitty corner with no shade and little foot traffic. Still, it beat all hollow mucking out saloon toilets.

After a week of nickels, dimes, quarters, and rare folding money, on an afternoon when he had a circle of maybe a half-dozen people, a policeman watched from a few paces off before he scattered Pierre's marks. His name was Herlihy. Herlihy explained that Pierre had to buy a license. Every dancer, every trumpeter, every banjo picker, and every spoon player Pierre saw on Herlihy's street had purchased a license.

"Your street?"

"My street."

"This is not a public street?"

"Not while I draw breath, boy." He drove the blunt end of his baton into Pierre's solar plexus, enough to take Pierre's breath, but not so hard as to damage him. He must have been an expert. "It's known to one and all to be my street. Will you do the proper thing or will I need to give you a lesson you won't forget?" Herlihy lifted the flap of his long blue police coat. Brass knuckles beside his handcuffs peeped out at Pierre.

"How can I get a license?"

"You're in luck. It's me that sells them. Some fucker named Eddie just had his license expire, so he's been run off and my street needs a game of Monte."

For two dollars a day or ten a week in advance, Pierre could do business on St. Ann, a better spot that come May would hold the sweet smell of oleander and jasmine thick at his back. Pierre would have the additional satisfaction of having made a contribution to the NOPD Retirement and Welfare Fund that Herlihy person- ally ran. In exchange, Herlihy offered savvy business advice and an iron-clad guarantee that Pierre would never be robbed by any snatch-and-grab nappy-headed pickaninnies. "The road to riches and health runs through Herlihy," Herlihy said, "if you take my meaning, a fact Eddie wanted to forget." He gave Pierre a second peek at the brass knuckles.

"Are you sure your name is not O'Hara? The last O'Hara to do me a favor like this set me up to get my throat cut. There were two of them. I thought every cop in New Orleans was named O'Hara."

"Only the ones that can't be trusted. Those would be your dagos pretending to be micks. Your dago constabulary is unsavory, to be sure." Herlihy's chest puffed out. "Your mick, on the other hand, will sell you a license, completely above board and never fuck you over. Think of your license as an insurance policy, but mind you if it rains that's your hard luck. The NOPD Retirement and Welfare Fund don't give refunds. Now, I have to ask you, lad. You aren't car- rying any firearms, are you?"

"No sir."

"Good. I discourage firearms. How about a blade of some sort? If I were to pat you down, might I stick myself?"

"You might. It's for shucking oysters. It's on my ankle."

Herlihy laughed. "That's a new one," he said. "As long as it ain't no bayonet. Oysters my hairy Irish ass. You make sure that pig- sticker stays where nobody can never see it. If someone gives you grief, you keep a sharp eye peeled for Herlihy, you inform Herlihy, and Herlihy will make certain the fucker regrets his impudence. Everybody stays happy and makes a living."

"Yessir."

"But mind me, lad. If I learn of anyone robbing decent folk at knife point, I'll know where to go. It's bad for business. Bad for everyone."

"Why did you come here? To New Orleans, I mean. That's quite a brogue."

Herlihy boxed Pierre's ears and faked a side kick to Pierre's hip before the blunt end of his baton again found Pierre's solar plexus, this time with enough force to make Pierre gasp. "Mind your business, lad. I am the law here is all you need to know. You seem right enough, but a personal question can change a man's attitude." He strode a few feet away, stopped, and called back over his shoulder: "It's known to one and all. If you play on Herlihy's street, Herlihy gets his due."

Pierre took to wearing a cheap, gray porkpie hat pushed to the back of his head. It had been abandoned on a bench. Crown crushed, the sweatband stained the color of rust, he thought he must be crazy to keep it, but perspiration seeping over his forehead and trickling down the back of his neck and into his eyes could break his rhythm. He needed something, and here was the hat he'd need.

Pierre grew a mustache, but it looked like a caterpillar had starved on its journey from his left ear to his right, so he shaved his lip clean, He carried a small tin of talc to keep his hands dry in the pocket of a tuxedo vest he found in a pawnshop. Since hand cramps could have lasted for days and left him stone broke and still owning Herlihy his dues, he swiped an empty milk bottle to fill with water and threw down salt tablets.

Herlihy had given good advice, he had to admit. A good day on St. Ann attracted tourists and soldiers and sailors out for casual strolls and the cooler air of Jackson Park.

Pierre was breaking down his setup when a woman said, "Ten dollars?"

"You look like a million," Pierre said, "but whatever you are selling, I ain't buying."

She laughed mirthlessly. The snaggletooth on the upper left side of her mouth seemed pointed at him. The curl of ink-dark hair she pushed off her smoky eyes immediately limply fell back. Maman's days at a cosmetics counter had taught Pierre enough to know that her burgundy full lips were a failed effort at distraction from the tooth and the shallow crow's feet surrounding her green eyes.

She might be thirty-five, Maman's age, or she might be a little younger, but not by much. Like Maman, the woman's face had been fashioned by troubles that were using her up, but she was gamely fighting time.

"No, *cher*, I meant, 'Did you make ten dollars?'"

"You counting the money in my pocket?"

"Handsome, too. If Doris' hand sneaks into your pocket, it won't be to squeeze your wallet." She stared at his crotch. "From the look of it, that might not be a waste of time, neither." She grinned. "You look a little young, *cher*, but that's how Doris likes them. I'm Doris and Doris ain' no one but me." Her tongue moistened her lips. "One grifter to another, *cher*, what was your rake? Whatever it was, I can double it for you. Your hands got speed, but you ain' got enough style. You need help."

He hid his two pine crate boards behind a hydrangea bush. The raw wood spiked a shallow splinter into the crease of his thumb. He winced, picking at it with his fingernail but only drove it deeper into his flesh. "Nine and a quarter," he lied, licking his wound like a dog. "Slow day."

"You don't need to count it?"

"No."

That much was true. No matter how fast the action, the running total in Pierre's head was more reliable than a cash register. People who could not manage arithmetic in their heads suffered some sort of deficiency, like blindness or palsy. His rake that day had been a pitiable six dollars. Summer heat kept the action slow, though the longer daylight hours were making little difference. At this rate, he'd soon risk Herlihy's wrath or be back mucking saloon toilets.

She lifted his injured hand palm up. "*Allons, cher,*" she said. "Doris ain' going to bite you. Not yet, anyway. And not there, neither." She lifted his thumb close to her face. Her soft grip was firm enough to immobilize his hand. "You throw those cards good. You good at it, *cher*. Maybe too good. Doris knows talent when she sees it. Your hands beat my eye, but no one can win like you win without bein' a mechanic. Doris sees you lose cheap but win big when a sucker plunges, too. Luck don' work that way. You workin' your luck so good it ain' be no luck at all."

The hat-pin she produced from her scuffed purse might have doubled as a weapon; it was longer and had more of a point than any hatpin ever needed. Pierre supposed she scraped it against a brick to keep a point as a weapon for a woman whose brunette tresses had never been gathered under so much as a sunbonnet. "Quit wiggling, *cher*. I can't have you bleeding all over your cards." The hatpin probed his flesh.

"You'd be Our Lady of Jackson Square, the Patron Saint of Card Mechanics?" he asked.

Great orbs of hard jade, her eyes took him in across his palm. "I'd be Saint Ann herself, Grandma to Jesus. Ain' this my street? You'd best light a candle for me." She lifted his thumb to her lips and sucked it hard, squeezing a bead of cleansing blood from the wound. "I collect the crutches cripples throw away, then I sell 'em. Ol' Andrew on his horse over dere takes forty percent when his horse don't shit on me." Her tongue whorled on his skin until the splinter softened with saliva; then she spit the splinter to the ground. "That's why he be tipping his hat. Andrew on his high horse, an' ol' Duke on his hind legs, but Andrew is a gentleman. He is that. He thankin' Doris for his crutch money. Duke don't shit on me near as much as he shit on ever' one else, but Duke be a horse, can't always help himself, horseshit being horseshit."

Her lips closed softly once more around his thumb to the base of the joint, while her tongue whorled to tickle his flesh in a different way. A tissue wiped her lipstick from his hand. She pressed it against the puncture. "Direct pressure stops bleeding," she said.

"They teach all us girls First Aid at Civil Defense." Without asking his permission, she rinsed her mouth with the last of his water and then chucked the empty milk bottle behind the bush to join Pierre's orange crate boards.

"Civil Defense?"

"Yeah, and I dance at the USO, too. Doris is a patriot who likes horny boys with lots of energy. The band ends ever' night with *We'll Meet Again* and Doris turns into mush. It's that dreamy trombone. Doris just wants to cry at how some of those boys will never again see home. Sometimes, I let a soldier-boy get lucky. Doris don't never charge a soldier for what comes natural. That's patriotism." She turned to leave him. "What's it going to be, *cher*? You want a partner or no?"

"No sale," he said.

"F'true?" She shrugged, surprised. "See you around, Butch."

"Pierre."

Her step slowed as she turned his name over. "'Butch' suits you better." She thought a moment. "You need some good green felt, if you can find it. I'd say Kresge's but who knows what the war is taking away at the Five & Dime. Green felt persuades the marks you run a classier game. When a man loses his pay across green felt, he believes he got his money's worth. Across splintered wood, he believes he was swindled. Don' ask me why. You don't need but a yard."

"What for?"

"When you fall off the turnip cart, be sure to land on your head. You don't want to hurt the brain in your ass. Butch, make a betting layout from the felt with white adhesive tape. No more splinters for you, and your game looks more honest. If that pretty thumb gets infected, you won't be throwing cards long. Peroxide. The secret to long life is peroxide."

Her dark green cotton skirt switched left and right and left and right again as she walked away. His throbbing thumb vainly tried to explain to the rest of his anatomy why he'd passed on what he'd passed up, but the rest of his anatomy was throbbing on its own.

Two days later, Doris showed up on the arm of a Marine. "Come on, sugar," she said, "Let Momma play." Her fingers touched the mark's chest between two buttons of his khaki shirt.

The small circle of non-players opened for Doris to drag the mark near. The guy put down a dollar. It was not much, but Washington might have older cousins. Abe, Alex, and Andy somewhere in that same wallet. Pierre had yet to toss cards for Grandpa Benny, but he was unafraid to try.

For a single dollar, Pierre tossed cards flat and honest. The mark would have to have been blind not to see the Ace of Spades fall at the array's center. Doris pointed and Pierre flipped the card over. "The lady has a sharp eye, sailor," Pierre said. "Back her play again? Double or nothing? Give a man the chance to pull even."

Doris found the Black Ace three times in a row. Pierre pushed his porkpie hat back as if he was amazed by her skill and his own bad luck.

The danger was that the chump was the son of a dairy farmer from East Bumfuck, and so might be happy to push one buck back and forth across the felt for most of a day while corn ripened. On Pierre's orange crate, under a pebble the size of a bottle cap, three crumpled singles lay undisturbed by the summer breeze. "Oh, I like this game!" Doris said. "Sugar, what say we win enough for Momma and you to have a swell time?" She whispered a suggestion never uttered in Arkansas. The Marine turned crimson, the color rising up his chest and into his face.

The eager sailor dropped a ten onto the felt, Pierre loosed the cards, and the mark pointed to where he believed the ace had fallen. He'd have been right if he'd received an honest drop, but Doris fumbled with his shirt pocket looking for his cigarettes, just enough distraction that Pierre could palm the winning ace and replace it with the Ace of Hearts.

The mark's arm circled Doris's slight waist. She was a narrow woman; her conical breasts above her flaring hips under a taupe pleated skirt. The Marine withdrew his wallet and extracted an-other ten, sure he could get even, but Doris urged him to double to teach the gambler a lesson. "Didn't I win t'ree in a row, *cher*? You can do it. It's easy."

"Who wants to back a Marine?" Pierre asked the circle of onlookers. Twenty dollars in side bets materialized, all with the serviceman. Pierre's layout promised 4 for 5 for any side bet, with or against the dealer. "Who'll back a hero just back from Guadalcanal?"

The Marine was too green to have been anywhere near Guadalcanal. If God loved him, he never would be. The only people back from Guadalcanal were missing limbs or eyes; some would stay on Guadalcanal or in the surrounding ocean forever.

Pierre beat him twice more for a total of fifty dollars. He also cleaned up on side bets for another seventeen. He crumpled handfuls of small bills into his pants.

"I am thirsty, sugar," Doris said—the plain signal to Pierre that it was time to close the books. She had her own schemes to further lighten her Marine's wallet. Her arm went round the soldier's waist. The two abruptly plunged into the darker shadows toward Bourbon Street.

As Pierre broke down his setup an hour later, Doris materialized out of the murky evening.

"Where's your Marine?" he asked as he carefully rolled his green felt playing field.

"He gone home to Arkansas to fuck Maybelle. Maybelle is a sheep." She withdrew what had been the Marine's wallet from a skirt pocket and toyed with the fake pearl buttons of her white blouse. "He ain' fuckin' Doris, is all Doris knows. Fresh down from Beauregard. They getting him all ready to ship out on a tub. He don' know to where, but he t'ink North Africa."

"Are you a spy?"

"*Merde*, no, that is not Doris. But it came up. It's amazing what a horny soldier will tell you when his dick is under your hand and he thinks pity will make you spread your legs. He might just be scared and miss home and his sheep. I hope he gets laid before he ships out."

"But not by you."

"Not by Doris. No, not by Doris. He don' have no dollars left. He don' even have his wallet. The boy just don' know that yet."

She spread the wallet's seams with her thumbs, found a hidden twenty, and then threw the tattered wallet's remains beneath a bush. "Doris did not marry him, neither."

"He proposed?"

"No, but I didn' propose to him neither. A girl Doris knows is married to six sailors. She collects the Cracker Jack rings and cigar bands they use at the chapel. If they die in action, she gets their GI Life Insurance. If they live, when we win this war, Doris is heading down to the dock just to watch the reunions when all them soldiers an' sailors come lookin' for the same wife. It's sweet, but Doris won' work a con that pays off if the boy is dead. Doris is a patriot and has principles. Besides, getting married all the time wears a girl out with all those honeymoons."

She put out her hand, palm up. Pierre peeled a ten from the roll in his pocket. When she did not withdraw her hand, he peeled off a second ten. She shrugged and took the money. That still left him with the best day he'd had since he'd first set up on the east side of Jackson Square.

"Did you roll him?"

"Doris is no thief." Pierre placed his porkpie hat on her head. She did not remove it. "He gave me his last twenty for a room. He expects change. He may still be waiting for Doris. Do you t'ink he knows his wallet is gone yet?" She neatly folded the bills Pierre had given her and pushed them down the front of her blouse. "Butch, you buy me a cold one and Doris will call it even."

"Twenty is not enough?"

"Doris never gets enough."

The saloon was dark, cool, and would soon grow crowded. If the bouncer recognized him as the boy who'd been mucking toilets, he made no sign. They sat at a small table far from the front door. Doris toed off her shoes before her leg and bare foot found his knee under the table.

"Explain that side bet stuff," she said.

It seemed simple to him, but to most people, it was not. "Your mind has to be fast to work it," he said. She stared impatiently at him. "Okay. Look. If a player bets either side of a four for five proposition and there are equal bets on either side, the players are betting against each other, not me. And I get to keep …"

"One out of five," she said, completing his sentence. "You pay the winner with the losers, but some money sticks. Doris is not so stupid as you think."

"One out of ten," he said, "but I'll grant you are not stupid. The more action, the better. If the bets are really lopsided, if I have to, I'll make sure the heavy side loses and I'll keep that much more. Today, the play was lopsided. Everyone wants to see the house get beat by a soldier."

"But that ain' happening."

"Damn straight."

She chewed her lip. Her errant incisor gave her the look of a wolf. Her toes explored his crotch. "You that smart? Where'd you learn such a thing?" Her muddy eyes in the dim light transformed to green pools. The pink point of her tongue traced a path across her teeth. She sighed. "A brain and fast hands. Any more gifts? Doris wants to know all there is to know about her Butch."

"Everything?"

Her eyes boldly held his and once more the pink tip of her tongue wet her lips. "Doris' foot tells her all she needs to know. Is that really all you, *cher*?"

Later, his shirt off and her blouse draped limply over the back of a chair, both spent and slick with sweat in the close heat of her apartment, she whispered: "How old are you, really? Is Doris getting arrested for cradle robbing, *cher*?"

"Old enough. Why do you ask?"

"Ain' nothing that sags."

Her leg went over him. She bent to draw her tongue along a slow path from below his ear, down his neck, and across his hairless chest, her teeth lingering to close on a nipple. The slower she went, the more excited she became. Her lips and warm breath skipped over him with slow kisses down his ribs to his belly and below to where her hand held him. She abruptly sat up, straddling him, her eyes lighted by inner heat. "*Mon dieu. Mon dieu.* You are beautiful, *cher.*" He was in her, her eyes closed, and she braced herself with her hands at his chest. "Don'you get tired? F'true, f'true, f'true, Doris is going to jail for baby-rape, f'true."

He had money enough to pay Herlihy for three weeks when he escaped the Y into an illegal apartment. The landlord asked to know his draft status. "I'll be here until I finish my ministry." The older man shrugged, not at all caring.

"Thirty a month on the first," he said. When Pierre held his gaze, the man said, "Twenty-eight. That's less than a dollar per day, you being a man of the cloth." Pierre held his gaze. "All right, twenty-six, but not a penny less." He added the favorite phrase of every chiseler. "There's a war going on, you know."

The two rooms stacked one above the other at the top of a hexagonal turret were close to Audubon Park. Convex windows warped his view in five directions. The apartment was illegal because the water closet was on the lower floor beside a few pantry shelves of raw pine. Daily, Pierre filled two blue and white china pitchers and a glass bowl with water that he carted sloshing up to his bedroom. The sluggish toilet had rust stains, and his sink was less than a foot in diameter. He could barely turn in the metal shower stall, but the water ran hot and the stubborn drain worked, if slowly. He stocked the old Kelvinator with a bottle of buttermilk, eggs, and a loaf of bread so in his landlord's frying pan he could prepare a breakfast of sorts on the two-burner propane stove. Most days, the garret filled with the aromas of oil and diesel fuel, tabasco, the park, or faintly the river itself. The chipped parquet floor was warped. The private entrance was secured by a simple padlock, and the entire building was behind a fence. A pry bar could open the stairwell, but Pierre owned nothing worth stealing, not so much as a radio. Best of all was the garret's four-poster brass bed and its unstained mattress.

He envisioned Doris naked on it, sinuous arms reaching up to him, the checkered white fluttering café curtains the same unapologetic green as her eyes. He liked the place's quiet. He read books and followed the war news in print from *The Times-Picayune* while he nursed his morning chicory coffee.

On her first visit to his garret, Doris bounced naked on the squealing springs like a kid on a trampoline. Her body was tight as a teenager's. Kneeling behind him on the mattress, she kneaded his shoulders. She wondered at the neatly piled books on the floor under the windows surrounding his bed. "*Cher*, you read all these? Tell Doris, f'true. How is a book gonna make you rich?"

Pierre read three or four books at a time, turning to each with his mood. He could not imagine a circumstance when he would discard a book. Barbarians discarded books. Hitler burned books. Jews, he had read admiringly, buried worn books as if they were cherished family members.

His days haunting the Napoleon Library ended the day he finished *The Death of Ivan Ilyich* and realized he had to own it but could not steal from a library. On a rainy day when he'd have no players, the *louche beau gamin* with his sweat-stained porkpie hat hunted treasure in the used bookstores that rimmed the French Quarter. He made Tolstoy his own.

Rain wounded his income, but it also set him free. Either a book or Doris or both lying beside him, the garret windows open wide, the steady hiss of raindrops on his street, cleaner air stirring the thin cotton of his café curtains like lazy flags—there was nothing better. If Doris was with him, after a morning of love, they'd put on only enough clothes to avoid arrest, stroll to a patisserie on Magazine where they lingered only long enough for desire to rekindle.

They talked about anything and nothing, but Pierre never mentioned his mother to Doris, while Doris never mentioned her past. Their lives began the day they met. Doris accepted that he was 22, and he accepted that she was 27. Fabricated histories left them a mere five years apart in age, when the reality was more like sixteen years, the same age difference that lay between Pierre and Maman, a fact Pierre acknowledged but did not like to think about.

Eventually, Doris asked how he did what he did with cards. "Doris wants to know all you know, *cher*."

He showed her seconds, dealing from the bottom, and how to ice a deck. "It takes practice," he said. "A person who makes a clumsy move can get his hands busted."

She nodded. "But once you have the skill, you have it always."

He asked her to move in with him.

"You're too much a citizen, Butch," she said, very seriously. "An address and a library card. Next thing, you'll join a Mardi Gras krewe. Someone is going to put the draft board onto Pierre, *cher*. Then Doris would be in the street."

"Why would anyone do that?" Was she planning on blackmailing him?

Her hand curled beneath his chin. "They love their boy who is shitting in the same foxhole where he eats; they want to know why you ain' shitting wit' him. Doris has eyes to see. Do not tell Doris about your flat feet. You have beautiful feet. Your feet are about as flat as Doris' ass." She slapped at her round hip. "*Mais non*, a place to stay in New Orleans is not so easy to find that I can give mine away. So Doris thinks we keep separate addresses."

Weeks later, he left her asleep and went down the stairs to refill the wash basin. When he returned, the garret smelled sweeter than burned sugar. Doris was naked and cross-legged on the bed, a short candle sputtering under a bent spoon. One end of a rubber siphon tube was in her teeth; the other end was tight around her skinny bicep. Her index finger tapped the soft flesh inside her elbow to raise a vein. She looked up. Their eyes met. She held out the bent spoon, but he would not take it. She shrugged and carefully placed the spoon on the bed stand. "I thought you went for bread." She bit the rubber siphon tight and her free hand slowly pushed the piston of her glass hypodermic needle. A form of ecstasy he'd never before seen crossed her face. Her eyes rolled up.

"Cocaine?"

She took a moment to answer. "Horse, *cher*. Doris is a simple girl."

She booted the rush by drawing the hypo's piston in and out without flushing the heroin fully into her vein while not removing the needle from her arm. Her eyes rolled a second time. Her breathing was shallow.

"White people don't use heroin," he said.

"This be The Big Easy, *cher*. The gumbo is all salt with pepper." A crumpled brown paper bag was on the bed beside the blackened tin spoon. "You don't know what Doris has seen and done. You'll never know." Her voice became faint as she struggled not to nod off. Her eyes fluttered. "Doris tells her fine boy-lover with his beautiful hands that nothing he sees is what it look like, *cher*." She fell in slow motion like a feather in an updraft until she was flat to her back, her skin whiter than his sheet, her head propped on his thin pillow. She rolled slowly to her hip, booting the drug a last time. Her blood whorled currents in the glass syringe. Her eyes rolled to whites; her toes curled. She trembled just as she trembled when he entered her.

"Why didn't you tell me?" he asked. He had to repeat the question.

Her thin blue lips, the corners caked with dry spit, barely moved. In the middle of a word, she blanked out, then suddenly revived. "Nothing to tell you. Doris kicked a long while ago, *cher*. This is what you do not know. Doris swears, f'true. Today was just a taste. Just a taste to get Doris through. I can quit any time. Just a taste. Come, *cher*, lie down beside Doris. It will pass. Lie beside me, my beautiful boy-lover. Take a taste, Butch. Know what Doris knows."

He lay beside her, his fingers laced behind his own neck. Her head lay on his chest where she drooled. He shut his eyes and heard only her labored, ragged breath. Her legs fell open. He thought to take her, but that would be like fucking a corpse.

She fell asleep beside him.

He went for a long walk, found a *Times-Picayune,* sipped chicory coffee at his usual black wrought iron table on the cobblestones before his usual café.

Doris had a lover she would never leave.

Hours later, his checkered curtains floated on the lazy air. His bed was unmade and the apartment felt empty of life.

Pierre continued to insert five single dollar bills into folded thick note paper every week so the thieves at the P.O. could not see Maman's money was cash even if they held the envelope up to a candle. He fabricated a continuing story for Maman about the wonderful yellow-haired girl he was courting. But when Maman wrote back for elaboration about Kathleen Josephine, a name he took from the *Picayune* society pages, his imagination smacked into a wall. What did rich people do?

He mailed Maman's notes and money to Gulfport General Delivery. Her letters to him were sporadic, badly printed in grease pencil on yellow school notepaper. She wrote news about her chickens or his classmates who had gone to war, but never a word about Charlie. Over time, Maman's notes became less frequent. Pierre, too, wrote less and less.

What could he write? *I sleep with whores and junkies. I cheat at cards. If Charlie hits you I will come home to kill him.*

1944

On New Year's Day 1944, Pierre turned 18. It seemed important to pay a whore to help him celebrate, but he learned what he'd always known, he could take no easy pleasure from a business transaction.

Herlihy doubled his tithe. Pierre complained for form's sake, but received no relief on the Irish Tax. "There's a war on," Herlihy said, parroting the justification for shortages and prices that rose for bread, milk, paper, heating oil, and every other consumer good. Black markets soared. Pierre tried dealing Blackjack at his spot on St. Ann, but Herlihy intervened. He advised not-so-gently that "There is them that will tolerate no competition. That's a game that belongs in a gambling house, not on my street. Stay with what you know, boy."

"I'll cut you in for thirty percent."

"Not even for forty."

That winter, when Pierre was not on St. Ann stamping his feet and pulling his collar up rubbing his hands for the warmth, he was in his garret with an emery board scraping his fingertips tender. Despite the cold, he needed every quarter if he did not want to go back to mucking toilets.

Slapping his hands together and sucking on his own fingers made Pierre's hands more sensitive, faster than anyone's eye even in cold. His false shuffles left a deck colder than a nun's privates. He sliced the edges of cards to precise widths so that his fingers could feel aces, royalty, and ten-spots, though the different widths were undetectable to any casual eye. He meticulously resealed shaved decks in their original cellophane so he could undo a new deck no one could question, though in reality the cards were truly iced.

By mid-April, up or down river, Jackson Square loudmouths were offering odds on where and when Eisenhower would invade northern France. The smart money looked hard at Calais on May 8, to take advantage of favorable tides and mild weather. Everyone claimed a cousin with a friend whose kid sister's high school girl-friend typed Top Secret messages, so their scuttlebutt was superior stuff, as rock solid as the inside word on a maiden colt to be tested over 5 furlongs at the Fairgrounds along with seven similar glue factory refugees jockeyed by pink-assed monkeys.

The day the black Cadillac parked a few feet from his game on St. Ann, Pierre's fortunes began to turn. The car gleamed with pre-war chrome and hummed, perfectly tuned. Pierre kept his patter steady, challenging a bettor, flattering a girl, allowing her a small win so her sailor would lose far more. The Cadillac's driver circled the car's front end to stand at the outskirts of a small knot of people who watched Pierre work his porkpie hat, tumbling it up and down his arm like a circus juggler. The driver's left cheek-bone looked as if it had had an unfortunate collision with Joe Louis's right hook. He was tall; from the crowd's rear, his lifeless gray eyes took in everything. Despite the unrelenting sunshine, he wore a rumpled unbuttoned camel hair coat and a better fe-dora gray as his eyes. The coat was lousy camouflage for the bulge at his left lapel that betrayed a holster. He would want to reach across his own chest for his weapon, so he had to be right-handed. The coat was unbuttoned to allow air to circulate, but that gave glimpses of his pearl gray pinstripe suit, same color as the hat. The *Times-Picayune* was neatly folded under his arm. His black wingtips looked spit shined.

The Cadillac's opaque rear window rolled open a few inches. The cragged silhouette of a man's face floated in the shadows. Riding shotgun, a third man extended his arm to adjust the passenger side-view mirror, enabling him to see forward and back without spinning his head. His reach exposed a starched white shirt cuff, a gold watch, and gold cufflinks. His suit sleeve was funeral black.

Herlihy could be no protection against such men.

The driver came forward to bet a fin. Why screw with a guy on a medium-cheap bet when the heat under his lapel could take every dime Pierre had? Pierre gave the gunman an honest drop, and the man pointed to the facedown black ace. The driver said, "Again." Of the ten dollars still on the array, Pierre was playing against five of his own.

The semicircle of observers drew closer. Ten dollars was not a small bet for a spring afternoon. Watching a swell play a street game offered high drama. This was no drunken sailor on shore leave.

He won a second time, said, "Again." Pierre was now playing against fifteen dollars of his own money.

Side bets began to mount. Pierre announced he would accept no coin wagers; quarters and dimes would slow his action. He supposed his real mark was the man hidden by the car's shadows, but he could not figure what his best play was. Chauffeured Cadillacs did not ordinarily turn up on St. Ann with passengers eager to play 3-Card Monte on an orange crate. These were the kind who owned the game.

A curl of cigarette smoke snaked lazily from the car's partially opened window.

The driver picked out the black ace a third time. Pierre was in the hole for thirty-five dollars, though the side bets were easing some of his pain even if the side action was beginning to lean toward the player. If the man doubled down again, Pierre would have to risk a cheat. He was a mouse trapped by a mean kitten. Seventy dollars would be a lot to lose in less than two minutes. But then the man scooped up his winnings, turned a moment toward the car, saw a signal Pierre did not, nodded, and then turned back.

"Mr. Carolla wants a word. Go ahead, kid. Your stuff is safe with me."

"Who is Mr. Carolla?"

"Nobody likes a wiseass, buddy." He pointed with his thumb. "Get in." When Pierre hesitated, he smirked and added, "Please."

The man in the front passenger seat stood on the sidewalk to pat Pierre down. Before he'd find it, Pierre said, "Don't cut yourself. There's a knife strapped to my left ankle." The driver very professionally lifted Pierre's crotch, his hands floating left to right and front to back. He removed the knife but left the leather sheath strapped where it was. Then the rear door of the Cadillac yawned wide.

The crushed velvet upholstered seat was softer than an angel's ass. His mother had sewn enough dresses for Pierre to appreciate the subtleties of cloth. This was pre-war goods, preserved and rubbed so well was either a miracle or contraband.

"You've got the good hands, Herlihy says. Now I see." Mr. Carolla gently lifted Pierre's hands by the fingertips.

"I just lost to your guy. How good can my hands be?"

Carolla almost smiled. His lips barely parted when he spoke. "Smart mouth, too. You Italian?"

"Never had the privilege."

Mr. Carolla released his fingertips. "You're dark enough to be Sicilian, but, okay, French, then."

"Partly. Mostly. On my mother's side. There is some Creole in there, too."

"Your father?"

"Never had the privilege of knowing him, neither, but Maman tells me he was a white man."

"Mothers lie."

"Not to me."

Carolla's grin exposed his yellowing teeth. "Brass balls. I like that. You might be the guy I need to do me a favor. As soon as I meet a guy, I know him cold. It's a gift, kid." His snap brim hat lay crown up on the seat between them. The man's gold pinky ring was set with tiny glittering opals. Carolla's double-breasted suit was unbuttoned, the lining lush cream-colored silk. His receding hairline shaped a widow's peak. His restless black eyes only stayed on Pierre briefly. "Herlihy is not too bright, but a beat cop like him has his uses. I never met the guy, you understand, but I am told Herlihy knows what he knows and he has his eyes on the street. He reports you have fast hands and a good eye. Is the mick off-base?"

"I don't think so."

Carolla's wolfish grin appeared a second time. "No false modesty? That's better than smart. And here I am in a bind. I need a new smart boy no one knows with fast hands and a good eye. So far, you fit the bill. Take it easy. I'm not asking you to strangle a nun. Can you use a few dollars?"

"Who can't?"

Mr. Carolla patted Pierre's cheek. His fingers smelled of nicotine and lilac. "I like you more and more, kid. So here's the proposition." He looked out the window and talked. "Someone who I want to work with is in town and wants a game. Some guys get laid; this guy likes high stakes poker. I need to arrange his diversion. Private, but he wants a professional dealer. That's my look out. I can't trust the little cooze he wants to deal, but if she does not deal, he will not play, and if he does not play, the other guys I need to be at this game stay away and the whole deal goes to shit. Tits and a nice ass are great in the sack, but dealing cards at a game I run? I am not so sure. It's my rep on the table, not hers. So this is a delicate situation. The cooze may be balling him, for all I know, but he says not. Business is business, but I don't want to say, 'Dump the mouse.' You follow me? But I can't afford a mistake and let her rob the table. These are friends, important friends. My associates. If they even think things are not on the up and up and that they cannot trust me, I will have the kind of trouble no cooze is worth. *Capiche?*"

"Sure. You need a face no one knows to keep an eye open for you."

Mr. Carolla nodded. "I trust nobody, kid, least of all you, but I do trust mutual self-interest. You make me happy, I will make you happy. Why should anyone be less than happy? It's just good business. We'll call you the relief dealer. The mouse needs to pee, you keep the cards in motion. Nothing fancy. We don't need a mechanic, but my bet is you can spot a mechanic from a mile away. You can see what no one else can. Am I right?" He did not wait for an answer. "Just deal fucking poker and keep an eye on her."

Mr. Carolla withdrew a sealed pack of cards from his interior jacket pocket. He peeled away the cellophane, handed the pack to Pierre, and told Pierre to riffle the new deck four times. Mr. Carolla cut and instructed Pierre to take out the King of Hearts. Pierre found the king. "OK, kid, put the king back, shuffle two more times, let me cut, and then show me that king again."

Pierre shuffled. Carolla cut. Pierre set the pack beside the upturned hat on the crushed velvet seat between them. Carolla snapped the top card face up.

"That's the six of clubs, kid."

"You didn't say you wanted it on top. Try again."

Carolla snapped over the next card. King of Hearts. "Seconds," Carolla said. He pursed his lips, impressed. "Herlihy did not lie. You know why they call the King of Hearts the Suicide King, kid?"

"His sword is in his own skull. My mother told me he died for love."

"No disrespect to your mother, but I hear he got careless, tried to show off and fuck over his friends. He had to do himself in before they put his nuts in a vice. Do you ever get careless? Maybe show off to a girl how you are a big deal? Brag about the people you know?"

"Wouldn't think of it. I stay to myself. I can't even remember a face and name after a few minutes. Ten minutes from now, I'll forget this conversation. It's a problem I have."

Carolla nodded and stroked his clean-shaven chin with the knuckles of his right hand. "All right, then, kid. We will take a chance on you. Sit in, keep an eye peeled, let Mario know if you see anything off the beam."

"Mario?"

"My driver. The guy who beat you at your own game."

"If I see anything, Mr. Carolla, I'll let Mario know."

"You don't want to know the pay?"

"I figure you'll take care of me."

"You're right, but that's the first stupid thing you said. Don't butter me up. This is business. I need straight shooters. Take some advice from Silver Dollar Sam. When it comes to money, take nothing for granted. What's your name, kid?"

Pierre told him.

Mr. Carolla nodded. "Loyalty is the most important thing, Pierre. Never fuck your friends, and never get careless. It's worth a century note to me. What's it worth to you?"

"About the same."

Carolla suddenly snatched and turned Pierre's wrist downward to look closely at Pierre's hands again. "Get your nails cleaned tomorrow morning." He named an address in the Garden District. "Tell Ida that Sam wants you should have a manicure, then forget you were ever there. You need to look professional. These guys will rip your arms from your chest to look up your sleeve if they think you are a mechanic, and if they see anything they will beat you to death with your left arm and shove your right arm up your ass. Get a decent shirt, too, linen, something soft." He paused to think. "And when you deal, you deal honest. You own a bow-tie?"

"I can get one."

"Never buy shit. Shit is anything second best. Like that asswipe shirt you got on. What is that? Burlap? And that hat. You look like a carnival guy who rides runs the merry-go-round and grabs at fourteen-year-old ass." Carolla tossed Pierre's felt hat out the limo window. "Go to the place on Carondelet. It's nice there. The tailor is my cousin. I have a lot of cousins. It's a big family. Get a white linen shirt and a velvet tie. Tell them who sent you and they will send me the bill." Carolla touched his lower lip. "And get a fucking haircut."

"Whatever you say."

Carolla reached across Pierre and opened the Cadillac door. "How much did you lose to Mario?"

"Thirty."

"You let him win?"

"He won legit."

Carolla's thin smile converted his face to inverted V's, hairline, eyebrows, eyes, lips. "I like you, kid. But I guess if you lost the money fair and square, I do not owe you shit. Are you sure you did not let him win?"

"Mr. Carolla, if I had won, would you ask me for your money back? I don't welch."

Carolla's lips pursed again. "Stick with that attitude, never fuck with Silver Dollar Sam, and you'll do just peachy." He peeled off another twenty. "Take tomorrow off. Sleep late. You need to be fresh at ten o'clock. Be at this spot. Mario is good at finding people." Carolla grinned like a wolf. "He will find you."

The three-story gray-and-blue house stood among several similar ivy-covered homes in the Garden District, most with porticos above faux Greek columns. Down the street, kids running across lawns and through hedges kicked a ball and shrieked, wild as the chained barking dogs that tried to run after them. More than one house had a rope swing hanging from a bough. Kids, bicycles, balls, willow trees, moss, and money, the life he'd never know.

It was hardly a neighborhood for sporting houses.

The wrought iron gate squealed on rusted hinges as Pierre pushed it back into thick purple and white wisteria. A wasp eager for its chance at the Bougainvillea in the lattice work hovered lazily by his ear. The garden was overgrown with pink oleander. The perfume of flowers held an undercurrent of damp rot.

Pierre perspired. It was not so long a walk, but the hot morning made it feel like miles. He mounted three wooden stairs and dropped a brass knocker on the newly painted white door.

The large woman with steel gray hair could only be Ida. She might have been 50; she might have been 70. She inhabited a cloud of jasmine and inspected him skeptically.

"Mr. Carolla sent me."

"Oh?"

"For a manicure."

"Is that what Sam is calling it, these days?"

She disappeared into a room beyond two large French doors where she whispered into a phone, burst into a raucous laugh, and then emerged to gesture that Pierre follow her. "A manicure, it will be." They walked a dim hallway. Early morning in a whorehouse had the place less than immaculate. Pierre stepped over a wine glass and a man's shoe.

Ida shouted up a winding flight of dark oak stairs for Verne to turn the damned radio off and haul her skinny ass downstairs right now this second.

Two bare statuesque legs appeared. As the legs descended, the rest of Verne was revealed. She seemed to float above the floor in an unbelted green silk kimono. Ida said to Verne, "This is the genuine article," Ida said to Verne. "He's no Vidalia: the man needs a manicure."

Verne looked puzzled.

"I have no idea why, so don't ask. A manicure, and nothing else. He has no name, so don't ask that either. Do you get off on manicures, sonny?"

"No, ma'm," he said.

Ida snorted and left him to Verne. They went a few feet further down the hall to a white-tiled kitchen. Verne and Pierre sat across a white wooden table. The table's paint was scratched. Verne's bare neck was exposed toward the half-open window behind her. In the yard behind the house, a square of coarse string marked a vegetable garden. Maybe Ida ran the only whorehouse in America that served homegrown peppers, tomato, snap beans, and lettuce. The sparkling glassware in a wooden drying rack suspended from the ceiling above the kitchen's twin porcelain sinks rattled faintly on a light stream of air that passed through the open window. "Oscar pours drinks at night," she said as Verne reached to the glasses. "But he is not here. You want something?"

Pierre shook his head.

Verne's high cheekbones did not hide her tired blue eyes. She was about his age, but far from girlish, at most 20. Like everyone else, she assumed he was older. Everyone called her Verne because her hair fell over her eyes, "like Veronica Lake." Ida called dates *Vidalias* because she was crazy. "It's not like she thinks you're an onion. That would be really crazy. Even crazy for Ida."

Verne inspected his fingers in the identical way Silver Dollar Sam had, though her touch was far more pleasant. She talked without looking up about how she heard that out west every working girl was a fake movie star. Doctors carved the girls up to make them look right, but while Ida was crazy, she was not that kind of crazy. "Them doctors are creepy, you ask me. Not that anyone is asking, but it sounds like a house filled with Frankensteins with all those tiny silvery scars on the girls' faces. Creepy, right?" Looking a little like Veronica Lake was her good luck and hurt no one, so she did her hair over one eye and Verne she would be until someone told her to be someone different. "Then my name might change. I hear there are lots of Vernes and Lanas and a truckload of Laurens, like Bacall. But for now, I am Veronica, Verne to my friends. I have either a lot or a few friends, depending on how a body counts friends. I mean, you ask me, and nobody is, but if you ask me once we have been naked and balling, I ought to be able to call a customer a friend, am I right?"

Pierre did not go to the pictures much. He figured Veronica Lake and the others had to be movie stars. People were wild for movies, and while Pierre could enjoy watching handsome men and pretty women act their stories on a screen, he preferred his hours in the library to hours at the Saenger down Canal Street way.

"My mother liked Louise Brooks," he said.

"Do tell. Who is Louise Brooks?"

"A star. From the silents."

Verne shrugged her shoulders. "I'm taller," she said. "By a lot."

"Taller than Louise Brooks?"

"Taller than Veronica Lake. Most everybody is. She is real short. That's why she plays with Alan Ladd. He's real short, too, but since she is under five foot, he looks tall next to her. I'm near five-seven. It's the gams." She hiked her kimono to show her leg.

When Verne stood up to adjust herself, the unbelted green-and-blue silk kimono fell open. Verne smoothed her satin white teddy flat against her hips and belly. Her sheer silk underwear left nothing to Pierre's imagination. Had she bleached her pubic hair or shaved herself clean as a baby? Verne smoothed the kimono under herself and sat again; those legs that seemed to start at her neck crossing at her knee. The garter belt that circled her left thigh held no stocking, the scarlet elastic startling against her flesh. Her neck was slender as a show horse.

She massaged his fingers one at a time; then with a tiny scissor trimmed each of Pierre's nails to the same length. She filed the edges smooth before she curled his fingers into a shallow dish of clear dish soap. "Softens your cuticles," she explained. Under her gardenia perfume, he smelled her Juicy Fruit gum.

She pushed a length of her very white hair from over her eye with her wrist. It stubbornly fell back. She did it again, it fell back again, and she pouted her lips to blow the unwelcome bangs off her eyes. Her hair persisted in falling back. They waited for his cuticles to soften until she held his hand up to inspect his fingers in the sunlight coming through the window over her shoulder. Every movement slid the spaghetti strap of the chemise further off her shoulder, but she seldom tugged it back up. She was the whitest woman Pierre had ever seen. Except for her crimson lipstick and the touch of rouge on her cheeks, she could have been made of porcelain.

The lazy electric fan oscillating at his left blew across a tilted tray of ice. Runoff melted slowly into the sink. With every pass of the fan her hair scattered and her robe fluttered. Pierre got an eyeful, but if Verne cared she gave no sign. The eyes of strangers had roamed over her before. What was one Vidalia more or less?

An orange stick pushed back his cuticles while she chattered about how she was from New Jersey but only just last week they sent her here to New Orleans. "Ain't that a hoot? Me from the Garden State and now here I am in the Garden District." Life was filled with little surprises like that, if a person looked for them. New

Orleans was too goddam hot, even in April, if anyone asked her, not that anyone would, but it was a free country and she was entitled to an opinion, right? It was not yet summer, but she needed shower baths all day long, but could never use soap because soap dried a girl's skin. Her hair wanted to be straight, but all this humidity made it kink up. Life was crazy that way: most of the girls needed permanents to have their hair curled and bobbed like Betty Boop, but Verne ironed her hair to have it straight as Veronica Lake's. The girls helped her iron her hair in late afternoons. They were swell kids who looked out for each other, but hair was hair and how much could anyone do? Thank God she would not be here more than a month. How did people live through a summer in New Orleans?

She wanted to be sent to Chicago. She had family in Chicago. Maybe in Chicago she could get a fresh start if her aunt would give her the moola to pay the boys off, but the boys might send her to Kansas City, first. She begged for Chicago, and while no one said *Yes*, no one said *No*, neither. There were operations in Chicago, there were operations everywhere, so why not Chicago? She had to do as she was told, she just owed so much, and the interest mounted up and up and up. Every meal, her transportation, every little thing down to the last penny, they charged her and put it on her very own page in a ledger. At least they were not too tough on her, no one wanted to damage the merchandise, but she owed what she owed, so she was so far behind the 8-Ball she might never get out. Right after she arrived, Ida had shown Verne the ledger. "That page follows me everywhere I go. I drop dead, St. Peter will have my ledger. It does not matter where I am, how many dates I have, or the number of dates who swear they left a tip with the landlady: My bottom line never budges. Can you figure that? I can't."

Thing is, her life was a mess, but she was straightening things out now that her boyfriend the shitheel was out of the picture. She owed all that money to start with because the shitheel was an idiot, you ask her, not that anyone was asking. That was why she needed to get to Chicago where she had people. Back in New Jersey, the shitheel had big, big plans but a small brain. Maybe he was still back in New Jersey. She did not know. "What's it to me where that 4F is?" All she knew was she always got stuck with the shitheels, fellows with small brains, big plans, and tiny dicks. She held her thumb two inches from her index finger. One day the shitheel told Verne she had to go with these guys or they were going to kill him, so what else could she do? "Now look at me. This is what I get for taking pity." She buffed Pierre's nails and blew on them like they were dice. She squinted close, and Pierre realized she was near-sighted.

"My problem is my big heart. One minute I am eating popcorn at Monmouth Park; the next minute the shitheel takes all my money, borrows a truckload more, and plans to win enough to buy the next Seabiscuit. You know how that works out, right? Instead of cashing winning tickets, I blink and when I open the peepers again, I am in Atlantic City studying hotel room ceilings, if you catch my drift." She critically squinted at his hand before she ran a fresh emery board across the edges of a few fingernails. "I know. I know. It's my own fault. A girl with a brain would know the draft-dodging shitheel wisenheimer 4-F was a stinker when he put a pencil through his eardrum." They must have slipped her a mickey in Atlantic City, too, because one day she wakes up on a train with three other girls and two guys on their way to New Orleans. "My clothes are still in New Jersey, but you can bet they got my ledger sheet on the train. Oh boy, they'd never leave that little item behind." The ledger sheet started with what the shitheel owed, and when the little wisenheimer 4-F put her name on all the paper he had out, they bought the paper at ten cents on the dollar, a deal that kept him out of concrete overshoes but put her on her back with her legs in the air.

"It's that interest. Interest makes no sense to me. I am no Einstein, but I am smart enough to know not to piss off guys who know where my sister lives. She is a sweet kid." Verne tenderly lifted the damp fingers of his other hand, pursed her lips and jetted breath on them, and told him to relax. "If our old lady ever saw the pictures they took of me after the mickey, she'd shit, just shit, rollover, and die. I never did half of that stuff before, and unless someone comes across with half of Fort Knox I will never do them again. At least, not when I am conscious, I won't. It gives me the willies just to think about it, so I say thank Jesus I can't remember any of it. I wish they didn't take those pictures, but they did. That's the day I learned to keep my head down. Let my mother wonder where I run off to. I sent a letter so she knows I am not dead, but that's all. That's better for her than the boys visiting my sister, Gina. Gina is fourteen. They'll scoop her up quick as a wink if I step out of line, tell Gina I am dead, and start her off with all I owe on a ledger page all her own. Gina is not one hundred percent in the head, if you know what I mean, but she is right enough to do what she is told and she is prettier than me. A real looker. She'd have plenty of pizzazz if she could get that grin off her face, but she'd have to be better in the head for that. Maybe they'd sell her to some jag-off thinks he wants to see Shirley Temple doing tricks in a garter belt."

Verne softy held the fingertips of each of his hands, considered her work from several angles, pursed her lips with satisfaction at the result, and said: "I don't argue. A girl who argues can lose a nose or her lips or something, and then what can she do?" She glanced out the window to the overgrown garden, and then turned to Pierre again. "Things are not so bad, I guess. I get my three hots and a cot. Some do lots worse. Am I right? Or am I right?"

Pierre thought she was done with his hands, but she said to wait a minute, went upstairs, and came back with a small jar of clear polish. She swept the kimono under her as she again sat at the white kitchen table, one long leg tucked under her as well. "You have nice half-moons," she said in that nasal New Jersey voice. "I wish I had half-moons like that." Her hand cradled his while she applied the polish with a small brush, cool and smooth. She asked him to flap his hands to help the polish dry while she scooped two clean jelly jars into the melted ice-water tray to fill a cold drink for each of them. When the polish was no longer tacky, she buffed his nails a last time. They shone.

He imagined she held his fingers longer than she needed to. "You know you look like that guy in that movie with Ingrid Bergman. *Casablanca*."

He'd seen that one. "Bogart?"

"No. The other one. Not the cop. The other other one. Bergman's husband. The one leading the Free French."

Pierre had no idea who she meant. He'd come away thinking nothing could be more stupid than *Casablanca*. Letters of transit with Hitler's signature that no Nazi would question? No one would forge them? Every gestapo agent recognized Der Führer's hand-writing? And fog in the desert? What con artist wrote such shit?

When Verne was truly finished with him, she patted his cheek. "You come back and ask for Verne because I never get them as cute as you. I can't give you a discount, but you better do that quick be-cause any day now I might be on the train. I hope it will be Chicago. I deserve Chicago. I have people there and they will help me."

They offered to monogram the white linen shirt's pocket, but how could it be a good idea to have his initials where anyone could see them? The offer reminded him of the Yellow-Haired Girl Who Looked back: he wondered again what KJ could stand for. She'd looked like a Katherine. He was almost sure she was a Katherine. But Jones did not fit, and she did not look like a James. Kathleen?

He already owned black slacks, but they needed to be pressed. He paid careful attention to the clerk's instructions on how to knot a black velvet bowtie, had the man repeat it, and though they gave him a little printed card with directions and pictures, he'd never again need to refer to it. Their mirror showed a young man who looked professional.

By afternoon, white thunderheads piled above the city. April in N'awlins could be either postcard-pretty or bring air thick as gumbo. His shirt-box under his arm, he jumped aboard a moving trolley to Central City. The passing breeze was a relief.

With Carolla's money burning a hole in his pocket, he lunched on a half-dozen oysters at the Monteleone Swan Bar, as much for the horseradish as the shellfish. Then his face wrapped by a coiled hot towel, he dozed in a fully reclined barber chair while a barber shaved his chin and throat, something Pierre hardly needed, but Carolla's money made him a swell. His Florsheims were new, but he sat in a chair for a shine anyway. The bootblack got twenty-five cents, but Pierre tipped him a full dollar to have his shoes gleam like glass. As Pierre went through the hotel lobby, he looked again into a mirror to admire the louche swell looking back at him. What would Maman think of her *beau gamin* and his gleaming fingernails, his unparted hair smelling of faint lemon pomade brushed straight back by twin military brushes, his shoes shining, his neck smelling of Lilac Vegetal?

It would have been nothing to head home by trolley, but Pierre felt too good to end the day. He strolled across the train tracks to the greensward at the riverside. From a shaded bench he watched the Mississippi flow. Hatless and relaxed, his arms fully extended across the bench's back. The fading sun touched his face.

When he opened his eye, for the second time in his life, he saw The Yellow Haired Girl Who Looked Back. She came toward him from no more than hundred feet to his left. It seemed like he'd fallen into a dream.

A towline of taut sight stretched between them. Every detail of what he saw embedded onto his mind. Her saddle shoes had flopping red laces, the toe-box an impossible white, her bobbysocks turned down to her ankles, her gray wool skirt, a red-and-yellow tartan, swirling easily around her mid-calf. The gray wool cloche tight over her ears failed to contain her golden hair. How did she endure wool and a hat on a day of such heat? Her unbuttoned jacket flapped below her hips, the empty patch pockets gapping. She clutched three thick books flat against her narrow chest.

At an arm's length away, she smiled that smile Pierre still dreamed of. His brain went to Novocain, but a stride past him she stopped, turned, and said: "Do I know you?"

On a day filled by miracles, here was the greatest.

She thumbed off the cloche; her hair cascaded free. Two plastic begonia pins stayed the curls jouncing by her eyes and face. The

New Orleans air was humid enough to slice with a butter knife, but The Yellow-Haired Girl Who Looked Back was more crisp than October.

The truth was too ridiculous. He could not say *I once saw you in the street and have thought about you ever since,* so he said: "I don't think so."

"I never forget a face," she said. "I just can't think where it was." She sat beside him. Behind a tugboat that pushed a barge downriver to the open sea, the river water dappled into flashes of sun. She pouted in thought, then smiled as if the sun broke through clouds. "Do you go to school here?"

She had to repeat the question. He'd been struck dumb looking at her eyes. "I don't go to school," he said. He was closer to her than he'd ever dreamed of being. Her eyes were miraculously blue.

She stacked her books on the bench between them beside the box that held his new shirt and bowtie. "Well, that's refreshing. Every boy I knew in school is nothing now, but expects to become something else soon. So I suppose it is not possible we met at that one of those dreadful Tulane dances. Fraternity boys once lured my girlfriends and me there, but all they wanted was to get us drunk and paw us. But you must be in the service if you are not in school. In civvies on shore leave? That violates a regulation, doesn't it? Let me guess, Navy?"

"I am waiting to be drafted. Just watching clouds drift by, today. If you look high enough, you'll see where colder wind shreds them. There's no wind like that down here. In the stratosphere, cold air blows all the time. Pilots have to know things like that." He babbled, unable to stop himself.

She palmed wisps of her unruly bangs flat, but they sprang back. She leaned back to study clouds with him. "The boys I know join up as soon as they can. The boys at Tulane are all 4-Fs. I do pray for them, the 4-Fs, too. I don't think that does anyone any good, but prayers can't hurt, either."

"I take care of my mother, so I may not have to serve right away."

"Oh. Then they may not take you at all. Is she very sick?"

Two tugboats eased the barge further downriver. Seagulls called to each other. Propellers in the channel churned bottom mud to turn the river bronze. A locomotive behind them labored to pull cars of coal and timber, the last four flatcars loaded with tanks and jeeps, all beneath fluttering camouflage netting.

What could he say that would not be a lie? He faced the same problem with Maman. The truth of his life was impossible. *I run a con game on the street with playing cards. I cheat. I am very good at cheating. I take up with whores twice your age. I did meet one today only a little older than you; she manicured my nails. They make her up to look like a movie star, but she may be the only one to not believe she will die when they are done with her in the white slave traffic. The only woman I ever came close to caring about was the same age as my mother, but she turned out to be a heroin junkie. She was a demon in the sack when she was off her drugs, though. But none of that matters because at night I dream about you. Not that way. Well, only sometimes that way, but not all the time.*

"What are you reading?" he asked, and nearly wept to think a conversation so obvious had nearly evaded him. Books! She carried books! He read books all the time! You could not go from his room's door to his thin bed without tripping over a book. When he thought to offer to show her the stacks of books in his bedroom, he realized how that would sound. With no experience of respectable women, his mind was empty. Pierre knew passing streetwalkers, Doris, and a string of willing country girls he'd left in Gulfport, but they were the only women he knew, and he did not know them at all in the way he wished to know The Yellow-Haired Girl beside him.

One of her books was four inches thick. Chemistry. The other two were about mathematics. He riffled the browned pages, his fingertip relishing the feel of old paper. Nice to the touch, they may as well have been written in Sanskrit.

"Used books cost so much less. My mother and I need to save nickels. Mother asked that I tell no one that. It's about appearances. I'm supposed to say it is my patriotic duty as part of the war effort to save paper, but the truth is we are broke and now I have math books where someone penciled the answers in the margins. Mother has designs on a man who cannot be allowed to guess how broke we are. It would spoil all her plans. I hate that her plan is to trap another man. I can't understand that. A modern woman should plan on taking care of herself. People should at least be honest with each other when the world is sliding into Hell in a handcart. Can I trust you with my secrets?"

"Have I ever betrayed you, *cher*?"

She clapped her hands and laughed happily. "Oh, at last! A boy who can make me laugh! I started at Catholic school here, but they did so bad a job I had to do an extra year at Hotchkiss in Connecticut, the people who put *bore* in boarding school. That's nearly done. It's Spring break up north, so I am home for a short visit, but it all feels like a mistake. I am visiting my aunt. All the girls call the school *Hot Kiss*. Definitely not a religious place, thank God. Isn't that funny? 'Thank God I am an atheist.' I hate the place. It's just too hard to make new friends if you start years after everyone else. Cliques were formed before I was born. So I came home for some fun, but the boys I used to know are almost all gone, except the 4Fs. College or war. The girls, too. I seem always to be in the wrong place at the wrong time. These books are for college next year, though. As long as I was home, my mother saw a chance for us to save a few dollars. New Orleans, it turns out, is great for food and secondhand books."

"College?"

"Wellesley. I start at the end of August. A year late. The usual for me. I am not sure I will enjoy it, all that rah rah rah silliness seems so wrong with a war on. I'd love to be of more use than cheering from the sideline. I do love to read, though. Do you know *The Robe*? Everyone at Hot Kiss was reading it. It's a story about the Roman who nailed Jesus to the Cross."

"I don't know it." Would she believe he owned a four-volume edition of Aquinas? The pages were onionskin thin. He'd underlined and reread it again and again. His favorite passage read: "Beware of the person of one book."

"*The Robe* is not a religious book, though," she said hurriedly. She leaned toward him to whisper: "I am not a believer. If the nuns knew that, they'd pray for my immortal soul and then call me *incorrigible*. Isn't that the most lovely word? Incorrigible." She laughed again. Her fingers along the bench back brushed the underside of his wrist, though Pierre did not kid himself into believing the slight physical contact could be anything more than a happy accident. "With mother in the north, now, and Daddy gone, I had to find excuses to come home, though now that I did that I can't imagine why I did. I believe my father bought clothing at the same place you do. I recognize your shiny box. Daddy is gone. Not 'gone' like 'away.' It's not like he is overseas in the army. Dead is a different kind of gone."

Her fingers traced the slick edge of the glossy Joseph A. Banks shirt box with its elegant silver script lettering on glossy white.

"I am sorry."

"Well, don't be. It's not as if you killed him."

If he opened his mouth, he'd sound like an idiot. Should he mention that he shopped where he shopped because a mobster with a pearl gray tie in a limousine with crushed velvet seats staked him to a better shirt, a haircut, and a shoeshine so he could spy on a dealer at a high stakes poker game organized for visiting mobsters?

"Daddy was blown to pieces by a bomb in London. The Blitz. It's been a while now. No one is willing to tell us what he was doing in London before Pearl Harbor. There wasn't enough left of him to bury. Blown to bits. We did get a handwritten official letter of thanks on embossed stationary signed by Mr. Donovan. Mr. Donovan uses bright blue ink. America wasn't in the show yet, not officially, anyway. I am over it. Or at least I don't cry myself to sleep anymore. I suppose Daddy was a spy. Daddy went to Yale. On the day he got a phone call, he packed a leather bag and was off to London to be blown to pieces. Well, country, God, and Yale, right? That's how Mother describes it. *'His country called him long distance. He went. Now I am a widow. We all make sacrifices.'* Anyways, next September I have to go to Wellesley because everyone in my family attends the best schools before their men are blown to bits. Mother went to Bryn Mawr, though I don't see what good it did her. She's never done anything except marry Daddy and pop me out two years later. That's what the women in my family do. They get educated, pop out babies, drink like fish to the end of their days because there is nothing left for them to do. While I visit I am staying with my aunt and I am so bored I am ready to jump in the river."

Pierre feared to ask exactly where Wellesley or Bryn Mawr might be. His goal was to be louche, not a lout. Judging by the books she carried, they were good schools up north, the kind of schools that had women studying Calculus.

"Did you visit because you miss your boyfriend?" He thought he was being clever.

"Yesterday, I'd have given you a different answer but my so-called boyfriend is the real reason I think this visit may have been a mistake. We broke up weeks and weeks ago. Freddie sent a long sobby letter asking me if I was sure, because he wasn't. So last night we got together. Freddie is a dear, but he is also a goon. Most of this morning he followed me like a lost puppy before I hopped off the trolley right over there at the very last second. But at least I lost him. For now, anyways." She looked anxiously over her shoulder. "Aren't I clever? I jumped off the trolley to ditch a boy I don't like, and I walked here and found you. Freddie is a 4-F. I am not sure why, but that does not surprise anyone who knows Freddie. He is making me hate a place I once loved."

"He's following you? Do you need me to help you?"

"Oh, now that's a scream. Protection from Freddie? Freddie is as threatening as Mickey Mouse. That was part of the problem. Being with Freddie is as exciting as tapioca. Then last night he got annoying."

"How?"

"The usual, I suppose." A cloud passed and her eyes turned a deep turquoise. "Will you go to school?" she asked suddenly. "I mean someday. In Lafayette? When the war is over?"

"Maybe in Lafayette," he said, wondering what *the usual* meant to a girl like her, guessed he knew, and could think of no way to ask.

A formal education was something he might want, but knew could never happen.

"Oh, that's a lovely college."

What school was in Lafayette? Why was it lovely? Pierre marveled at the scheming that had the red of her lipstick match the red in the pins in her hair, which matched the red of her scarf, which matched her shoelaces, and all for a casual trip on a very hot day to a used bookstore while running from her 4-F ex-boyfriend who probably got his wrist slapped when he tried to put his hand under her skirt.

The April sun slipped behind some trees; their bench fell into dappled shade. "Before the end of summer, we will move to Uncle John's place on Martha's Vineyard. If Prince Charming comes to rescue me, he'll have to arrive on a ferry. I don't think Uncle John will be my uncle for very long. He is Mother's boyfriend. I don't think I can call him 'father,' but if mother insists, I will, but not for very long. Once I start at Wellesley, they are rid of me, and I say thank God for that. John and Daddy were in Skull and Bones, something nobody is supposed to know but everyone does. Isn't it funny how things work out for the best?"

Skull and bones? "Do you truly believe things always work out for the best?" Pierre asked. He'd come across the ridiculous notion in his reading. He'd been reading Voltaire. Pangloss, the compulsive optimist who dies of syphilis, was a total fool. At that moment, the best of all possible worlds was divided into Axis and Allies with their hands at each other's throats. There was not much hope for anyone, anywhere. The best of all possible worlds was a steaming pile of explosive crap.

Gulls and pigeons wheeled overhead and came down to strut at their feet. The birds waited to be fed, saw nothing forthcoming, then indignantly flapped away. Conditioned to beg, like most people they'd starve if they had to be on their own.

The Yellow-Haired Girl scowled. "You make me laugh and then you can be so serious! No. I definitely don't believe things always work out for the best. It's just something to say because otherwise life is dreary. I'm sorry I said it to you. People in Washington called on Daddy because they needed him, he went, now he is dead. If it was his duty to be blown up, I don't see any good in it." In the river, a scow's horn blasted, a flock of seagulls took flight off the river. "You're easy to talk to," she said suddenly.

"Thanks," Pierre said, knowing he had said nothing. What he did was listen. Would she want to see a card trick?

"Are you dangerous?"

"I don't think so."

She pouted. "I think I'd like a boyfriend who was dangerous. Being dangerous is better than being a bore." She leaned to look directly into his face. "Now here I am babbling away. I've told you my biggest secrets, and I don't even know you. I get tired of being so darned pleasant all the time." She pursed her lips. "I mean so *damned* pleasant. Isn't that better? Being pleasant is too much damned work. My mother says a woman's job is to smile and be pleasant, but with a stranger, I don't have to be pleasant. I can be myself. I can say 'damned' if I mean damned. You must think I am awful."

"I don't think that."

"Maybe at Wellesley things will be different. Wellesley is all women, you know. There are no men to be pleasant for. That will be a relief. We can smoke cigarettes and say 'damned.' None of it matters, though. Right now, I just want this war to end and for people to stop being killed. If I were a boy, I'd be a conscientious objector. I really would. Everyone would hate me, but I'd do it. I went up to Sacred Hearts to visit Sister Agatha. She filled my ear with the news of boys she knew who were in a hurry and signed up. Two are dead, and one is blind. The blind boy used to play tennis. Sister Aggie called him 'lucky' because he is still alive after a jeep windshield shattered and bits of glass went into his eyes. That's what she calls 'lucky.' She prays for us all. It must be wonderfully simple to be a nun. No matter how bad it gets, all Sister Aggie needs to do is pray and have faith that God has His mysterious reasons. That makes life simple, doesn't it? God has His purposes that are none of our business. All we need to do is suffer and die." She gazed out at the river. "Am I terrible?"

"You're fine. You can tell me anything."

"Ten years of Catholic education, this war, and Daddy's death can leave a mark on any girl, and now here I am on a park bench with a complete stranger telling him how I want a boyfriend who is dangerous and believe religion is a fraud because my father was blown to bits too small to find." The slate-gray water of the Mississippi flowed past. "So, no confession for me, but I do my penance. I knit hats and socks for boys I will never meet. If they get blown into pieces, at least their heads and feet will be warm. The lucky ones will only be blind. I hate it. I hate all of it. I don't want to know any more blind boys, and I don't want to kiss anyone at the USO because they are so far from home and there is no one but me to say good-bye to them."

"Maybe they just want to kiss you."

"That kind never wants to stop with a kiss." She stood to peer through the haze above the river to Algiers Point. The labored sound of the freight train behind them passed and was fading.

"Maybe we can see each other again," Pierre said, his heart flinging itself at his ribs.

"If we do, it will be your turn to tell me your secrets. That's only fair."

"I will."

"Tell me something secret, quick, right now. Anything. Please. It does not have to be a big deal. No thinking. Just out with it."

She'd be gone in a moment. "My mother was sixteen when she had me, younger than I am now. Younger than you are, I bet. We were poor. She nursed me until I was six."

She seemed startled, and then clapped her hands. "Oh how marvelous! Thank you so much! Now there are only two people in the world who know that. You and me!" She drew a deep breath. "To get to Boston I take the Panama Limited to Chicago, then the 20th Century Limited to New York, and finally an express from New York to Boston. But you can see me off. Do you want to see me off? That would be lovely. Someone to say good-bye to me, for once. I am always the one saying good-bye and someone else is going places. The Panama Limited has a dining car that will serve anything, but I have already decided that I am having a cold lobster for lunch because the ticket is being paid for by Uncle John and I am happy to spend Uncle John's money as fast as I can. Mother reserved a sleeping berth; I go to sleep and wake up for breakfast in Chicago. But if you come to Union Station tomorrow at 10:30, I will write my address on a piece of paper and then we can trade letters." She thought for a second. "And secrets." She thought a second more. "Yes. Secrets. And a kiss. I promise a kiss on one condition."

"What's that?"

"I don't have to tell you my name until after we kiss. I have always wanted to share a kiss with a boy who does not know me."

"I'll be there."

She laughed a third time. "You won't, but you are good to say so." For a moment, he thought she would kiss him right there, but she blushed and fumbled with her books.

"Let me help you," he said. He undid his belt, wrapped it twice tightly around the three books, and pulled the belt taut. "All you have to do is put this over your shoulder."

She grasped the end of the belt. "I don't know if that's clever or ridiculous. What if your pants fall down? Oh, how you make me laugh!" The corners of her lips and eyes crinkled with a kind of mirth he'd never know.

"Will I see you again?"

"If you come to the station. A promise is a promise. 'I'll be looking at the moon, but I'll be seeing you.'" She recited the song lyric with no irony in her voice, pulled tight her cloche, then slung his impromptu book strap over her shoulder smooth as a longshoreman hooking a burlap bag of Texas rice. She leaned forward to trudge up a gentle incline and across the railroad tracks, the belted books bouncing off her hip with every step.

At the top of the rise, she turned and looked back as he knew she would. Strands of her hair free of the cloche fanned into a rippling golden apron. She waved once and vanished into the crowd.

Pigeons flocked and strutted, cooing at his feet, trapped by habits, conditioned to expect anyone on a bench wanted to feed them. Pierre had nothing to give. The Yellow-Haired Girl had looked back at him for the second time in his life.

The steeple clock over Jackson Square read 10:03 when the Cadillac's rear door swung open silent as a crypt. Mario and the man who'd patted Pierre down were vague shadows. Dimmed streetlights were a late gesture to the reality of U-boat warfare in the Gulf. N'awlins loved its nights, but even The Big Easy had come to understand that shipping silhouetted by the city's lights benefitted only Nazi commanders at sea.

Mario stood with a leg in the door and his elbow propped on the car roof. He gazed through the gloom beyond Pierre. Pierre ducked his head to step into the car, but Mario blocked him with an outstretched arm.

"Wait a second, buddy. Do you see that?" Mario asked, pointing across the street. "That's the Lower Pontalba." The three-story red brick building was black in the nonlight, but Pierre faced the building for so many hours on so many days that he knew its every feature. "*Mi nonno* and *nonna* lived there when they got off the boat. From Palermo. She was fourteen and pregnant. Nine kids, eventually, every one of them baptized in St. Louis, right there behind Jackson's horse's ass." Mario crossed himself. "People like *mi nonno* don't exist anymore. I never go by here that I don't look up to remember."

"What?"

"Ghosts. Uncle Vito died there when he was three; Uncle Biaggio died the same year. Yellow Fever, both of them. They were kids. Do you see that stone archway into the courtyard?" Pierre lied and said he saw it through the darkness. "The courtyard is over-grown now and the fountain is filled with dirt and dead leaves. I'm told it once flowed with the sweetest water."

"Sounds nice."

"Don't be a fucking idiot. The water was for the horses. The courtyard stank from horseshit. *Nonna*, may she live forever"—he crossed himself again—"said to me the flies were big as sparrows. Nine kids, God bless her. The old lady is blind now, but she sees more than the rest of us put together. Her spaghetti gravies can't be beat. We moved her and *Nonno* upriver and then lakeside. Nice. Nothing fancy, but nice. They would not know how to live fancy. The old man lasted a couple more years before we put him in the dirt. He wanted the old country's dirt, but there was no point to shipping him to Italy. At least we planted him in dry ground. I hope he isn't disappointed. At Easter *Nonna* still makes those cookies so good they are the reason Christ rises." He kissed his thumb as he crossed himself one more time. "Never mind God's promise of eternal life. Jesus rises because He loves anisette. All *Nonna* still talks about is the great times in the old Pontalba. I think maybe not so good for Vito and Biaggio, but the old lady remembers it as the best time in her life. That's what it is with old people. No matter how much life shits on them, what they remember is the feeling that does not come back anymore. They were young. They were strong. Nothing hurt when they stood; nothing hurt if they took a crap." Mario's Ronson flared as he cupped and lit a cigarette.

Pierre stooped a second time to get in the Cadillac as Mario slapped his palm to the car's roof. Pierre sat alone in the rear seat. Mario drove. He twisted in his seat to face Pierre. "I've never been in the fucking Pontalba. It's a shithole. The guy who owned the place blew his brains out, which saved me the trouble. Remember that."

"Why should the kid remember that?" The silent guy in the front finally spoke.

"Nothing is more important than family."

"I meant the part about the guy who owned the place."

"What the fuck is your problem? It's part of the story, no?"

The guy shrugged. Mario said: "*Bene*. Now shut the fuck up." The Cadillac shifted smoothly into gear.

After most of an hour they were well south of Lafitte, deep into bayou country. Some of the road was paved, but most was rutted dirt. The car's headlights were Civil Defense approved for blackout driving, black cardboard with slits radiating light like cat's eyes. The nameless guy in front chain-smoked. He licked his thumb and forefinger and extinguished each cigarette with a pinch before the shredded cigarette's remains were flicked spinning into the moonless night. Then he withdrew a new cigarette from a silver case in his inner jacket pocket, tamped the cigarette three times at each end, and lighted it with the wavering liquid-blue flame of a Zippo. Every cigarette the same. Always tamped three times. Never four, never two. Three. In the flare of the lighter, Pierre saw the swollen black burns on the pads of his fingertips.

They crossed railroad tracks before they rode over a steel plate spanning a shallow drainage ditch and parked beside a cinderblock building that faced the road. The car rolled to a stop on a patch of hard sand barely higher than the swamp. The building's windows were the only light for miles in any direction. To the north, despite the blackout, New Orleans glowed like a faint green gemstone at the edge of darkness. The air smelled faintly of salt and kerosene; as they drew closer, the air from the waterside of the cinderblock shack carried the overpowering grease stink of rotting fish trapped in tidal pools. Pierre and Mario walked on ground covered by crushed clamshells; the nameless third man stayed in the car, slouched low in his seat, and tugged his broad-brimmed black fedora over his eyes as if he were sleeping, though it was hard to imagine that man closed his eyes, much less ever slept.

"You still wearing that pig-sticker on your ankle?" Mario asked.

"Yes. Do you need to take it?"

"Hold on to it. Guys can get testy. These places in the middle of no place give me the willies. Why they don't gamble in a decent hotel with fans and air a man can breathe beats the living shit out of me, but what Silver Dollar Sam wants, Silver Dollar Sam gets."

Someone peered at them through a barred peephole. Muddy yellow light spilled from the opened door.

Three guys with shotguns across their laps sat in cheap rumpled suits on easy chairs. They nodded to Mario and eyeballed Pierre. The shack's flickering electric lights drew power from a sputtering kerosene generator. In a larger room further to the rear, the game had already begun. The piles of chips before the players were roughly equal, which meant the game had to be young. Six men and a female dealer sat at a green-felted poker table.

The dealer was Doris.

Her white shirt was starched and her hair had been dyed screaming peroxide blond, but there was no mistaking that snaggletooth. She slowly blinked when she and Pierre made eye contact, then, as if they were strangers, she returned to the business at hand. "Ante up, gentlemen." She expertly spun two cards facedown to each player, then followed those two hole cards with a third spun smartly face up. The game was Seven-Card Stud. Every card landed just where it should. Her touch was perfect. "Queen bets," she intoned, but kept her eyes where they belonged, strictly on the pile of money at the table's center.

They played for cash money, not chips. Part of Doris' job was to be sure no errant fingers lightened the pot. The house banker beside Doris extracted the house cut after each hand before a player could rake in his winnings. The longer the game continued, the more the house withdrew. If a game went long enough, eventually the house would have every dollar. Any pause in the action was, therefore, lost money. A relief dealer meant that Doris could take a leak, fix a sandwich, or drink a beer, but the game could not stop.

Backs to the wall, Pierre and Mario sidled along the room's periphery. They stepped around high wooden captain's chairs. Mario introduced Pierre, calling him *Buddy*. Doris's eyes narrowed imperceptibly as she tipped two fingers to acknowledge the new guy.

A slender gold wedding band was on Doris's hand; her fingernails were as neat as his. Her hair was cut shorter than Pierre's. Their white shirts were near identical down to the French cuffs.

They wore identical black velvet bowties, as well. She looked more hollow-cheeked than when he'd last seen her and her skin was wax-white, but her new hair color did little to hide her sunken eyes. It might also have been her eyeliner or maybe the faint rouge on her cheeks, but Pierre did not doubt she was pale from the horse still regularly burning through her. She would not be the first junkie to deal poker, though her hands were rock steady.

The shack's third room at the rear held a bridge table in a make-shift kitchen with a slop sink that ran salt water. Top shelf liquor bottles stood like sentries beside a platter of sandwiches under crinkled yellow cellophane. Plenty of ice was in the sink. Mario gestured that Pierre could help himself, but Pierre took nothing. He was working and would drink only ice water, not even coffee.

He settled back onto his bar-height oak captain's chair against a whitewashed wall directly opposite Doris. It was the best place to do his job, which was to watch her. Mario did the same, but from behind her. Mario's teeth savagely came together through a deviled ham sandwich on a Kaiser Roll. He washed it down with Jax he'd pumped from a steel barrel into a pilsner glass. His chair tipped precariously back, then his eyes shut like a sleepy spectator at a dull baseball game. Pierre felt sure that with his eyes closed Mario saw more than most people saw wide awake.

Pierre focused his attention on Doris's hands.

In the next forty-five minutes, the six players hardly spoke, though they smoked a lot. At least $30,000 in cash was on the table, surely why they were out in the boondocks at a secret location. The high stakes also explained the additional three guys with shotguns across their laps in the kitchen. Only a crazy person would roust a game like this, but this was Louisiana where crazy was routinely stirred into the gumbo.

Doris snapped cards like gunshots. Like any good dealer, Doris softly chanted the play of each hand. *Three hearts, straight building, paired the five, cowboys.* Her skills as a mechanic had become very, very good, but while her fingers were lithe and fast, and they might fool most, they could not fool Pierre. She must have known that, but it did not stop her. Someone was paying her for a dishonest game. She had to continue. She was relying on Pierre to cover for her.

She dealt ruiners to a single player. The con was odd because it did not make any player rich, but made a certain player poor. Doris did not deal the mark bad cards every hand, but often enough. Maybe the guy already owed money, and this would tip him over an edge where he'd fall broke into someone's pockets.

The mark's voice was Kansas City flat. He twisted an emerald ring on his left small finger when he was anxious. The tell should have been enough for a decent card player to empty his wallet, but at this level of play, the tell might be a deliberate false signal. A mechanic like Doris pushing out losing cards was prudent insurance. The ring looked to be worth more than Carolla's Cadillac.

Carolla had told him that someone had insisted on the mouse to deal. How much was Doris raking to dump the game? And by whom? Did the arrangement include that she had to sleep with some guy, or was she being paid in heroin?

Four large was in the pot when Doris busted the mark's four-flush in diamonds; on another hand, Kansas City bet into his low pair and an ace looking to improve to a high two-pair or three-of-a-kind, but Doris's fine hands delivered a six from the deck's bottom that left the mark sucking on a worthless pair of treys.

"I can't catch a break," he muttered and stood.

"Piss call," Mario said.

The pigeon pointed at Pierre. "He can deal. Why stop? What the fuck is a relief dealer for?"

Mario's chair scraped the floor as he stood. "Piss call," he repeated.

It was 1:30 AM.

Hands balled into fists deep in his sport coat pockets, Mario walked with Pierre out the rear door into air heavy with the smell of sea salt. The hard sand under their thin-soled shoes hardly yielded. It was a hell of a way to treat new Florsheims.

Pierre's ribs quaked with damp cold. He turned down Mario's offer of a Lucky Strike Green. Mario cupped his hands around his lighter as if a Nazi sniper lurked in the darkness waiting to draw a bead on the flickering flame, then held the cigarette in his lips while he pissed into two inches of brackish water. "I hear that crickets that make noise are boy crickets asking girl crickets for a piece of ass."

"I heard the same," Pierre said. He filled his lungs, hoping brackish salt air could clear his mind as easily as it cleared his lungs.

"That's nature for you." Mario zipped his fly. "Well, what do you say, buddy? Does Mr. Carolla have a problem or is the game on the up and up?" He exhaled tobacco smoke.

Pierre gave Mario the details of what he'd seen. It was too much to be bad luck. He did not mention he had taught the dealer everything she knew.

What else could he do? Suppose this were a test? What if they wondered how much they could count on the Cajun kid? For all he knew, Doris could be in on it. It made no sense to go to all this trouble to test him, but there was no way to know what was what.

Mario peeled a shred of tobacco from his tongue. "Absolutely sure?"

"How much trouble is she in?"

"A lot, and it is the worst kind, buddy. The guy from Kay-Cee is practically family. We can guess who is paying her, but we need to be sure, and that means you have to be sure. There is no going back from a thing like this. You're either the best like Herlihy tells us, and that means you are also stand-up, or you're a punk who wants to stay out in the rain with vegetable crates."

Pierre said he was sure.

Salt air cloyed at his face and eyes. Beyond the shack and far from the shore, a dark wall of pine trees loomed. They stood on a strip of hard sand that may as well have been 50 yards from the edge of the world. Doris needed to know she was in shit, but Pierre dared not tell her until the game was done. Any sooner, she'd panic and run, and then Mario would know Pierre tipped her off. Instead of one person drowning in shit, there would be two.

To tell her what she needed to know, he'd need luck and perfect timing. Once the game ended, Doris would have maybe a half hour before they'd come for her. If they had driven her down here, she would not have that long. The timing was impossibly tight if Pierre planned to be at Union Station by 10:30 when The Yellow-Haired Girl who Looked Back would tell him a secret and give him a kiss. He had to be there. She was off to her new life up north. Her green eyes would be searching for him on the platform. He'd never see such a chance again at a real life. Doris-the-junkie was his past, but the Yellow-Haired Girl Who Looked Back, the college girl who studied higher math, was his future. Someday they'd have a house, they'd have a dog, they'd have a tree in a yard, and they'd have kids who would make him laugh and happy to be alive. He'd get an honest job. Stranger things had happened.

Mario cupped his hands around a second cigarette as they turned up a pebbled path away from the shoreline. The path went from hard sand to harder cement beside the whitewashed concrete wall. Out front, the spotlight on the Caddy flared into life, blinding them both. Pierre stayed in shadow while Mario leaned into the Caddy's open window.

"If there is a kraut with eyes to see out there, expect a torpedo in about a minute. Turn that fucking light out." He glanced at the radium dial of his watch. "Tell the boys they need to wait another half hour," he called to Pierre. "We need a phone that's up the road. No game until I am back. Have something to eat, buddy. Try the liverwurst. You did good."

"What should I tell the players?"

"I have to spell this out for you? Tell them it is business. Tell them we are sorry. Tell them to fuck themselves. Tell them any fucking thing you want, but nothing happens until I get back."

The Cadillac's door slammed shut, the engine growled into life, and the car's big white-walls slowly rolled over gravel and mud until it gathered speed and carried the two men away.

The players grumbled, but seemed satisfied enough. The mark who did not know he was being screwed was least patient.

Pierre went for a ham sandwich in the back room. Doris was alone in the kitchen waiting for him, her hips braced against the sink's edge behind her. "The shotgun guys went for a nature hike," she said and crushed her cigarette against the bottom of her black shoe before she pumped enough salt water to wash the cigarette butt down the sink drain. "Why would you pump seawater into a sink?"

"They clean fish in the sink. It's not for drinking."

"That makes sense. What's up wit' you, Butch?" she asked. "Why we waitin'?"

It was his chance to tell her what was going on, but if they came back and Doris had cleared out, he'd be a gallant hero but very dead. They could run together, but only on foot. They might get a half mile. "Beats the shit out of me," he said. "I like your hair."

"F'true? I'm not so sure of it. For now, okay." She backed onto the riot bar on the shack's steel back door. It swung open and banged against the exterior rear wall. "I'm saving up to get this tooth fixed."

He followed her until they were out of any light. Ten minutes earlier, on the same spot, Mario had been pissing. Doris suddenly gripped his face in her two hands. Her kiss was so forceful their teeth clicked. Her tongue ran deep into his mouth, as urgent as it used to when she came, straddling him as they made love. She'd once sucked his tongue so hard he thought she'd tear it out by the roots; more than once she'd bitten his lower lip until it bled.

Her hands went to his belt.

"Doris ..."

She unzipped his pants, and her hand went into his shorts. "Holy shit, Butch," she said. "Did you get bigger or did Doris just forget? God, Doris will die of lockjaw. Right here. Right now, Butch. What do you have to give to your Doris, *cher?* What do you have? Ava is new and she wants to know if what I tell her is the real truth."

She dropped to her knees, but he stepped back. "You're married."

"*Merde, cher.*" She stood and held out her hand to him. "That ain't nothing but a Cracker Jack prize to keep hands off'n me. It doesn't stop some, but Doris has her reason to say '*Non.*' I tell them Ava is in love wit' a sailor boy who is far away." She gripped his face again and nipped his lower lip.

He pushed her away to roll up her shirtsleeve.

"When did you join the po-lice, *cher*? Nothing to see. No track marks. Doris has been clean for months. F'true, *cher*. Weeks, anyway." In the darkness he could see nothing. Besides, a clean arm might mean the needles went to veins between toes. Or in her gums or hips.

She reached deeper into his pants. "We're running out of time." She started to laugh. "It will be a kick to go back to those sorry bastards knowing we got laid on the sand, right? I mean, think of it, *cher*. Sand in your shoes and my scent on your joint."

He near ran, her laughter clattering down the beach like marbles down a washboard.

"It's your game, buddy," Mario said, one foot on the bumper of the Caddy. "Ava has an appointment she can't miss. I'll be back to pick you up at sunup. I hope you like waffles."

The mark from KC had less luck in an honest game than he had when he was getting screwed. Doris had not needed to do a damn thing. At sunrise, each of the players tipped Pierre a hundred dollars. Mario returned and folded two one hundred dollar bills into his hand, lifting Pierre's take to $800 for a night's work, more silver than Judas earned.

They sped north in the Cadillac. "I should split tips with Ava, no?" he said to Mario. Damp morning blew through the open car windows. There was no sign of the third man.

"She'll be taken care of."

Pierre wanted to believe there was still be time to warn Doris and for him to get to Union Station, but as dawn turned the world pink and then into clearer light, Mario drove straight to a diner in Algiers. "It's too early to wake the wife and kid. For what? She'd only give me all kinds of shit."

Pierre's heart sank.

The diner was a converted railroad car. They climbed three chipped concrete steps, pushed through swinging doors, and took counter seats near a rotating fan across from the pass-through from the kitchen over the grill. Mario balanced his hat on a counter stool and then indicated that Pierre sit beside him. A green crayon on yellow note paper brittle with age was taped to the clear pie cloche. *Hommade Pecan.* It seemed a fine place, smelling of fresh coffee, warm biscuits, and sausage gravy. Their distorted reflections were on the thin high-polish stainless steel wall plates; the diner's counter was hard pink plastic trimmed by yet more stainless steel. "They put eggshells in their coffee. It cuts the acid. I don't know where in fuck they get the coffee, though. Maybe they have not heard there is a war going on. You can't beat this place with a stick."

Mario ordered two eggs over-easy on a ham steak, beans, and a double order of toast. He thought a moment and added a short stack of pancakes. The counter girl was a washed out teenager who was more interested in chewing gum, but she called Mario *mister* and Pierre *sweetheart.* Her smile was a narrow crowd of crooked teeth; her red lips gnawed a pencil.

Hoping to speed things along, Pierre ordered a simple Danish and coffee. It was just 7:30. He needed five minutes apart from Mario and a telephone booth.

But Mario disapproved of his breakfast order. "This is the most important meal of the day, buddy. Keeps your pecker up. A pastry and coffee, you'll drop dead." He gestured the counter girl to come back. "My friend forgot he was hungry. Bring him some pancakes. You like waffles, buddy? He's going to go with the waffles and a side of bacon. Crisp, from the oven not a frypan. And bring us two glasses of that orange juice you squeeze back there. With the pulp." He turned to Pierre. "Best damned juice I ever had. Wait until you get a taste of it."

More food than Pierre ate in a week materialized in front of them. Everyone in the place must have been longshoremen chowing down for a day of physical labor. The place was thick with cigarette smoke and the slow talk of working men, many of whom to steady their morning shakes poured whiskey from hip flasks into coffee.

"I bring my family here once in a while," Mario said. "That's how good it is."

"It's a nice place."

"I never thought I'd say this, but I like my family. You get a little older, you should have a family. My boy thinks he's Gene Autry. He's four." Mario produced a wrinkled photo from his bulky wallet. "That's Vincente. He looks like me, you think? Look at those eyebrows. Has to be my kid. Creepy kid, though. He runs around on a broom handle like it's his horse. And he sings. Nobody can make out the words, but the kid sings. Vincente the Singing Dago Cowboy. My wife thinks this is cute, which is the only reason I have not dropkicked the kid into Pontchartrain. I love my wife, when I don't want to strangle her, I mean. She is expecting again. I look at her sideways, and she gets knocked up. The boy is handsome but dumber than rocks. Nothing wrong with him, just stupid. Someday he'll make a great doorstop. Maybe run an elevator, if he can keep the numbers straight. You tell him 'Don't jump on the bed,' but the minute I look at the *Morning Telegraph* to dope out the Double at the Fairgrounds, Vincente is bouncing like he is trying out for Ringling Brothers."

Mario drained his scalding coffee as if its heat did not affect him, looked into Pierre's cup, saw it was near full, but nevertheless gestured to the counter waitress that Pierre needed a refresher. "I can't ask the wife to control him. Her bladder is down to a walnut, so she pees every fifteen minutes. Up and down all night. If I try to sleep anywhere except next to her, she cries. She understands I can be away for a few nights on business, like last night, but if I am home, if I don't stay next to her, she cries. Family shit makes a man crazy. What do you think? Can I get her to lock the kid in a closet until he is sixteen?" He cut his ham steak into a half dozen small pieces and scooped a fork of scrambled eggs into his mouth. "I can't read the fucking paper; I can't listen to the fucking radio because fucking Gene Autry is on his broomstick running figure eights around my ankles. Then he crouches behind my chair and croons '*Back in the Saddle Again.*' At least he knows most of the words. That must be the all clear, though. Not a redskin in sight for good old Gene. The first time I heard Vincente singing, I thought the kid was cute. I'm his father, right? I like my Vincente, I swear to God, but when he sings that fucking song for the ten thousandth fucking time, I am ready to take the little creep for a ride, lose him in Mandeville, and take bets on whether he finds his way home. Don't get me wrong. I love my boy. Family is the most important thing. Here, look at this again. He's me, all right, but he got his mother's nose and lips. But that fucking song. He did not get that from her or me. All I know is if I hear it again, the real Mr. Autry is going to have a visitor who will explain how brass knuckles work. He won't be crooning so good with his teeth hitting the floor like Chuck-a-Luck dice. You think maybe that's how Gabby Hayes got to be Gabby? He says, 'Yer dern tootin'' in the wrong place, and the next minute Gabby is sucking oatmeal through a straw."

"Gabby Hays is with Roy Rogers."

Mario looked hard at him, then smiles. "Fuck 'em both. All I know is that my house drops dead when Autry is on the radio. You ever listen to that show? Total shit. The kid sits on the wife's lap. I can't step out; the wife cries if I don't join them, too. Fucking Autry is the only damn thing gets Vincente to sit still more than a minute. I sit smiling like I am downing sugar-dipped shitcakes." He tapped his fork on the edge of the plate. "But how about these waffles? You want pecans? Bananas?" Mario's fork cut a three-inch wedge of waffle that dripped egg yolk and maple syrup. "But what do you care about my troubles? You are a kid and you are single. Get laid a lot, buddy. Get laid. When you are older you will need the memories. The nights can get pretty long."

"What will happen to her?"

"Who?"

"The dealer. Ava."

"Not your problem. You saved Mr. Carolla some embarrassment. He won't forget you. How old are you, anyway? F'true, now.

I told Sam I figured you for 22. He said 'Younger. Twenty.' I couldn't believe he was trusting a guy who was twenty. But that's Sam. He's all instinct. You should put more syrup and butter on that. F'true, they drive the maple syrup from Maine all the way here just for ham-and-eggers like you and me. The orange juice I can figure, but the coffee is a fucking mystery. I know people who know people who know people, and I can't get coffee like this coffee." He gestured for a refill. "You did good last night, kid. Relax. So how old are you? There's a sawbuck riding on your age. Sam wants I should get the real number. The over and under on you is at 20."

This was not a guy to lie to. "Eighteen," Pierre said.

Mario stared at Pierre's reflection in the mirrored stainless steel behind the grill. Crockery rattled onto the counter in front of them.

"No shit? I owe Sam a sawbuck. Jesus. You got big balls, buddy. You should be on a bicycle dropping-off tonic to old ladies with the vapors, not bird-dogging a cooze poker mechanic. I'll be damned. Eighteen? No shit? You sure you don't want some extra bacon? Here, have some of mine." Mario patted his stomach. He was cement-hard, a 35-year-old welterweight with a broken cheek and full head of black hair, partial to a gray fedora and an unbuttoned double-breasted sharkskin suit. Mario loosened his tie and undid his shirt collar and shrugged. The hand-painted tie showed a sunrise, or maybe it was a sunset, over a tiny island in a lake. A loon crossed the sun above the lake; the lake sprouted cat tails. A tuft of wiry black hair bristled above the neck of his undershirt. "Why aren't you in the service?" He swiveled on the counter stool to face Pierre.

Pierre thought how the train would leave at 10:30. It was near 8:30. "I'm waiting for them to find me."

"Are you yellow?"

Mario asked the question without malice.

"I don't think so," Pierre said. "When I was a kid, I figured I'd kill Hitler. Save everyone some trouble."

Mario sopped up yolk onto his toast to draw it dripping to his lips. "'When you were a kid?' That's rich. When was that? Last week? So you're not some pussy conscientious objector?"

"No. I'd kill someone for the right reason. Give me my shot at Adolf, and I'll end the war. I just don't see it as my job, and I can't see getting killed to make it happen."

"That's good to know."

He repeated, "I am not yellow." Pierre thought to tell Mario of the Yellow-Haired Girl and her blind lacrosse player and her father blown to pieces, but then he'd be playing a card he could never sweep from Mario's table.

The diner clock was racing: 9:12.

Mario touched his lower lip. "I did not figure you for yellow, buddy. Relax. Avoiding being killed is not being yellow. It's smart. If there is some other guy who gets killed in your place, well, someone should have looked out for him. I missed the last war because of connections. I have no regrets." He added. "Do you know this ham steak comes direct from Virginia? Comes down on the same truck that brings the maple syrup. They make the trip to Maine four times a year, I am told. In a car with refrigeration and dry ice. They pick up the ham on the way back. See this?" A piece of pink meat quivered on the tines of his fork. "This is what America is about. Maybe this and baseball, but that's the whole deal." He chewed a bit of ham. "Buddy, maybe we can help you out. You want a job on the pipeline? Vital war work. You get a deferment."

"I don't need a job."

Mario gestured to the waitress with the pencil between her lips. "Get my friend a cruller. He needs to sharpen his common sense. And I'll have a slice of the apple pie. I know, darlin', you have told me the pecan is better, but I am watching my weight." The waitress laughed. Her two customers had eaten enough for a logging camp. Other men had come and gone. But they were still ordering dessert after breakfast. "Don't be a dope, buddy. You'll never touch a wrench. I mean we can get you papers. We know the people who know the right people in the union, the pipeline company, and the draft board." His voice dropped to what Mario would consider a whisper but for the rest of the world was normal conversation. "Everybody signs off and you become a part of the war effort. Make your family proud. The pipeline guys will put your pay in an envelope every two weeks and all you have to do is hand it over to us. We take our piece and give you back enough. It's government work, so no one loses. All we ask is you keep yourself available. Odd jobs come up. You have skills. Your phone might ring. We owe you one. F'true, you'll be free and clear, but Silver Dollar Sam likes to help out the people who help him."

"Mr. Carolla can make that happen?"

"Silvestro Carolla can make anything happen. It's government. No one gives a fuck, and no one is asking you to be muscle. It's just a way to clear some dough. Just like last war, when this one is over, just like last time, there will be regular guys who got fucked and a smart guys who get rich. Be a smart guy. I can always use a dealer with good hands, even if he is fucking eighteen. Nobody is eighteen, anymore, but if you say so, I guess you are."

Pierre chewed his cruller but hardly tasted it. His freshened coffee raised a blister on his palette. "What will happen to the dealer?" He tried to sound casual.

"Eat, buddy. Live easy. Don't worry about things you have nothing to do with. Troubles have a way of taking care of themselves. Trust me. You did your job, that's finished, and now everything is just jake."

Mario slurped down his third coffee, lit another cigarette, and stretched his arms over his head. He was a man finished with a job well done. They sat quietly until he lighted a fresh cigarette and finally dropped too much money onto the counter.

Mario's Caddy shuttled across the river to where Mario had picked him up. It was just shy of 10, almost twelve hours to the minute since Pierre had climbed into the car. Lawns and streets still shone with dew.

"We'll be in touch," Mario said, leaning across the seat. "You done good."

The moment the Caddy rounded a corner, Pierre sprinted to a café. He elbowed past a half dozen customers to slap a dollar on the counter. He needed nickels.

Pierre closed himself behind the accordion door of the phone booth. His nickels were piled on the metal shelf beneath the phone; he lost sight of the one that fell and rolled across the floor. He jammed a coin into the slot and dialed what he hoped was still Doris's number. The operator asked him for a nickel more. Doris's phone rang and rang and rang. He slammed the receiver onto the claw and repeated the entire process.

There was no answer.

The café wall clock read 10:10. He'd have wept if weeping were not a waste of time. He still believed he could do it all, but knew in his sinking heart he could not.

Doris or the Yellow-Haired Girl? Past or future?

He was kidding himself. The choice was life or death; his life and Doris's death. That was a choice that should have been easy.

He hurled himself back out into the streets wet and slick with dew. He told himself Doris was not answering because she was asleep, was all. Sure. That made sense. Doris was asleep. She liked to sleep late, f'true. He knew that. Running all the while, while he created a tissue of unlikely circumstances that meant she would survive. He could not abandon her.

He would say, *Get your ass up, girl*, and, yes, he'd have to tell her why, and, yes, she'd think he was dog shit for ratting her out, but that was small beans compared to the need to persuade her to put New Orleans far behind her. He'd lie and promise to join her if a lie would hurry her. They'd run to Omaha, or Denver, or someplace where no one ever said, *Never fuck with Silver Dollar Sam*.

Pierre's new Florsheims gave him no traction. The soles were barely scuffed. He slid to a stop, bent to catch his breath, and left the shoes on a sewer grating. The pain between his ribs was a straight razor. He undid and then dropped his bowtie somewhere. He was running in his socks. The stitch in his side never eased, but he straightened up to run again.

As he rounded a corner, he lost his footing and fell to his hip. He ignored his pain, rose, and ran again limping. The stitch in his side was a claw. His trousers were ripped where he'd fallen. He bent double. His vison blurred, his lungs burned, his ribs ached.

The single flight of stairs to Doris' rooms was torture. He pounded his fist on her door, put his hands on his knees and bent double to breathe. His thighs quivered like a sick dog's.

An old guy on spindly legs wearing boxer shorts and an undershirt opened the facing apartment's door. He drew on a loosely rolled cigarette and carried a can of Jax. "You're scaring the crap out of my dog, podner." The dog, part Pomeranian and mostly rat, barked wildly.

"Doris," Pierre said, gasping.

The guy exhaled and nodded. "Doris. Doris. I knowed her. See, how I used to live upstairs, but took this place when it opened up. Why walk up three flights I says to myself if I can walk up two? Am I right or am I right? When I live upstairs, I watch from a front window. They charge extra for being in front. I'd see that gal come and go, you know what I mean. I was not spyin' on her, but she was easy on the eyes. Nice gal. Had dark hair. But one day I sees her and see she is blonde and she tells me her new name is Ava. The girlies get to do that, you know. First one thing and then another. It never fails. You think you know a girlie until you finds out you know jack-shit." He snapped his fingers and sipped from his beer. "I don't think she comes in last night, though. I'd have heard her. I'll tell her you was here, though. Just stop making my dog crazy." He gathered the Pomeranian into his arms as the door lock clicked irrevocably shut.

Pierre's knee oozed blood. The speckled skylight two flights above the stairwell ignited dust motes with sickly daylight. Someone boiled cabbage. Salt sweat dripped from under his hair down his face. His shirt collar was sodden. His new linen shirt clotted to his back. He cradled his head in his hands and remembered the Yellow Haired Girl.

He had to try. She'd never care that he looked like hell. Someday he'd tell her why, but they would be old friends by then and she'd forgive him anything.

So he bolted shoeless into the street once more, half running and half walking to Union Station, praying the train was late. Trains were late all the time, weren't they? Gradually, his injured leg loosened up and his knee hardly hurt at all.

The Panama Limited had indeed departed for Chicago ten minutes late, but that was still fifteen minutes before Pierre near fell through the station's big doors into a marble lobby, crowded with servicemen, children, and sad women. Redcaps eyeballed him and his torn white shirt, saw no luggage, and turned away.

Pierre sat on a wooden bench worn smooth by a million people. He'd have surprised The Yellow-Haired Girl by buying a ticket right there on the train. He was crazy enough to have done that. He'd have sat on her left, the late morning sun streaming through the railroad car window brilliant behind her darkened profile, a silhouette ignited by loose wisps of her golden hair. His protective arm would encircle her shoulders as she napped against him as they passed rolling fields of corn and wheat reaching as far as anyone could see, the train lumbering through all the country behind red brick factories and mills, clattering over bridges that crossed canals and streams of black water that emptied into the Mississippi, his past falling away behind them.

Had those green eyes searched for him in the shadows of the station? What might he say to her if they ever again met? *I missed your train that day because I betrayed my lover the junkie poker dealer who cheated. I loved her a little, I admit. She was my partner in a street con. Her last words to me were about how she wanted to screw me for old time's sake. She was my mother's age, which sounds odd, I know, but it felt natural. I failed to tell her to run. I failed. She might have saved herself, but I failed.*

Four days later the papers carried notice of a woman's corpse, victim of a maniac, was found in a salt marsh. The corpse had rotted for several days while crabs ate her face and eyes. The NOPD presumed she'd been killed elsewhere and her nude body dumped; they hoped for a missing person's report because they had no means of identifying her. Her teeth had been smashed and fingertips cut, maybe while she was still alive. She had been gagged with her own clothing, the newspaper euphemism that meant "panties." The

Picayune speculated she was a transient prostitute. Surprisingly, there was no evidence of sexual assault, a detail chilling in its implications. Doris's killer had taken his time killing her; his sole pleasure was her agony and death.

Over days, the story ran out of legs. First it migrated to the paper's back pages; then it disappeared completely.

On the street, however, the story lingered. Word circulated that her hands and ankles had been hogtied with piano wire looped tightly at her throat. The more she struggled, the tighter the wire at her throat. She'd been worked on with pliers and a blowtorch before she was dropped into the shallow marsh, still breathing through her gag. Her struggles tightened the wire through the flesh at her neck before it severed her windpipe. She'd not been strangled, but her lungs had filled with her own blood. She'd drowned.

Two sleepless nights passed before Pierre returned to the Garden District cathouse. In some way he did not understand he was hopeful of absolution from Verne.

Ida, the landlady-madam, stood with one hand on her ample hip in the center of the doorway. "Verne? We never had any Verne here. I've got a Lucy, and an Iris, two Renees, and tonight a blonde German gal in black boots named Marlene. Genuine blonde, too. You can get close as you like and look to prove it. They are clean as a whistle. But a Verne or Veronica? Hair over her eyes and face like a movie star? A manicurist from New Jersey? That's rich. Are you on the pipe, kid?"

Never fuck with Silver Dollar Sam.

1948

Two weeks before VE Day in April 1945, with the Allies and Italian communists in hot pursuit, Benito Mussolini, 61, and his mistress, Clara Petacci, 33, made a run for it through the anarchy that was the defeated Italy. The country had more parties in its political ragu than there were churches in *Roma*. They fled in her German-made Audi hoping for neutral Switzerland but made it only as far as the southern shores of Lake Como. Their German escorts abandoned them.

Benito and Clara were dragged from their car and placed under arrest for most of a day until Italian communists put them and fourteen other *fascisti* against a wall and opened fire with submachine guns, a messier death than shotguns, a far messier end than a polite military firing squad. Just as Mario was thorough, the partisans pumped the shredded corpses with additional pistol shots to the head before the bodies were hoisted to the roof of a gas station and suspended by their ankles from meat hooks. For modesty's sake, the mob bunched and tied Petacci's skirts below her knees, though modesty prevented no one from urinating and spitting on her corpse prior to it being hauled aloft, her lifeless arms dangling below her head.

Il Duce's fascists were in part brought down by powerful men like Charlie "Lucky" Luciano in New York and Silvestro "Silver Dollar Sam" Carolla in New Orleans. Pissed off at the their decline in power and profit in Italy, American mobsters had agreed to *la familia* joining the resistance in the dusty hills of the old country. Wehrmacht officers stupid enough to lower a staff car's windshield were decapitated by piano wire strung taut from tree to tree across the rutted roads of Sicily as Montgomery and Patton raced to Palermo. German heads bounced in the dust like bocce balls.

For his patriotic service to America, Silver Dollar Sam Carolla was deported in 1947, one and all agreeing that a return to the old country was a better deal than a penitentiary cell in Atlanta, further agreeing it was far better than being suspended by the ankles from a meat hook.

Leadership of the New Orleans crime family fell to Carlos Marcello, the chain-smoking silent bodyguard who'd expertly patted down Pierre before Pierre climbed into his new life in the rear seat of Carolla's limousine. Marcello was the man with dead gray eyes who had blackened his thumbs pinching lighted cigarettes with spit and bare fingers and probably entertained himself for several hours by extinguishing his cigar on parts of Doris who, unlike the unfortunate Clara Petacci, was still alive and wishing she wasn't when Marcello suspended her from a ceiling meat hook.

By the war's end, Pierre still fancied himself the louche romantic, but even a louche romantic knew when vengeance was beyond his reach. In his 20s and bearing down on his 30s, Pierre acknowledged he had grown fond of breathing and saw no pressing reasons to pursue a course of action that might free him of that habit.

His patron, Mario, maintained plenty of influence, but not being a sadistic psychopath he was insufficiently vicious to keep a large organization in line. If called upon, Mario would not hesitate to decorate walls with brain spatter by a bullet through a skull, but Marcello would only administer the coup de grace after he'd sliced your eyelids away to make certain you could not turn from seeing your children suffer medieval agonies.

Pierre slept to late afternoon. By night, he dealt blackjack or poker wherever he was needed in any of the half-dozen casinos run by Mario. Every Friday, Mario had a wheel guy drive Pierre and three others to collect his cash pay at a trailer in front of the gate of a construction site. Someone would ask him if he owned a hardhat, and when he said he'd forgotten it, the someone would say he could not be allowed onto the site itself, so what he should do is go home; then they handed him a brown envelope filled with money. Mario's wheel guy kept all but ten percent.

But Pierre was trusted to do more than place cards on felt. The major security problem in any gambling operation is employees who believe they can steal from their employers. Every dealer, croupier, table manager, floor manager and up, including Mario, had at least two pairs of eyes on him. It was the managerial structure used by Stalin. Mario kept Pierre moving around and asked Pierre to keep his eyes open.

"Why me?" Pierre asked.

"You're smart enough to do it, and stupid enough to be honest." Mario puffed on a Cuban and gazed at his ceiling. "An Italian guy will always look for an angle, but you think you're Sir Lancelot. Are you honest?"

"As the day is long," he said. "But I'm not muscle."

"Muscle is cheap; smart is harder to find. No one can find honest. But I've never seen you forget a name."

"It's a talent."

"It is that."

At first, Pierre dealt low stakes at sleazier joints. He kept the games moving fast enough that even at lower stakes his tables turned a steady profit. He kept an eye on employees and the kind of cheat who filched a chip from his neighbor. Most cheats could be intimidated by a warning, but from time to a cheat would try it a second time and be stupid enough to try it in front of the dealer who never forgot a face. Instead of tedious explanations of the rules, Mario had two guys built like handball courts in cheap suits who could make drawing a deep breath difficult for the time it took bruised ribs to heal. Pissing blood for a week was not unheard of.

Women who cheated—and there were plenty—puzzled Pierre. His age and even younger, they seemed to believe that clear eyes, a slender ankle, and a flirtatious smile could buy them a pass. Despite warnings, if she were stupid enough to believe her good looks kept her safe from harm, she might find herself in a nearby alley with most of her clothes removed wishing she owned roofer's knee pads. The most astonished were the younger women who showed up with an alderman or a judge, a ward boss, parish bigwig, or some other political parasite who summarily washed their hands of a young woman not their wives.

Pierre's regular habits, honesty, and demeanor advanced him into Mario's upscale casinos. It did not hurt his career that if he were told which player needed to lose and which to win, he could make that happen. A bag or envelope of cash was outré, but a run of extraordinary luck could descend on the right man like a miracle. Pierre's good looks, polite manner, and soft voice attracted a few loyal female players, well-to-do genuine wives or daughters of those same influential men. He slept with a few, though not as many as Mario believed he did. Not wanting anything more complicated than a peccadillo with the dealer with dark eyes and long fingers, they coupled in a dark rear room, a stairwell, or outside in deepest shadows. Women went home, thrilled that they had navigated an interlude through a demimonde of jazz, cocaine, and gamblers, and Pierre was not unhappy.

He was stashing a pay envelope in his trousers when he asked Mario how he managed so many places at the same time.

"Buddy, a monkey can supervise a casino," Mario explained. "The games have percentages that favor the house. But managing a place to squeeze the most out of the investment calls for a more delicate touch. It is nothing to us to lose few hundred to a mouse while her boyfriend drops a few thousand. Don't ask me why some palooka would bring his wife here, but stranger things have happened. She'll nag him to come back because for her the place was lucky. You think we don't know about you and your women? You're a better asset than a rigged roulette wheel. Think of it as a job benefit. I just don't want to know about it. It makes me jealous."

"Jealous?"

"What can I say? I love my wife."

Each of Mario's casinos had the same office smelling of lemon oil and cigar smoke. The same gooseneck bank teller's desk lamp curled above the same leather blotter on the same glass desk guard. Mario was partial to ox-blood red leather furniture. It dried and cracked, but he kept the overstuffed blocky furniture forever. "It's Stickley," he explained, and Pierre nodded as if that meant something to him.

One night in 1948, with his feet crossed at the ankles on his desk beside his fedora, Mario said to Pierre: "Go home early, buddy. Rest up. We need you at a private game." He wrote a Metairie address on a small slip of paper. "Eat that paper when you get there."

Pierre glanced at the address, crumpled the paper, and burned it in the ashtray.

"I don't forget numbers. You know that. Not a hotel?"

"Not this time. A guy what owes us is making his place available. This guy loves his wife and he loves his little girl, but he loves the ponies a little more, so we are borrowing his home while they are away." A fresh ice-cube rattled into his Maker's Mark. On the bookshelf behind him, a framed photo of Mario's pretty wife looking haggard with overwork and his two boys looking happily overfed stood amid several decanted bottles of better liquor. The mahogany gleamed. If Mario owned a book to put on those shelves, Pierre never saw it.

"But the ponies do not return his love?"

"You got it." Mario saw the questions in Pierre's eyes. "Look, buddy, the game is on the up and up. You shuffle, you deal, I pay you, you collect tips, you go home. I know you can make the Jack of Diamonds stand up and sing *Pagliacci*, but all we ask is that you keep it simple and honest. There's a friend of a friend down from New York who can't be seen in New Orleans because he isn't in New Orleans. You might think you see him, but you are suffering an illusion. If certain people knew this Irishman was in New Orleans, they would wonder why he was here, and that could be trouble for everyone. The Irish do not appreciate good food, so they do not come to New Orleans for a meal. It is a good thing he is not here talking business. But as it happens, this Irishman who is not here plays poker to relax, and he has too much dough to relax for penny-ante stakes. In fact, he would be pissed off mightily if the game was rigged for or against him, as a rigged game tests no one's skills and he thinks of himself as a shark. He might be right. Who would disagree? So we are offering an old friend we have never met who may become a new friend an accommodation. A few players we know and trust will join him, also honest players. We're taking the usual vig, nothing extra. In a day or two, we will finish our business, but in the meantime nobody can know he is here. Because, as I said, he is not here."

"Just a friendly poker game that never happened?"

"Exactly."

"There is no such thing as a friendly poker game."

"This is sadly true." Mario cracked his neck and his knuckles. "If life were more simple, we could get him laid, but life is never that simple."

He tossed Pierre car keys. "It's the Packard in the back. The convertible. The guy who donated it had a foolproof system for roulette."

"There is no such thing as a foolproof system for roulette."

"True again. If everyone was as smart as you and me, we'd have to work for a living."

The candy-apple red Packard was a sweet ride. The ragtop was white; it floated on marshmallow whitewalls. The push-button radio was all chrome, and the car's front grill made it look like a wild boar. Despite the chill that March night, Pierre lowered the top and ran the car's heater at maximum. He had warmth at his feet, and cool night at his face.

He stopped the Packard beneath a palm close to the address in Metairie where the poker game was to be played. He was early. The unpaved parking lot near the sandy lakeside beach was abandoned in winter. Windblown chop dimpled the lake's unsettled green surface. His eyes grew heavy and he drowsed, the first time he'd slept outdoors since a million years ago when he spent a night on a bench his first hours in New Orleans.

He bolted awake a little stiff, saw he still had plenty of time, stretched himself loose, shrugged out of his windbreaker, rolled down his white sleeves, attached his faux pearl cufflinks, tied the knot in his bowtie, checked himself in the rearview mirror, and then drove to work. The address was a mostly brick house with a curtained white-trimmed bay window that faced the lakeshore from behind well-trimmed hedges. The house was fronted by a circular gravel driveway. For the guy who owned the house, life could be worse.

The front door had been left unlocked. Furniture had been moved to make space for the octagonal poker table beneath an ornate pewter chandelier in the formal dining room. Packs of unopened playing cards were stacked on the felt. Against the wall, a small credenza was crowded with top-shelf liquors and a sweating silver ice bucket. There was no sign of the people who'd done the setup. A better spread than most Pierre had seen was on a kitchen table, sandwiches speared by toothpicks under a crinkled yellow cellophane tent on a silvered cardboard tray. Bottled beer swam in ice in a zinc bucket, mostly Ballantine, a sure sign of a New Yorker come to play. He probably was a Yankee fan. Now that the war was done, whatever they paid DiMaggio, it wasn't enough. The house's kitchen's window overlooked a fenced yard, mowed grass, a willow tree beside a kid's jungle gym, and beyond that a trellis of miniature roses at the gate to a private hard-surface tennis court.

Why would any citizen who had this much put it at risk? What thrill could the ponies offer that he put himself in hock with Marcello's people? What could he win he could not already buy?

More help arrived. They congregated in the kitchen, loosened their ties, removed their hats and sport coats, and helped themselves to bottled beer. Though no stranger could be stupid enough to knock over a game like this, they kept their shoulder holsters. It would be an easy night with cold cuts, cold beer, gun talk, sports talk, and the usual lies about women.

Artie the Jew was the night's banker. He was no Hebrew, but may have been Albanian or Yugoslavian or something else like that, but his nickname reassured players their money was carefully watched. Pierre knew him from a few other games. His alligator suitcase was fitted with a wooden rack of rattling poker chips. The case matched his shoes. Artie also wore a white shirt and a cordovan shoulder holster that held a black .38 Colt automatic.

Within a half hour of each other, the players arrived. Their coats hung in a row in a hall closet as if they were in Metairie for a wedding to be conducted on the tennis court beyond the rose trellis. Pierre could not guess who was the big dog down from New York. No one looked Irish. They drew cards for table seats. Artie the Jew very publicly counted out chips so each player could be certain that every chip represented the same fifty dollars. The buy-in was three grand, after the ante of $50, the minimum bet was $100.

At precisely eleven, Pierre put the wheel in motion. They played five-card draw-poker, same as cowboys in Deadwood where Wild Bill Hickok took a .45 through the back of his skull. Artie the Jew watched the action over Pierre's shoulder. The muscle in the kitchen yammered mostly about how this Williams kid might do it for Boston. Somebody had to beat the Yankees, right? Not that the fucking Yankees weren't the smart bet, no argument, the DiMaggio kid being a force of nature, but DiMaggio did not play alone. Besides, Boston was long overdue.

At one-fifteen in the morning, four men masked like Jesse James' Gang boarding the Glendale train arrived, two through the front door, two through the back. Unlike the James Gang, these cowboys carried pump-action assault shotguns. Pierre had just enough time to register the puff of smoke-free air from outside that followed them in before he riveted his eyes to his folded hands. Pierre Doucet would never die defending someone else's money, but he was surprised that the protection in the kitchen drew no weapons. Then he heard automobile engines and realized they left on cue. There were simpler means to committing suicide than knocking over a Carlos Marcello poker game in Metairie, but that was not what was happening. This was a different kind of setup.

The masked gunmen neither spoke nor hesitated. Three players took 12-gauge blasts from close range to their chests. Their chairs carried them through back flips to the floor. A fourth player half stood, but before he managed a step most of his skull and all of his brain spattered the dining room's grass-cloth yellow wallpaper. Dead before he hit the floor, he spun from the ankles with his arms spread like a martyred saint, then sprawled face down over the poker table's green felt. The fifth player, who might have been the alleged Irishman from up north, had sat with his back to the door, the position that had proved fatal to Hickok. He fared better than Wild Bill. He draped his suit jacket over his shoulder, went nervously to the entrance hall closet, carefully took down his fedora, and tiptoed swiftly through gun smoke past the killers. His car coughed into life before the sound dopplered away.

"Artie, Artie, Artie. For a smart guy, you are awful stupid. You know better than this," the tallest of the masked men said as walked around the table and put a round from a .45 Browning automatic into weeping Artie's ear. Artie's skull exploded. The stink of gunpowder mixed with the iron stink of blood. The tall guy then walked calmly around the table to carefully put an insurance round behind the ear of each of the shotgunned players. There would be no miraculous survivals.

Hail Mary full of grace, the Lord is with thee. Blood and brains mottled Pierre's white shirt and forehead. *Blessed art thou amongst women, and blessed is the fruit of thy womb, Jesus.* A salty rivulet of gore snaked from above his eyebrow into the corner of his mouth. He sat rigid with his hands over the pack of cards in front of him. *Holy Mary, Mother of God, pray for us sinners.* Blood and brains seeped across his scalp and nose into his eye. A puddle of blood from four dead men pooled at his shoes. *Now and at the hour of our death.*

The shortest of the three gunmen jerked a thumb at Pierre. "What about this asshole?"

The tallest man said, "There's no contract on the dealer. He's all right. Did you see anything, buddy?"

"How can I see anything in Metairie if I am on Bourbon Street?" Pierre said.

"I don't like this," the shorter gunmen said. He pushed two fresh shells into the firing chamber. "Dead men can't talk even if they change their minds."

The tall man sighed. "Buddy, my friend who is suddenly particular about details needs to know you won't go blood simple. How about you stop praying and shoot someone?" Pierre looked up and confirmed what he already knew. That black, wavy hair with a pompadour could be no one but Mario. "If the dealer shoots somebody, will you be happy? I do not want you should be unhappy. Will that make you happy?"

"There is no one left to shoot."

"I will grant you that. Our guys from the back room are already halfway back to Corpus Christie. They know how things work and they are happy to be on their way home. They were also on Bourbon Street, regular tourists in New Orleans who have never heard of Metairie. They drank Hurricanes, enjoyed some music, got laid, and are on their way back to the wife and kids. They know we know where they live. They gave no guarantees. Trust is simple when it is a matter of mutual benefit. They will keep their mouths shut, and we will not need to kill them, their wives, or God forbid, their children just to make a point." He paused, and scratched his nose under his red kerchief. "Will it make you happy if the dealer shoots someone who is already dead?"

The stock toward him, the guy who could only be Mario handed Pierre his gun. The GI issue Browning was heavier than he imagined it would be. Pierre stood behind the corpse that had spun to lay face down on the poker table. Then, as directed, his arm trembling, once Mario showed him how to release the automatic's safety, from two feet he put a round through a dead man's lower back. The big gun made the loudest damned noise Pierre ever heard, the automatic leapt in his hand, the body bounced a half foot into the air before falling back. Then the corpse slipped from the table to the floor. The dead man's arm had impossibly wrapped around a table leg. Pierre's ears hummed; his eyes watered from smoke. He handed the Browning back to Mario, stock first, just as it had been given to him, but one shot lighter. His hands no longer shook.

"Enough?"

"That does not mean shit. The guy was already dead."

"I say it was enough. The only live guy I see here he could kill is you. You aren't arguing with me, now, are you? Who in holy fuck put this hair up your ass?"

The smaller man shrugged. "If something goes sideways, it's on you."

Mario sighed. "Have some faith. What can go wrong? There is a gun, we have a body with an extra pill in it, we have the dealer's prints on the gun. To seal the deal, I will give you the gun. Put it in your hope chest. It will be your Get Out of Jail Free card forever. If you get pinched for jaywalking, you offer it to a district attorney, and the D.A. will be grateful."

"I don't see how."

"The gun has prints and matches a bullet taken from the Metairie Massacre. What can go sideways?"

"This little prick dressed like Charlie McCarthy is only a dealer, am I right? That dummy is made of wood but talks a blue streak. I'd feel better if the dealer were permanently silent."

Mario sighed. "This is a very good dealer. Almost family. Nothing is going sideways. I would be grateful to end this bullshit. I am due to go fishing at sunup with important people who expect me way the hell down in Lafitte. We are out for seabass by Turtle Bay. The bass bite in the morning before they have their coffee and they believe every fucking lure is a dragonfly or a beignet, but by eight-thirty you have to be a magician to get a nibble. I do not want to miss this boat, but I will discuss this matter further with you if you are still unhappy."

"I don't know." The guy's shotgun started to rise.

Mario ended the debate with a single swift shot between the guy's eyes. He back-flipped to the floor. The other gunmen hardly blinked.

Mario holstered his automatic. "Now that everybody is happy, the discussion is finished, and we all trust each other. If it is all right with the rest of you, I would like to get some biscuits and gravy. There is a place on the road to Lafitte has a machine that squeezes oranges right in front of your eyes. The oranges roll down a chute like bowling balls, and orange juice flows out of a spout like water from a fountain in Italy. Who is in?"

The gunmen still wore their bandanas. No one used names. They broke their shotguns and pocketed the unspent shells.

"Burn those shoes, buddy," Mario said to Pierre. "Bourbon Street can be an awful place. Ruin a man's best Florsheims."

Seconds later, the front door clicked shut. The hum of departing cars left Pierre the sole breathing occupant of an expensive lakeshore suburban spilt-level with a private tennis court. The walls and floor house were awash in gore. The dead lay grotesquely twisted at his feet in puddles of thickening blood that left the floor slippery.

Pierre turned the cards over. The guy whose corpse he'd shot would have drawn a full boat, treys over fives. "You're a winner," he said. The bloody cards stuck to his fingers. He wiped his hands on his handkerchief, and ignored the gore to gather the deck into a paper napkin. He wiped his hands clean again, and put the crumpled paper napkin and the playing cards in his trouser pocket.

No record of Pierre Doucet's fingerprints or identity existed anywhere, but there was no reason to have a police jacket on those fingerprints opened. One day he could be stopped at a railroad crossing and be rear-ended by a near-sighted little old lady on her way home from the fruit market. An ambitious cop could become inquisitive and someone might find Edward Duquesne prints on a gun used at the Metairie Massacre and then he'd be in the shit. Pierre carried papers that named him Edward Duquesne, a name lifted from a badly weathered headstone from a small church graveyard outside Vidor, Texas. The grass had been sparse and the ground uneven where the cheap tiny coffin had cracked underground and caved in. The child's grave was ill-tended because who had the heart to revisit such terrible grief? The real Edward, God rest his soul, had come into the world on July 14, 1923 and died that same year eight days later. Since birth records were never crosschecked with death records, Mario had arranged for a draft card, driver's license, and union card for poor baby Eddie. Pierre even obtained a library card for Eddie. He never told Mario about the day when Pierre rode a bus to Vidor to slide a fifty dollar bill into the slot of a rusted donation box bolted to the churchyard's iron gates.

Pierre stepped over the man with the neat hole between his eyes. If the noise from the shootings alerted anyone, the police would have already arrived, so Pierre was in no special hurry. His pulse stayed steady. The local police might have been on the pad, but Pierre doubted that the murder of six citizens in an expensive suburb could be ignored.

At the base of the stairs to the second floor, Pierre stepped out of his shoes. His socks were sticky with blood. On his way up, he left a wet crimson footprint on each oak step. He looked down from the landing and thought how the stairs behind him looked painted by the Devil's cloven hoofs. Pierre was careful not to touch the handrail.

The bedrooms were orderly, the smallest all pink with a four-poster beneath white taffeta and lace. The bed and shams lay beneath a heap of stuffed animals, the largest a white bear on a maple rocking chair large enough for an adult. A glass-topped vanity had a skirt of the same pink-and-white taffeta. The bear had a pink ribbon tied at its throat. Pierre used a silver hair comb to open the jewelry box filled by the treasures of a little girl, her red bead necklace, hair pins, and a rhinestone tiara. He watched the twig-sized ballet dancer twirl before jewelry music box mirror to the Dance of the Sugar Plum Fairy, then with the same comb snapped the box closed.

A wild man covered mottled with gore stared back at him from the vanity's larger mirror. In the little girls' bathroom he found her jar of fragrant pink and yellow soaps shaped like seashells. Pierre washed his face and hands with a lavender-scented soap. He stuffed the blood-stained towel into his trouser pocket and dropped the soap into the toilet.

A safe was bolted to the floor of the master bedroom's walk-in closet, its door hanging open. The room smelled of potpourri, rose, pine, and ginger. The safe's metal drawers were hanging empty and several were on the floor, so the guy who owned the house must have planned to tell the police how jewelry and cash was stolen while he and his family were on the beach near Havana, when, in fact, the jewelry had been placed on the nose of a nag at the Fairgrounds so slow it might still be running. Pierre wondered if the wife knew her house was loaned for a poker game; for certain, neither the wife nor the guy could have known it would be used for a hit. Three slender banded stacks of cash were still there, no bill larger than a ten, supporting evidence to a story for the police and an insurance company of the thousands taken by phantom burglars.

F'true, the degenerate gambler would be implicated in the murders, but he could not be so stupid as to name his loan shark, not if he wanted the little girl and the wife to live. Daddy would go away, but Pierre doubted he would live to see a trial. The reach of Carlos Marcello passed through prison walls, and Marcello left no loose ends.

The master bedroom's nightstand held a half dozen glossy, blurry, semi-nude black-and-white photos, almost certainly the wife. In a lacy garter belt and mesh stockings, she was a looker. The pinup pictures were made for fun. One showed a shadow of pubic hair, but only one.

What kind of *fonchook* pisses away so good a life?

Downstairs again, Pierre rechecked the kitchen. If you overlooked the corpses, the overturned chairs, and the lakes of blood, the first floor still looked as if the house was waiting for the neighbors to attend a penny-a-point Bridge party. Pierre soaked a dishcloth, bent to drink cold water from the faucet rather than touch a glass, then wiped his face with the wet cloth, drying his face on his shirttail and his palms on his trousers. He unbuttoned and removed his blood-stained shirt to wipe down the wooden lip of the poker table, every surface of the chair on which he'd sat, and then any other surface in the room he might have touched. He wished he'd thought to look for rubbing alcohol while he was upstairs, but he could not bring himself to climb those stairs again and once more pass the pink and taffeta room.

He fixed a sandwich of Italian salami and *capicola* on a Kaiser roll, loading it with Swiss cheese, lettuce, and extra mayo, then realized how hungry he was and so added coleslaw, sliced bread-and-butter pickles, pitted olives, and a red pepper, but decided not to risk washing the Dagwood down with a Ballantine from the zinc ice bucket. He needed to stay completely sober, and he dared not leave a single careless fingerprint.

He chewed his food slowly, thinking. He'd always known Mario could kill, but seeing him at work clarified Pierre's vision. Mario was a family man who ran casinos who would spatter a guy's brains onto a wall with one shot, but the guy had made himself Pierre's protector.

His head was in a friendly tiger's mouth.

Pierre remembered to lift his shoes from the winding staircase's bottom step with his two fingers. Then in the kitchen he opened the oven, extinguished the pilot light, turned the gas on full for all six burners and the oven itself, took a fresh cigar from the pocket of a dead man, puffed it cherry red, then wrapped it in a cardboard matchbook before placing the burning cigar on the kitchen floor. He surrounded the cigar and matchbook with a pile of wooden matchsticks. When the cigar burned low enough, the paper matches and then the wooden matches would flare into a room by then filled by kitchen gas. He stuffed a towel against the bottom of the kitchen door to trap the gas. There might even be a small explosion. He did not know how much time he had, but it could not be long.

Outside at the house's rear, he bundled his shoes, trousers, and shirt in newspaper he found in a trashcan so no blood could smear the Packard's interior, then he pushed the trash can inside and shut the door. A halo glowed around the quarter moon hanging golden ripe above Pontchartrain. Weather was on its way, but no rain would be here on time to extinguish the fire in the house in Metairie. With the damp washcloth from his pocket he swiped the house's brass front door handle. Mario never gave him bad advice; Pierre would not have thought to burn the shoes straightaway. Then again, Mario did not advise him to burn down the house.

Pierre breathed the clean air and caught the faintest aroma of the collecting gas. He cringed as he started the Packard for fear the ignition spark might set off a firestorm with him in it, slipped the Packard into gear, and followed the circular driveway out front, careful to stay on the gravel and leave no tread marks in softer lawn.

The Packard had carried him east along the lakefront no more than a half mile when his hands began to shake. His shakes spread over his ribs and down his arms and then over his belly. His skin twitched around his torso. He forced his hands to grip the wheel, but that only aggravated the crawling snakes that took possession of his chest.

He allowed himself to look back. A column of black smoke curled like God's finger into the sky. There had been no blast, but a gas-fed inferno was burning.

He pulled over to allow fire engines going the opposite way. Near Live Oak, he stopped again to pull up the convertible's top. It was too dark and too early for him to have the bad luck of being seen, but anything was possible. The sun was not yet fully risen. Half-dressed and barefoot, he climbed the grass to the top of the levee at the lake's shore. His willed his pulse to slow. Streamer clouds in the east blushed a pink near the same as a little girl's taffeta.

He waited. Pierre would begin to feel all right, but then the shakes would start again. Losing control of his own body was like sickness, and sickness always reminded him how when he was a boy he'd chewed towels until his gums bled while Charlie beat Maman.

By the time he tossed his shoes, shirt, playing cards, and the dishtowel into a metal ashcan on the apron of a closed gas station, he was steady enough to kick through the service station's glass door to steal a tin of lighter fluid. He dropped his socks in the ashcan for good measure, sprayed the lighter fluid, and realized the percentage play was to burn every garment he'd worn. He'd have to do that closer to home. He already looked like a railyard bum in an undershirt and boxer shorts; he could not look like a crazy man driving stark naked. He warmed his hands on the small fire in the trash barrel, took a piss of heroic volume against the cinderblock wall, and left.

Two days later, he went to Mario to return the Packard.

"Keep it."

Mario's feet were on his desk. "It says here in the *Picayune* that the murderous thieves missed a significant amount of cash in the death house before they burned it down. They are calling it the Metairie Slaughter and guessing it was a mob hit. They haven't yet identified the bodies. Too badly burned. Have you read the story?"

"I saw it."

"Why do you suppose the guys did not take the cash?"

"Maybe the guys do not want blood money."

"Money doesn't know shit about blood. Money knows only about more money." Mario reached for his decanted Maker's Mark. "Sometimes I think you must be a fucking communist. This McCarthy prick would stare up your ass and just might find Stalin. You think too much. It comes from reading, a nasty habit unless you are studying the sports pages or doping out the daily double in the *Morning Telegraph*. At least when you are done with a newspaper, you can wrap fish or line a birdcage. What can you do with a fucking book?"

Pierre waved away an offer of bourbon. He never drank if he was scheduled to deal. "You can put a book under the short leg of a table," he said. "Keep the soup from spilling."

"There is that, I admit. This is what I admire about you, buddy. You pay attention to details and you are smart enough to think of them all."

"Books become pals." Pierre waved away a second offer of a drink. "A pal is a guy who lets another guy know what in fuck is going down rather than springing a surprise that has him struggling to keep his asshole closed. A little trust goes a long way between friends. Friends are not family, I admit, but trust goes farther than even a Packard."

Mario pursed his lips to consider the point, shrugged as if he reluctantly acknowledged wisdom not his own, lifted his bourbon, and said, "*Salut.*" He slammed the shot glass to the top of his desk, opened the deep drawer on the right, and withdrew a bundle wrapped in rags and tied with coarse twine. "You'll want this, buddy. Maybe take a boat ride down river to drop it overboard. Salt water erodes metal faster. This is even better than trust."

A few nights later, Pierre booked a tourist dinner cruise for a party of one on a side-wheeler. He enjoyed most of a bowl of bouillabaisse before he walked the deck nodding to couples who smiled at the neatly-dressed young man who seemed alone but not unhappy to be in New Orleans, a tourist like themselves. He wore a new brown hat low over his eyes. At the moment the ship finished its cruise upriver and turned bank-to-bank to return to its dock, at mid-channel above the deepest water, Pierre braced his elbows on the stern handrail, looked from under the brim left and right, and allowed the rag bundle that held the .45 with his fingerprints to slip overboard.

When the side-wheeler docked, Pierre aimlessly drove the candy-apple red Packard with its toothy chrome grill out of the city, the white top down and the cool night blustering about him. He drew his collar up and turned on the car's heat, but once again he did not wish to put the convertible's top up. Cold air lashed his face. Into the smallest hours, his long fingers loose on the wheel, Pierre idled on the south shore of Pontchartrain at the same grass-covered levee he'd been days before. He cupped his hands against the wind and lit a Lucky. Dawn peered over the horizon, extinguishing stars as the sky paled from gray to rose to pink and finally, a blue so clear it took his breath away.

Pierre stood on packed cold sand. The narrow line from pole to pole that separated shadow from light, night from day was immobile, but the world turned through what was called the Terminator. As the planet spun, the Terminator passed through him, through Mario, through Doris's bones, through Verne whom he devoutly hoped was in Chicago, through the Yellow-Haired Girl wherever she might be, through Charlie and Maman, through all of the French Quarter with its fishermen, musicians, careless children, crooked police, heist specialists, carpeted casinos, embezzlers, extortionists, sports fixers, racketeers, professional killers, pool hall hustlers, shopkeepers, cheap whores, second story men, boot blacks, Murphy men, jockeys, mothers, youths drunk on hope, drunks sunk in despair, booksellers, waiters, pimps, call girls, madams, teachers, tap dancers, chefs, tailors, bare knuckle pug boxers, fortune tellers, bakers, pickpockets, singers, young toughs, old women with secret memories of who they had been before they became respectable, and sad old men whose memories were nothing but regret for all the things they did not do.

The line could be calculated to the width of a thread. At the precise moment the Terminator passed through him, Pierre believed that if anyone might live forever, it would be him.

1950

RUNNING DAILY DOWN A FLIGHT of stairs for a basin of water was bad enough, but Pierre could not cross his room without tipping over a ziggurat of books. The towers rose from his warped wooden floor. Pierre dearly loved his wraparound windows that captured any breeze, but he had outgrown his garret. He found a second story apartment on Prytania, east of Audobon Park. The house was walled; having the nearby park close was like having a giant private lawn. The landlord asked for no references when Pierre paid cash.

Pierre's book habit amused Mario. "They have an aroma," Pierre explained.

Mario grinned. "Like pussy. Maybe I should get a library card."

"Sure. Just like pussy." Pierre reminded himself to never again explain anything dear to his heart to Mario.

The pride of his book collection was the complete edition of Scott's Waverly novels he'd won at an estate auction. The bindings were pasted with thumb-worn green marbleized paper, the top edge smoothed with gold gilt. *Rob Roy* was better than *Ivanhoe*, but in Scott's world of ruthless cads, damsels in distress, and Robin Hood, Pierre was immersed in a world very much like his own. Scott's heroes adhered to a simple code: protect the weak, never lie for advantage.

From time to time Pierre gazed over the top of a book at nothing so he might wonder what the Yellow-Haired Girl Who

Looked Back had read at her far away New England schools. She lingered in his mind like the dissipating scent of a gardenia in a half-forgotten dream.

Pierre read every day. He took spare meals in unspectacular restaurants, often with a single glass of burgundy and a book. He exercised as if he were in isolation at Angola, squats, push-ups, and sit-ups, all exercises that needed nothing but a floor. His flesh remained tight; his back and joints flexible. He sprinted 100-yards five times each for three days per week either along a levee or the lakeshore before his morning cup of chicory and a half beignet. He employed housekeepers and a laundress.

As a favor to Mario, he accompanied a young woman to Brennan's for Bananas Foster. She was an innocent, but Mario had cautioned him that if anything more than pleasantries occurred with the teenage girl whose visiting father had a friend who had a friend in St. Louis, Pierre might awaken in a ditch to find his testicles had migrated to his mouth. The dessert proved to be delicious and the innocent girl remained innocent. Not so Pierre. Brennan's occupied the one-time home of Paul Morphy, in his day the world chess champion. Chess became a lifelong obsession for Pierre.

It was not sensible, but Pierre allowed himself to feel kinship. Morphy taught himself chess by simple observation, became world-class by 12, and was acclaimed best in the world when he was 21. In Europe, Morphy consorted with kings and queens who doubted his identity because of his youth, until he beat their best national players flat. He returned to New Orleans, but at the top of his game gave it up. Thirty years later, on a hot New Orleans summer day, he lowered himself into a chilled bath in the house that became Brennan's, the very same house he shared with his mother, and in that chilled bath he died of a stroke. Now they served Bananas Foster one story below where Morphy was found dead in a copper tub surrounded by a semi-circle of women's shoes.

No other game had so deep a recorded literature. No other game yielded complete information to competing players. There were no dice, no element of chance, and while that could be said of checkers, no other game offered infinite complexity. With a slip of paper that he moved down the page to expose each White and Black move played in a game recorded a hundred years ago, he tried to teach himself to think like a grandmaster. When he moved the paper and discovered he'd calculated the next move before it was revealed to his eyes, he exulted. While he learned the openings, the truly deep moves, the art and beauty of the middle game, evaded him.

Chess confirmed what Pierre already knew, that cold calculation contributed less to any victory than human instinct. The game pitted powerful personalities against each other, and they dueled through assessment of patterns. Morphy played by feel, his style marked by Romantic speculative gambits and sacrifices that subsequent cold analysis proved to have been faulty, but in the heat of play across the board came at an opponent fierce as a desert storm.

At Mario's insistence, Pierre installed a telephone. His number remained unlisted, and his telephone bill went to a post office box in the name of PM Enterprises, a name chosen to honor the chess prodigy who too much loved his mother, though he let Mario think PM stood for Pierre-Mario. Pierre made no outbound calls. Mario called him rarely and then only on business. He shared the phone number only with Maman, placing it on a slip of ivory notepaper he slipped into the monthly envelope which also held a folded a fifty dollar bill.

Maman telephoned him only once. She'd had to walk to town to find a pay phone and then called collect. Her voice slurred as if her jaw was stiff, and though he pressed her for details she insisted she was peachy. Her *beau gamin* needed to stay away. "You come here, you make trouble, then you gonna go right back to New Orleans, and 'linda has more trouble. Den what am I doing? So you stay away, but know your Maman loves you."

The massive final hemorrhage that exploded from Kolinda Doucet's mouth sprayed a shower of blood and lung tissue across her chest and the thin, flowered, cotton bedspread under which she lay undiscovered for three days. The textile fibers she'd inhaled during her factory days had done their work.

Maman was 40, Pierre 23. No one had told him how ill Maman had been or that the strong woman who'd carried him to a country road to escape Escambia County had grown frail and prematurely old.

Tante Gertrude's call came precisely at 8 AM. Maybe it had been *Tante* Esme. He had no memory of any of the women Maman called *les grosse z'oie*, "the big geese." She must have been staring at the clock since dawn, waiting for the stroke of 8 to place the call, neither too late nor too early.

She asked if Pierre were alone.

The lips of the woman asleep in his bed were parted, a rivulet of drool snaking from the corner of her mouth across a pillowcase. Pierre sat cross-legged with a blanket over his bare lap trying to recall his companion's name. She'd flirted with him most of the night over a blackjack table. The curve of her hip was startling. "I'm alone."

" 'linda dead. We brought her home to Pensacola, but last night we found this number in 'linda's cigar box. It had the letters you sent her tied with a bow with a black ribbon. Charlie brung the cigar box with him to bury with her, but the old fool never thought to look in the box except to find money. He says there wasn't none." *Tante* Gertrude said, "If you leave at once, there is time enough for you to get here. We'll wait one extra day."

She went on with unsparing details. Evidently, Charlie slept beside Kolinda's corpse for two days before he notified the sheriff. His aunt shared that detail as if Charlie were a saint; the more probable explanation was that the *couillon* was on a bender and never noticed Maman was dead. His aunt revealed a detail Pierre knew could not be true. "She'd been reaching for her rosary, so there is that. God rest her."

Rosary? If there was a Hell, Maman was at the front door kicking at the Devil's shins.

Maman's final journey to Pensacola was as bereavement freight, her first and only train ride. She'd arrived two days ago. Charlie was allowed free fare from Gulfport as long as he sat beside the coffin. He lied about being Maman's husband.

The eyes of the woman beside Pierre fluttered open. She yawned, stretched her arms, and stroked him under the cotton blanket. She reeked of tobacco and something inexpensive. Chantilly? Tea rose? Her green mascara smeared across his bedding. She was missing a false eyelash.

His aunt supposed the import-export business would keep him in New Orleans and far too busy for his simple family who were plain folks. 'linda boasted he was in Paris and Rome and London and whatnot. It was a miracle they had found him at all after reading through all them letters. "Your mother, God rest her, never stopped lording it over us how you flew around the world at the drop of a hat after you were discharged." She snorted. "All those secret missions; you'd think you won the war alone." She paused for breath. "Well, the past is past. My sisters and I need to know if you will be joining us, or would you prefer that we send you a bill? There's Charlie's ticket, the box, and the man we 'spect to hire to say a few words. Nothing comes cheap, though. It's a scandal. I can't never die because I can't afford it."

"I'll be there," he said.

Surprised, Gertrude held her breath a beat, then said the address of a mortuary north of Pensacola. When he said he did not need to write it down, the telephone connection abruptly broke.

The woman beside Pierre wanted breakfast, but he told her she had to leave. Her breath was sour. She stuffed her nylons into her bag, shimmied into a dress, and tried to apply lipstick, but Pierre gave her the bum's rush. As his door closed firmly behind her, she called, "Asshole," but he was already neatly folding what he'd need into a small brown leather suitcase.

"It's your mother, buddy," Mario said. "Everybody gets one, but only one. Do what you have to do. I'll see you when I see you." He reached into a desk drawer to retrieve a crumpled wad of spare bills that he pushed into Pierre's hands.

By the time Pierre set out, the red Packard tracing the shoreline of the Gulf on Federal 90, the sun was low at Pierre's back, white sand beaches on his right. The car carried him eastward, backward through time, from New Orleans, to Gulfport, Biloxi, Mobile, and a thousand no-name towns in between, the places where his life was shaped by no one but Maman.

Eventually, the Packard's headlamps probed the dark Pensacola Holy Cross Cemetery, a treeless flat field beside a non-denominational chapel. A steeple stretched heavenward through the gathering October night.

The mortuary director, a young guy no older than Pierre, was eager to please. He and his pregnant wife had just purchased the business with a loan he was able to obtain only because he'd taken advantage of the GI Bill, so he apologized for having no associations in nearby places to stay, being a recent arrival himself. His father was a mortician in Montgomery. "But you know how it is. The wife wanted seashore." Pierre was welcome to stay with them, however; no trouble at all. Pierre thanked him, knowing that for a pregnant woman an unexpected houseguest was nothing but trouble. Pierre said he preferred to sit with Maman on a metal folding chair beside the gurney on which his mother's plain pine casket had been set.

The rosary with which she'd supposedly died was wound through the folded fingers on her chest. The mortician had done a fair job with her face, but her skin remained sallow and her cheeks wizened in ways Pierre did not recognize and could not be ordinary on a woman who died so young. Her lips were colored wrong; Maman, who'd worked a cosmetics counter at the Five & Dime, would have wiped her face clean of all that crap. She'd been a tough, pretty girl who'd been worn down by troubles. Pierre half-expected her to sit up with annoyance.

He loosened his tie and put his legs out before him on a second folding chair to sit the night beside Maman. He spoke with her ghost and jerked awake from dreams and memory that were an improbable mix of playing cards, hugs, kisses, soda fountains, and the times when they suddenly and swiftly moved from one place to another. He'd been sixteen in New Orleans before it occurred to him that Maman was regularly fleeing landlords. That night in the chapel he dreamed he played Boo-Ray with Maman, making her laugh by riffling playing cards while telling her stories about street musicians, a good crawfish boil, the people who knew and liked him, how his good friend Mario hated Gene Autry, how they went fishing together from time to time, like gentlemen, not working fishermen, and of a special yellow-haired girl whose name he did not know. Maman read his fortune. As ever, he was the Knave of Hearts who would disappoint many women except the last one, the Queen of Diamonds. The riches she was to give him would not be money but the depth of her soul. Maman's ghost studied the cards. The sun was the hint of a suggestion of the new day coming. "I will see you when I see you, *mon beau gamin*," she said. "Do not hurry to join me, though you must make space for another in your heart. Maybe she be this yellow-haired gal."

As dawn burst through a stained glass window, the tiny chapel exploded with color. The funeral director appeared in the chapel carrying a small wooden breakfast tray that held a buttered roll wrapped in a white cloth napkin beside a small blue porcelain cup of cold milk. He hoped Mr. Doucet did not mind they had no coffee, but he and his pregnant wife drank none and were unused to guests. Mr. Doucet was welcome to what they had. Nothing was hot because the aromas of food in the morning nauseated his wife. The man refused Pierre's offer of money for the roll and milk, and listened carefully to Pierre's comments about the color of Maman's lips. "I did what her sisters asked, but I will take care of your changes. I promise you."

There would be no wake. She'd been dead for several days and needed burial. Pierre approved an open coffin in the chapel followed by a short walk to the gravesite and a brief service there. Since the walls of the pine coffin were porous, Pierre paid for a dark-stained walnut water-tight casket lined by white satin. Maman's head would forever rest on a lace pillow.

When next he saw her, Maman's lips had a paler hue. She'd been in a cotton shroud because Charlie had not thought to bring any of her clothes, but the mortician dressed Maman in a white cotton choir dress. Her hands were in thin cotton gloves. "My wife suggested the dress. It's all we had ..."

His three *tantes* remarked on how well Maman looked, just as she had in life, though Pierre knew that none of Kolinda's younger sisters had seen her for more than twenty years. None of the Doucet girls had ever married. If Pierre had cousins by Maman's siblings who'd left Pensacola before she, they were far away and lost to any family connection or history. His uncle the bootlegger was a good story, but he too was long vanished.

The pitiless eyes of the hardscrabble sisters peered unblinking at him from under black veils. They clucked with disapproval mixed with envy at the showy candy-apple red Packard convertible, but that did not prevent a recalculation of what they thought they knew: 'linda's fairytales of Pierre's mysterious success were possibly true. No poor man drove a red convertible. Gertrude and Filomena's nostrils flared annoyance at their wayward sister's final victory. They lacked all talent for hiding how they felt. When Pierre's impassive eyes fell on them, they turned away, their eyes dull glass.

Graveside, a pastor who never knew Maman turned to the gospel of John, reading *For God so loved the world, that He gave His only begotten Son, that whoever believes in Him shall not perish, but have eternal life*, and then went on to explain how that meant that sinners were eternally damned, the faithful would rise to be with Christ Everlasting, but even the worst sinner could be forgiven and gathered unto Jesus if they would only repent.

The words moved Pierre, though he was sure Maman would have fumed to find the rosary entwined in her grip. Somewhere nearby a dog barked wildly. Charlie's shaky hand gripped his, and then Charlie stood beside Pierre, nervously turning the straw boater he held before him. Had he grown thin, or had Pierre's memory magnified the man? His aunts buzzed nervously about how Negroes and whites rested in the same ground at Holy Cross, an indignity they'd have avoided if only they'd known their nephew had substantial means, perhaps investing in a plot beside their own mother who had preceded Kolinda to her eternal rest by only seven years, perhaps even a plot that might someday hold all the Doucets.

Four Negroes lowered Maman into the earth. Pierre dropped a single rose and a spade of brown earth rattling onto her coffin. The mortuary director had without asking arranged for a single rose and a dozen gardenias to be delivered to the gravesite. The white flowers fell on Kolinda.

Charlie wept unrestrainedly. The sisters lingered, wondering what more could be done or said. Esme suggested the members of their close-knit family find a restaurant to set a bit. "Maybe just cherry pie and to tell you tales of how your grandmother and your uncle were so loved. You never knew either of them because of your mother's willfulness," Esme said, then hurried to add, "She loved you so."

"My grandfather is the one who killed himself. Is that right?" The sisters looked anxiously at each other. "And my uncle, that would be Uncle Andre, the bootlegger?"

Filomena ignored him, but proposed a Doucet Cousins Club to do charitable work for unwed mothers. "'linda, God rest her, believed nothing was more important than family."

"My New Orleans associates expect me."

It became plain Pierre would have no truck with them no matter how much they clucked or wheedled. With a billow of black taffeta and snapping parasols, Gertrude, Filomena, and Esme sat hip-to-hip in a pre-war black Ford and sped away, convinced more than ever that their sister's son was fathered by a soulless mulatto of indefinite blood, a fact that accounted for his lack of feeling and unwillingness to part with a dime.

Charlie thrust his hands in his trouser pockets and said, "Holy Cross was the onliest place the sisters could afford 'lessen you helped out. No one never heard from you, so they made all the decisions. I didn't know it took so much money to bury nobody." Pierre said nothing, so Charlie added, "I did the best I could, like always. 'You find Pierre and it will all be all right,' is what I said to those women. 'He's a good boy and will do right by you and his mother.' A fella in Gulfport took my last dollar to box her up, we rode the train, and that's when your aunt called you." Charlie held out his canceled train ticket.

"Where are her things?"

"I sold what I could to pay for the train. There weren't much." Charlie danced from foot to foot like a child that needed to pee. "Look, son, I can't afford no boarding house and figured to skip out, but now that you're here … There's no reason for us to make the Greyhound people rich, is there?"

Pierre agreed to pay his bill and drive Charlie to his shack north of Gulfport.

He left Charlie in the sun in the Packard while he paid the mortuary director with the cash Mario had pushed into his hands. When was that? One day ago? Two?

"Thanks for the gardenias," Pierre said.

"I took a liberty," the man said. "Your sisters said 'No,' to the flowers, but the moment I met you, I knew you'd say 'Yes.' If you can't afford all of it right now, we can work something out." He held out a neatly handwritten itemized bill.

Pierre read only the bottom line. With the same dexterity that enabled Pierre to ice a deck of cards, he slid an extra hundred dollar bill into that good man's side pocket, thinking, *Thank your wife for her kind breakfast. This gift is for your baby.*

It was still late morning. While Charlie retrieved his pitiful belongings from the boarding house, proud to be able to pay his bill even if it was with Pierre's money, Pierre drowsed in the Packard. Maman came to him. She warned him that the October afternoon promised storms, no hurricane, but there could be a blow. She also told him there was more good than evil in the world, but she admitted it was harder to find.

I am sorry I never visited, Maman.

F'true? What was here for you?

Forgive me.

There is nothing to forgive, mon beau gamin. Her cool hand swept back the hair that had drifted over his eyes; her lips touched his forehead, and the spot stayed warm to his touch.

Clattering hail awakened him. The street was blanketed by scattered melting diamonds. The hail quickly stopped. Charlie chose that moment to dash from the hotel porch to rap on the Packard's window and toss a carpetbag into the car's rear seat. He settled beside Pierre and wept again, great heaving sobs that reeked of cheap wine.

"Your mother's troubles are over, but mine ain't. Where will the likes of me find another like her? How am I going to get along now? Exactly how, is what I want to know. God takes the good young, and has no pity for the living," he muttered. "That priest might be right about sinners being forgiven, but what are we supposed to do in the meanwhile? That's the way of it, am I right? Heaven is for the sweet by and by, but you and me have to live here and now."

They were west of Mobile Bay when Charlie asked, "Do we have any of my medicine?"

Pierre kept his eyes on the road.

When they crossed into Mississippi, they stopped to take a leak into the roadside dust. In the three hours since they'd set out, the sun had grown more fierce and the unsettled weather receded behind them. Pierre lowered the convertible's top. Further west, they stopped a second time at a roadside stand that sold all manner of things, including Charlie's preferred medicine, a pint of George Dickel.

The Packard was rolling again when Charlie's shaking hands broke the seal on the metal cap. His Adam's apple bobbed when he drank, his head way back for a long swallow before he wiped the bottle mouth with his filthy palm to offer the whiskey to Pierre. Pierre waved it away. "I told your Momma you was a good boy," he said, stifled a belch, and leaned back for a second long swallow.

The liquor and sun persuaded Charlie to remove his crumpled blue sport coat and toss it into the read sear with his straw boater. The cheap hat soon was lofted on the wind and sailed away. Then Charlie stripped off his shirt and balled that into the back seat as well. He was bare-chested except for blue suspenders, his ordinary mode of dress, his dark neck pitted with angry red and black scars where boils did their work. His arms sagged a sickly fish-belly white. Maybe they'd been muscled long ago, but this shrimper had not been to sea in many years. Pierre wondered how he had ever been terrified by this little, fat, sorrowful, broken rummy in a tattered undershirt.

Charlie drained the Dickel and sang. Unable to remember any lyrics, he mumbled the chorus over and over.

> *Bang bang Lulu*
> *Lulu's gone away.*
> *Who's gonna bang bang Lulu*
> *When Lulu goes away?*

When the empty bottle was cast onto the highway, shards of glass spun behind the Packard. The foul-smelling drunk fell asleep, twitching, snorting, snoring, sweating, his shoulder wedged against the passenger door.

Maman's life came unbearably clear, her sacrifices for her *beau gamin* leading into a final trap, Charlie. Trapped by a pregnancy, trapped by the Depression, trapped by her love for Pierre, too old and too alone and too tired to fight free of Charlie, enduring the drunk for what she had imagined was safety.

Why hadn't he brought her to New Orleans? Why not? He'd had it in his power to set her free. Mario was fond of repeating, *Family is the most important thing,* but Pierre had arranged his life so *family* meant *no one.* Never mind what he did to live; Maman need never have known.

On the outskirts of Gulfport, his self-loathing mounting, Pierre never stepped from the Packard. He gave Charlie a ten dollar bill, more than enough for a late lunch and the local bus that would carry Charlie to the no-name road and the shack where Maman had breathed her last. When Pierre had been ten, he'd gone barefoot through the crumbling dust that filled Charlie's front yard, a place where dogs bayed at the yellow moon and where Maman knew Charlie's unforgiving hands.

The Packard left Charlie standing with his hand shading his eyes, but ten miles further west, once Charlie's stink had been blown clear of the open car, Pierre twice steered onto the road's gravel shoulder. The second time, his mind made, he twisted the wheel and turned the Packard around.

Every rut on the dirt road north from Gulfport jarred Pierre's bones. His teeth clicked shut until he clenched his jaw. The Packard sped past sad, desiccated cows.

Charlie's shack was a ways back. A wreck of a Ford pickup was rusting in front, the tires and doors long gone. The Packard bounced over weeds and brown grass to stop within a foot of Charlie's sway-backed porch. Pierre took the two crumbling cement steps with a single stride.

Charlie saw him coming. With a river rat's instincts, he scrambled away, but he was too drunk to stand, near unconscious on the wooden swing hanging lopsidedly from two chains. Charlie had walked from town to save the bus fare that he spent instead on a fresh pint of Dickel. He fell back onto the swing that hung above his half open carpetbag on the porch's weathered wood.

Pierre's hands found Charlie's throat. Charlie kicked out, but his feet found no purchase. In Pierre's grip, eyes bulging, sweat running free over his face, the stupid son-of-a-bitch chose that precise moment to say, *Son, she left nothing worth nothing, I swear it.*

Pierre grabbed a handful of the seat of Charlie's pants to force Charlie to bend forward, then kicked him into the dark beyond the shack's unlocked door. The shack's three rooms smelled of cat piss and rotting food. Flies buzzed in fury. This was where Maman had taken to her bed never to rise; this was where Charlie left her in darkness and filth. A towel on the kitchen floor was stained black, crusted with Maman's blood. The blanket onto which she'd hemorrhaged was balled in a corner, covered with insects. Every corner of the shack mocked him.

Louche? He was the selfish piece of crap who'd never thought to rescue his own mother. Kolinda Doucet died without ever knowing her *beau gamin* as a man. Instead of making her life right, he'd sent her money. She'd fabricated stories to account for his absence and why he had to abandon her. Remorse and self-loathing filled him.

Charlie squirmed in Pierre's grip as Pierre swept the rummy's feet from under him. He lifted Charlie from the floor, knocked him to the ground, lifted him, and slapped Charlie senseless. The drunk curled into a whimpering ball. Blood flowed from his scalp over his eyes. Pierre did not plan to kill him, but he left Charlie in a puddle of vomit long enough to go to the porch and pulled a doubled porch swing chain free of its hook. He gripped Charlie by his hair, braced the drunk on his knees, and whipped Charlie like a dog. The howling drunk collapsed facedown to the floor. He whimpered, his pants darkest where he'd pissed himself.

Murder would bring out bloodhounds, but a thorough beating of the town drunk would disturb no one. His showboat Packard had surely been noticed, but even if someone in Gulfport recalled the numbers on the stolen Texas tags, there would be no successful pursuit. By the time anyone discovered Charlie, Pierre's trail would be cold.

Pierre left Charlie in the back seat of the rusting wreck that lay before the shack. When the Packard left, Charlie was alive. If he could stand he might walk. The rest was up to God and an unhappy swarm of hornets.

He planned to drive through the night, Maman's spirit beside him. She asked why her *beau gamin* needed to beat the worthless *couillion*. F'true, Charlie deserved all Pierre gave him, but if everyone received their due, Hell would fill.

The Packard rolled past white sand beaches and sparse overarching palms. Surf broke on the shallow shore, wavelets receding to break again. The seascape was so monotonous that Pierre could not be sure he moved at all. Humidity sucked skyward massed into darkening thunderheads. Late in the day, the first hiss of rain first dimpled the sea, then the sand, and finally moved shoreward to fall fat on the blacktop two-lane highway. Pierre lifted the Packard's top, then cranked shut his window. The car grew steamy; the sky the color of a bruise. Twice, the Packard slid on rainwater that covered gentle curves.

He came to a badly paved parking lot beside an open-air bar, not much more than a thatch roof on driftwood pillars set in a cement slab. Pierre needed a place to wait out the storm. This place had no name. He doubted he was being followed, but he nevertheless steered the red Packard behind tall hedges hidden from sight.

You worry too much, Maman whispered to him. *Ain' no one even found Charlie yet, and if they do Charlie the fonchock be talkin' no kind of sense.*

Pierre left his shoes and socks on the Packard's front seat to run barefoot for fifteen feet without shelter. His white dress shirt soaked translucent. He shivered like a wet dog.

The bar held five stools, two vinyl bench booths, an illegal dime slot, two ceiling lamps set in the center of lazy rattan fans, and a bubble machine Wurlitzer. Pierre dropped a nickel for Jo Stafford's melancholy "I'll Be Seeing You." He settled himself onto the stool at the bar's end and doubted that The Yellow-Haired Girl Who Looked Back all those years ago could possibly approve of beating a helpless drunk. She'd felt it her patriotic duty to kiss boys goodbye at the USO. Maybe Jo Stafford had been singing. Would she understand there were some things that simply needed doing? The song led him to recall Doris and her many husbands, those pitiful marks in an insurance scam orchestrated by their ever-loving wife whose eyes were eaten by crabs.

He was among the ghosts of the only three women who'd ever mattered; KJ who was the Yellow-Haired Girl Who Looked Back; Doris whom he betrayed; Maman whom he'd abandoned.

You did all you could, Maman whispered. *Everyone starts wanting to be good, jus' life be changing them. Ain' no one sets out to be evil.*

Am I evil, Maman?

No, beau gamin. You be human.

The bartender was the cook, dishwasher, and waiter, and proudly noted he was also the proprietor, owning the place free and clear. There was little enough business on weekend, and next to nothing weekdays, but he liked to be behind his bar because there was no better place to be. "Ilene, the wife, passed over two years ago, God bless her. Always had a laugh in her."

When Pierre turned down a drink, the bartender brought him coffee. "For the chill," the little bald man said. He was right. He needed to grip something to stop the cold shakes, ripples of movement across his chest and down his arms. Pierre's fingers laced around the chipped porcelain mug. He said how he'd just put his mother in the ground, then he draped his wet shirt on the back of a chair. Ever since Clark Gable took off his shirt in front of Claudette Colbert, no man worth the name any longer wore undershirts. Doris's ghost appeared in the bar's speckled back glass, grinned wickedly, puckered her lips, and wordlessly admired Pierre's physique. Had she forgiven him? But her ghost disappeared before he could ask. He hoped so. His tan trouser legs slowly dried, as did his back and chest. Wind drove pattering rain a foot or more under the thatch roof and across the cement slab floor, but he was beyond the rain's reach. Pierre blew into his closed hands.

"Conch chowder, podner. Take the chill out of your bones. Just the thing. I boiled it up this morning. The celery is fresh. I cut the potatoes myself. Lots and lots of pepper. Guarantee you gonna like it."

Pierre dropped oyster crackers and Tabasco into the steaming chowder of conch, vegetables, and what he was sure was a trace of lime. The owner would take no money from a man who had just lost his mother. "I'm glad for your company," he said.

He was reaching for his wallet anyway as Maman's ghost urged him to not insult the man. *Accept his hospitality.* He slipped his arms into his still-damp shirt.

It was pleasant to be in the shelter of the thatch roof, to be outdoors in wet weather but dry. The chowder warmed him from the inside. His hands and ribs no longer shook. He insisted on paying for the second cup of chowder. When his host suggested brandy, Pierre accepted. They drank to Maman and the departed Ilene.

The bar's lights flickered with a close lightning strike. The last of the setting sun appeared below the black clouds, and then the rain slowed and stopped. Runoff from the thatch roof became a steady trickle.

Pierre might have departed, but he moved instead from his bar stool to one of two rattan Empress Chairs set to face each other across a tiny driftwood table. He'd barely slept for two days. Heavy as the air, his shirt tail hung off a chair. He shut his eyes; brandy flowed through him.

The soft-looking woman with black hair who joined him was barefoot and dark-eyed. At first he believed Maman's spirit was beside him again, but he looked more closely and guessed this woman might be Greek or Portuguese. "We may have a rainbow," she said as his eyes took her in.

His brandy-loosened tongue started to explain the physics of rainbows, one of those facts he had read in one of his books, but the dark woman laughed at him for being so serious about something so beautiful and touched a finger to his lips. "It's God's promise of peace," she said. They talked about nothing at all, but managed to do so for a very long while. When she seemed certain of him, she placed one light hand on his bare shoulder and with the other lifted his hand to her breast before she led him over pebbly dirt beyond wild saw palmetto to her place out back, two leaky rooms under a badly pitched terracotta roof. Square holes in her concrete walls served as windows, but held no glass. The hut was also the bar's storeroom; cases of soft drinks and whisky were stacked against the walls. Drinking water flowed from a brass pump on top of a green copper pipe that ran through the limestone beneath the topsoil. The gushing faucet emptied into a cement trough at one room's center.

Her unpinned hair fell about her shoulders as she removed his clothes. He inhaled the soap smell and the orange peel essence behind her ears and between her breasts. Her thick hair was perfumed by simple soap. She rolled him face down on her bed, straddled his hips, and kneaded his shoulders until she rolled herself beneath him and to take him into herself. As he entered her she said, sighing: "*Cherie, mon dieu, herie.*"

Her scent, the aroma of rain, the fragrance of night, and the smell of the sea in the onshore breeze eddied about them. His fingers gripped her hips until, sated, she fell onto him to curl into sleep. He peered upward into the darkness while he smoked one of her cigarettes. Had Maman sent her? He did not want to think about why the only women he trusted were heavy-chested dark-haired whores while he clung to a spiritual connection to a yellow-haired girl closer to his own age to whom he'd spoken once and whose name he would never know.

Hush, beau gamin, Maman said, her voice in the sound of the surf. *You t'ink too much.*

The hut overlooked the beach where moonlight played over wavelets, igniting them to silver. The sea broke onto the shore, receded, and broke again as the tide climbed over sand to reach the seaward edge of the two-lane blacktop that rimmed the Gulf.

Some hour in the night, closer to morning, Pierre left the sleeping woman to walk the dark beach. He wore nothing. He floated on his back in the sea, the salt water holding him between the earth and sky. The moon was set; the sun not yet risen. It would have been nothing to allow himself to drift offshore and into the night, but Maman urged him to strike out for shore and live.

Before the dark-haired whore awakened, he pumped enough well-water for the woman's day. Together, they emptied four pails into a larger overhead zinc bucket, then stepped beneath a trickling shower. The water was sweet; the air redolent of wild grasses. She took her time soaping his back and shoulders and then controlled the water's flow onto him with the pull chain fixed to a wooden handle. Her wet hair was even more black than it had seemed the night before; the skin at her chest was unapologetically white, though her neck and ankles were burned dark. When not whoring, she must have done fieldwork. Long ago, Pierre and Maman had harvested strawberries. He could not have been eight years old, face down on a palette, picking with two hands, a bucket at each side, buzzing yellow-jackets hovering at his eyes. The back-breaking labor had left them, too, with sunburned necks and ankles.

An angry white scar crossed on the woman's belly. "My boy," she said. "did not wish to leave me, so I was cut. I lived, he did not." She held her finger to his lips because she would talk no more about that.

A terry cloth and a large natural sponge rinsed him clean. She coaxed the last trickle of water from their overhead bucket and tiptoed to kiss his neck. "Your skin is so dark, *herie*," she said. Then, in full view of the roadway if anyone slowed enough to peer beyond the row of bottle palms behind the wild grasses, her back to him, she leaned to one side while she wrung water from her hair, twisting it dry. Her breasts swayed loosely. Her nipples were large and dark; her hips broad. When he went to take her again, standing, she laughed and slapped his hands away. "Do not spoil it," she said.

Pierre was behind the Packard's wheel when she leaned across the open car to him. Last night she had worn a simple blue scarf knotted beneath her chin when she came to him in the nameless bar, but now in the morning with no brandy to sweeten his eyes, he saw she was older than he'd have guessed. Her sad gray eyes hid nothing from him. He asked her name; she put a single finger across his lips yet again.

"You need no name, *ma très beau gamin*," she said.

Her lips touched her two fingers, and her two fingers touched his forehead, her blessing. She asked for no money, so he gave her most of what he had, folded bills that disappeared into her apron's pocket. He promised he would come to see her, but they both knew he would never pass that way again.

With every yard the car moved closer to New Orleans on the final leg of his journey, he watched her in the middle of the road diminishing in the Packard's rearview mirror. She stood one arm raised in farewell. Distance made her seem ever smaller until she was no more than a shadow's shadow. Then the shadow extinguished, and all that was behind Pierre was a long, twisted road.

1952–1956

PIERRE SAT OUT THE KOREAN War in the same way he'd missed World War 2. His conscience did not make it easy for him once the world knew about Nazi death camps. He was no pacifist.

"Why make yourself crazy when the assholes who run things did not lift a finger?" Mario said. "It's not as though Roosevelt or Churchill or Marshall or Montgomery even Stalin popped wood to rescue Yids and gypsies. They knew, they had to know, but they had other things on their minds."

"Hitler was evil."

"No argument from me, buddy. Who kills children by the gross? But even if you had been a G.I., you would only have been riding to the rescue if you disobeyed orders."

"What if everyone thought that way?"

"Then you'd be one dumb fuck to figure it any other way." Mario gestured with a breadstick. "Other than a talented girl with knee pads, a decent jambalaya, a good ragu, making five consecutive passes at craps, or a solid tip on a pony, what should anyone's life be about? Keep your causes. I have sent both my idiot boys for Holy Communion, I do not beat my wife—shit, I don't even dare to argue with her—so while I will never be square with God, my family has their chances. I fight for my family and one or two close friends. End of story."

"Your family? Like Marcello?"

"That's *mister* Marcello to you and me. It is a large family, I admit. Like the Irish say, buddy, 'This is the life we have chosen, and none of us expect to see Heaven.'"

They were sopping up clam sauce at Mosca's. Mario wiped his plate clean with a heel of crusty bread. "By the way, as long as I mention it, you get a chance Tuesday, look for me at the k'grounds in the grandstand. Put at least a yard on Mikey's Bad Idea. Across the board is a good bet."

"You're doping it out?"

"Doping out the horses is a pastime, but this is better than that. There's a steward who will suffer a moment of blindness when he checks the tattoo on the horse's lip and so, by mistake, will pass a stallion coming out of the four slot who is not Mikey's Bad Idea but is a class shipper down from Arlington. Poor Mikey was a plater never finished any better than fifth before he found purpose in a glue factory. Our shipper ran a work on a closed track yesterday that made the trainer think his stopwatch was running backwards. Come Tuesday, there may be a speedball as insurance, and for double insurance the boy will be carrying a buzzer."

"So it is a sure thing?"

"No. There is no sure thing. Have some more Ruffino. This is a horse. The day jockeys carry thoroughbreds on their shoulders and run six furlongs, it may be a sure thing, but right now the jocks ride the horse, not the other way around. Just like you and me, horses have heart attacks. They step in gopher holes at the top of the stretch and snap fetlocks. A busted fetlock makes it hard to finish no matter how much heart and Lasix is in the animal. If you ever see a sure thing at a racetrack, we'll go for oysters at the Monteleone." He ran the edge of a matchbook between his teeth.

Mikey's Bad Idea paid $22.40. Pierre had $500 on the nose, and another two hundred bet to place. He treated himself to a two-tone Bel-Air Impala, white and robin's egg blue, another convertible, the first car he'd ever paid for. The top was cream-colored. Running at 80 mph around Lake Pontchartrain to Mandeville from Metairie, the car damn near took flight, though it handled like a dirigible in a hurricane. But Pierre found he could not live without it until the '56 Bel-Air came out with its fins like a condor's wings. After that, he never owned a vehicle more than two years off the lot.

In 1956, Pierre and Mario took an evening break to smoke outside one of Mario's better clubs.

A casual observer would have seen two guys from the neighborhood out for a smoke and probably discussing Dietzel's strategy to put the LSU Tigers in the Sugar Bowl, though a casual observer would have been wrong.

"You are a good dealer, maybe the best in town and the best I ever saw, but buddy, you need to grow. As a brother, I tell you that you can't go any further. You'll be spinning playing cards across felt another ten years, your hands will get stiff, you will have nowhere to go."

"So you are offering me a pension?"

"Don't be a wiseass. I trust you with my kids' hearts in your hands, but some guys who look over my shoulder will not. They will take my word only so far." Mario stared closely at the burning end of his cigar. "Be more independent."

"How?"

"A guy who knows a guy who knows a guy wants someone to do some wet work."

"Wet work?"

"Wet work. You put holes in someone, the floor gets wet. He needs his partner dead."

"Why?"

"If you are in I can find out for you, but I tell you, buddy, I cannot tell you dick until you are in. It's an opportunity. I thought of you. What else do you need to know?"

"Why are you so good to me?"

"I worry about you. You have been moping around for so long that when I shave, your face is in my mirror. I expect to see you at breakfast eating Cheerios with my boys calling you 'uncle.' You are smarter than that. A regular dealer will hang around for six months, two years at the outside, and will either fuck up or decide to drive an ice cream truck. I knew a guy who did that. Christ as my witness. Saved his money, now he rides around in a white truck that plays 'Pop Goes the Weasel' all fucking day. I do not understand why he does not put his neck on a trolley track, but I hear he is happy, children smile, so what do I know? Are you saving up to buy an ice cream truck? Or maybe you are in the market for a few horses? How about a bookstore? You read every fucking thing. You never talk about what you read, but I know what I know. Buddy, there is no serious money in a bookstore. It's a business for old ladies who like lilacs. Tell me, how long do I know you, buddy? What is it? Since the war? Almost fifteen years?"

"Twelve. But I am not counting."

"So I have to wonder, 'Why is Pierre hanging around?'"

The question had occurred to Pierre. The best answer he came to was that he had no other plans, and that, he was sure, was an evasion of the real issue. Sleeping at the back of his mind was the idea that he would choose to make his exit as had *grand-père*. His life was never going to be about a dog, a wife, kids, and a lawn, but what it might be about was dark monotony, emptiness, and the end of surprises. He was more than fifty percent to the finish. Before boredom eroded whatever soul he still had, he'd eat his gun.

"Have you ever thought of going independent?" Mario said. "F'true, buddy, since you are not blood family there is a limit to what you can know and do for the family."

"You mean I am not Italian."

"And here I thought your people came from Napoli. It must have been that olive skin. Look, buddy, I have a real brother who if he tries to cross the street will break his foot. The jag-off collects nickels from pinball machines. It's the most I can trust him with because Frankie is too stupid to skim. I can find stupid-but-honest on every street corner, but Francis is family, so we do not have to go to any street corner because we give him the master key to the machines and hope he does not get lost on the route. I love him, he is my brother, but the boy plays with half a deck. It does not matter how old we get, he will always be 'the boy.' F'true, it goes back to when I held his head in the oven and I turned on the gas. You know, typical kid stuff. If he would have given me his fucking roller skates like I asked, I would not have had to hold his head in the stove a few minutes and maybe today his left eye would not be staring so hard at his right eye. He screamed like a son-of-a-bitch until I calmed him down. Our father took the razor strop to me. I went to confession, and I had to say Our Fathers and Hail Marys for weeks, but God did not fix Frankie. My father made me swear I would take care of Frankie because of what I did. You ask me, he was dumb as shit to begin with, so I took a bum rap from our father, but I promised. You know what it is with fathers, right?"

"Actually, no, I don't."

"I forget. No insult intended. Anyway, what I wonder is if going independent will snap you out of the mopes. You have the balls, the brains, and will keep your mouth shut. Did you sniff oven gas when you were a kid? No. So there is only one more consideration."

"Which is?"

"Do you have the heart? Balls, no question, you'd run into a burning building to rescue a little girl's ragdoll, but to kill a guy right you have to be up close enough to smell his breath, which is easy for a guy with balls, but you have to live with yourself afterwards. That takes heart."

"I have heart."

"Sometimes you say shit makes me think you may have a conscience. Conscience can make you hesitate at the worst possible moment. Next thing you know, you are the one leaking from bullet holes instead of the other guy. Trust me on this. Conscience is a liability."

Pierre had never told Mario about Charlie, the rummy shrimper who beat Maman. One year, on Maman's birthday, Pierre had yielded to nostalgia and made inquiries. Someone at the other end of the phone asked Pierre if he were willing to contribute to Charlie's upkeep, explaining how the state sought support for its indigent residents, especially its veterans. They would be happy to look at Pierre's income tax records to set a fair rate for him to pay. Pierre explained he'd called in hopes of learning the shrimper was dead, then pressed down the phone's claw to listen to the hollow buzz of a dial tone for several minutes.

That hollow buzz was the sound of his conscience.

Pierre and Mario stood on a soft lawn before a nice house on a nice street lined with nice private homes. The place's interior had been gutted and soundproofed to serve as a casino Thursday to Saturday nights. Otherwise, it looked like every other place on the block, someone's idea of a Mexican hacienda, three buildings surrounding an open courtyard where a few palm trees and barrel cactus were made unnatural by red, green, and blue lights half hidden in hedges. The casino's neighbors were annually gifted with Christmas turkeys; they did not complain at the lavish block parties on July 4th and Halloween that served up bratwurst and sausages, supplied confetti, costumes, and kiddie rides. Mario directed funds into a Mardi Gras Krewe, as well as making sure local houses of worship collected outsized anonymous donations. No neighbor complained that weekends brought drunks who puked or peed on their sidewalks because, fact was, mob proximity bolstered real estate values. Trash was always collected; the streets were safe at night; cars moved at slower speeds; petty crime simply never happened. A burglar peddling loot taken from the wrong house would find no fence stupid enough to take the stuff off his hands. More likely, the thief would be found alive but broken, alive to deliver the message to the overambitious.

Mario puffed on a Montecristo that enclosed them in a cloud of cigar smoke. His hands were folded at the small of his back against a palm tree. Pierre faced him from his seat on the fender of a DeSoto. When a police cruiser crawled by, its white spotlight fell on the two men. Mario raised his hand in greeting; the two policemen waved back familiarly.

"What do you think, buddy?"

Pierre extinguished his Old Gold against the bottom of his shoe, then dropped the butt in his pocket. "You have guys for wet work, Mario," he said. "I met them, remember? I damn near crapped my pants and had to burn my clothes because wet work is wet. I haven't been able to eat sweetbreads since. Look, I deal cards and I am good at it. That's enough for me," he lied.

"All right. but I recall a guy had to shoot a dead man and his hand never shook. I still tell that story; it always gets a laugh." The cigar glowed bright red. "It also gets respect."

"I see your point."

"But for me, the impressive point is how all these years you never once bring up the day Artie the Jew and his friends had to disappear. Bones and blood all over you. It could not be helped, but you never complained, did not run, and took care of things that needed to be taken care of. Most guys would have run screaming down the beach, but you burned the whole fucking place down."

"I ate a sandwich before I left, too."

"No shit? Turkey or ham?"

"Italian salami and *capicola*."

Mario shook his head. "I never knew that, but you prove my point."

"What happened to the guy who owned the house? He was into the shys because he loved horses more than the horses loved him, right?"

"Now that's a sad story. The asshole thought he was paying off by lending his house, but instead he gets slammed with second degree murder. He hanged himself with a bedsheet. We did not have to help him do that. He was in his cell when they found him."

"The wife and kid?"

"Who in fuck knows? The life insurance was gone long before you burned their house down. The asshole borrowed against it for a sure thing that is still running. Maybe the wife is doing that act with the donkey in Havana; maybe she crochets doilies. For sure, she is better off without the degenerate gambler." Mario stood away from the palm tree. "I am not heartless. I hope the kid is doing fine. I wish she had a smarter father."

"I do too. She had a nice little room. All pink."

"I never saw it, but I am glad to know that." Mario softly brought his hands together. "But listen. The biggest danger doing murder for hire is not a failure of nerve, it is a remorseful client. One night they sweat through a dream of Hell and wake up in the morning with the need to confess their earthly sins. Do they roll over and sleep it off? Most do, but some do not. I cannot understand it myself. They are away clean and the mark is pushing up daisies, but for reasons that make sense only to that doctor Freud, they need to confess. You step out on your wife, you get hit by conscience, you light a candle, and you perform an act of contrition. Maybe you build an orphanage. But these assholes wake up and realize that, while there are missteps God will forgive, murder is not among them. Make someone dead, you can build a hundred orphanages, but the dead guy stays dead. So the biggest danger isn't your conscience, it's your client's conscience. This is why my guys only get into this line of work as brokers. We need to believe that nothing can ever get back to us."

"Who is 'we'?"

"You know better than to ask that."

"I don't see how it can be guaranteed that nothing ever gets back."

"It can't, but precautions are possible that make the odds long and you a better bet. I wouldn't even discuss this with anyone unless I thought the guy was one hundred percent. Balls, brains, and heart can guide a man through a world of shit. You have all three in spades. Then there is trust."

"You're flattering me."

"No. F'true. Assassins are lone wolves whose hands do not shake and who never look back. Murder is like flu; it rots your whole system, except for guys who cannot rot. This is why I thought to ask you, buddy. If you take the job, you make an easy score, very good money, and everyone is happy. I'd be your handler, not your partner."

"How about the guy who is erased. How happy is he?"

"He does not know he is unhappy because he is dead."

Pierre cupped his hands around a fresh Old Gold. His Cartier lighter had been a Christmas gift from Mario. They had joked at how the space for a monogram was deliberately blank. "You think I have no conscience?"

"Maybe you do, but not that I have seen, no. You are the only guy I ever knew came back from burying his mother without a single story to tell about what a good woman she was. You went to work and never looked back."

"She was a good woman. I don't like to talk about her." Pierre slid off the fender and stood on the grass, challenging.

Mario nodded. "Take it easy, buddy. I am sure she was a saint. You keep a lot to yourself that another guy would broadcast. It is not easy to find a man willing to do murder who has no vices. No dope, no women, no gambling. The past has a way of coming up to bite a man on the ass, but if you have a past, you are the only person who knows it. Your idea of excitement is to read a book, and usually it is a book no one else can understand."

Pierre was growing irritated. Mario knew him too well, though not in the way or as deeply as Mario thought. He would never reveal how anger and rage had led him to beat Charlie, but that, of course, was exactly what Mario admired. Pierre kept what he knew to himself. "I am not some fucking machine, Mario."

"*Marone.* You can tell me I have my head up my own ass anytime you want." Mario's palms slapped together and he held them out as if his hands were newly washed. "Feel free to say, 'Mario, you have lost your mind.' You say it, and I swear on my kids' eyes I will pour you a highball so we can forget this conversation ever happened. We will drink the good stuff and be as square as we were yesterday."

Pierre thought a minute. "I need to meet the guy who is paying."

"No, you do not. I am your handler, you are the seller, he is our buyer. You do not need to know or meet the guy. Never mind regrets and conscience, but some miserable night they will stop that prick because he has a broken taillight. To avoid a cellmate named Bubba who thinks your guy is the bee's knees, he will roll over on you faster than Fido licks his own balls. But he cannot give you up if he does not know you. You are a smart guy and so before you ask me why he would not give *me* up, I will tell you that he knows that if he gives me up, I have an organization and an airtight alibi while you did the work, and we have guys strong enough to bend him to lick his own balls same as Fido. Maybe I was fishing in Havana, maybe fishing in Michigan, and maybe he also knows my organization can arrange for his ever-loving wife to vanish with no trace except for the glossy photos of her swallowing five well-hung dicks before she is attached to old plumbing and dropped into the Gulf. His kids will be tricking in Morocco. Make no mistake, buddy, terror and self-interest keeps most everyone in line. Those are our specialties. We are a wolf pack, but a pack is better at terror than any lone wolf ever was."

"Terror?"

"Terror. Fear. Whatever you want to call it. It is called a contract because there is consideration on two sides of a proposition; money for us, and a dead guy for him, but no one goes to court to sue if someone does not deliver. No one needs collateral if there is terror. You can't have a contract without guarantees, and terror is a guarantee."

"You'd do that? To a guy's wife, f'true? Just because she married an asshole?" Mario did not answer. Cigar smoke eddied around them. Pierre scratched his head. He knew better than to ask if it had ever happened. "How do you think of that shit? Jesus, Mario, you can be one scary fuck."

"It's in the blood, back to ancient *Siracusa*. You figure the emperors were on the straight and narrow? Fed only bad Christians to polite lions? Served tea and toast to the rest?"

"There's an expression in chess you ought to know. 'The threat is more effective than its execution.'"

"Who gives a crap about chess?"

It was true of chess or fending off rapists at the YMCA, but this was not the moment to educate Mario. Pierre knew he would take the contract when he heard himself ask: "The mark is not a woman?"

"No. I can tell you the mark is not a woman." The night was gentle as a baby's kiss. "You want to sleep on it? I can't tell you a cunt hair more until I know you are in."

"I don't need to sleep on it," Pierre said, "I am in."

Mario did not take his extended hand. "You cannot change your mind. You do not want to fuck this up."

"I said 'I am in.' I am in."

As Charlie had taught Pierre to wield a knife, Mario taught contract murder as an art form.

"Every move needs to become a reflex. If you are thinking, you are not ready. A wolf does not think about his next move. No, it's pure instinct. Be a wolf. Read all the books you want, but if you are killing a guy you do not want to think at all. If you start wondering about his wife and his kids and whether his grandmother will miss him, you can be sure grandma will show up on time to put a hole in you with her 20-inch Winchester pump gun while you are considering the ins and outs of putting a hole in her favorite grandbaby." Mario poured two fingers of Jack Daniels for each of them. "There is very little theory. When you open a hole in a guy, if the hole cannot be closed, sooner or later the guy is dead. We want him dead sooner rather than later, so placing the hole in a guy in some locations works faster than others. A pill through the pump or brain is best; after that, an artery in the neck. Precision requires you to be close, but you need enough distance or position so that after the hole opens your drycleaner never has to wonder how your slacks became so stained."

"You once advised me to burn my best shoes in an ashcan. I never got to any drycleaner."

"Another reason you are the guy for the job. You listen good. But your job will be different from blowing holes in a guy with a shotgun. F'true, your mark will be just as dead, but you are not sending anyone a message; you are just making a corpse. Get this straight. You are not Davy Crockett shooting heads off turkeys from 300 yards. You come up close enough to know whether the guy prefers Old Spice or Aqua Velva, and then you shoot the fucker in the pump or the mouth or the eye or the throat or his ear. Your contract does not include a mean look in the eye, clever remarks, or, God forbid, a message from your employer who wants him dead. If someone wants to send a message, tell him to call Western Union. Give the mark no chances; forget fair warning. Once a mark is twitching on the ground, or even if he is not twitching, put one more cap in his ear because you do not want he should ever get up to discuss the situation with you." Mario dipped the unlit end of his cigar into a brandy snifter as he crossed his legs at the ankles on his glass-topped desk. Purple tobacco smoke filled his office. "Your best hit looks like a robbery gone bad. Some hophead lost control and the mark is a random victim. All the police need to do is round-up enough hopheads who can stand for the killing and they will think their job is done. Doesn't matter if their hophead did not do it. No one gives a shit about junkies, and the cops will be all square with the public and the grieving widow. So a robbery gone bad with a small caliber pistol puts a junkie in the frame, the evidence does not need to be solid, and the homicide squad orders extra donuts and uncaps the Bushmills. Just don't screw the pooch."

"I won't screw the pooch. Why not a larger caliber?"

"Because a hophead with a gun bigger than a .32 would rather sell it than use it."

Pierre balanced the burning half of his Old Gold on the lip of a large ashtray. Yellow light was captured in the polished wood of the wall panels and desk.

"But there are alternatives, most shitty, but let's get them out of your mind." Mario pointed to his index finger. "Strangling a guy is dicey, but if you get to him from behind and use a garrote which also slices the veins in his neck, your garrote has the virtue of total silence. Two handles and baling wire, loop, turn your back, bend forward, and the guy's feet leave the ground. His weight closes his throat; with his throat closed, he cannot holler. His instinct will be to struggle with the wire at his throat, but that will only kill him faster because he should be struggling with you but he thinks he needs to breathe, which is not wrong, but also hard to make happen when there is a wire slicing through his throat. By the time he realizes his mistake, he is dead. But I tell you, buddy, since you are shorter than most, unless the contract is a midget, I cannot recommend the garrote to you. You'd have to struggle for leverage, and a guy whose feet reach the floor just might kick hard enough to tip you both over."

He pointed to a second finger. "A knife across a man's throat is sure, swift, and silent, but it makes a mess. This is murder. Neatness counts." Pierre hoisted his trouser leg to expose his shucking knife. "You still carrying that pig-sticker? Why do you want to fight like a pimp?" Pierre barely smiled. "Buddy, the problem with gut-stabbing a man is that his pump has not heard the news that he is cut, so when you have opened his veins his blood spouts like a fountain in *Firenze*. Why would you want to roll around in the dirt with some screaming cocksucker whose hands are around your throat and his teeth on your ear while his guts are spilling out? He may be already dead, but that will not stop him from trying to take you with him."

Mario pointed to a third finger. "Poison is for women. Don't even think about it."

A fourth finger. "Blowing up a car draws suspicion because it does not appear to be street crime. Cars do not explode by accident. They have guys who do nothing all day long except to put the pieces back together to see what the bomber forgot, so I do not recommend attaching explosives to some asshole's ignition. Besides, guys have been known to send their wives out to start the car, and then the worst thing that can happen, happens: the mark knows someone is trying to punch his ticket."

"How about the wife?"

"True, it is not a happy day for her, either." Mario pointed to a fifth finger. "So I recommend a gun. For a pro, it is the only thing. A .38 is plenty; a .45 is always certain; but if a man knows his business, a .22 works peachy. Up close, a .22 Magnum with a 40 grain charge has enough firepower to send a round through a skull but not enough for it to get out. The bullet bounces around like a bazooka shell in a tank, scrambles the guy's brain, and since it is a small caliber leaves so little blood spouting from his nose and ears you can clean up with a handkerchief. But for crissakes, whatever caliber you go with, use a revolver. You do not want to hang around to police the brass from your automatic because unless you wear rubber gloves like some fucking proctologist, when you load a clip, you'd leave your prints on the shells. Sure as shit some sunny day you will be snatched for jaywalking and your prints will come up because they were lifted from your brass from a murder so long ago, you forgot you did it."

Mario loosened his tie and came as close to raising his voice as he ever did. He pointed the tip of his burning cigar at Pierre. "Leave a body where it falls. Say it."

"Leave the body where it falls."

"Say it again."

"Come on, Mario, I am not a kid."

"Say it."

"Leave the body where it falls."

"Good. Remember, you are not being paid to make a corpse vanish, you are being paid to make a man a corpse. And Holy Mother of God, do not keep the gun. Some guys are more fond of their piece than of their dicks. Keep a piece and you can be sure that somehow, somewhere, someday, your sweetie will forget the toast and your house will burn to the ground. Firemen will sift the ashes hoping to steal your jewelry and then tell you nothing was recovered, but if they find your gun, the next thing you know you are in Angola lifting steel plate in the yard with a guy who wants you to be his wife and will knock out your teeth for that extra smooth feel.

So unless you enjoy the feel of a locomotive up your ass, take the fucking gun apart, wipe it down, and throw the pieces away, two, three miles apart. Why amateurs are not smart enough to figure this out is a mystery. Salt water rots everything. The deeper, the better. You can always get another piece."

"That's what you asked me to do with the gun that shot a dead man."

"And did you?"

"Yes. Off a dinner cruise."

"What did you have?"

"The mussels in white wine with garlic."

"I'd have put out eight for five that you'd remember. Every detail after you kill a man stays with you. Reds are more red; blues more blue; the songs on the radio are better than they ever were."

"It's probably the adrenaline."

"No one gives a fuck what it is. Geez, buddy, dumb down a little. Remember, this is a business like any other. You plan ahead, you do the job, and you build a rep. Strictly word-of-mouth."

Mario's wheeled office chair rolled back easily when he pushed away from his desk to stand. He sprayed soda water into his brandy.

"*Salut*," he said. "We are at the good part. Once the deed is done, be sure to take a vacation, maybe go down to Cuba, drink rum, get your dick sucked, maybe arrange to have a hotel register indicate you got there two days earlier. Get seen in places where they put paper umbrellas in coconuts with cherries and a pineapple, the waitresses all have big tits, and little Cuban girls giggle while they jerk you off with their feet."

"I do not own a gun."

Mario nodded. "I can get you what you want, but it's better if you buy what you need. This is America, thank God. A law-abiding citizen can arm a Marine battalion at a corner gun store. If you buy a bazooka and a mortar from some hophead out of his car trunk, you will buy a world of shit. Even if you do your job perfect, when your gun-guy fucks up, you can count on him trading your name for conjugal rights while you take 20,000 volts up your ass. Buy what you need. Keep it simple. Keep it legal, except for the fake name. Buy quality. Buy it in Texas. In Texas, they sell Kalashnikovs to junior high school boys for squirrel hunting, and they throw in a free bayonet in case the squirrels counterattack. In America, if a real man wants a weapon, he buys it. In America, we are free to shoot any asshole we want."

"Tell me about the client."

Mario sighed. "Do you really need to know?"

"Yes."

Mario knocked on wood. "I guess it is time. As I hear it, the client has a kid who has polio. The kid is a girl, nine. Polio is expensive. My two boys are healthy, praise God. The older one is so stupid he cannot bait a hook or swing a baseball bat without hurting himself. He is taking another try at senior year in high school, and the younger boy never shuts up. Still, if you were standing between them and good health, I'd turn you into a grease spot in a New York minute. That is what the client needs done."

"I don't understand. How does erasing a guy cure a kid's polio?"

"The mark is his partner. Two Yids who are green grocers. Our guy needs dough for his kid's doctors and wants to sell his half of the business to the mark, but the prick Jew-partner offers him ten cents on the dollar."

"The guy is squeezing his partner whose kid has polio?"

"Iron lungs and braces cost. I did a little research for you. The mark has some chippy in a place he visits maybe two, three times each week. She lives on the third floor of a walkup." He wrote an address on a slip of paper, slid the paper across the desk to Pierre, then took it back, set fire to it, and dropped it flaming into the ashtray.

"You are not making this up?"

"Hand to God."

Pierre marveled. He was going to make a guy dead because the guy would not let go of his carrots, onions, lettuce, and a side of pussy.

Mario would never have thought to complete Pierre's education with a book, but Pierre did, an old edition of *Gray's Anatomy*. At an antiquarian bookstore, the clerk guessed an early edition might cost between one and three thousand dollars, depending on its condition if they could find it. She assumed Pierre was a well-to-do recent medical graduate, but he corrected her. "I am an artist. I need to study the color plates." She said she'd put out a query to their network of stores, and then suggested something about expanding his study of anatomy to living subjects. As he left the shop, he pretended not to understand her. Her eyes bore twin holes in his back. The clerk looked as if she'd have been a treat, the bold ones usually were, and maybe she told no lie about having been an artist's model, but Pierre wanted nothing about himself to be memorable.

The book arrived with worn bindings, but the color plates were exquisite. They made it plain that Nature or God or Chance had designed the human form to be frail. The most vulnerable organs were protected in cages of bone, the skull or ribs. Pierre thought to razor out the color plates for framing, then thought how his primary obligation was to keep the volume intact. He owed any book that much.

That same night, Mario sent word. He was in business.

Pierre stands in shadow, half-sitting on a Ford's fender, wondering if his own Chevy parked blocks away from the ferry even fitted with stolen tags was a mistake. He left the car's ragtop down in a spot with little sun. He does not imagine he will be down river in Algiers long enough that the Bel-Air will get soaked in a storm.

Trees limbs sway. Afternoon clouds had gone from white, to pink, to crimson, and were about to sink to invisible black, but they promise no rain.

Pierre tugs a broad-brimmed Panama hat is low over his eyes. He smokes a Chesterfield, not his usual brand, but he is nevertheless careful to place his extinguished cigarette butts in the stolen car's ashtray. He wears a short-sleeved white dress shirt and tan trousers, the evening air is velvet on his bare arms.

This is not his first evening in this shadow.

A week earlier, after Pierre told Mario he was headed west to Texas, he drove east to Mississippi to buy a five-shot .22 magnum revolver. The revolver weighs less than a half-pound, has a wooden grip and no trigger guard. The sales clerk hardly looked at Pierre's driver's license for one Jean Baptiste, a citizen of Corpus Christi. Behind the gun shop, Pierre fired several rounds at a distant target. The trigger is quick, the cylinder's action smooth.

Four nights later, Pierre hotwired a Ford, raising its hood and closing the ignition circuit with a four-inch screwdriver. Fords are easiest. Pierre stored the boosted Ford on a street three blocks from where the mark lives. With the same screwdriver, Pierre lifted the tags off a nearby Dodge to replace the tags on the stolen Ford.

Three cars for a single killing.

On several nights over a span of ten, Pierre sits in darkness in his own Bel-Air to observe the grocer's habits. On the nights he appears at all, the grocer appears at 7:30 and parks off the main boulevard near his girlfriend's. Her house fronts the boulevard's neutral ground. The grocer climbs four cement stairs to three green front doors that open on a common porch. She leaves the entrance door at the extreme left unlocked for him. The randy grocer then leaves no earlier than 9:30, but never later than 9:45. Pierre doubts they make love every time they meet, but he is sure the grocer believes his regular habits protect him from his wife's suspicion. In fact, his habits will kill him

This final night, he left his Bel Air blocks from the ferry and crossed the river to walk to the stolen Ford. While the grocer is upstairs, Pierre passes time with a pocket chess set. He carries it in his shirt pocket, red versus black disks that cling through thin vinyl to a magnetic board that closes like a cigarette case. Pierre is working his way through a book of chess puzzles drawn from actual games. The corner streetlamp fifty yards away sheds enough light, though like any good chess player Pierre does not need to see the board; the moves play out in his mind. He slides the magnetic discs physically only to be certain he has solved the position.

*As the chippy in her negligee rises to her toes to kiss her lover fare-
well, Pierre sees that the mate in four imagined by Capablanca requires
an elegant two bishop sacrifice. The combination never was played across
the board, however. His opponent was good enough to see his end and
had the dignity to resign before the* coup de grace. *The New Orleans
night air is suffused by jacaranda and lilac.*

*The chippy's shape is not bad. Backlit, her negligee hides little, but
she cannot be twenty, so it is plain what the grocer is about. She pretends
her grocer will leave his wife; maybe he even believes it when he tells
her so. The fairytale ends with them living happily ever after bagging
rutabagas and asparagus.*

*Love is the opposite of chess. Nothing remains hidden on a chess-
board and there is no chance of bluffing. Love is a blindfold that obscures
all that the rest of the world sees stark and plain. Lovers imagine stories that will go one forever; chess players prepare positions and imagine
moves that end an opponent's game.*

*Pierre steps away from the Ford as the mark passes. Pierre's hands
are steady, his breathing measured and even. From behind, in a single
fluid movement he has practiced a hundred times, Pierre grips the guy's
chin with his right palm, holds the mark immobile, lifts the revolver
with his left, and squeezes two shots into the center of the guy's lower
back, a vulnerable spot he chose after studying* Gray's Anatomy. *The
book tells no lies. The bullets do not emerge from his body, but with his
spine severed, the mark slumps like wet laundry. If he had tried to cry
out, Pierre's hand held his chin closed tight, but the grocer did not try. His
legs twitch, his legs gone spastic.*

The grocer is heavier than Pierre imagined. Deadweight *has new
meaning. The grocer slides through Pierre's grip to the ground.*

*Pierre removes the grocer's wallet from his trouser pocket and slides
the man's wedding ring from his hand. Blood oozes from the grocer's
lips, a sign that his heart still beats. Pierre supposes a bullet ricocheted
from a bone to perforate the guy's stomach or maybe a lung and the blood
is from an internal hemorrhage. The mess the guy made in his pants
smells foul. Pierre holds his breath and drags the guy behind a hedge
by his armpits. Pierre kneels to pop one more round into the back of the*

mark's head. A sliver of bone from an eye socket and some brain seep into an overgrown lawn.

Heart steady, hands dry, Pierre leaves the stolen Ford on Valette beside a cemetery where no street lights burn. He slips into his sport coat so he is no longer in shirt sleeves when like any citizen he knots his tie, removes the spent shell casings from the cylinder, then smashes the revolver against the Ford's metal dashboard until the cylinder hangs loose. It was a fine weapon.

With a dime pinched between his fingers, he squats to remove the car's stolen tags. He walks six blocks through the damp night to the ferry where, with his weight on his elbows on the chin-high white wooden barrier at the wharf's end, he drops bullets and shell casings one by one into the dark water, pennies cast for wishes.

The ferry's screws churn the water into a yellow and phosphorescent green wake. The air reeks of diesel and river rot. The gun's cylinder vanishes from sight over the fantail. Mid-river, the stolen tags from under his sport coat slide free of his grasp. Before the ferry docks at Canal, the remainder of the gun, his screwdriver, and even the dime drop into the accepting Mississippi.

Walking home, thinking he will wash himself with rubbing alcohol to be rid of gunshot residue, he lights a final Chesterfield and considers the gold wedding ring. It was engraved with a single word, Forever. He wipes the ring with his handkerchief before he flips it like a quarter into the air; it chimes like a glass bell when it strikes the sidewalk. It bounces and then rolls several feet. Someone will find it; someone will feel lucky.

Two days later, Mario's voice crackled in Pierre's seldom-used telephone. "Where y'at?" Pierre told him he was sleeping like a baby. Mario asked Pierre to join him at Mario's favorite casino. In Mario's office, Pierre's accepted his manila pay envelope, the same kind of envelope that carries his pay as a pipefitter, the same kind of envelope that carries his pay as a one of Mario's dealers. This night, the envelope contained forty hundred dollar bills, four month's pay earned in a few hours. He never thought to ask what he'd earn.

Mario's thumbs hooked his suspenders. He leaned his creaking chair back, and placed his big Broughams on his glass-topped desk. "*Salut*," he said. "Brains, balls, and heart. But what would you have done if the mark had hired you for a contract with a story that went the other way?"

"Polio. The little girl. Iron lungs. All bullshit, wasn't it?"

"This is real life, buddy. You do not get to be the Lone Ranger every time you mount a horse."

Bourbon scorched his throat. He had known all along Mario's story had been bullshit. He wanted to believe it was something else, but this was real life.

His life.

1974

A HALF-ARM'S LENGTH AWAY FROM HIS lover, her back to him, Pierre's eyes roamed the familiar curve from her hip to her waist and up again to her bare shoulder. His eyes lingered on each knuckle of her spine, lingered again on her ribcage, expanding and collapsing at each breath. His gaze was tactile. Nothing could be more exquisite than to touch her skin. Being in bed beside KJ was akin to being in an art gallery where fingertips on great work was not only expected, but encouraged.

A year had passed since that first morning together when he'd been immobilized by what had seemed a delicate question. They'd spent weeks charting their way through an old-fashioned courtship, neither of them hurried, both increasingly wanting something that would endure. He'd called her "Kels" then. They'd dined at The Palm, took in the Knickerbockers, cheered racehorses at Aqueduct Raceway, and picnicked at the Cloisters.

One night, Pierre's hotel concierge obtained unobtainable seats four rows back for Colleen Dewhurst in *Mourning Becomes Electra*, the first production of a limited run in the new theater, Circle in the Square.

After three rounds of standing ovations, they remained silent in their seats as the rest of the audience shuffled to exits. He'd become accustomed to her gray sweatshirts, jeans, and black basketball sneakers, eccentricities that only made him love her that much more. A grown woman, she dressed like a 14-year-old boy. What of it?

He fell deeply in love with her when she breathed, "Devastating." He knew no one so deeply affected by theater; he knew no one who could express what he felt so deeply within himself.

That same night, the chaste kiss of departure they usually shared in her elevator became something more. Up to that moment, they'd been guarded, but the beast was unleashed by the time her elevator doors parted. His shirt hung open, his chest was bare, and their mouths pressed so hard together that their lips bled. They tore at each other's clothes like kids on a hot night in the back of a Chevy. Her hands and fingers lingered at the plane of his belly and over his arms and legs. She whispered her confession that he was her first man in a long while as she fumbled with his belt, freeing molten need so deep and so long ignored she believed it had been extinguished. He undressed her until they fell together across her creaky brass four-poster. As the sun rose, they made love a third time. His hands held hers flat on the bed above her head. He felt good inside her. She glided rudderless across a sea whose waves rose and fell and rose again within her.

On that same morning, when she'd asked, she accepted Pierre's explanation that his New York employers required he be armed.

"Knife and gun?"

"Knife and gun."

Then Pierre asked if she bleached her pubic hair or if she was a natural blond. The fact puzzled him. By then she was in her bathroom. "Why do you dye your hair brown?"

"Are my roots showing?"

"No, *cher*. Not in the way you mean. You're blonde ... down there." Sure he sounded like an idiot, but could think of no delicate way to say what he meant without sounding either coarse or as clinical as *Gray's Anatomy*. There was no part of her body he had not tasted, stroked, or explored, yet the language to describe what he meant escaped him. Cunt? Vagina? Pubic mound? *Mons veneris? Dieu*, words failed him.

He propped a pillow against her brass headboard and decided against a cigarette. He had already outlived Maman by three years, but he was ever-mindful of how Maman's thin lungs had burst to drown her in her own blood. Pierre limited his use of tobacco not because he feared death so much as denial was a discipline to strengthen self-control. Not so many years ago, he'd planned live forever, then he planned to swallow his gun at 50. Now he again planned to live forever.

Her laugh came back to him through her apartment. "Well, you were in the ideal spot to notice. But my hair is not brown. That color is 'espresso'."

Pierre mentally shrugged. Brown was brown. Only women saw distinctions like brown and espresso and russet and walnut.

He'd assured her he was unmarried, nor was he sleeping with anyone else when he was gone from New York. She'd not asked, but he felt she needed to hear it from him. She took him at his word.

One languid arm over her head against the bedroom doorframe, wrist limp, weight on her left leg, an unfastened terrycloth belt dangling to the floor on each side of her bare feet, her hair mussed. She pursed her lips to blow at her errant bangs. "Why do you ask about my hair?"

She made no move to gather the open bathrobe. His view of her exposed belly confirmed what the murky light of a candle had put on display. Kels was a natural blonde.

"In my experience, women go from dark hair to blonde, not the reverse."

"And why do these women do that?"

He did not need to think, but said, "They imagine they need to start fresh."

Could his new lover be on the run? Pierre was in the business of arranging fortunate accidents that expedited child custody disputes, inheritance issues, and eliminated stubborn husbands. Did the lawyer she'd mentioned need an accidental fatal encounter? He'd arrange it *pro bono*. Kels need never know.

With a flourish more dramatic than she needed, she knotted the robe at her waist and turned to her apartment's kitchen. Morning aromas filled the apartment: frying eggs, toasted English muffin.

His feet found her thin carpet. He pulled on his white boxer shorts and pushed his head into an undershirt. In her bathroom, he urinated noisily while he touched the stubble on his chin. Four days had passed since he'd last shaved, about average for him.

"And you know this about women how?"

"A scientific survey."

He settled onto a maple wood chair at her tiny table. As ever, coffee smelled better than it tasted. Could they find chicory in New York? A small carton of real cream stood beside his cup. She should have flowers on her table. He resolved to send her flowers at least once each week no matter where he was.

"Would you care to share how this scientific survey was conducted?"

"Careful observation. Thousands of subjects. I take notes."

She tapped his cheek with a mock slap.

Once again he wondered why he'd sputtered his identity to a bookstore clerk he did not know and simultaneously blessed himself that he had. Doris, the junkie who became a poker dealer, had also known his real name. Then there were Maman and Mario. Though no woman was good enough for her *beau gamin*, Maman's ghost had let him know that the bookstore clerk was tolerable.

Her foot beneath her breakfast table lifted to his bare thigh. "First I cut my hair, then I colored it. That's what women do. They cut their hair. Tell me, lover, what do men do?"

"They sleep with someone new."

"That's my scumbag-ex," she said, suddenly serious, her foot no longer touching his thigh.

He sipped his coffee.

"I had a friend, Eugene, who saved me a fortune in therapy when I was getting divorced. He was a crossdresser. Dressed as a woman, Eugene became Ginny. The best female friend I ever knew had testicles. If not for Ginny, I'd be a lush in Scarsdale screwing Mexican gardeners." She stirred heavy cream into her coffee. "I came to the city, found the bookstore job, and made new friends. They happened to be gay. I was Wendy for the Lost Boys of Never Never Land."

Pierre looked puzzled.

"Like in Peter Pan, Mary Martin on TV twenty years ago? Clap for Tinkerbell?"

Pierre nodded, though he had no clue as to what Peter Pan on television was.

"Does any of that shock you? My secret life with homosexual men?"

"I'm from New Orleans. Nothing shocks me."

She bit delicately into the last of her muffin. "Nat was the leader of the Lost Boys. He was a little older and had money. He swore he'd slept with most of the male stars on Broadway. I may have been drunk the time I offered to sleep with him, but he nearly fainted with panic." She wiped her fingers on a paper towel. "When I was teenager, I took the attention my blonde hair got for granted. I was in college by the time I realized that the men I met on the street who urged me to smile hoped one thing would lead to another and they could fuck my brains out. Total strangers. Why not take a run at the blonde? Blondes, more stupid, hotter in bed, and a lot more naïve."

"I cared for only one blonde in my life. Two, actually, but the one I knew well was not a real blonde."

"Tell me about her. Please. I know so little about you. I want to know everything."

"There is not a lot to tell." His teeth tore a deep crescent in his English muffin.

"You seem dangerous. Not to me, but dangerous. Like a boiling pot with the lid held on. Are you dangerous? I've never known a man who carried a gun and a knife."

"I am terribly dangerous," he said, and she grinned. Better false-hoods were truths that would not be believed. He began to massage the ball of her foot that rose to rest in his lap. "No lies?"

"No lies."

"All right," he said, uncertain he could deliver on that promise. He made a play for time. "I will tell you about my blondes, but you must go first. Tell me about your marriage."

"We met young, still students. Jack became a lawyer. A total shitheel, it turned out. A lawyer who became a shitheel. There's news, right? We had a child, but when she discovered her father was a shitheel, she took off. Seven years, now."

"A child?" It surprised him, but he liked it.

She lowered her eyes. "I imagine I talk to Buckles all the time. Abigail, actually, but she picked up the nickname, 'Buckles.' I can't think of her in any other way." She'd not talked about Buckles to anyone for years, not even Nat or Eugene. Being able to be open was a reason she was falling in love with this Pierre Doucet. He healed what had been broken.

"Did Buckles clasp things together?"

"More like blew them apart. She left me a note about her father and his girlfriend and ran off to San Francisco. She was seventeen. All the kids were doing that, but she never came home. I don't even know if she made it there. It was stupid."

"Brave, maybe. No daughter of yours could be stupid."

She had never thought of Buckles as brave, though she supposed she had to have been in her way. "She is alive out there some place. I reach out to her spirit. We talk. It's like telepathy, but not with words. Does that make sense?"

"I talk to my dead mother. Why not talk to Buckles?" His eyes narrowed and darkened to a deeper shade of brown. "Maman died young. The night before she was buried in Pensacola, she came to me to say she looked forward to seeing her *beau gamin* again, but not too soon. She visits me and I talk to her." His free hand lightly touched the softer skin of her ankle in his lap. "This is why people never die. Memory makes the very good and very evil immortal."

"And the rest are forgotten?

"It's all they deserve."

"The last time I was in a church, I prayed for Buckles." Her two hands circled her coffee mug. They sat in silence until she said, "This is too grim. Let's change the topic. Can we get back to my pubic hair? I could shave it, if you like. On a morning like his, why can't we choose to be happy?"

He stood to toast a second muffin. His back was to her when he said, "Will you want half?" She said she did, then added that when she'd been in college the girls in her dormitory played a game called *Two Truths and a Lie.*

"You say three simple things about yourself. Two have to be true, but one has to be false. That's the lie, of course. Maybe a game will make it easier for us. I'll go first. You'll see how it works."

Pierre's heart was already committed to truth to this woman, so he agreed to play. Mario would have called him a *gavone.* Mario was seldom wrong.

"My father was a spy. I went to Wellesley. I like to cook."

"Wellesley? Really? I assumed NYU. The sweatshirts."

"No. Wellesley. Up near Boston. That statement is true."

He sat back. "Forget the game a minute. You had yellow hair, were a schoolgirl in New Orleans, and went to Wellesley. Was there a boy who gave you his belt to carry your books the day before you left? A boy who said he'd meet you at the train station?"

His hand rested on her foot.

"I kept that belt for a year," she said. "It was you. It was you." Her eyes widened. "You were such a beautiful, beautiful boy. Why didn't you meet me at the train?"

He'd been pressed by mobsters to monitor a dealer who turned out to be his former lover, the other blonde in his life. Then he told the truth about her because he had to, and the truth betrayed killed her, horribly. "I tried," he said. "But I could not get to the station on time. I did get there, but the train was gone." He said: "You became a symbol to me."

"A symbol? Of what?"

"An ideal. Of something pure in a world where there is none. You had a monogram of your initials on your blouse. KJ."

"I am Kelly Jo. No one calls me KJ anymore, but it would be nice if you did. Call me KJ, if you wish, but I assure you I am far from any symbol of purity."

Bluish smoke curled from the toaster where the muffin burned.

"Can you also let your hair grow out yellow again?"

"Don't ask me to do that. It would be going backwards." Her fingertips caressed the fine hairs on his arm. This beautiful man at her breakfast table with fine hair on his forearm had been the beautiful boy who did not appear at Union Station. She'd wept all the way to Chicago. She was ready to weep now at the loss of a life that might have been.

In his dreams he had lain a million nights beside the Yellow-Haired Girl Who Looked Back. That first morning after the first time they made love, Pierre stood to kiss the softest depression at the base of her throat and then kissed her bare back.

His dreams were no longer dreams.

Fate had granted them the rarest thing, a second chance.

On a warm August night when sleepless New Yorkers turned pillows to the cool side, Pierre said he was ready to complete his turn at Two Truths and a Lie.

"It's just a silly game," KJ said, and kissed the tips of his fingers. She wanted to be done with games.

"I want to finish," he said. "But I warn you I may cheat a little."

They were on an evening urban hike north from Plaza Circle on Fifth Avenue, holding hands like high school kids as they went from puddle of yellow light to puddle of yellow light cast by streetlights. When the ripe smell of the Hansom cab horses and auto exhaust fell behind them, they sat on a splintered wooden bench with its back to the Park's shoulder-high granite block perimeter wall.

The tri-color flag of France hung heavily across Fifth Avenue from them at the Consulate, a Gilded Age four-story townhouse with glowing bow windows. KJ's stringy denim cutoffs, sandals, and a sleeveless cotton blouse wafted in air that barely stirred. Pierre bent forward, his long fingers laced between his knees. His un-tucked rumpled unbuttoned white linen dress shirt fell loosely over his belted khaki slacks. Sockless in his loafers, he appeared, *louche*, the word he'd explained to KJ was for him more than a fashion statement. His earth-brown felt trilby rested on the back of his head. When her fingers touched his neck, they came away damp. Perspiration spread along his hairline.

KJ expected a confession. As long as he was not married elsewhere, how terrible could it be?

Pierre said, "My father was a Navy pilot, but I never knew him;
when I was a boy before I dealt poker in illegal casinos, I hustled
cards near Jackson Square and cheated; I kill people for pay; I collect old editions of *Gray's Anatomy*."

KJ laughed, relieved. "You're making fun of me. That's four
statements, and one is an absurd lie. If you do not want to play, you
do not have to, but, please do not make fun of me."

"I said I'd cheat a little. You remember the bench near the
French Market? Central Park does not smell like the Mississippi,
but with a French flag before us, we are in much the same place as
when we started." He drew a deep breath. "It's a good place to begin
again. That day you asked me to tell you something that no one else
knew, and I told you my mother nursed me until I was six. I've never
lied to you. Never will."

His face hung in shadow. Her hand traced soft circles on his
shoulder. Whenever they were together, some part of them touched
the other. "This is too easy. You do not kill people."

His silence weighed heavy as the humid night.

"Not every day, and not because I am a maniac, *mais vraiment,*
people hire me to smooth things over for them by erasing a problem in their lives."

"Now you *are* making fun of me."

"I have a talent for it. I have never killed a woman."

He sat more erect to turn toward her, his face still dim in the
humid half night. KJ grew annoyed. "Stop it." But her heart had
gone cold because she was less sure of him than she had been minutes ago. "Tell me instead about your father."

"Never met him. I like to believe he wasn't an asshole, but I
think must have been. My mother says he was handsome, but she
might have made that up. I was born on New Year's Day, so she
must have had a one night stand with a pilot when she was sixteen.
For a very long time, I thought my father would drop out of the

clouds to fly me away in his airplane. In my dreams, he looked like Lindbergh in that leather cap and wearing a white silk scarf."

"He had to be handsome. French or Italian by the look of you."

"Maybe, but Maman was dark, Cajun, and probably part Creole, but her family would never admit to African blood. I met her sisters when we buried her, but my aunts were pale as geese and twice as stupid. Kolinda, my mother, said my father was her first man and then I came along. She was thirty-two when she told me. I thought she was old. She had had a few drinks and called herself 'Fertile Myrtle.' The only reasons she told me as much as she did was that she needed to be sure I knew that the drunk we lived with was not my father and because I wanted to join the Marines. I was personally going to kill Hitler. A year later I lived in the streets of N'aw Leans. I did all right for myself at cards by Jackson Square. Maman taught me to play and to tell fortunes. I taught myself to cheat."

"Never joined the Marines?"

"They would not have me because I was too young, but by the time I was old enough I found other ways to live."

Night thickened. Taxis slowed as drivers hoping for a fare eyeballed the couple on the bench, but Pierre waved them away.

"I believe you about *Gray's Anatomy*, too. The store always has copies for new medical students. Paper quality and glue change, but not anatomy. Doctors require a desk reference."

"The 1858 quarto has color plates."

"Oh, now you see? You've given yourself away. Only a real collector would know that, and no book collector kills people. So that's it. The game is over." She pointed at separate fingers to prove her logic. "You never knew your father, that's one truth. You collect old anatomy books, that's a second truth. And, lover, I know your hands have never been callused and I've seen you do card tricks, so the part about dealing cards in casinos and cheating at a game in Jackson Square must be truth number three. I hope you will tell my fortune. But those are your three truths, and they leave only one possible lie." Her fingers traced another small circle on his back.

"Bend the rules if you want, but, you can't be killing people." A bus groaned south.

He gently folded her fingers into a fist and held her hand. "KJ, all four are true. The game won't work for me. I cannot lie to you."

"Stop now. It's stupid. We are finished with it." She kissed the tip of each of his fingers.

Not that evening, nor the evening after that, but on a following summer night they went west to east across Central Park. Guidebooks cautioned tourists of the perils of the park in darkness, but Pierre refused to be intimidated. "The best way to ensure safety in Central Park is to fill the place with people, not warn them away." KJ wondered if he were truly brave or if he wanted to impress her. Probably both.

They'd taken the night air for another of their urban journeys, this time to the Dakota, the stately apartment house at 72nd Street where *Rosemary's Baby* had been set. Pierre had read the book before they saw the movie together at a revival house near Times Square, but now he wanted to see the place. "Any place that spawned the Devil will welcome me," he said as they grew close. Pierre, usually quiet and contemplative, talked of how the life of the film's director, Roman Polanski, imitated his art. A year after the film was released, his pregnant wife, Sharon Tate, was among the dead slaughtered in the Hollywood hills by Charles Manson's "family," that group of devoted, harebrained women who painted the walls with Tate's blood.

In the day's fading light, they observed the Dakota from several perspectives. "Blood and lust," Pierre murmured. She shivered as he took her hand and they slipped into the cooler shadows of Central Park.

Trees rustled. There were crickets. Pierre's arm circled her shoulders. She felt sticky with heat.

Her lover took an odd sidestep when he placed himself between KJ and a young man who coalesced out of nothing. No more than a shadow born from deeper shadow, he came toward them. Pierre's .22 pistol rose from his trouser pocket. A bullet went into the man's open mouth. He clutched at his throat as he fell. Then Pierre pivoted to send a second round into the eye of a second man five yards behind them. Her lover moved like a dancer as he killed two men. His pistol made very little noise. *Pop, pop.* Pierre knelt beside each of the young Hispanics to place a shot through the softer flesh at the base of their ears. The *coup de grace* sharply snapped their heads. Brains and blood oozed onto the dirt.

"Hold this," Pierre said and handed KJ his pistol. Pierre tossed a mugger's knife into the roadway, then stood to smack dirt from the knee of his tan trousers. Pierre's gun barrel was hot to the touch. Beside them, a crawling line of cars passed them on the park's crosstown road.

KJ had had no chance to be frightened, but now her heart raced. "You just killed two men." She stated the fact it as if she read a back page story from a newspaper.

Two men lay dead in Central Park. She needed to pee. She wanted to run. It would not matter where, just run.

Pierre pulled the corpses out of the glow flares of car headlights. The dead men's shoes gouged shallow parallel lines in pebbly soil. Pierre kicked at dirt and leaves, then slapped soil from his knees a second time. The bodies would not be discovered by casual passers-by until morning, if then.

"We ought to call the police."

He gently used two hands to pry her fingers apart to remove his gun from her grip. "To do what?" He wiped fingerprints from the pistol with his long shirttail. "All the police can do is make it hard for us."

His eerie deliberateness both frightened and calmed her. What could be more ordinary than a stroll on a summer night in the deepest gloom of Central Park with her Cajun lover shooting muggers? Some other night, they might trap lightning bugs in a fruit jar. What could be more ordinary? She touched the soft flesh under her ear. When Pierre's tongue found that spot, a thrill raced through her entire body; it was something to realize a bullet in that same spot finished a man.

She was lightheaded. Pierre was too at ease to be anything but a practiced murderer. He moved like a dancer. The hands that thrilled her took life expertly when they killed. When they made love, his face took a slight reddish hue and his pulse hardly rose, the same as when he shot a man.

"The *gros couillon* should know better than to smoke cigarettes and set up an ambush. The smell of tobacco gave that one away. Where there is one, there is probably two."

Behind her eyes, her mind became a passenger riding at the top of her body. She'd smelled nothing. Were Pierre's senses more acute? They walked from the park at a pace neither leisurely nor hurried, heel-toe, heel-toe, heel-toe. His arm encircled her narrow shoulders just as it had before he'd fired his pistol.

"He could have been asking for a match," she said.

"I feel like someone needs to pay me money."

KJ walked hip-to-hip with Death's own agent. At the park's east edge, she brought herself up short. "Will you need to shoot me?"

"*Mais non*. Remind me to tell you about the time a guy made me shoot a dead man to feel safer about himself by insuring my silence. Do you want to go back and shoot a dead man?"

"What good would that do?"

"Instead of being a witness, you'd be a killer, too."

"But they are already dead."

"That is exactly the point my friend made when a guy wanted my prints on a murder weapon."

"What happened?"

"The short version is that my friend in the room got tired of his complaining. He ended the conversation by blowing the guy's brains out." KJ halted again. "It scared the crap out of me, but when I burned my clothes to be rid of any blood or gunpowder evidence. I knew I was happier to be alive than he must have been to be dead."

"Burned your clothes? How do you know so much about this?" Her hand was trembling in his as if she were cold.

"I burned down the house, too. I just placed myself between you and a bullet. Why would I shoot you now? Besides, I won't kill a woman."

In a dark place under a broad tree at the park's edge, he removed the 5-shot cylinder from the revolver. He did not share with KJ the possibility the two muggers had been set to find him. It was unlikely, but not impossible. On Fifth Avenue, as if he bent to tie a shoelace, he removed the remaining cartridge and dropped the cylinder through a sewer grating. Then he dropped the live bullet into another sewer. It was an ordinary summer night, air thick as flour paste, and he was deliberately disposing of the murder weapon that left two muggers dead in the dirt. Pierre explained the importance of being rid of her clothes. A single drop of blood could have floated through the air and settled on her. The chemistry of the park's dirt might give them away, so even her sneakers would need to be burned. They could not be too cautious.

"How many men have you killed?"

"Many."

"More than ten?"

"More than ten. Many more."

"Are you a psychopath? Don't you feel guilt?"

"No. I get no pleasure from killing. It is not as though I dream about my next hit and look forward to it. Killing is my job. I am good at it."

"It is cold-blooded."

"*Certainement.* Passionate killing is dangerous. There are mistakes. Cold blood is better. That is why I am good at it."

When Pierre asked himself who might want him dead, the list in his mind grew long with people whose names he did not know. They'd only know him if Mario had given him up, but Mario would never give him up. Mario himself had no reason to want him dead. Besides, if Mario wanted him dead, he would not hire two New York punks to do it; he'd do it himself.

So say the odds were eight-for-five that the street punks were nothing more than street punks. Who else might be so stupid as to set up a trap and smoke cigarettes while they waited? It was Amateur Night in Central Park.

The grip of his pistol dropped through a subway grating on Lexington Avenue. At 77th Street, while KJ waited on the street, Pierre went down a flight of stairs to the subway platform, bought a token for the turnstile, walked to the edge of the platform, and tossed the firing pin, side plates, and several more tiny parts onto the tracks as an IRT local shrieked into the station to grind the gun's disassembled parts to twisted, unrecognizable bits of metal. On another block, before a D'Agostino's, the pistol's safety found its way into a trash barrel filled with rotting lettuce.

Guns were a bargain compared to the cost of being found with one linked to a shooting. Rifling marks on bullets matched to a barrel were enough to have a man executed. "Keeping a weapon is strictly for amateurs," he said as much to himself as KJ.

They crossed a footbridge over FDR Drive at 78th Street to the shore of the East River. Across the black water, electric lights on Roosevelt Island twinkled. It was a romantic spot. With hardly any movement of his hand, the last pieces of the pistol skittered over gneiss rocks to disappear into the black water of the East River. He'd need another pistol, though obtaining a gun in New York was a pain in the ass. He felt exposed.

"Killing is evil."

"That's a matter of perspective."

"It's a Commandment."

"Then the Devil must love generals."

"War is different."

"I doubt it."

KJ chewed her lip. "That makes no sense."

He kissed each of her eyes. "Making sense is overrated."

He walked her home but did not stay. Just as Pierre left her, she heard herself say: "You make me feel safe." She wondered if he heard her, but as she lay down and folded a wet cloth onto her brow, she realized she felt safest beneath the leather wings of a practiced killer.

KJ quit constant sweatshirts. By fall, her closet overflowed with sweaters in blues, scarlet, and meadow green. She left the bookstore. Nat gone, the fun was gone, too. It had taken years to end her sense of dependence on Jack, but she could no longer recall why she'd ever felt that way. Though there were dozens of plausible explanations, none could stand against simply turning and walking away. What had she feared?

Being the kept woman of a contract killer was nothing like being a suburban housewife in a vine-covered Scarsdale Tudor. One night, after watching unmemorable television while gorging on Rum Raisin, Pierre told her fortune with a pack of cards. She cut the cards, but his quick hands arranged every array to have the King of Clubs appear beside Queen of Hearts. The Queen of Hearts was the only queen in the deck holding her flowers on the left, a sign that meant the queen of love might choose to go her own way. The King of Clubs was devoted, honest, and a good provider. When she'd asked how he knew all that, he lowered his eyes and said his mother taught him that the cards never lied.

Pierre gave her access to his numbered account in Switzerland. His other accounts were in the Caymans, but the Berne account was the big one. "It's our Fuck You money."

"What is Fuck You money?"

"Like a pension. There will come a time when we will want to say 'Fuck you' and vanish."

"A life insurance policy."

"We'll stay alive to enjoy it, *cher*."

"It may be more like a bribe to not report you to the police."

He shrugged. "What would you report?"

"That you are a professional killer."

"Oh? Who have I killed? Name one."

"You did not tell me that part."

He kissed her lips. "Nor will I, *cher*. For your own safety."

"What about the two muggers in Central Park?"

"Maybe. But there is no physical evidence. For all the police know, you did it and want to frame me to save yourself."

Pierre asked only that if he vanished she wait for three years to access the numbered Swiss account. "I might be in hiding and not want anyone to find you."

"I could rob you blind, you know."

"That's right."

"You're pretty sure of yourself, *Monsieur* Doucet, aren't you?"

His eyes smiled at her over the lip of his coffee.

On nights when Pierre was absent, her bed felt empty. In sleep, her Catholic schoolgirl education came on her as the weight of sin, a leering demon on her chest. She'd pull her sheet over her head, but it was no protection.

She loved a killer.

But what of it? KJ would have chosen eternity with Pierre in Hell than to be at God's right among all the angels of Heaven.

Pierre rented a pale blue Corvette. They set off for a picnic to New Jersey, the green spot of ground on the Palisades, the cliff high above the Hudson River where Aaron Burr shot Alexander Hamilton. Looking back across the river, the George Washington Bridge was at their left; to their right the mouth of the Hudson broadened to the sea, shrouding in haze the Statue of Liberty, Ellis Island, Governor's Island, and rising like a cat's back from the harbor, Staten Island. Directly before them, the spires of Manhattan seemed to rise directly from water.

Not quite facing each other, they leaned back to the Corvette's bumper. Whenever Pierre was contemplative, he spoke even more slowly. "Hamilton's mother was jailed for adultery, which was a fancy way of labeling her a whore. Hamilton never knew his father."

"Like you."

Pierre cupped his hands around a cigarette. "That's right," he said. "Like me. By the time Hamilton was twelve, he was on his own." He spoke as if to himself. "He was a hothead. Having children did not stop him from putting his life on the line for principles. In those times, honorable men did their own killing, but dueling was technically illegal. No one ever actually took a shot at anyone else. It was a pissing contest. Gentlemen did not kill other gentlemen. They shot into the air or into the dirt to see if either of them turned chicken. Hamilton was no chicken." He drew on his cigarette. "But Aaron Burr was no gentleman." Pierre toed a loose pebble that rolled away under the wrought iron fence, gathering speed until it disappeared from view over the side of the cliff. "One morning they rowed across the river with their seconds, climbed this steep cliff, squared off, took ten paces, turned, and discharged their single shot pistols. Burr was uninjured, but Hamilton took a shot in the belly. Bullets were slow moving and huge, compared to today. It ripped a hole in him. His seconds rowed him back." He pointed to the Manhattan skyline. "It took him a day to die, paralyzed. The ball must have severed his spine."

"Would you kill a man for honor?"

"I've only known one man I wanted dead, but I did not kill him." Pierre thought a moment. "*Mais oui.* I believe I could look a man in the eye and shoot him for honor, though Charlie would not know honor if it bit him on the ass. He was the drunk who beat Maman."

On a secluded bench in dappled shadows beneath a leafy tree, KJ opened the wicker basket that held their lunch. While Pierre pulled the cork from a bottle of tartly sweet Vouvray, KJ smeared soft bread with Camembert.

"You're an eighteenth-century man trapped in the twentieth century," she said.

"You may be right." He extinguished his cigarette and sipped from a plastic wine flute. Without their eyes meeting, he asked: "Would you want to come with me?"

"Where?"

"On a job. We won't be Bonnie and Clyde. We won't be writing doggerel to brag to newspapers. It's another grocer someone needs dead. This one is near Chicago."

"A grocer?"

"They are all grocers. Someone pays. He doesn't know who I am, and I do not know him. We never meet. There's a go-between who moves the money. It's simple commerce. There is no honor in it."

"Why would you want me there?" She studied her lover's unwavering profile. She leaned back on the bench and felt the faint sun shedding little warmth on her face.

"You should know this part of me."

They turned until their eyes met. She saw in his eyes with unerring clarity that her life with Pierre would end badly. It was like boarding an endless rollercoaster. Good sense said to quit the thrill ride.

"Yes," she said. "I'll join you."

KJ knotted her kerchief under her chin, then stepped into the waiting Corvette. Like a hand at her chest, acceleration pushed her back into the seat. Pierre kept the top down. The wind was fierce.

Mr. and Mrs. Worthington from Oneonta, New York take a lake-view suite at the Drake. For the sake of the desk clerk, Mr. Worthington pretends to be concerned at the expense, then yields to his wife. Yes, they will stay at the Drake. The uniformed desk clerk cannot hide her smile. They carry no supporting ID for KJ, but what could be more ordinary than a man and his wife combining business with pleasure? They have two pieces of matching luggage, bought new but deliberately battered by a hammer and scraped by sandpaper to look worn. The Worthingtons ask for and accept a recommendation for nearby restaurants. "As long as they are reasonable," Mrs. Worthington says. After a bellboy makes a show of switching on and off lights, Pierre gives the kid two dollars to get rid of him.

They make love with the drapery flung wide open, gray Lake Michigan stretching to the horizon. KJ has never imagined a lake where she cannot see the far shore. Why isn't it an inland fresh-water sea?

Her head rests on Pierre's bare chest. KJ as much feels as listens to her lover's heartbeat. He explains he has been Mr. Worthington two other times. Three is his limit. The fake driver's license will need to be disposed of after this final use.

A week earlier, without KJ, Pierre registered under another name at another hotel closer to O'Hare. He cased the mark, Weslajnick.

Weslajnick is neither rich nor poor. He keeps to himself in his modest home in Maywood, the leafy Chicago suburb. Someone is paying five thousand to place Weslajnick on the spot. It's no trick to eliminate anyone. He is just another doomed grocer.

Mr. Worthington rents an unremarkable gray four-door Mercury. They spend two consecutive evenings in Maywood parked beneath a sycamore to confirm what Pierre already knows; the mark walks his Golden Retriever at the same hour, daily. The dog is large, calm, and likes strangers.

Mr. and Mrs. Worthington wait for an overcast or rainy evening. Dogs don't insist on fair weather.

On their fourth day in Chicago, sheets of rain blow off the lake. Mr. and Mrs. Worthington use the miserable morning to take in Manet at the Art Institute. Manet's women are resplendent in hats and bonnets, reclining on Parisian lawns in city parks or in French countryside so sun-drenched the light crackles as if alive, but KJ supposes Manet's women are troubled, uncertain of their status, knowing the color in their cheeks and eyes will inevitably be extinguished. Pierre cannot see that in the portraits, but he comments how art will keep them forever as they are. Manet made them art; art makes them immortal.

KJ likes his observation.

The rain eases. They walk the lakeside esplanade in light drizzle, jacket collars up, shoulders hunched, Pierre's fedora low over his eyes. Their arms loop together. Ripples of light coruscate the gray water.

"Are you sure?" Pierre asks. "There is no going back."

A chill passes through her.

They leave The Loop and the lake behind. The nondescript Mercury turns right, rolls two streets off West Madison, and comes to rest in the unsettled shadow beneath what KJ has come to think of their sycamore. There is nothing to notice on this dark street in Maywood except a middle-aged couple necking like high school kids in the front seat of a Mercury. Yellow leaves clot on the windshield.

Swift as Death itself, in a single motion Pierre releases her, cracks open the car door, steps into the dark, and shoots Weslajnick in the back of the head. He holds the man like an unsteady drunk, lowers him to the ground, and puts a second shot behind Weslajnick's ear.

Weslajnick's Golden Retriever licks his hand. To make the killing seem a robbery gone bad, Pierre takes Weslajnick's wallet and wristwatch. There is no wedding ring. He turns Weslajnick's pockets inside out. The Golden Retriever sits puzzled but expectant, limpid eyes brimming, then licks the dead man's face.

Pierre scratched the dog's ears, then starts the Mercury.

"Not yet, mister," KJ says. "This was not our agreement."

He hands her the revolver. She steps from the car, squeezes her eyes shut, holds the gun with both her hands, and fires a round into the corpse's chest. The dog's sad eyes look at her. "Good girl," she says to the dog.

In the moving car, KJ takes Weslajnick's wallet apart, no more than a billfold. All she will ever know of the man dead in Maywood is in her hands. His only photograph is a crinkled black and white of a young boy and an older girl at what must have been the girl's birthday party. Neither kid looks especially happy.

KJ tears the photo into even, ever-smaller bits of stiff photo paper. The bits of paper drop like gray party confetti out the Mercury's window where they fall to the wet streets. It makes KJ sad.

KJ also separates the cheap wallet into pieces. She drops the bits of leather miles from each other in the same way Pierre disposes of revolver parts on distantly separated streets. The final drop for the wallet is through a sewer grating in Greektown.

At a restaurant named for a goddess, they drink Retsina, eat souvlaki, and cast white plates to shatter on the parquet floor. The pieces of ceramic spin at a belly dancer's slippered feet.

That night, the suburban housewife who'd been drying up in Scarsdale wears not a stitch to bump and grind before her naked lover on their hotel bed. When he tries to sit up, she presses his shoulders flat, then teases his erection before she takes him in her mouth. Later, her lover sated and asleep, she stands naked to peer out the hotel window. The storm having passed, unsullied moonlight lies on Lake Michigan.

Pierre returned to New Orleans without KJ. He still kept a place. Before he could leave the apartment to go to Mario's to collect his fee, Pierre's telephone with its untraceable number rang. It was Mario, calling from the other side of the world, Naples. No one else but KJ had his private number, and how Mario knew he was in New Orleans to lift the receiver was something Pierre did not want to think about.

"The wife and I tried Sicily, first. It's a donkey shithole. Sand in my fucking eyes, in my fucking nose, up my ass. It's too bad that Castro prick is still in Havana. I'd have liked Havana. I hear they still make cigars there by rolling leaf on the thighs of virgins. A guy who knows told me that so who am I to call him a liar? The best women are where you find the best cigars." Pierre looked through a rain-streaked dirty window to Freret St. Everywhere he went, it seemed to be raining.

Mario said, "Enough about me," Mario said. "Buddy, I called because I need a favor. My boy, Vincente, has a good heart, but not enough brain. I want you to look in on him. They are starting him in the business. No lie, but if you tell him I said he's an idiot, it will crush him. Maybe it's not brain. Maybe it is experience. He can be delicate. I swear, if they left it up to me, you'd be running at least the place in Metairie, but you know how it is. It was not up to me when I was there, and now that I am here, nothing is up to me. Can you keep an eye on my boy, make sure he does not fuck up so bad he wakes up whacked? I can't ask my brother Frankie. He never recovered from his head in the oven, so while he smiles and sings plenty, what can I do? Ask him to look in on Vincente? Frankie still collects coins from pinball machines, when he does not fuck that up. He dropped a dime, once, and spent two hours moving furniture to find it. A fucking dime. But look, I had to tell my boy, Vincente, who you were to be sure he'd listen to you and you are still going to need a handler, am I right? He already knew his Uncle Buddy was not just another *gavone* who worked for his old man, and he wants to be your handler for your business. Same percentage. I told him if he got greedy I'd kick in his cojones. So I gave him your phone. You should check on Vincente once in a while, is all I am asking, make sure he does nothing stupid and breaks his mother's heart. Look, you'd need to see him now and again anyway, right? Hand to God, buddy, I tried to get you one of the good places to manage, you earned it, but you know the fucking Italians. They'd slice the fingers off their grandmother's hands one at a time to make the old lady give up a nickel, and since you are not Italian blood, they will think their Metairie investment is gone." The long distance connection hummed and crackled. When that static cleared, Mario was still talking. "… and this Nixon asshole? He did what he had to do, am I right? Roll over and lose? For what? I miss the bread at Mosca's. They bake bread here, too, the crust is perfect. You dip it in olive oil. No butter, just oil. You smell the bread, you cream your pants, hand to God. You should visit. Bring a girl. Bring two. But keep an eye on my Vincente. I just want the boy should be safe."

Thirty-six hours after hanging up on Mario, Pierre obtained a legitimate phone number under the name of Morphy Enterprises. KJ had no idea she was the only person who knew it existed.

To keep a professional distance from his business required a professional handler, a disinterested but connected person who could insulate Pierre from an actual employer. He was left with Mario's boy.

Vincente still called Pierre "Uncle Buddy." In his late twenties, he had grown to be not half as stupid as his father had predicted, but what he lacked in brains he made up for by being shrewd, arrogant, and vicious. Vincente explained that his father's departure for Sicily was so sudden he did not have the time to arrange for Vincente to properly come into the business. It was clear he did not know his father had moved on to Naples, but Pierre was not about to be the one to break that news. If Mario wanted the boy to know, he would tell him in his own sweet time.

Vincente had expected to inherit six gaming houses, but as Mario set foot in Italy the word came down that Vincente was to be tested with only one. "It's nothing but guys with mustaches shitting on me," he said. "No trust. Why? I ask. Why? Five years I manage money on the street with airport baggage handlers, dock workers, and truckers. They try to fuck me over all the time for their shitty fifteen points, but no matter what, I pay upstairs every dime I am supposed to and never skim. Not like my old man. He pocketed plenty."

Like his father, Vincente put too much cracked ice in a tumbler filled with Maker's Mark. Without asking, he handed the same drink to Pierre. The glass sweated in his hand. Pierre suspected Vincente could never master the bookkeeping or the security needs of a first-class club. He was a smash-and-grab guy whose only tool for any problem was a Louisville Slugger. But that was bad for business. The same people rolling dice in a classy casino had their pictures on the *Times-Picayune* Society pages. They owned the clubhouse boxes at the Fairgrounds where they bet no horses because they owned the horses. If Vincente pissed off judges, judge's wives, or judge's girlfriends, the judges might stop coming back. Cutting into profits was bad enough, but jeopardizing the delicate balance of legal protection could prove fatal to all manner of enterprises.

Vincente ran the Metairie casino, the best one, right enough, but he still made coin with his old standbys, loan sharking and hijacking. The two rackets were hand in glove: a guy too far into the shys might choose to preserve his knees by giving up information about a truckful of better scotch or better suits being unloaded. A bay door might be left ajar. A watchman would feel the call of nature at the exact moment when Vincente's guys showed up. "It's peaches and cream, Uncle Buddy. Peaches and cream."

When after the war the Japs made a swift move from plastic water pistols to world-class electronics, Vincente saw the shape of the future. Handheld video recorders fortunately dovetailed with his hobby, girls as young as eleven but seldom older than fourteen performing sex acts ordinarily reserved for older, jaded whores.

Vincente made do-it-yourself videos with state-of-the-art Sony cameras. "There's no film to develop," Vincente said. "Great, right?"

The wall safe that never held less $200,000 of casino backup money hung open, the money behind a wall of white boxes neatly stacked like bricks. Each video cassette had a neat girl's name in black magic marker on the box's spine; a few repeat stars also had roman numerals in black marker. Linda I, Linda II, Clara, and so forth. Vincente reached deep into the safe and tossed Pierre's his payment for the Chicago job, then thought to impress his uncle. Vincente's office filled with light so bright it hurt Pierre's eyes.

"I had them installed for shooting," Vincente explained, and flipped the lights off again.

He described how he might rig a table game against a woman of a certain age and position, spot her the money she needed, then wait for her to get in over her head. "Second wives about to get put on the shelf for wife number three get nervous and play harder. They lose harder, too." He moved to the desk and slid a tape into a deck set below a large television. "You have to see this."

Vincente sat in the captain's chair that had been his father's to swing his broughams onto the glass top of the Cherrywood desk in the same way his father always had. He also wore the same white socks and had the same growing gut overhanging his belt, same bristling eyebrows that looked like warring black centipedes above the bridge of his very Roman nose. Mario, however, used expensive cologne; Vincente bought cheap stuff, maybe by the gallon at a drugstore in a fancy box with a cellophane window to show matching soap on a rope. Vincente favored neon purple or chartreuse shirts with pointed collars and tightly knotted patterned neckwear, the kind vicious toughs in movies wore.

As far as Pierre knew, Mario never entrapped a woman. Even Doris had paved her own road to Hell. Pierre believed a gambler deserved whatever came to him—that was why it was called gambling and everyone knew at the outset that debts had to be paid. So, it seemed wrong that a woman played against a stacked deck so Vincente could take advantage. "These women have lawyers and bankers who negotiate everything for them, but a debt to the casino is different. They don't get it. There is no negotiation."

Vincente touched a button on a remote in his desk drawer and the TV screen struggled to ignite.

"This Linda was twelve. Scared spitless. Look at those eyes. But once her mother told her she had to do what the nice man asked, she came around. Dark rum and some Coca-Cola helped. Hand to God, three drinks and she went from woozy to enthusiastic. Think of it! Her mother the society lady pimped her kid to me. 'Just do what the nice man says,' they tell them and leave. The kid moans like a street whore when I bend her over the desk, but she comes for real three times." He kissed his fingertips. "This was why I installed the good lights. Her second and third tapes show those little nips stiff as beads. You think I need microphones?" He paused. "Do you think I should interview their mothers, too?"

He dropped fresh ice into Pierre's bourbon, grinning as if he expected Pierre to admire him. "You have to see their faces when they realize that the only way they can keep the country club, the nice car, the husband with the bottomless checkbook, and the mansion with the big driveway and two uniformed maids is if their kid takes it up the ass. I'd edit to a shot of the kid choking on my dick. More interview, a shot of the kid on her hands and knees. Like that angle there." He gestured toward the screen. "Stuff like that is artistic. I need to get a better video editor." He scribbled a note to himself on a large yellow pad.

The safe held two Carols, two Susies, and one Princess that Pierre could see. More were stored with the cash at the safe's rear.

Pierre wondered if a slug into Vincente's eye and leaving him dead on a pile of his tapes might persuade police not to pursue him. Pierre touched the handle of his knife at his ankle, Charlie's knife, the same blade he'd stuck in the floor of the YMCA twenty years ago. Gutting the little punk would be more appropriate. He'd squeal like the pig he was. It might be understood as a public service. The cops might even give him a pass, but the organization never would. Vincente was family. His little hobby could be indulged until it put profit, not wide-eyed little girls, in peril.

"I can get you a playback system. They fall off trucks all the time. Borrow a few tapes. Hell, keep them. They are easy to copy. But you have to see Linda number two. She sucks like a hoover."

He tossed a white box to Pierre. "But we also need to do business, am I right?" He handed Pierre a manila envelope fat with fifties. "Count it."

"You wouldn't short me, would you?"

"Not my Uncle Buddy."

The boy seemed anxious. Pierre waited. It came soon enough.

"I need you to do a special job for me," Vincente said.

"Where?"

"Right here in N'awlins. It's a guy I'd like to not see anymore."

"A civilian?"

"No. that's why it is special."

"Vinny, with respect to you and your father who I love like a brother, you know I don't work that way. Strictly civilians." Pierre knew there was no winning this. "You have guys for wet work, am I right?"

"Yeah, yeah. Sure. I just don't want anyone to know. You're my uncle since before I can remember. I trust you. The others, not so much."

Pierre shook his head. "I don't think I can help you," he said.

A shadow of rage crossed Vincente's eyes. He was unused to anyone denying him anything, much less someone who had just tucked an envelope of cash he had just given him into his coat pocket. But he seized control of himself, the darkness in his eyes dispersed. "It was just a thought," he said mildly and shrugged. "Look, it's simple. Let me persuade you. A guy is scheduled to testify to a grand jury against another guy. The work has to be done in three days."

"Like I said, you have people for that. Has the canary got police protection?"

Vincente pursed his lips and shrugged. "Probably, but I think I can arrange for that to go away. We still need the favor. You are the best."

Already knowing his answer, Pierre said, "I'll get back to you."

"That's all I ask. But by tonight. This problem has to go away in three days."

Pierre dropped the video tape through a sewer grating and walked rapidly away, thinking that if the vicious little shit knew his phone number, the little shit could find Pierre's address. Morphy Enterprises was no party line, but all it would take was a conversation with the right person in the right office and, if he did not already know it, Vincente would have the address where Pierre lived. Pierre put the odds on his address already being in the wind at eight-for-five. It was two-for-one that the vicious little shit had someone tailing Pierre, and the odds on a tail were that high only because the little shit was so arrogant he might believe he could locate Pierre at will. It was hardly chalk, but Vincente's requested favor might be a set-up to have Pierre killed. Pierre could be on the spot. The odds there were no longshot, either. Three-for-one at best.

Pierre saw no percentage in trying to ascertain the facts. All that mattered was that he loved KJ and so for the first time since he was a boy, he had reason to live.

He alternated running and walking the route to his place, walking heel-toe, heel-toe, heel-toe then rising to the balls of his feet to jog three hundred yards before speed walking again. He perspired from more than exertion. All his exercises to augment his wind and endurance were paying off. He moved through side streets that were eerily quiet; certain unwelcome eyes probed his back.

A call to Mario for help could do him no good. Between Pierre and Vincente, Mario could choose only his son. Maybe the grocer in Chicago had been no grocer. Maybe an orphan somewhere was intent on revenging a father. Maybe a long-ago-satisfied client felt over-exposed and had contacted Vincente and offered money to close the books. Where Mario considered *omerta* a binding oath that would seal his lips, Vincente would consider Pierre's life an expendable asset, one ready to cash in. It was equally probable that Vincente was just an asshole wiping the last trace his father's dealings from his own life. He'd want Pierre dead because he could make it so.

Pierre entered his apartment with caution. He took a very fast shower with his pistol balanced on the lip of the sink, but had no time to linger under the hot water for as long as his kinked neck needed. He'd never get clean enough. He touched for the last time the covers of Walter Scott, so like KJ's skin, and began his long-rehearsed disappearing act. He donned a white linen suit and with only the blue satchel walked two blocks to use a payphone to call a car service he'd used only once. Then he waited at an interior table with his back to a wall.

He sat in the taxi's rear seat with his pistol against the back of the driver's seat ready to put one through the driver's heart and spine and then spatter the man's brains across his windshield if he so much as made a wrong turn.

Vincente, the little shit, fucked little girls and bragged about it. It was better than even money that could not stay hidden forever, as close to a sure thing as there could be. The little shit owned a growing collection of incriminating evidence. How butt-ugly stupid was that? Eventually some guilt-stricken mother would spill, or get drunk enough to write a note and cut her wrists, or one of the little girls would tell her girlfriend about the man who taught her all a preteen could want to know about sodomy. The little shit's arrogance blinded him to how a small crisis could expose more than a gambling operation. Corrupt unions, whores of every sex and age, drugs, and vices even Pierre did not know could be tolerated in the Crescent City, but local citizenry drew a line at sodomizing children. Higher-ups in Vincente's family would come to see him as a liability, one they would remove from the books with an anchor chain wound around Vincente's ankles and a midnight cruise on Pontchartrain.

No wonder Mario had called. Mario must have known that Vincente would overreach and had no other way to warn Pierre.

But the odds were sure that if Vincente himself was not after Pierre, when his hobbies caught up to him and it came time for Vincente to squirm out of that after-hours cruise on Pontchartrain or become the wife of a black weightlifter who liked a sissy to lack teeth, Vincente would turn state's evidence. To do that, he'd need something to trade.

That would be his Uncle Buddy, the mass murderer.

Pierre emptied his safe deposit boxes at the Whitney on St. Charles, tying three bricks of cash in tight red rubber bands that he stuffed into his blue satchel along with a half-dozen documents that established false identities. He exited the banks walking sideways, his back flat against stone walls before he quickly ducked into his waiting cab. Every passing vehicle looked like a threat.

Pierre closed accounts at The Gulf Coast Bank and Trust, the Metairie Bank, and Jefferson Financial, the large balances wired to numbered accounts in Switzerland and the Caymans. If he did not make it back to New York, KJ had the account keys and would know what to do. If he did make it, though Pierre wanted nothing between him and KJ, explaining the little shit who bragged about buggering little girls would be like dragging her by the hair through an open sewer.

As his car made its way through the early evening, Pierre thought how he would have liked a last meal at Mosca's or oysters at the Monteleone's Carousel Bar, but there was no time for fatal sentimentality. Vincente was stupid and vicious, but it would not take the little shit long to realize that by asking Pierre for a favor, he'd tripped his play.

Uncle Buddy needed to vanish faster than Gene Autry could outrun a tribe of marauding Apaches.

Pierre flew via Pan Am to Miami. From Miami, he caught an Eastern Airlines flight to Charlotte. He flew the red-eye from Charlotte to Newark International. Each ticket was under another name; as soon as he landed, he dropped the shredded ID papers into a Men's Room toilet. Powered by caffeine, between flights, he sat in armchairs with the longest view of the terminals.

He and KJ would need to disappear. The only questions were, when, and how to accomplish that with the least chance of pursuit. Pierre's numbered accounts in the Caymans and in Switzerland were enough to sustain a man and woman with simple needs for several lifetimes. KJ would want for nothing. Never mind knowing where the bodies were buried, Pierre had put them there.

In Newark, he passed on the first two taxis waiting at the gate and asked the driver of the third car to drop him at the Port Authority Bus terminal at 40th and Eighth Avenue in Manhattan. The driver was bitter. It was a long cross-river drive. Pierre withdrew two hundred in cash from his blue satchel. The cabbie took him through the Holland Tunnel and north on Eighth Avenue to the Port Authority Bus Station.

Pierre walked into the station from Eighth Avenue and out again on 42nd Street, then hailed a cruising cab on Ninth Avenue, an old-fashioned very comfortable Checker with leather seats, dangerous because he nearly fell asleep. He rode the Checker downtown and east to Penn Station, where he went down a flight of stairs to the train level, crossed the entire station, then reemerged onto the street. A new cab took him to the St. Regis—where he registered but never saw the room—and took his last taxi directly to KJ's apartment, the only place he was sure of.

"You're back sooner than I thought," KJ said.

"I missed you," he explained.

1968–1974

O N A STOLEN BMW MOTORCYCLE named Lilith, haunted by the notion that the FBI had a set of fingerprints that could someday with a single wrong move connect her to the criminal assault and attempted murder of a government agent, Abigail "Buckles" Sinclair crossed the continent. She looped south to escape winter in the mountains and moved west across The Great American Desert to elude her inescapable past. The sun baked her by day; cold penetrated her bones by night.

She adopted Grandma Dot's plan, never traveling in the same direction more than three consecutive days, never on major highways, and doubling back whenever it suited her. Her route took her over scrub and brush in southern Colorado, New Mexico, and Arizona, and arid roads that snaked through the landscape before delivering her to California.

The flower child from Scarsdale hitching to San Francisco to smoke a little weed and make a little love had become a desperado, a woman in black leather boots and black leather jacket who carried a fake driver's license in her wallet, a spring action switchblade tucked tight against her belly by her garrison belt, diamonds camouflaged by rhinestones embedded in her cheap sunglasses, a few thousand in cash in her saddlebag, and—in a soft flannel-lined interior pocket over her breast—a scrap of brown paper torn from a grocery bag that was a crude treasure map of one shore of Lake Tahoe.

Once the vegetable greens of the Midwest, those bountiful fields of corn and soy, had faded to miles of mesquite and monotonous chaparral, Buckles felt safest by night twenty yards off the road flat on her back on her thin bedroll. Her three weeks in the annoyingly stupid Girl Scouts where she'd learned to nurse a campfire were proving handy. She spoke only to gas station attendants and servers in diners who, once she removed her helmet, saw the rider in black leather was a blue-eyed young woman with little left of once-yellow hair. Buckles kept her eyes averted from theirs and asked where she could score a little smoke. As often as not, she was sold a small amount of weed from the supply that every pump jockey across the Southwest seemed to have in his oil-stained overalls. She kept one hand on her knife while she exchanged dope for money. More than a few figured a fuck could be part of the deal; they were all disappointed.

Kneeling at her meager campfires, her cold-stiffened fingers thawed, Lilith hidden behind an outcropping of rock or trees and later behind cactus, with a joint in hand, Buckles contemplated the velvet dome of heaven. Each star was a nuclear furnace that in time would consume itself in its own fires. In the desert, her heartbeat slowed and she made peace with the idea that whether she lived or died meant very little. The stars had been burning long before she passed into the world unnoticed and would continue to burn long after she was gone. Then she would join them, for Buckles, like all who lived, was no more than stardust.

She could take little rest. No one would believe nor care that the FBI agent she left with two broken knees had been intent on rape and blackmail, so she learned to do her business squatting where she was and paid cash for a roof and room with running water when weather required it or when her own stink threatened to become overpowering. After the luxury of a bath, she slept on a chair, her eyes locked onto a roadhouse's flimsy, hollow door, sure relentless pursuers were close behind. Beds had become too soft. She swore to her absent brother-in-arms, a gay Army deserter nicknamed "Pussy," that the bastards would not take her without a fight. She hoped they did not hang Puss.

On the bike cutting through the monotonous landscape, Buckles was left with much time to think. Her dreams of peace and love had been flattened. Big Bill and Levi proved what she'd always known: safety existed nowhere. Evil was normal. Evil was as American as cherry pie. She wondered how any one girl could screw up in so many ways. At her very worst moments, she thought how her troubles might be done if she headed home, where Daddy could fight for her in court and Mom could protect her. Just a kid who made a few bad decisions, why not resume the life where she had not crippled a government agent and go back to preppie concerns like stuffing a bra with toilet tissue to snare a nicer boy? They'd marry, own an Irish Setter, and live in a gabled house with a yard behind a picket fence. Buckles could drop a litter of babies and drown in a sea of safe diapers, safe A&D Ointment, and safe easy recipes for meatloaf.

Grandma's ghost cackled laughter. When the old lady smashed Buckles' rearview mirror, she'd been about more than teaching Buckles to drive.

She ran out of birth control pills, but her period, once reliable as the moon itself, had stopped. She nevertheless kept a sealed box of tampons in Lilith's left saddlebag against the certainty that anything that could happen would, and at the worst possible moment. She stopped shaving her armpits and legs. She'd lower herself into the occasional motel room bathtub of hot water, her sunburned neck against cool porcelain, submerging all but her face, her eyes growing heavier and heavier. She'd snap erect to avoid sleep and emerge from the tub with her skin radiating heat, smelling like a bowl of potpourri set out in her mother's guest toilet.

She took up cigarettes in Gallup. Going for tough, she tried unfiltered Luckies and near coughed her lungs onto a sidewalk in front of a Circle K. After four more cigs that first day she awakened the next with a bad case of glue-mouth. She crumpled the Luckies pack and dropped it onto the road. Virginia Slims were hopelessly girly. Marlboro seemed wrong because Buckles had no intention of growing a penis and no plans of becoming a cowboy. She settled on Winstons in the soft pack, keeping them rolled under the sleeve of her T-shirt at her left shoulder. She valued the ritual of urging one cigarette from the pack, tamping it, lighting it, and exhaling a first satisfying blue-gray cloud of smoke. Lighting even a single smoke allowed her the extra few seconds she might need to sharpen her mind before committing to anything, no matter how petty; speaking, standing, sitting, turning left, turning right, or what she learned was the best response of all, doing nothing at all.

Cigarettes also occupied her hands when she could not sit still, which was most of the time. She'd treated herself to a cheeseburger and noticed her knee bouncing. She also cracked her knuckles; it was an act of sheer willpower to not bite her nails. She'd stooped so low as to buy moisturizer and once she'd peeled off her black lambskin motorcycle gloves might spend thirty or forty minutes working skin cream into her hands. Her wrists were burned deep brown by the sun; her hands and forearms remained ivory white. She nearly kicked a jar away when it occurred to her she was turning into her mother. What was next? Raisin cookies or some shit, but with hashish? If someday she had rug-rats of her own, they'd be stoned and peaceful as hippies singing *Kumbaya*. Her cookies would be the surprise bestselling treat of every school baked goods fund raiser.

But the soothing ritual of moisturizer, like the harsher rituals of cigarettes, quelled the panic that always seemed about to rise and overwhelm her. Running an emery board across each of her fingernails was a strange habit for a runaway felon on a motorcycle whose idea of a meal was a can of beans dropped into a fire and then sliced open with a switchblade, but her rituals brought some momentary peace to her fluttering soul.

Crossing the empty desert on a motorcycle made things plain. She might be going crazy, but crazy and stupid were very different things. By night the desert air carried the indistinct voices of her mother and Grandma Dot, so she was sure she could not be totally sane. So what? A bouncing knee, a little sleeplessness—she'd survive those, though the girlish things she did to calm herself attracted and repelled her at the same time. She rolled to her hip on her bedroll and wondered if when she ran out of road she'd have to hurl herself into the Pacific, but she took solace from knowing that the best thing about being unfiltered crazy was that she knew she was unfiltered crazy; it explained worlds.

She crossed from Arizona into California, through Needles, Barstow, and north to Bakersfield along flat roads laid out by compass and ruler. She circled the Mojave, went through Tehachapi, but bypassed Death Valley, certain any place named for Death was nowhere she wanted to be.

Some trucks passing her did 100 mph, their blowback wobbling Lilith at her maximum speed of 90; she drafted the big rigs when she could, redlining Lilith by being sucked along the cone of less resistance as a truck punched a tunnel through air. A few drivers gave her a thumbs up when they saw her in their side view. If they guessed she was a woman, they sounded their horns, but if they slowed to waggle their tongues at her, she flipped them her middle finger, gunned Lilith and passed any stupid bastard who believed that having testicles might persuade some random woman in black leather to spend time with them. Twice, when that happened, they'd put the hammer down speed to pass her again, slow, and she'd slow until she was confident Lilith could breeze by the slowing truck, a kind of game and road-dance she actually enjoyed. Big Bill was dangerous because he had been a meth freak and she had been trapped in his cab; as long as she was aboard Lilith, she was beyond danger.

As a phony college girl in Illinois, at Web's and Celeste's urging, she had read Mao. He wrote, *Power comes through the barrel of a gun.* Mao was not stupid, either. She had to travel a larger highway, but found a gun shop north of Fresno and south of Berenda, a place the sun could kill and the dust could choke, though pipeline water and constant sunshine made the deserts of southern California into Eden. The grapey aroma of vineyards and sweet jacaranda surrounded her. She set Lilith's kickstand, balanced her helmet on the seat, and went into the gun shop. Evaporating perspiration raised the hairs on the back of her neck.

She lingered over a glass counter in the dark shop's rear. The store owner, a short bald man whose narrowed eyes gave him the look of a man calculating his chances to beat the Devil, eyed her up, down, and up again. Her heavy leather jacket flopped over the counter. His eyes raked her again, from forehead to feet and up again, but this time stopped where her nipples puckered beneath her sleeveless T-shirt. She was visualizing how if he came within arm's length she would cut his throat with her Piranha knife.

"How about a .38, little lady? Five shots in the cylinder, light-weight, it's ideal for personal protection. Fits in your purse."

"Do you mind if I smoke?"

"Don't care if you burn."

Buckles smiled as if she thought him clever. She took her time unrolling her Winstons from her sleeve. When the salesman produced a lighted match, she gripped his wrist and lit up. A physical touch could yield a discount because he was the kind of asshole who believed a touch of hands was foreplay. A gun to fit in her purse? Purse? What fucking purse was that? Buckles had not carried a purse since she could not remember when.

She pointed wordlessly at a display of Berettas lying flat in a glass case.

"That's not cheap," the gunsmith said. She exhaled smoke. Grandma's money gave a woman certain confidence. "That's the Modello 952, a fine pistol, but a lot of gun for a little lady."

She drew on her cigarette again and thought of how a little lady might instead of cutting his throat gut him. "Tell me about the gun."

"That pistol takes 9-millimeter ammo, sweetie. Eight in the clip and one in the chamber. Quite a wallop. It will stop a charging rhino if you hit it between the eyes, and slow it down if you hit it anywhere else. The kick might set you back on that pretty derriere, especially if you set it to rapid fire. See this button on the side? That's not a safety; it selects how the gun will fire. It will empty the clip before you can blink." He grinned and moistened his lips.

After his teeth shattered, she'd kick splinters of enamel down the softer tissue of his bleeding throat, but she grinned back. Grandma had taught her well. He was now her mark.

In the abbreviated firing range in the shop basement, silhouette targets were clipped to a pulley. She held the pistol with two hands while a second, younger store employee taught her the gun's operation. His arms went around her, a forearm brushing against her chest only slightly more than his hands needed to. Her third shot put a hole through the silhouette's heart; a fourth shot went through its head.

"You're a natural," he said.

She pretended to gush at the compliment, put in a fresh clip, and set the gun on rapid fire. With a single squeeze of the trigger, the target was shredded in two breaths.

This was the gun she'd need.

"Most people think that's a problem," the young clerk said. "Don't tell Ed upstairs I said so, but it's impossible to fire short bursts."

"I like it just fine," she said.

Upstairs, the shop owner said to make the purchase she'd need an ID. When he saw the hundred she peeled off the roll of bills she took from her pocket, and added two more than the price of the gun, he forgot any laws. He gave her three empty magazines and two boxes of ammo when she peeled off a fifty and snapped her red rubber band back into place. The bank was closed.

"Are we good?" she asked the gun dealer whose eyes drifted again to her chest.

"I already forgot you were here. What did you say your name was?"

Buckles did not answer him. Blue eyes, tits, and a roll of cash could take a woman most anywhere.

With the automatic tucked into her belt at the small of her back, her knife still hidden a her waist in front, she shrugged into her leather jacket, snapped the chest flap to its grommet across her collarbone, and steered the BMW further down the road. At a second gun shop, she picked up a cleaning kit that included an instructive pamphlet, a bore-brush, a can of gun oil, a gun rag, and two more boxes of 9 mm ammo. In the shadow of a billboard just out of town she guzzled water from a half-gallon jug and loaded all three spare magazines.

She had enough firepower to take out an Oakland SWAT team.

She left the paved highways and headed east and north over un-paved dirt through groves of pecans, walnuts, cherries, and peaches. As long as enough water could be stolen for irrigation, anything that grew could be coaxed from California dirt. She shot at cans and rocks. Whenever her target flew into the air three times, she backed up ten feet. Her marksmanship improved; eventually she could hit anything within forty feet with the gun in either hand. More distance than that, she'd want a sniper's rifle, but while she toyed with that notion, while a telescopic site with hairline cross-hairs intrigued her, she decided she could never be an assassin at a distance. Her style would be to blast and blast and blast. Maybe she'd buy a second automatic, either another kind of Beretta or a Glock. Browning made a nice gun, but they had a nasty reputation for jamming. With the Feds on her tail, two pistols might get her out of a tight spot.

That night, and the night after that, she squatted at her small fire to finish her days by running her brass bore brush and an oiled cotton pad through the muzzle. Cleaning the Modello proved more soothing than applying moisturizing cream, though cleaning the Modello had the added benefit of allowing her to visualize putting a hole in Big Bill's forehead to see how bits of his skull and brain matter might drip down his window, no different than the juice of fat, giant Ohio bugs that had smeared their greasy yellow lives on *Donna May*'s windshield. Armed with a rapid-fire pistol, Big Bill's Little Cherry Lollipop could have left his dead ass where the crows could find it.

But the closer she drew to San Francisco, the more a final bit of business demanded attention. It might have been the sun, being part of startling beauty of the stark Southwest, or Lilith's incessant thrumming between her legs; or maybe it was something as simple as her drinking pure water and eating simple food, but her hormones were rousing. She took being horny as a sign of health, though she'd believed she was done with all that.

All that, however, was not done with her.

She'd awaken from vivid dreams with a phantom lover's arms around her. In that short interval when she was neither awake nor asleep, her mind and body were in his probing hands, his lips moving on her with perfect pleasure. The sensations stayed with her for miles after she was awake. However pleasant, being rangy as a feral cat was distracting.

With her gun in her belt tucked tightly against the small of her back under her leather jacket, Buckles felt safe enough to stop at a dark no-name roadhouse, a gray wooden shack behind a row of dirt and barrel cactus. She left her helmet balanced on the bike's saddle to bake in the sun and told herself she was thirsty. Her eyes ached from distance and dust.

The bartender, a young woman with lusterless dark hair and bad skin, did not trouble Buckles for evidence of her age. Buckles quietly smoothed a ten onto the polished bar and then, with one Doc Martens boot on a brass foot rail, told the bartender she'd need tequila and a PBR. On the bar was a plate of salt and slices of lime. Buckles took what she needed. The tequila ignited her blood; the beer slaked her throat. When the bartender lifted her eyes expectantly, Buckles gestured that she do it again. Buckles prepared the lime and salt on her fist, slammed back the second tequila, felt fire in her blood, gulped the beer, then lighted a cigarette before she turned to inspect the room with her elbow on the bar. She walked real slow to feed a dime to the jukebox where among the usual shit by Patsy Cline or Tammy Wynette she found CCR's *Fortunate Son*. She bent over the clear plastic of the jukebox, her ass so high she may as well have pinned a target on it.

She was playing so hard at being the badass slut, she hardly knew if she was still Buckles, the weekend preppie teenage hippie who visited headshops in Greenwich Village to score some weed before a retreat to safety on a commuter railroad to Scarsdale. The tequila obligingly numbed her upper lip while her eyes came to rest on the seat of a pair of very loose jeans on the very bony hips of what might have been a cowboy bent over one of the three pool tables in the darkest recess of the L-shaped bar, though he was more likely the farm boy who drove the weathered Ford pickup at the front door.

He was playing pool alone. Buckles found three quarters and snapped them flat on the game table's edge, the signal she'd learned a million years ago in Champaign that meant she wanted the table next, and since there were no players at either of the two vacant tables could mean only that she was spoiling for a game with him. He could not have been 26. The crown of his straw hat was stoved in, he needed to shave, and his dust-covered boots were steel-toe Red Wings. His checkered blue shirt had two pockets; the left held a drawstring pouch of flake tobacco, the right a pack of rolling paper.

The 8-Ball fell hard; then he banked the 3 to a side pocket to clear the worn green felt. He lifted his eyes to grin at her. His blue eyes were deep as her own, blue as the Pacific she had yet to see. His teeth were even as tile but not as white. When she saw his teeth she knew the tequila had delivered the courage she'd want to fuck him blind and leave him for dead, and she was not troubled that Bobby—he said his name was Bobby—seemed to assume that was coming, but he was not rushing anything, taking the time to curl himself around her to show her how her fingers could hold the cue stick steady, and that the key to shooting pool was to take a long, slow, even, level stroke. She hoped he did not fuck that way. She pretended to know nothing so Bobby had to curl his lean body and arms close around her. He smelled like a working man, tobacco, sweat, but nothing unclean. She pretended not to notice his erection through the two layers of denim that were their jeans, though she did wiggle against him.

It was dusk when he asked if she would like to share some of the good Hawaiian weed he kept in his truck's bay. "That your bike?" he asked outside, and she said it was. "That's a lot of bike for a little lady."

"I'm a lot of lady." She almost smiled, but she did allow her tongue to moisten her lips. They'd have to move quickly. Alcohol-courage could drain away as quickly as it rose.

The day had cooled. Gray storm clouds were thickening, water sucked from the earth for a brief desert storm. "Gully-washer coming," he remarked.

His big hands circled her waist as, easy as you please, he lifted her onto the flatbed. She kissed his lips and he kissed her throat and tongued her ear while the light grew eerie-dim, nothing like the greenish light of a Midwestern tornado that she hoped to never see again, but nevertheless light that held the certainty of no-nonsense weather. The flatbed smelled pleasant. "Peaches mostly," he said. He joked that they were lucky he did not haul manure. They lay down and shared a joint, then squeezed and touched and kissed, then probed and stroked and gripped. Though his skin was smooth, the muscles beneath were iron. Her nameless need moved here to nameless urgency. *It may as well be him as any other.*

Fat slow raindrops fell, then thickened and fell faster. Bobby snapped a canvas tarp to the sides of the truck that protected them in the bay in a space only three feet deep. Rain drummed the tarp over them, deafening. Somehow her jeans were undone and off. The vice of her thighs clenched his hips while his tongue traced lines of fire across her throat and belly, all while cold, fat rain drummed faster and faster on the canvas over them. His breath rasped and she could not tell if the pulse she felt was her surging blood or his. Her body found the rhythms it needed as all troubles and doubts and fear left her, and this Bobby became an unassuming sweet boy whose hands roamed over her, his tongue in her, his teeth closing hard enough on her but never harder than that while her fingertips ran over his damp scalp and down his back to grip the knots of his behind. Her hips and pelvis moved in ways she never suspected they could, not even in her dreams. Her toes clenched; her eyes squeezed shut.

She reclaimed what Big Bill had stolen.

She grinned wickedly to recall how unseen she'd moved her gun under her jacket while he fumbled with a condom, and when it was over, she told him she'd follow his truck to where he lived so they could do it again, do it right, do it until morning, do it with all their clothes off instead of an awkward tangle, and take it slow and easy and then hard and fast and then slow and easy again, but once they were moving she asked Lilith for the speed she needed to pass the Ford until her mirrors showed only black night. She grinned to think how Bobby would try to keep up until he realized the best sex of his life was beyond the Ford's headlights.

After an hour of running in the dark, the desert night went cold because of the passing storm. Still a little drunk, she forgave herself, and swore to never again drink tequila. She could not remember if she'd given him a name to know her by. It was simple. A girl could be fucked, could fuck, or could make love. Buckles would never again be fucked, but the terror and doubts of fucking had been vanquished. Should she ever find someone worth her true heart, she was equipped to make love. The knowledge reassured her, though the last thing she needed was to become enamored of a steady diet of dick. Inevitably she'd come across some asshole who believed that if he had it once, he owned it. Abigail "Buckles" Sinclair had been fucked and would never be fucked again, but while she might wish to get it on from time to time, her heart and mind would forever stay her own.

Lilith, the Lilith of legend, was right. Sex was a mess. Trying to visualize what she and Bobby must have looked like made her nearly swerve off the road, giddy.

Buckles twisted the throttle. The BMW's front wheel popped two feet off the ground as the rpms rose, the soul of the BMW surging with the soul of its rider. Her unfastened leather jacket fluttered like batwings. As night flowed over her chest and belly, it seemed to be the last ash residue of her past blowing free into the desert night.

Buckles ran out of continent where the desert ended on the eastern edge of a northbound road and the western edge of the road met gray surf. Straddling Lilith, she felt the immensity of America pressing at her back. The sun struggled to rise over the horizon behind her. She dismounted to walk toward the murmuring surf, sat on dirt to pull off her Doc Martens, stood once more to shed her clothing into a puddle of worn black leather and softer cotton. The organic smell of the morning sea settled over her as she stepped over a line of seaweed left by a diminishing tide. Cold water cramped her feet, water colder than she thought it would be. She walked forward until the water was at her knees, then went forward again until it topped her thighs, then forward again as the water rose to her waist and she dove forward through a gentle swell to stand on the last shelf of land where her head could stay above the surface. She plunged through a new swell, surfaced, and her feet found no bottom. She kicked out, strong and certain. When she turned about, the sun was half a hand's width over the land. Lilith's long shadow reached her, and she swam back to lie beside her machine.

When her eyes opened, an old woman sat on a large rock beside Buckles' clothing. "Quite a show, young lady," she said. "Quite a show." Seawater had pooled around Buckles' shoulders, back, hips and legs. "Do you feel better now?"

"It's good to see you, Grandma. You are supposed to be dead, but here you are again."

"Dead as a doornail."

"That water was awful cold."

"A cold sea purifies better than fire."

"I feel burned through."

"You're as naked as a jaybird, asleep on brown sand, chatting with a ghost, and while I am sure the sun feels good, you need to open your eyes and be on your way. What if John Law comes along?"

"Just another minute," she said. "Just one more minute. Will you stay if I wake up?"

Her eyes opened. Grandma's cackling laugh lingered like seafoam on the shore.

Lilith's slow roll down Haight Street passed rheumy-eyed kids who slept in parks or sprawled across the back seats of abandoned cars after wearying days of selling themselves for brown rice and watery soup. Celeste had advised her to avoid San Francisco, and now Buckles saw why. At the sound of the BMW, a few mustered enough strength to shuffle into the street to beg, but when they saw Buckles' black leather jacket they backed off. Over much of western America, biker criminals trafficked speed, smack, and girls. The Aquarian Age delivered a perfumed tide of Flower Children to the City by the Bay; as the tide receded it left in its wake addiction, scabies, lice, herpes, chlamydia, gonorrhea, syphilis, blindness, sterility, and death.

The Summer of Love had ended before it began because America would rather fuck its children than feed them.

Buckles heeded wise Celeste's advice. She headed across the Bay Bridge to Oakland, an unrelenting city not much more than a waterfront, bars, and naval shipping. San Francisco chewed up hippies; Oakland shit them out.

She found a partly furnished second-story room in an Oakland building that looked like a failed layer cake. It faced Alameda. Most of the furniture was blotted with cigarette burns. The hallway was dark, the stairs creaky. The salty ocean air reeked of diesel. It suited her.

Buckles needed to sell the smallest of Grandma's remaining diamonds. So there could be no suspicion she might be a thief, she dressed in a girlie-girl dress she bought in a consignment shop, took BART into the city, and, still a natural grifter, squeezed out tears to tell a tale about how her fiancée stepped on a landmine in the DMZ. His family knew nothing about her; she was desperate, alone, and needed kindness. A respectable Brannan St. jeweler took one look at the untraceable stone and like any less-respectable fence offered her one third of what the stone was worth. She held out, inflicted her tale of woe on two more jewelers and settled for enough cash to pay her rent for most of a year even if she did nothing else. Home in Oakland, she balled up the pantyhose and put it in the back of the apartment's sole closet. She stole some California license plates and then garaged Lilith and her new tags nearby.

Finding the Revolution or Celeste's Chicago friend, Bernardine Dohrn, was not easy. She fantasized mustering comrades to spring Pussy free from under the tons of concrete the Feds must have piled on him, but there was no way she could lift that weight alone.

Flyers announcing community activity were stapled to telephone poles near churches and schools. For Pussy's sake, she attended several to drop Celeste's name at meetings devoted to better daycare or developing job skills for mothers who had none. At one meeting in a church basement clouded by cigarette smoke, she identified Celeste as a Black woman she knew back east. Neighborhood activists stared at her blankly. Revolution was more local than the weather. Many assumed she was a lesbian on the make. Buckles felt like the Scarsdale-cracker who believed all Black people knew each other.

On the way out of one meeting, a white woman took her elbow. They went for peppermint tea.

"Celeste. Celeste from Nebraska?"

"No. Wisconsin," Buckles said. "Said she knew Bernardine Dohrn in Chicago."

"Red hair, right?"

"No. My Celeste is a Black woman. A big girl. I am Flo, by the way."

The two women shook hands. "Can't help you, sister. Never heard of her."

Before they went their separate ways, they chatted about one thing and another, never exchanging contact information.

But one month later, though Buckles could not find the Revolution, the Revolution found her.

A manila envelope appeared under her apartment door. The small hairs on her neck stood. How had they figured out where she lived? A check of her bona fides must have traveled from the Peppermint Tea Lady, to Dohrn, to Celeste, who must have let it be known her old comrade, Flo, left an FBI pig in an alley broken and chained to a rusted Edsel. Though Celeste had never trusted Flo's Illinois identity, Celeste must have vouched for her favorite ofay, even though her ofay had taken Lilith. No other explanation for the envelope's appearance seemed possible.

Flo was reborn as Abigail Carpenter, the pride of Fair Oaks, Sacramento County, California, U.S.A., now down a little on her luck. She'd must have once told Celeste her real first name: how else could they have known she'd feel easy about the dorky *Abigail?* She had a fake high school diploma from Bella Vista High, class of 1966. Abigail had been a cheerleader for the Bella Vista Broncos. A forged birth certificate had been wrinkled soft and stained with Lipton tea to appear old. Her favorite teacher had been one Iris Murphy, a real-life retired social studies teacher who as part of the Movement would swear to recalling Abigail and her eleventh-grade term paper about the Napoleonic Code. Miss Murphy was disappointed that her favorite student had not gone to UCLA, but understood how an unplanned pregnancy had turned Abigail's life inside-out. Abigail Carpenter lost her baby to a sad miscarriage the summer after graduation, shortly before her parents move to Bend, Oregon. A pencil note in the envelope instructed Buckles to memorize the street names on a map of Fair Oaks until she could direct a stranger to the Dairy Queen. The driver's license indicated she was qualified to ride a motorcycle. A bit of notebook paper ripped from a spiral-bound pad read MEMORIZE AND BURN.

Celeste's name had been worth more than Grandma's diamonds.

But diamonds could not last forever. For wages and to seem ordinary, she packed groceries. It was not like selling out: they paid exploitive cash wages to employees with no social security numbers and asked no questions, but she was allowed to take sacks of unspoiled milk and cheese near expiration with her. Her coworkers who spoke some English were nice enough if not terribly bright, taking a break from the tougher gig of panhandling. A few boys she came to know talked surfing, fast cars, and easy girls. They believed The Beach Boys were keys to a unique California philosophy.

Buckles periodically purchased weed from the acne-ridden dork-wad who worked with her behind the grocery's deli-counter. They all wore hairnets. He believed no one noticed he stroked himself every time a high school girl ordered a sandwich. She gave him a plastic canister of *Phisohex,* but he said thanks and did not get the insult. She wondered if he collected *Playboy* centerfolds.

Reborn as Abigail Carpenter, Buckles moved to a second furnished room and changed jobs so not even the invisible army that invented Abigail Carpenter knew where she was. She stored her unloaded Modello in a shoe box beside the balled pantyhose at the rear of her closet. Like Buckles, the gun rested ready, but unused.

Abigail Carpenter, the once knocked-up cheerleader, worked 25 hours each week as a clerk in a headshop. A headshop in Alameda was no different from a headshop in Greenwich Village—crystals, dayglow, dashikis, essential oils, and joss sticks. The aroma of frangipani left her mildly nauseated by day's end. The clean-cut kids who came in trying to score weed made her smile; in New York, she'd been that kid.

She kept her hair short, but allowed the yellow to return. She covered her head with a knit seaman's watch cap and purchased a woolen Navy surplus coat, the warmest garment she'd ever owned. She evened her hair until it looked feathered rather than a chop job hastily administered by a desperado fleeing across the Mississippi into Missouri. Her blonde hair grew in more dull than it had been. That did not trouble her: her straw-yellow hair had never brought her anything but trouble.

From time to time she followed Otis Redding's advice, sitting in the morning sun on the dock on the bay smoking a joint to cultivate a mellow buzz. These were not scrawny New York joints that could not get a ferret high; these were bombers that could lay waste whole Mexican villages. Buckles also wore a seaman's cabled sweater with a rolled collar that came to her chin beneath her black leather motorcycle jacket or under her Navy peacoat. It was so goddam cold in sunny California that the skin over her ribs quivered and jumped. Her nose dripped like a junkie's. Navy ships rolled in and Buckles watched them roll away again. Only an occasional passing prick noticed Buckles was a woman, and if he said something smartass she did not so much as shift her blue eyes in his direction but did raise her middle finger. When one overconfident asshole came within ten feet of her, without a word she showed him her knife. He turned away, remembering he had other plans.

Every girl in America needed the gift of a combat blade at her Sweet Sixteen. Fuck that, when the girl reached twelve. This was the Land of the Free and the Home of the Brave, where girls either grew up fast or they did not grow up at all.

In Otis's honor, Buckles mused on how an aircraft carrier might be blown up with common kitchen chemicals. All right, if not a big honkin' aircraft carrier, a least a submarine. An itty-bitty one. Did not even have to be nuclear as long as she could have the ship do a belly roll to put its dripping screws in the air like the legs of a dead dog. She'd like to see that, she would.

Though Lilith was garaged with stolen plates, Buckles was unable to resist going on two-wheeled day daytrips. Even then, Buckles could never summon the will to go north, not even to explore Abigail Carpenter's hometown of Sacramento. Grandma's treasure might be buried at Lake Tahoe, but the map might be another of Grandma's delusional dreams. True enough, the black plastic sunglasses held genuine diamonds, so it was a fair bet the lockbox existed, but Grandma also claimed to have crossed the Atlantic hustling backgammon when she slept with Omar Sharif who had not yet been born.

The Patty Hearst story puzzled her; the Charles Manson family killings more so. Buckles found no source she trusted. *The Berkeley Barb* was crazier than *The Village Voice,* but neither was reliable as Grandma Dot, and Grandma Dot regularly modified reality. Everyone knew stuff Buckles did not because Buckles owned no television and spoke only to strangers she hardly knew. The whispered buzz in dive bars and greasy spoons started with an exchange of information, but usually ended with a beery offer for a quick fuck. She turned them down. No one was even close to being as sweet as Bobby, the farm boy she'd screwed blind in his Ford pickup smelling of peaches.

Still, no matter where she was, Buckles read books. She'd spent hours in small-town libraries, her only rule being that no matter how much she liked what she read, she would not steal from a library, a rule that did not extend to bookstores or college libraries. She'd once lingered at some forgotten town to finish *The Grapes of Wrath*. The town's name was long gone from memory; the journey of the Joad family stayed with her forever.

She discovered City Lights, a downtown San Francisco bookstore that reeked of cinnamon and strong coffee and unwashed poets. The place was holy. She sat on the floor and, recalling Kafka's *The Metamorphosis* from her days in Champaign, she read *The Trial*, a book with wisdom enough to prove that punishment and guilt had nothing to do with each other.

She paid real cash money to buy and tape a green and purple blacklight poster of Che Guevara to her wall. Che also rode a motorcycle, which figured and, in some stoner way, explained so much. When she saw how stupid an unlit poster was, she liberated a blacklight from the headshop where she worked. Stoned enough, mouth salivating over the delicious words, she chanted Ginsberg's *Howl* aloud to Che over her creaky bed. She slept under Che's glowing blacklight eyes, aroused as a novice in a convent clutching her crucifix beneath the Sacred Heart of Jesus.

Che inspired her.

On a misty morning before dawn, Buckles apologized to Lilith for her neglect and liberated the motorcycle from its storage space. She puddled Lilith's tarp on the floor, dusted off her helmet, tugged her black leather gloves tight onto her hands, flipped her tunic collar high, and strapped on her leggings for what she intended would be a short ride. Lilith had the power to clarify her mind; Lilith who'd argued with God.

The BMW wove through traffic that seemed motionless, cars carrying ordinary citizens in mobile cages. The further Lilith carried her from the Bay area, the easier it was to let the throttle full out. It was sweet to once again be crossing the scrub desert. All right, she'd never find the Movement, and, all right, she'd never free Pussy, and all right, the war in Asia would go on forever, and, all right, the Feebs would run her down until she fell dead of exhaustion, and, yes, all right, all right, all right, Big Bill and the legions of dick-swingers preying on women needed to be brought to accounts, but, all right, all right, all right, she needed to seize control of herself and the situation.

At a greasy diner south of Salinas she ordered ham and eggs over-easy, sipped black coffee mean as her acidic mood, and smoked two cigarettes. The plate glass window framed an empty landscape. She considered her alternatives and concluded she had to blow some shit up.

She ground the second cigarette out into the runny egg yolk thickening on her plate and left a dollar on her table.

Pipe bombs required a workshop she did not have. Pipe bombs also frightened her, but not so much that she would not do what Che had requested of her in a dream. But how? One mistake with a pipe bomb and she'd be blind or lose a hand. There were chemicals she'd heard of, but coming by them was complicated and would leave a paper trail that led to her. What could she easily obtain that could reliably explode? If she'd ever found the Revolution, she could have asked someone. Alone, she'd have to figure out the smallest detail. Che would be her guide.

Outside the Salinas diner, she took several Mae West Coca-Cola bottles from a wooden rack that leaned against a stucco wall beside a vending machine. The empties clinked in Lilith's saddle bags. At a cove near Carmel by the Sea where wave after wave broke on the black rocks at the base of a mild cliff, the gray Pacific charged the shore, churned to green foam, receded, and charged the cliff again. Out to sea, the rising sun hammered the gray sea into uneasy copper. Several hundred yards to her right, surfers in black wetsuits paddled out, waited, bobbed on water, called to each other, dove, swam, caught mild waves, and paddled out again.

The grip on a Coke bottle's neck was good; the size was right, but the green glass was too thick. She threw it, but could not get a bottle to shatter. If all she planned was to shatter a plate glass window, they were perfect, but Buckles had more in mind.

The surfers had left empty wine bottles at the base of the cliff, cheap fruity stuff once sealed by screw tops. Buckles threw several in a high arc over the black rocks. They fell and shattered with a satisfying sound. She dipped one end of Lilith's rubber siphon into the motorcycle's gas tank, then, careful to inhale none of the fuel, she sucked on the siphon's other end. A cup's worth of gasoline flowed into what had been a bottle of Boone's Farm Apple. But when it shattered on the rocks, all she had was a greasy smudge that the ocean quickly washed clean.

She felt like a fool. Gasoline required ignition. She'd need flame.

Like a Vietnamese peasant squatting on the road's sandy shoulder, feet flat, knees before her face, she gave the matter more thought. Surfers bobbed on the incoming tide. She envied them. What could it be like to be at one with the wind and water and float weightless? She walked the beach as the puzzle's answer revealed itself. Fire and fuel had to meet on impact, so the ignition, fuel, and bottle had to be a single object. She found another empty bottle.

A flaming rag soaked in gasoline stuffed into the bottle's neck would do nicely. She felt the heft of the wine bottle. She tore a two-inch wide ribbon from the waistline of her T-shirt and stuffed it into the neck of the bottle, but even before she lifted the firebomb over her head she realized that with a gasoline-soaked flaming rag, a bottle held overhead could be relied on to eventually spill. It would surely spill on her. She'd torch herself before she torched her target. Buckles was no Buddhist monk making a statement. She was working at becoming Death itself.

She poked around Lilith's black saddle bag. Beside an Allen wrench and a tire gauge, she found a box of tampons she must have thrown in there, what, more than a year ago? Perfect size, perfect shape, perfectly absorbent, perfectly flammable. Equipping a Molotov cocktail with a flaming tampon as her personal blow against the Empire also had symbolic appeal.

Her first successful firebomb went into the woodie the surfers bobbing on the waves had parked at the end of the cliff road. The car had no windshield or glass, to accommodate their long surfboards. There wasn't a woman among them, so fuck them. These were the future business executives who expected to own the System, the kind of boys who listened to The Beach Boys and played cheap guitars at bonfire parties so they could fuck nice girls who wanted to fuck nice boys, drop a litter of nice children and then grow old in Newport Beach before they were nicely dead.

If any of the floating surfers had looked up, they'd have seen a black-clad motorcyclist hurl a bottle that spun like a flaming pinwheel. Her bomb bloomed into a burning rose that in the car licked itself into a frenzy. God's own finger, a column of black smoke, curled to the sky as Lilith and Buckles sped away.

She went through San Francisco and discovered *The Anarchist's Cookbook* at City Lights. She even paid for it. This was no time to be busted for shoplifting. William Powell, the author, gave up the real goods. She'd gotten all of it, but Powell added a finesse she never would have come across on her own. A fire bomb became meaner if Styrofoam was introduced to the fuel. It dissolved to a syrupy, flammable paste in gasoline. The homemade napalm was hard to extinguish. She felt like a fool at not having found the book before she went hurling Coca-Cola bottles, but then again, even if she had been reinventing the wheel, she trusted her own results far more.

A day more passed while she reflected on how the dick-slingers had driven her from Peace and Love Flower Child to Revolutionary to a blooming Anarchist. The dick-slingers squeezed power in their steel death grip. The so-called System was a fairytale invented by men to mindfuck women into spreading their legs for an endless parade of power-mad rapists.

Shit had to change.

If she did not prevail, at the very least she would burn the System to the ground and then blow up the ashes. Her weapons were powerful—stealth, cunning, silence, and the unequivocal certainty that no matter what surrounded her, she would forever be alone.

She found an engraved Zippo in an Oakland pawn shop. The nickel finish on one side held the eagle, globe, and anchor; on the other side was etched, *Yea, though I walk through the valley of the shadow of death I will fear no Evil, for I am the meanest motherfucker in the valley.* No wind could blow that flame out. She wondered if the Marine who'd owned it pacified villages by setting fire to thatch huts, but more likely he'd been on shore leave and drunk if not broke. She practiced flicking the top and striking the flint one-handed. With a tampon-stoppered bottle braced between her legs, she could light a bomb with one hand while Lilith kept her moving. The bike's speed gave every thrown bottle plenty of heft for impact. Buckles might throw like a girl, but astride Lilith she'd be lethal.

Buckles went out once more, this time circling Lilith north. Fresh out of surfer-wagons, she tested herself by igniting and hurling a firebomb from the moving bike. Once the bomb left her, tumbling end over end through the air, she twisted the throttle and was back up to sixty even before flame flowed across the highway behind her.

Buckles stowed three capped wine bottles of gasoline wrapped in thick layers of newspaper in Lilith's right saddlebag beside her store of tampons.

The very next day, three mailboxes in Oakland mysteriously burned. Though she might never find the Revolution, it had found her. At least she was ready.

Tampax joined the Revolution.

Bobby Seale, Huey Newton, and Eldridge Cleaver, the core of the Black Panther Party, were the real deal in Oakland. Feeling the Power's heat, Cleaver, the Minister of Information, retreated to Algeria to await the inevitable second American Revolution. A white woman who could not be totally trusted, Buckles was content to serve breakfast to children in DeFremery Park. It was a revolutionary act. Food came from local storekeepers who had been persuaded to support the community that supported their stores. Shop windows stayed intact. Buckles felt good doing her part in a world movement that extended to northern Africa. Revolution was that simple.

By not shaving her armpits and legs, she was becoming a blond gorilla, but at least she was no longer the weekend Greenwich Village hippie-kid who fled her corrupt ticky-tacky life in a ticky-tacky suburb. She smelled like a woman, not a bowl of potpourri in her mother's guest toilet.

Peace, love, flower-power, bombs, feed the poor, and keep handy a rapid-fire 9 mm automatic pistol. The path to a better world lay open before her.

But months stretched to years. Buckles drifted, disconnected.

Freddie, the headshop owner who hired her, was impressed by any-one who could make change, as this was a rare virtue in his circles. He bored her with his story, having started out as a runny-nosed street-freak with ambition and a tobacco-stained beard who had claimed as his own a patch of sunlight on a sidewalk by a BART station where he panhandle the quarters that went into his filthy paper coffee cup. His hands quavered like an addict's, but his sole addiction was to money. He eventually collected sufficient quarters for a run to Tijuana in a borrowed black Ford Galaxie that burned so much oil he needed to add a quart every four hours, about half the time it took to get to Mexico. He smeared fresh dog shit over the spare tire, believing dogs finding pungent dog shit on a spare excited only the dogs, but seldom interested border guards unwill-ing to investigate damp dog shit. Freddie returned to Oakland with some mediocre weed in the spare tire's wheel well. He sold most, smoked some, and repeated the trip when the spirit moved him. Eventually he moved enough weight to afford his first Oakland storefront, a space off a main drag and up an alley that was the cor-nerstone of his real estate empire.

A late sleeper, Freddie hired a series of wall-eyed hippies to open the store for him at the crack of noon, the latest of whom was Buckles.

Freddie kept the headshop's money in the Dutch Masters cigar box he stowed under the counter. Buckles counted the cash on hand as soon as she opened and checked it against the note Freddie left her when he closed. Usually, the numbers matched. After verifying Freddie's money, she brewed a pot of espresso on a hot plate on the counter, free for anyone willing to risk the diseases sure to linger on any of the three ceramic cups. Now and then, as a gesture to public health, she rinsed the cups. Like the headshops of Greenwich Village, the store sold blacklight posters, ornate dope pipes, lava lamps, bongs, crystals, fancy roach clips, wiseass lapel buttons, frangipani oil, tarot decks, body lubricants, and anything else that was not weed, mostly to college boys and high school girls, each of whom assumed marijuana was for sale if they knew the right people. Not even Freddie was stupid enough to sell weed that way. Sailors on shore leave had better dope from Vietnam or Hawaii. Most of her customers were underage teenagers stocking up on lilac lubricant.

Buckles worked twenty-five hours each week. Freddie showed up more or less at six. Once Buckles made it plain that no matter how dull life might become she was not going to screw him to hold a job that paid $2 per hour, he let her be. Buckles lifted the rattling iron grate over the storefront glass and unlocked the shackle of the big Master padlock with the key Freddie left on doorframe's lip; it was the first place anyone would look, but Freddie was Freddie and Freddie was the boss. He assumed that by day's end Buckles' fingers dipped into the till, and he was right, but petty theft hardly rose to the level of crime in Oakland.

When the storefront beside the headshop was occupied by someone new, Buckles allowed herself to make a friend. A hand-lettered sign with random triangles, a spiral, and what Buckles supposed might be palm trees around a desert oasis was hoisted over the door, *Ishtar's Readings*. Ishtar turned out to be a stoner who wandered into the no-name headshop to offer the store her dreamcatchers. She stayed for the free espresso. Her dreamcatchers were raggedy topaz skeins of yarn wound in distorted rectangles on a frame of two crossed dirty sticks knotted together by coarse twine. Buckles hung a dreamcatcher on a wall near the cash register where it caught more dust than dreams.

Ishtar returned for more free espresso and left with a crystal ball, a tarot deck, and a promise to pay eventually. Since Freddie kept no inventory, Buckles saw no harm in letting her take whatever she wanted, When Ishtar confessed to being a lesbian, she waited for Buckles to express interest, and when Buckles remained impassive Ishtar shrugged and took her usual place on a brown Naugahyde director's chair. Buckles did not care if the woman slept with Paddy's pet pig. She was glad for her company, and giving away Freddie's goods did not seem a high price to pay.

Ishtar was busty, short, had waxy bad skin, stringy unwashed hair, and mud-brown eyes that fixed on something far off no one else could see. Big as Mama Cass, and as likely to choke to death on a tuna sandwich, Ishtar was smart but oddly vulnerable, a combination that could never sustain the ruthlessness a revolutionary required. Ishtar could never be a comrade, but offer her a hit of Freddie's dope and Ishtar would bang a platoon of Marines, all at once or one at a time, their choice. So while Buckles missed Celeste's big laugh and her steadying presence, Ishtar was the best Oakland could offer her as a comrade. If Celeste ever appeared in the Oakland headshop, she would pop Ishtar in the nose, call her an idiot motherfucker, and ask why white girls had to be so damn white.

One drizzly day, Buckles asked how Ishtar managed without earning money. The dreamcatchers were hardly a hot item, and few people entered Ishtar's small shop for readings. Either no one cared about their futures or the dust and the store's arid interior kept customers away.

"I grew up on a lakefront in Connecticut," Ishtar said as she peeled a curl of lemon rind into a blue-and-white cracked demitasse cup that also held a stick of crystalized sugar. "I get some family support, still. But there are expectations, which I try hard not to fill. We had a dock, a rowboat, and trees that changed color in fall. I lost my cherry in that rowboat. You have no idea how hard it is to grow up with money."

"I can't imagine," Buckles said, recollecting her idle summer days swimming laps topless in the Sinclair's isolated backyard pool.

Ishtar lit a fresh joint and leaned forward. "I could read your palm, if you want."

"That's a scam."

"No shit? And here I thought I was gifted with vision. But accuracy is not the point. It's fun. I could tell you all about the mysterious lover who is coming into your life or how you will be wealthy someday."

The choices seemed bleak. "I'll pass."

The track marks ulcerating at Ishtar's forearm were the evidence of how she skin-popped smack now and again. Buckles waved the joint away. She seldom smoked weed unless she was alone. Weed was good for fucking and for talk, two activities Buckles did not trust herself to do safely. It would be too easy to say the wrong thing to the wrong person, and the next thing she'd know a pack of rabid jackal Feebs would be at her ass. What if she blabbed information to some lover to come with her to see Grandma's treasure map?

But she was not chaste, either. Buckles held her left knee firmly in contact with her right knee as long as she was able, a few times lapsing for one-night stands with servicemen on shore leave. The war supplied her with a steady supply of lovers far from home with toned bodies, nice shoulders, stamina, and better weed than any Buckles could supply. If they offered the crazy hippie with black-light posters and candles money, she never accepted it. They'd share cigarettes to recuperate enough for a second round of love. Buckles found Grandma's rule to hold true: people were always eager to tell their own story. Her lovers enjoyed that as much as screwing, some-times more. As an added benefit, the second time they got it on was usually better and less awkward. A third hookup was possible, but after that as a rule she had to tell the boy they were done. If they asked, not all of them did, she told them she was *Daisy*.

Hours could grow long in Freddie's store. Buckles waved away Ishtar's burning joint. "So where'd you pick up the name 'Ishtar'?"

"Goddess of fertility, love, war, and sex. That's me. She also has them big floppy titties. I picked the name myself. It's cool."

"Your butt is big enough. You could be a fertility goddess."

"Go fuck yourself." Ishtar smiled, coughed, and spit. Phlegm arched over the counter to the store's wooden floor. Then she suddenly asked: "You trickin'? You have money enough, and it ain't from this shit job."

"No."

"Selling dope, then? This would be a good place for that."

"Would not dream of it. Smack will kill you."

"They want us to think that if you come close to heroin you'll be an addict for life. Like saying every addict started with weed. Fact is, every addict started with mother's milk. Maybe you are holding up the 7-Elevens?"

"Yeah. That's me. The Slurpee Bandito. For real, why 'Ishtar'?" Her own name having changed so often, she wondered how other people managed.

"At my bat mitzvah, I was Mary Jane Baumgartner."

Buckles' laugh rocked her chair back and nearly tipped her to the floor. "Mary? For a Jew?"

Ishtar shrugged. "It was a mixed marriage."

"It must have been really mixed."

"About as mixed as a marriage can get in Connecticut. Mom's people were old money Congregationalist. Dad was her second husband. I have no idea what evil shit happened with her first husband. I think he beat her. Then she married Dad. He is an engineer at Sikorsky, the helicopter place. He escaped from Europe on a ship from Austria just before Hitler took Vienna. He can't say the letter W, so our cleaning service included a *vindow viper*. They live in New Canaan, so Moms spoke with a Fairfield accent."

Buckles wondered if Ishtar could be persuaded to get blueprints of the Sikorsky plant, even if that meant hauling ass all the way back to the East coast just to throw a Molotov cocktail, but realized that if that could do any good, if would have already been done.

"What's a Fairfield accent?"

"You wear a riding helmet and talk without moving your lower jaw. It's like holding warm cum in your mouth, but more genteel."

April from Connecticut, the bitch Daddy had been boinking, must have had that trick down pat. Buckles wondered if Daddy might be still with the bitch.

"My mother thought it would be *avant-garde* to marry a Yid who escaped Hitler and name her first child after a candy bar. Mary Jane? The molasses thing stuffed with peanut butter? One bite and you are guaranteed to lose all the fillings in your teeth."

"Better than being named for the shoe."

Ishtar shrugged. "I had an older sister who died. Kidney disease of some sort. I can't remember Iris, but it became my job to be two daughters. Iris the Good, and Mary Jane the Fuckup. That's what my shrink says, anyways." She took a Winston from Buckles' crumpled pack, lighting it with the burning tip of Buckles' last cigarette. "The party after my bat mitzvah cost more than the GDP of Honduras."

"Those things are a terrible waste of money."

"Not really. You ask the caterer, the waiters, the musicians, the baker, the busboys, the florist, even the rabbi, and they'll agree it was money well spent." She said: "The one sure way to waste money is to never spend it." Ishtar took a deep breath, coughed, and went on as if preparing to overcome Everest. "High school was a fucking nightmare."

"High school is a nightmare for everyone."

"I had acne, bad hair, and boobs that came way too early. I did what girls do when they need love; I worked my way through a forest of dick. Fast Mary, the Blowjob Queen. My shrink said I was compensating."

"For what?"

"Beats the living shit out of me. Shrinks tell you *bupkis*. You're supposed to discover shit at one hundred dollars per hour. Maybe if you pay two hundred an hour, they tell you. Didn't you ever have a shrink?"

"No."

"I thought everyone had a shrink."

Her parents back in Scarsdale had not believed in shrinks. At Dobbs, girls had competed to be the most screwed up. They worked at having eating disorders, anxiety disorders, tracing thin lines of blood like spider webs on their thighs or underarms, or cutting their wrists, never too deeply and always drawing razors across the arteries instead of down the length of their forearms. Opening an artery the length of an arm might have helped them die, but the ineffective cross-vein slash left plenty of time to be discovered, the status of a bandage, and the beginning of long careers of being fussed over. An army of shrinks did nothing more than steer fuckups to plans of how to unfuck themselves. The advice did not have to work; the shrinks collected their fees no matter what. People were eager to pay. It was a scam Grandma might have invented.

"Therapy is too much work. It's easier to stay stoned." Ishtar rounded her lips and managed a smoke ring. "My family preferred Iris the Innocent. She was dead before she could fuck up. On the other hand, I have life down to a simple science. When I am happy, I eat and fuck. When I am sad, I eat more and fuck more. One of my shrinks said I have to break through to find a *life-enhancing response*." Ishtar toked a fresh joint and held a thoughtful silence. "Short version? Bad luck turned my parents into assholes. I didn't turn out so hot, neither."

"Everyone's parents are assholes. They screw up. When people have a baby, they get an asshole license."

The door's Christmas bells rattled. A customer paid for a pack of Zig-Zag Rolling paper and left. It was near 7. Freddie was an hour late and nowhere to be seen. Buckles was getting bored with Ishtar's nasal whine, so she lied and said: "I have to close. I am having a dinner with someone."

"Like a date?"

"Like a date."

Ishtar tried not to seem insulted. The door's Christmas bells rattled again as she tugged the door open. Buckles flipped the door sign to CLOSED, then retreated to the store's back room to wait for Freddie.

Three days later, Ishtar was back in her director's chair. "It's your turn," she said. "You have to tell me how messed up you are. That's how it works."

The day had been cloudless. She wished she had been riding Lilith. "There is nothing to tell. I am Abigail Carpenter, the super-smart orphan cheerleader from Sacramento. Go Eagles!" She did a little shuffle, her Doc Martens stamping the floor. "Never Abbie."

Ishtar lifted her red-rimmed eyes. "I'd pay to see you in one of those skirts."

"No chance, sweetie. No chance. You are such a dyke."

"If you are so smart, how did you wind up behind the counter of a shitty headshop?"

"The family blew up in a gas explosion. I was the only survivor. Shit happens, you know?" Pussy would forgive her for borrowing his story. Ishtar looked amazed. Buckles embellished the story a bit, adding she was too young to remember any of them. On the spot she created a maiden aunt who took her in but never paid attention to her, being more interested in Anchor Steam Ale. "I was raised by wolves, then got knocked up just before I graduated high school. I lost the baby, then skipped college." Buckles shrugged, feeling overwhelmed by Abigail Carpenter's troubles. "Now if I go back to school I have to figure a way to pay for it." She mentally inspected her tale and liked it well enough, though she thought that if she were anytime soon giving a history of Abigail Carpenter, she'd skip the part about losing a baby.

So she quit there. No smart grifter elaborated beyond the bare minimum. It was too easy to lose the thread. Grandma had tangled her stories so badly that time and geography warped into impossibility. So Buckles created no bus stop departure from Sacramento nor did she put good old Abbie on the road with her thumb out. Who'd ever ask?

The talk needed to move to safer ground. "What do you know about Patty Hearst? The SLA?"

Buckles still longed for a taste of Revolution. All she had ever done was run and prepare, and prepare, and prepare for the day she stopped running and they caught her. She was uncertain she was even being chased. But she had accomplished nothing except to ladle oatmeal to kids. Breaking an agent's knees did not count; that was self-defense. Web must have known what he was talking about when it came to mustering up a revolution, but Web also believed the path to a better world of social equality and justice started at her crotch. Maybe Patty Hearst knew something more.

"I was new in Oakland when all that Hearst business started," Buckles said, "so I know jack. I don't trust newspapers. Newspapers are horseshit." *The Berkeley Barb* was not bad, but when Buckles departed New York her contempt for *The Village Voice* rose with every mile she put between herself and Manhattan. The idiots urged kids to go west for a summer of love. The entire country was a love-fest. The only detail they'd omitted was the petty thing about needing a combat knife to hitchhike. In that stupid song about San Francisco, Scott McKenzie needed a new stanza about how to avoid Big Bill's dick in your ass.

"They shot some brothers in L.A., right?" she said. "But the rich white girl got away. Is that it?"

"More or less. The Symbionese Liberation Army is a bunch of insane *schvartzes* who snatched Miss Patty right out of her student apartment easy, like they were shoplifting apples from Kroger's. You can't piss on the sidewalk at UCLA without wetting a rich white girl's shoes. You know about the Hearsts, right?"

"William Randolph. More money than Scrooge McDuck. Hearst probably paid to plant the bomb on the USS *Maine* himself."

"The *Maine*?"

"The battleship sunk in Havana harbor. 1898. Hearst wanted a war to sell newspapers."

"They don't teach that in schools."

Buckles shook her head, realizing she was doing it again; showing off how smart she was called attention to herself and would someday get her busted. She covered herself. "Great schools in Sacramento. AP History. And I read *Prairie Fire*. That's a book by Bernardine Dohrn and the Weathermen. The title comes from Mao who wrote 'a single spark can start a prairie fire'." She'd paid two dollars for the book instead of shoplifting it, the true sign of her reverence for it.

"What's the book say?"

Her tongue was outrunning her brain. "It's hard to remember. I read it a long time ago." In truth, she'd read and reread the damn book so many times that the cheap paste binding cracked and the yellowed pages were coming undone. In the night when Buckles was stoned and tried to conjure a revolutionary movement she could join, the printed words indicting Amerika flamed fiery red off the pages.

"What else do you know?" Ishtar asked.

Buckles knew that *Symbionese* was about as African as Johnny Weissmuller in a Tarzan movie shouting, *Ungawa, motherfuckers*, but she kept her mouth shut.

"They shot this black guy, a big mistake," Ishtar said. "All manner of motherfuckers need killing, but the SLA offed the superintendent of schools in Oakland. They mailed notes to all the papers. 'Death to the fascist insect that preys upon the life of the people.' Donald What's-his-face, calls himself General Field Marshal Cinque Mtume."

"That's not the Panthers?"

"Definitely not the Panthers. Not the Boy Scouts, either. 'Donald' is one shit name unless we are talking ducks." Ishtar sat erect. "Never mind Scrooge. Forget Huey, Dewey, and Louie. Daisy must be a slut. She may be a girl-duck but she still should wear underwear. Hey, do you like Donald Duck or Mickey Mouse?" As usual, the conversation veered off course because of the two joints Ishtar smoked for her breakfast when her feet had first hit the floor at two in the afternoon.

"I'm a Daffy girl," Buckles said. "Mickey is one squeaky little rat-fuck, but Daffy always gets the shitty end of the stick. I sympathize. Daffy can't win for losing."

"That rabbit is too sly."

"If Elmer ever catches the little motherfucker, I'll make the stew. Carrots, onions and lots of black pepper."

"Don't forget celery."

"You should come with me some morning. I ladle breakfast at the park. It's a Panther thing. We can volunteer to cook the free meals the Panthers serve."

Ishtar bummed another Winston from Buckles, unaware she had three cigarettes balanced and burning on the lip of their Coca-Cola can ashtray. "I don't know. Maybe. Mornings?"

"Yeah, it might be good for you."

Ishtar shuddered and sipped her espresso. "Anyways, the Panthers were thoroughly pissed off. I mean, the SLA wasted a black community guy with eight hollow-points laced with cyanide. You could waste Superman with a hollow point and cyanide if you had some of that stuff that knocks Superman flat."

"Kryptonite?"

"That's the stuff. Kryptonite. Hollow-point kryptonite bullets." Ishtar brushed an ash off her chest. "So the Panthers cut the SLA off. This Donald Whatever is in it for white pussy, but now he looks like a total asshole shooting a black community leader, so he tries to regain creds by snatching the Hearst bitch. He wants the ransom to buy his way back in."

"But the Hearst bitch screws them up."

"Not like you think. They decide to knock over the Hibernia Bank, but what shows up on the bank video but Princess Patty carrying a rifle and wearing a black beret. The Princess sure don't look like no prisoner. That girl *joined* the SLA. It turns out that a 19-year-old fox with a tight ass and a lot of coin can take just so much black dick before she will be happy to tote a brother's assault rifle. She changes her name to Tania, after Che's girlfriend. You know Che Guevara, right?"

"I've heard of him."

"All America wanted to know: can a rich white bitch be fucked into being a bank robbing outlaw?" Ishtar hooted with pleasure. "But listen to this! They screw up again. The L.A. SWAT team is not going to miss a chance to gun down some badass niggers, so they surround the SLA headquarters, fire enough teargas to choke West L.A., and set the place on fire. Then they shoot anyone who runs out the door. But when the smoke clears, no Pretty Princess Tania." She shook her head and laughed again. "Can you dig it? When they catch that girl, what will you bet that Daddy's money will talk? You and me can get twenty years for spitting on the sidewalk, but that rich white girl will never see the inside. Any white girl wants to change the world, all she needs is a tight ass and some serious weapons. Like you."

"Like me? Why would you say that?"

"Your clothes. The sleeveless T-shirt, the Doc Martens. They say a lot. And you have the ass. All you need is a rifle."

"I would not know where to start," Buckles said, and when Ishtar smiled added a question. "Have you been staring at my ass?"

"Only when you stand up." Ishtar hooted again.

"Let's hang out at Winterland tonight," Ishtar said.

"For what?"

"The Dead, girl."

"Who cares? I've never seen them."

"You live in the Bay area and you don't care about the Dead? Who raised you?"

"Nobody."

"That can be a problem."

"You have tickets?"

"Tickets? Tickets are for frat boys in Madras shirts and Bass

Weejuns. We'll hang in the street and look for a miracle. It's a tribe. Everyone cares about everyone else. Someone will give us tickets. It's the Dead. We really need to go."

Ishtar was again angling to sleep with her, but so obviously so it had charm. Her joint had Buckle's ears buzzing like a front door on Halloween. Her nose and upper lip had skipped town. Before she could think it through, she said she would go.

They agreed to meet at the BART station. Smart enough not to walk around with heroin, Ishtar planned to load her arm up at home. Busted for simple weed at a Dead concert was impossible because the pigs would have to arrest all of Oakland, the population of San Francisco, the band itself, and any military personnel stationed at the Presidio with a rank less than Major.

But Ishtar never showed up. Buckles waited half an hour, figured Ishtar nodded out, and then boarded BART.

She felt naked. Her sunglasses with her cache of diamonds disguised as rhinestones lay in a shoe box in her closet beside her Piranha knife which lay beside her Modello near its three 9 mm ammo clips. City pigs just might be checking for weapons because Mick Jagger had hired the Hell's Angels for security at the free Altamont Speedway concert where the bikers stabbed some poor bastard to death while Mick riffed on *Sympathy for the Devil*. Hiring the Hell's Angels for security had all the smarts of hiring Charles Manson to be your psychotherapist.

The starting time for a Dead concert was never more than an approximation. No one in the mob before Winterland was hurried. The three Valley girls who gifted her with a miracle were stoned, staggering, impressed by a short-haired girl wearing a grease-streaked motorcycle jacket. In an act of solidarity, Buckles swallowed the tab of psilocybin they gave her. The world began to hum like a cheap speaker with too much bass.

After what must have been several days of tuning with Bob Weir kissing the mic to say *test test test test*, The Band Beyond Description opened with *Uncle John's Band*. The first of several communal joints came to her from the left. It was not especially strong shit, but the acid laced in the syrupy jug wine that also came her way was potent. Fat, gushy purple notes floated from the Dead's banks of speakers. They moved magically into *I Know You Rider* which became *China Cat Sunflower* as her last sense of time said fare-thee-well, my own true love. After tuning up again for what had to be several hours, the band set sail into an intergalactic version of *Scarlett Begonias* that began in the Pleistocene Era to continue to that very moment, and would continue to the heat death of the universe at the end of time. Donna Godchaux, borrowed from the 12th circle of the Heavenly Host, led all of God's angels to a place where the sky was indeed yellow and the sun surely blue, a place to which Buckles willingly followed as more jug wine fueled a voyage on which Garcia discovered notes that had never before been heard by anyone mortal. Buckles floated like a red balloon tethered to a child's wrist.

She awakened on a soiled mattress on the floor under an opaque window painted pea-green, a curl of her drool on a thin pillow. She rolled away from the dim light to her hip and threw up into the galvanized bucket the naked man beside her must have provided. Dried semen caked her thigh. She itched and felt sore, checked, but seemed uninjured. Her clothes were neatly folded on a wooden chair beneath the window, except for her panties, balled in a farther corner. She stepped into her black jeans before she pushed her underwear into a back pocket. Once she laced her Doc Martens, she was able to stand, found a place to pee, washed her legs and belly with a miraculously clean towel, then brushed her teeth with her finger.

She thought to slip out a door if she could find it, but something smelled good. She followed her nose to wobble into a shabby one-window kitchen. The boy she'd slept with stood over his two-burner hot plate. He had more curly russet hair than Sasquatch and was totally naked.

"Do you like blueberries?" the boy asked.

"Are you the asshole who fucked me?"

"You insisted. There were three frat boys who were pissed off I got in their way. They all planned to fuck you, either one at a time or all at once, I could not be sure."

"Am I supposed to say 'thanks'?"

He shrugged. "Abby, right? You're amazing in bed, Abby."

A bit of bravado seemed called for. "I know," she said.

He poured pancake batter onto a hot skillet. "The trick is to watch for bubbles in the batter before you flip. I am the one who should say 'thanks.' If all the girls from Scarsdale fuck like you, I am heading east. Call me 'Dean.' Like the guy in *On the Road,* but my last name is Moretti." He extended a hand covered with flour.

Buckles hesitated, then shook his hand. It was a greeting of sorts. It's always nice to know the name of a boy you fucked, though she preferred the reverse order, name followed by fucking.

"Wasn't anyone with you at the show?"

"I was by myself."

"Big mistake." He balanced a stack of pancakes on a plastic plate on a scarred table and set his bare ass on a wooden chair. "It's a Dead concert. You go with people. There is always going to be acid, right? We are fresh out of butter or syrup, but we have some honey." He rattled through a cutlery drawer, found two forks, ran them under the sink, and offered her one.

"We?"

"Me and my sister. Terri stays here when she comes to town to check on her little brother. She undressed you before she took the bus back to Fullerton. I go to East Bay. It's a casual kind of place. They probably will kick me out again because mostly what I do is follow the Dead. Last night was my fifty-eighth show. I want to get to a hundred. With one plate, clean-up will be easier, right?" He reached between and under his legs to pull his chair closer to the table. His face lifted to hers. "Terri said to leave you alone to sleep it off, but after she left you got horny. I used a condom, but I have to ask. You're OK?"

"I take pills."

"That's cool, but I meant OK for VD. For me, I mean."

"Oh. Nothing I know about," she said. The pancakes were rubbery but edible.

He shrugged. "Well, it was a Dead concert. You may have been the only person there without crabs. Your hair is so short I wondered if you recently had head lice. Condoms don't do anything for bugs. The two pancakes at the bottom have the blueberries, so if you are allergic, be careful." When Dean scratched his ribs, his fingernails traced faint red lines on his skin. "What was all that shit about your grandmother and her treasure map? Terri and I thought it was weird. You were tripping. Do you live in Oakland or San Francisco?"

"I must have been really tripping. My grandmothers died before I ever met them. Do you want to put on some pants or something?"

"I'm comfortable, thanks. Do you want to get naked again? You were great stoned; how are you straight?"

"Do you give everyone you fuck a review?"

He grinned. "No offense. It was good, is all."

They ate off the shared plate. When she had her fill, she went to the door. Her hand rested on the glass doorknob.

Dean asked, "See you again?"

"Maybe on campus," she said, lying. "I go to East Bay for Accounting."

"That's cool. If you can't be with the one you love, love the one you're with, right?"

She headed down a flight of rickety stairs thinking Dean was a nice Italian boy so she did not need to kill him to keep her secrets, but if she did not want to kill someone else some other day, she would need to keep her head below the clouds and her knees together.

Buckles took Ishtar to the Free Food Collective of Greater Oakland to introduce the fortune teller to the possibilities of street activism. They volunteered for food prep. The community organization was loosely connected to the Black Panthers, though it had too many white people to be completely trusted. It was as close to the Movement as Buckles could hope for.

The Panthers were dedicated to community defense, dismantling the capitalist state, and to feeding the poor. Buckles made no bid for creds by mentioning she owned a gun, or that she once crippled an FBI agent or could hurl a firebomb with some accuracy from a speeding motorcycle. She did not dare to breathe the name "Celeste." Buckles might be wearing a motorcycle jacket or a Navy-issue peacoat, but if she brightly said, "Some of my best friends are Black," someone was sure to shoot her in the head.

The Free Food Collective occupied most of a two-story strip mall, a wood-frame cheese-box of a building in north Fruitvale. Student activists from Berserkly had once occupied the abandoned structure to declare it to be property of the People. The city of Oakland was delighted to have squatters convert a nontaxed eyesore to a nontaxed eyesore that fed homeless women and children.

Iron bars were riveted over the Collective's ground floor windows, whether to keep junkies out or keep rats in was a subject of ongoing speculation. Donations were extorted from local merchants to obtain a six-burner gas range, two stoves, and the FFC's pride and joy, a walk-in Westinghouse refrigerator christened "Lazarus." Lazarus emitted grinding noises and wheezed, but worked, most of the time. The entire Collective sucked illegal electricity down a line tapped across the back alley, another theft the city chose to ignore because Lazarus held gallons of milk destined for children. There was occasional ice cream, as well, labeled with masking tape and black ink: Children Only.

The door-free pantry beside Lazarus became Buckles' realm after she prepared her first batch of stew. Ishtar asked, "Where did you learn to cook?" and Buckles shrugged, remembering Southwestern stars impassively overhead when she'd knelt beside a small fire and dripped Tabasco through slits punched by her knife through the top of an otherwise taste-free can of Dinty Moore's Beef Stew. Held on a grating over an open fire, the labels burned and the cans burst, but the bubbling stuff became passable food. Now she fed welfare mothers and their children at St. Augustine's or in San Pablo Park. It was not as good as blowing shit up, but it was satisfying work.

Buckles became Mother Abigail when Huey Newton, free between murder trials and yet another hung jury, admired her stew. "He was just trying to get over on you," Ishtar said. "Did it work?"

Buckles demurely lied by saying nothing. She'd spent most of an unremarkable night naked listening to a lecture about how the Power hated the Panthers for feeding the poor because the Power needed the poor to be dependent, and here they were liberating people with hot meals. The Empire could be forced to its knees with a soup tureen.

The miracle of the fishes and loaves was nothing compared to the miracles Mother Abigail worked with lentils and potatoes. A crust of Mother Abigail's wholegrain bread and a wedge of food-bank white cheese could sustain a person for days. The world had much to learn from beans, all those colors and shapes simmering over low heat blended to become something more than the ingredients had been separately. That, Buckles believed, was how the world should work.

The FFC also offered special assistance to women and their children. No one was turned away. Most stayed for a few meals and to bathe in one of the two rust-stained tubs when water could be urged to rise above a cold trickle. As long as no imbecile clogged any of the three rusted toilets with sanitary napkins, most of the plumbing worked, though the pipes groaned like syphilitics passing water if the washing machine was running. Women slept on the floors curled three or four to a room like blind puppies sharing warmth.

Buckles quit her job at the no-name headshop after four days of waiting to give Freddie some notice, but he no longer showed up. She lowered and locked the mesh riot door that covered the storefront for the last time before placing the key above the door jamb. Weeks later, she stopped by. The key was where she left it. Freddie's bones were surely bleaching in some Mexican arroyo, a fate that had always seemed inevitable. Ishtar thought to liberate some of Freddie's inventory, but since unloading the stuff would take more effort than it was worth, she took only a box of rolling paper and a lava lamp.

Buckles maintained the secret of her address. She had money enough and ate but one meal per day standing over the Collective's steel sink. Her preference for cleanliness was a telltale sign of growing up bourgeois, an issue that came up at the mandatory weekly hour-long self-criticism sessions.

The required Monday morning hour of self-criticism was allegedly the means by which a revolutionary cell honed its members into an irresistible force, but at the Collective was little more than semi-organized bitching. They separated seeds and stems on an Olatunji album cover. No one had ever played the vinyl record, warped as a potato chip, but the membership felt duty-bound to honor the grinning African musician.

A bitch named Emerald with tightly knotted blonde cornrows and jailhouse tats above her neck done with a straight pin and a Bic at FCI Dublin rolled bombers thick as Buckles' thumb. Emerald lit the joint, sucked down some smoke, gasped, toked a second hit, and at intermittent various meetings charged Buckles with being too pretty. "Emerald just wants to jump your bones," Ishtar suggested, but Buckles worried more that the woman was a paid police informant hoping to prod Mother Abigail into making an angry mistake and some sort of admission that would topple her from prominence in the community's pecking order.

Ishtar laughed at Emerald's charge. She accepted a passed joint and said: "This is America. Ain't you heard? You can't be too pretty, too rich, or too thin. That's our Mother Abigail. Don't be forgetting that," she added with just enough edge to carry a threat that surprised Buckles.

When a criticism session ended, kitchen work began. Ishtar's two big bare arms extended shoulder deep into a tub of what would become coleslaw. She claimed the perspiration that trickled from her armpits and the dash of cigarette ash that sprinkled off her chest added flavor. "Ignore that bitch. Emerald peddles her ass all weekend, so by Monday the cum she swallowed curdles." She stirred the coleslaw with a paddle big enough for a rowboat. Buckles cut potatoes, carrots, and celery into a running sink, then scooped the vegetables into a tub, set the tub to boil, then turned down the heat. She thickened it with a half cup of flour. Stew, like revolution, could not be hurried, but only helped along.

Once the meal was simmering, they carried beers to Bad Girl's Beach, what they called the tarpaper and gravel roof. Reclining on mostly intact woven vinyl beach lounges, the two women peered over the surrounding rooftops. Squealing gulls wheeled overhead. The breeze off the bay cooled them. Oakland was a city of extremes: when you weren't freezing, you were baked. It was easy to believe that Fruitvale and the harbor were their private realm.

Ishtar lighted her habitual joint. Buckles stank like a ferret, having worked up the honest sweat that came with sweltering kitchen work. She wanted a shower. Buckles accepted the passed joint and took a long hit. It was unusually potent shit. She lifted her eyebrows in question.

"Nothing but good ol' maryjane, I swear. Hawaiian."

Buckles developed a light buzz. She could not risk getting stoned; she'd learned it loosened her tongue. She returned the joint to Ishtar.

"Of course you aren't too pretty." She was still criticizing the criticism session. "You're America's daughter in black leather, camouflage T-shirt, washed-out jeans, and Doc Martens. I could do you a favor and scar your face. Keep the motherfuckers away. Ever think that you catch shit because no one can figure you out?" Ishtar sat back, popped the cap on a first Michelob, and offered it to Buckles. "You ever going to tell me what happened at that Dead concert?" She tilted back her head and drained the bottle with a single swallow, then blindly hurled the empty over the roof's edge.

"What Dead concert?"

"The one we were supposed to go to but I fell asleep. You went, right?"

"I never got there."

Ishtar cocked her head to look at her. "You changed after that. You got ... I don't know, meaner? You sure you did not go? Something happened, right?"

"I met someone and fell deeply in love."

Ishtar laughed.

Whenever Buckles thought of the Italian boy and the life she could never permit herself, she grew sad. Enough of that, and she grew angry. What had been his name? Moretti? In a normal life she'd have stayed with Moretti for a month or more. Instead, she'd had to go on alone. Being alone was wearing thin.

Ishtar lifted another bottle from the six-pack, "I wonder if Emerald thinks you might be the bitch who carved up an FBI agent before you came to Oakland. That's where she thinks your creds come from. Right? The story is all over about this pretty white bitch who left an agent's nuts on the floor in one of those big square states in the middle. Iowa? Nebraska? Something like that."

Her hands shaking as if she had palsy, Buckles fished a bent cigarette from her T-shirt pocket. She had to turn the flint on her Zippo three times to light it. If the story was around, this was the first she'd heard it. The cigarette was an effort to will herself calm. She'd need to know where the rumor came from. This was not like asking if she'd slept with Huey Newton or what happened with Moretti. Who was repeating the story of a woman who carved up an FBI agent? Was there a reward? Who was fishing? Ishtar? Emerald? Betrayal could come from anywhere at any time. No wonder Grandma trusted no one, and no wonder she allowed everyone to believe she was no more than a crazy old lady in an Edsel convertible, the most impossible car ever made.

There was no such thing as safety. Her cover might be blown. If anyone drew a line from Abigail Carpenter the knocked up cheerleader from Sacramento to Mother Abigail or back to the desperado terrorist Florence Goodbody from Wisconsin, she'd be scooped up as the outlaw who aided a deserter and crippled a Feeb. The thread could unravel back to the Westchester preppie, Abby "Buckles" Sinclair, last seen with her thumb out on Rt. 6.

It took two hands for her to steady the unlit cigarette and her Zippo. Her hands trembled a lot lately. Muscle fatigue, she told herself, but lack of sleep and persistent tension were the truth of it. Two or three nights each week, Buckles twitched awake in damp sheets. Every morning required her to will her shoulders slack when she rose. She had aches and pains with no origin. In her night terrors, Big Bill and her mother somehow became one to confront her about stupid choices. Pussy and Grandma blended into a single figure to mock her. Pussy wept that Buckles abandoned him. Web and Celeste and Che Guevara came together to treat her with contempt for her inaction. She'd sit motionless in the dark and wonder what kind of idiot had been ruthless enough to shatter Levi's knees but lacked the smarts to realize that leaving an FBI agent alive to identify her was too stupid to be believed? In her night terrors, she stabbed the rapist FBI *agent provocateur*, but though the evil son-of-a-bitch spouted sticky hot blood, he grinned and refused to die, smirking as he pursued her on his deformed legs until he caught her while Big Bill knelt on her shoulders readying her for rape again while a horde of Grandma's faceless marks looked on impatient for the return of their diamonds. They would have the map to the Lake Tahoe lockbox, nothing less. She'd awaken sitting cross-legged to smell how sour she'd become. Limp and chilled by drying cold sweat, she snapped off her blacklight to extinguish Che's glowering eyes above her, his benevolence vanished, his penetrating eyes too much like her father's.

Now here was Ishtar telling her that her pursuers were no nightmare. The story was too much like her to be made up. Someone real, someone not a dream, someone who lived and breathed in Oakland was asking about the girl who left an FBI agent broken.

Ishtar rose from her plastic chaise longue to stand on tip-toe, her Jewfro wobbling in the breeze as she reached to touch a gull's nest covering a narrow chimney pipe. She threw a second beer bottle over the building's side.

Was it time for Lilith to carry Buckles north to Tahoe and then to Canada before she zigzagged south to Costa Rica? She'd been on the run for seven years, sure federal agents, cops, and MPs were close behind. They'd never quit. That was how they got you. You were neither trapped nor caught so much as run down until you fell dead.

Ishtar often drove the Commune's loaded Volkswagen bus to the park while Buckles hovered over two simmering pots on the propane stove in the bus's rear. Usually, four psychedelically painted vans set out for the park.

The unspoken agreement with the Oakland pig-force was to leave the FFC headquarters unmolested; but in the park where the FFC doled out meals, all bets were off because the free food program left the Power and their enforcement pigs with an unresolvable dilemma.

The Power needed to generate fear to sustain its authority. Obey or starve. Obey or lose your house. Obey or sicken and die. Obey or watch your kids sicken and die while you rot in a cell. This was the foundation of Pig Nation from Baltimore to Oakland and back again, but in a few California enclaves the Panthers accumulated power of their own by liberating citizens from the System's terror. All it took were full bellies. In the absence of the state terror called The System, why run on the treadmill?

Pigs were obliged to descend on the poor periodically to renew their reign of terror. Cops took special joy in spearing batons into women's ribs, the reminder that unearned meals could not be tolerated unless doled out by official white charities or food banks who could exact gratitude and obedience. With sufficient meals, terror might evaporate and, with it, the Empire might collapse.

The usual clot of cops congealed on the north side of San Pablo Park where they eyeballed Ishtar as she sloshed a final beer down her throat. She kept her other hand on the wheel, but a half-drained bottle of Michelob in the hands of some hippie freak behind the wheel was all the pigs needed. Ishtar's Volkswagen wagon train swerved and bounced over a curbstone to dig tread marks in the park's turf.

There it was: wanton destruction of public property. The pudgy kid with the Jewfro needed to be hauled in for questioning for drunk driving, disorderly conduct, public intoxication. She and her damned porridge could not be allowed to endanger the community. Who knew what was in the stuff?

The OPD rushed them. Cops wielding batons and riot shields hurled smoking canisters of tear gas into a mass of women and children who fled south and east as two black helicopters appeared overhead, a necessary show of force insofar as welfare mothers were known to become agitated when their children under 10 wailed with hunger. Teenage boys upped their game by throwing rocks at the helicopters, a gesture of defiance no self-respecting cop could allow without response, though no helicopter had ever been downed by a rock, a lesson firmly underscored by peasants in Southeast Asia.

Buckles found herself coughing in a nauseating yellow cloud, face down on grainy dirt, her eyes gassed into sandpaper, her chest tight. She had no memory of how she got there. Blinking did nothing to clear her vision; coughing did nothing to clear her lungs. Her eyes streamed. She wished she knew how to make a propane tank explode. She had her knife, worthless, but she'd left her gun at home, a precaution Huey himself had advised the one night they'd gotten it on when after this and that they talked about Pig-Preparedness. If she drew a weapon, she'd be dead before she hit the ground. "Those motherfuckers do not fuck around," he'd said and buckled his slacks, the best advice any girl ever received from a one-night stand.

Buckles managed to pry open one eye. Television crews and their vans surrounded the park. They'd not have known to be there without notice from Oakland's Finest, so the pigs had to have planned this ass-kicking well in advance of Ishtar's provocation. Their TV coverage was designed so the residents of Rock Ridge and Trestle Glen could see their tax dollars at work. Six cops on horseback pretended to be Czar Nicholas' Cossack Hussars charging Bolsheviks. Buckles' stew was dumped, a steaming puddle on darker dirt.

Buckles stood to help Ishtar, was knocked down, and stood again. That was the moment Mother Abigail was caught on one knee *in flagrante delicto*, snarling into a camera with her middle finger raised. Her woolen knit hat was pulled unevenly low over her forehead, her arms bare in her sleeveless camo T-shirt, her narrow waist cinched tight by her wide black garrison belt. Close by, pigs smashed the legs of Commune tables only because purpose-fully smashing human legs might look less than sporting on a news video.

The blurry photo of Buckles standing over a fallen comrade defiant amid havoc was picked up by *Newsweek*. A captain who had supervised the raid from the safety of the stationhouse boasted how the OPD had for a long time kept a close eye on that one, the rabblerousing ringleader, Mother Abigail, Huey Newton's white mistress. The captain enjoyed his airtime, shaking his head in sorrow at the ones who pursued violence for its own sake. In private, the captain shook his head in mock sorrow, muttering, "A white woman, no less," the police pejorative that meant a woman had gone mad for Black dick.

Mother Abigail was charged with inciting to riot. She gave her name as Abby Carpenter from Sacramento to the overworked sub-versive, pinko, puke public defender who wore the most hideous tie Buckles had ever seen. He represented nineteen other people that day. That night in the lockup, women threw up from the stink of tear gas trapped in their clothes and hair. Most of the time they made it to the seatless steel toilet, but not always. Since peeing was accomplished without anyone's ass touching anything, piss puddled over the holding cell's floor. Buckles spent the night expecting to be booked and fingerprinted which would surely connect her to the assault on an FBI agent years ago in Illinois, but the pigs fin-gerprinted no one. Instead, she and her cellmates spent the night singing *We Shall Overcome* and were released in the morning, the charges reduced to disorderly conduct from inciting to riot. A mush-head judge sentenced Buckles and the other alleged rioters to time served, a suitable punishment for ladling boiled potatoes, lentils, and carrots.

But the captain's sobriquet for Buckles had national legs. *Newsweek* pasted Mother Abigail's face on the Movement. She was white, she was pretty, and she did not frighten readers by wearing a black leather coat to cover automatic weapons, a beret cockily set on an unapologetic afro, or hide her eyes behind impenetrable dark glasses. No Panther leader, Mother Abigail was the girl next door gone astray, a story that in the absence of facts struck pity into the hearts of mothers in Beverly Hills, Oak Park, and, yes, even Scarsdale. Not filthy rich like the rifle-toting Patty Hearst, Mother Abigail was the high school field hockey team captain with a conscience, a Girl Scout who gave up cookies to pursue social justice. Hugh Hefner wanted her for a *Playboy* centerfold. Those perfect teeth set in a gleaming smile, that boyishly cropped hair, that snarl just shy of a smile with her middle finger raised at the entire country belonged in every college dormitory or taped to the back wall of a thousand auto repair shops, if only she'd pose topless. Hef dreamed of a photo feature: *America's New Daughters.*

Buckles told the pipe-smoking fart to jerk off without her.

The *San Francisco Chronicle* tracked her down for an interview at the FFC headquarters. "People want to know your story," the reporter said. Buckles told her to get the fuck off her roof.

Ishtar, however, was thrilled. She had a crush on a celebrity. The celebrity, Buckles, planned to split this scene because it could not be healthy. Abby Carpenter had to fire up Lilith and haul ass, the sooner the better. She probably should have already left when Ishtar wondered what she knew of that white girl who'd left an FBI agent crippled. She thought she must be getting old, comfort filling her with inertia and fatigue. It was only a matter of time until she was recognized, busted, or Ishtar betrayed her for a reward. She was too bovine to be anything like an agent, but she could certainly be bought, and cheap, at that.

Two days after Buckles invited the *Chronicle* writer to kiss her ass, Emerald—the syphilitic whore with dyed blonde hair braided into cornrows and jailhouse tats above her neck—stuck her ugly freckled face above the edge of the roof. She shouted down behind her, "She be here." Then Emerald submerged from view.

Ishtar extinguished a joint with a pinch of spit. Buckles crushed her cigarette to the sole of her shoe while her stomach flipped somersaults. Another reporter? The cops? Could she jump the two stories to the ground, not break a leg, and run? She wished she had her pistol. Damn Huey and his condescending advice. The damn Modello was a weight, but it was reassuring. On rapid fire she could get out of a tight scrape, and this just might be the tightest scrape she'd ever know. A single shot could buy her a few seconds; emptying a clip might be worth a minute while her pursuers sought cover, and that minute might be all she needed to hightail to Lilith.

She touched her switchblade nestled in the hollow of her garrison belt as a face popped over the rooftop's lip.

It was her mother.

San Francisco, 1974

THE NEW DOWNTOWN HYATT WAS a triangular tower with an atrium at its core. KJ and Pierre lodged on an upper story that on one side held floor-to-ceiling mist-covered windows that overlooked the Bay and beyond to Oakland. The other side of their room opened to the indoor balcony above the lobby. It commanded a view of the entire hotel from within. No dark corridors, no corners behind which someone could be waiting, the architecture added one additional precaution, a measure of safety unavailable at the St. Regis in New York or the Monteleone in New Orleans. The glass tube elevator shafts made Pierre feel as if he were a target suspended in a shooting gallery.

KJ and Pierre finished a room service breakfast in bed of coffee and rye toast.

"When do we expect Buckles?" he asked.

KJ stretched under the sheet of their unmade bed. "Later. There's no firm plan."

"Do you think I have time for a quick run?"

"Knock yourself out." KJ smiled. "You kept me up most of the night. A girl needs her rest, you know." She nestled further into the bed. "Do you think she's a dyke?"

"What difference would it make?" Pierre pulled on his slacks.

KJ thought a moment, and shrugged. "None. It's how she carries herself and what she wears that make me wonder. I'll just straight-up ask her. We are getting along so well. I just don't want to blow it."

"She'll take the question as a sign of acceptance. She's an adult."

Pierre wrapped his pistol in the box with the green-and-blue Aloha shirt KJ had given him the day before. KJ was already half asleep when he kissed her eyes. As he did whenever he left their room, he stood on the interior balcony and inspected the lobby, especially the escalator that brought people up from the street. Nothing alerted him. In the lobby, he handed the shirt box to the bell captain who gave him a chit, then descended to the street. He stretched his knees by holding first one ankle and then the other up behind his back while eyeballing the San Francisco financial district, long alive since before sunrise, and began fifty yards of walking followed by two hundred of jogging followed by fifty yards of an all-out run, then walking again while his pulse lowered. He followed Embarcadero, the street that hugged the crescent of the Bay around Telegraph Hill as far as Fisherman's Wharf, his mind a passenger above his body. He was thinking how despite a lifetime of studying the faces of gamblers who professionally needed to betray nothing, but always did, Pierre had believed he knew how to read people, but in the company of KJ and her daughter, he saw his delusion.

Pierre, KJ, and Buckles had enjoyed days of touristy things, long walks, cable cars and Chinatown. Buckles felt proprietary about the Bay area, enjoyed showing "her" city, though Pierre had seen it all before and never let on that he had. Their daytrips held a false touch of nostalgia, as if Buckles was again a teenager on vacation with her family. Wherever they went, the Sinclair women were magpies chattering about nothing in particular, then, later, KJ could explain all Pierre had missed, though he'd been present for every word. The two women's talk could careen forward, spin about, go forward again, weeping, laughing, scolding, explaining, explaining again, repeatedly retracing the conversation for greater clarity on a point that Pierre, in his naiveté, thought settled. Gaping holes in Buckles' story remained unexplained, but KJ never asked for more.

They held a delicate balance between complete communion and partial disclosure.

Their stories that emerged were remarkably parallel. Buckles did not wear clothing so much as she inhabited her olive green sleeveless T-shirts, her baggy camouflage pants, and shoes that belonged on a juvenile delinquent in a seedier alley in Belfast; KJ had for years dressed like a gypsy moth in Manhattan, faded jeans, a gray college sweatshirt, black basketball sneakers, and a knit seaman's hat she tugged low over her ears. She was only for the past year back in skirts and blouses.

Pierre challenged himself with a small detour and circled Coit Tower. You had to like San Francisco with its patchwork of neighborhoods even more closely packed together than Manhattan's, but far cleaner and free of shadows.

The Sinclair women were like tuning forks close by each other, resonating at the identical pitch without quite touching. Outlaws in spirit as well as fact, KJ and Buckles had over seven years independently hacked away their hair, choosing at one time to dye what had been standout blonde to mouse brown. Both women worked at being unnoticed. Buckles alluded darkly to names she'd taken other than the notorious Mother Abigail, names she'd adopted to dodge law enforcement for unspecified crimes. KJ said nothing about their suitcase of false driver's licenses and forged birth certificates.

Over white wine at an outdoor bistro, KJ told Buckles about how she had passed years as the leading fag-hag of Manhattan. "I was Wendy to the Lost Boys of Midtown, a group of beautiful and gifted gay men. I loved all of them." Buckles was intensely interested; this was not the mother she had left in Scarsdale. She said as much. KJ nodded. Then Buckles mentioned a roommate she'd had in Illinois who was arrested for lewd behavior. "His name was Pussy. That's a long story by itself," Buckles said, "but I loved him like a brother, and I still miss him. That was in Champaign, Illinois. We were hanging out at the university there."

"Do you want to go college?"

The kid laughed uproariously.

Later, when they were alone, Pierre had shared with KJ his certainty that Buckles could not be all she seemed, a selfless worker for the poor and those out of luck. In an age of rebellious kids, she seemed more deeply rebellious. Anger radiated from her cobalt eyes, a phenomenon he recognized from the face that had greeted him from mirrors his entire youth. Someone had wronged her, but when, where, and how remained hidden. She was too alive and too pretty for her to have ever been a hooker or dope smuggler, so she was not flirting with death, at least not in any of the ways Pierre ordinarily knew.

"And she is not gay," KJ said.

"How do you know?"

"I simply asked her. It's nice to have that level of a relationship with her. She took no offense, but did say part of the reason she wore leathers and T-shirts is so she can say 'No' to some cowboy because she sleeps with girls."

"Why would she say that?"

"I thought you understood women?"

"I used to think so."

That had been two days ago. He came now to a long downhill stretch that returned him to Embarcadero. Near the hotel, Pierre waited stop perspiring, stretching again, then took the escalator to the lobby and retrieved the shirt box. In the Men's Room he donned the shirt and slipped his pistol into his pants pocket, the familiar weight reassuring.

Pierre, Buckles, and her mother had agreed this day would be the day to stop talking old times and decide what was next.

For several days, Buckles daily rode BART to Embarcadero, the first stop in San Francisco once the train departed Oakland, but today she rode Lilith.

Last night she'd slept under Che's glowering eyes for the last time. That morning, she looped the beaded cord that held Grandma's sunglasses with its last two diamonds and a half-dozen rhinestones at the rear of her neck. She packed Lilith's right saddlebag with three tightly rolled black and camo T-shirts, a second pair of camo jeans, a baggie of first-rate marijuana, and her old friend, her desert bedroll. She was looking forward to again being in the desert's silence below a canopy of stars that hardly twinkled. She tucked her switchblade into the cavity in her garrison belt at her waist, and placed her automatic pistol snugly at the small of her back under her leather vest. She'd left her cabled white Navy sweater on a wire hanger in her closet. She would miss it, but the sweater would serve no useful purpose.

It was time to go.

Her life had stalled, and if the image of Mother Abigail had made national news potent enough to draw Kelly Jo Sinclair across the continent to reunite with her daughter, it was only a matter of time until some gnome in the CIA or FBI or Pentagon connected the dots. A SWAT team could easily blow up three square blocks in Fruitvale to subdue the 110-pound woman so ballsy she'd run with a fag deserter and then refuse to be raped by a government agent, splintering the agent's knees as part of her daring getaway plan, doubtlessly masterminded by the Weather Underground in league with The Black Panthers, the Symbionese Liberation Army, and Patty Hearst herself. Blowing up Fruitvale would become a matter of national security, superseding any and all considerations for ordinary human life. Any amount of destruction would be permitted in pursuit of the dangerous petite mad motorcyclist.

It had been the greatest disappointment of her life, but it was now clear why Celeste's friends had left her in the dark about who and how they had invented Abigail Carpenter of Sacramento. Buckles had learned the wisdom of being unable to betray people she did not know, but her ignorance left her outside the Movement. It rankled her; then again, Buckles had arrived where she was through panicky improvisation and dumb luck. She might yet have her time exploding shit.

She had blown a farewell kiss to Che and left her apartment door gaping.

She'd stopped at the Commune to dole out a simple breakfast of oatmeal, milk, and homemade brown grain bread, helped Ishtar with clean-up, and said to the woman who was the closest thing she had to a friend that she'd see her soon, almost certainly false. Ishtar deserved better but would never get it. Then she kick-started the BMW and said farewell to Oakland.

At her right as she crossed the Bay Bridge, the sky over the Pacific was indecently blue, the clouds impudently white, the sun defiantly yellow. The sleeping curl of a cat's spine rising from the Bay above steel-gray water was Alcatraz, no longer a prison, recently occupied by native Indians reclaiming land rightfully theirs because the Power no longer had use for it, a treaty provision no one but the tribes wanted to recollect. They had the crazy idea of converting The Rock into a cultural center and school. President Pig Nixon cut off power and water to the occupants who established The Bureau of Caucasian Affairs. They broadcast from Radio Free Alcatraz until, after nearly two years, John Wayne being unavailable, the Feds lost their sense of humor and invaded the island to quash the last Indian uprising.

If she could avoid it, Buckles never traveled to San Francisco on Lilith. In the open over the desert, Lilith could soar off road or on a highway faster than any pigs might care to pursue, but in congested city traffic, bridges and tunnels were rattraps. Buckles had to slow Lilith at the Yerba Buena tunnel because as usual the traffic was piled up by perpetual phony road construction, obviously phony because it was never completed.

Stopped motionless, her right leg nervously bounced while her left waited to tap Lilith into first. Stop-and-go was hell on the bike's clutch, but the dangerous desire to steer down a white line between cars that moved slower than a walk was a fool's play, one that surely would draw pig notice. Speed and mobility offered no escape if, when she emerged at the tunnel's end, she was greeted by squad cars and a thicket of drawn weapons. Lilith might be primed, but police radio traveled faster. A pig search would discover clinking wine bottles smelling of gasoline. She'd have to shoot several of the pig motherfuckers before they took her down.

She parked the motorcycle in a public lot beside the park on Drum Street. The BMW dwarfed the puny Yamahas and Hondas, the rice-burners left by the polished young men in polished penny loafers who before dawn had hastened to their desks in the Financial District, braced by black coffee and ready for the stock market's opening bell in New York City.

Money never sleeps.

She left her helmet clipped to Lilith's sissy bar and crossed open space in downtown San Francisco, nothing like open space in Oakland; one an airy grass-covered showpiece lawn crisscrossed by pedestrian pathways, the other a bare bit of dirt pounded grassless by children's feet.

An escalator carried her up to the lobby floor, an architectural design to keep the riffraff out. If riffraff were the kind who kept tightly capped wine-bottle firebombs in motorcycle saddlebags, carried automatic pistols and switchblades tucked under their garrison belts, she most certainly qualified as riffraff.

She saw Pierre at the far end of the atrium in the dimmer light under overhanging floors. He stretched, one ankle braced on the back of a molded plastic chair with his head bobbing to his knee. His wife-beater undershirt was tucked into a pair of baggy chinos held well above his waist by single strap suspenders. Over that, he wore the green-and-blue Aloha shirt KJ had given him. It hung on him like drapery. He bent his torso from his flat waist, looking pretty good for an old man. He waved to Buckles.

"Just back," Pierre said.

"How far did you go?"

"I run when I can. Nothing spectacular. Short distances. For my wind. Anything more and my knees swell. I made it to Fisherman's Wharf and back."

Buckles unsnapped her leather tunic, pulled her green camo T-shirt from her waistline to loosen up but keep her gun hidden at

her back. She sat at the small glass table. She unrolled her Winstons
from her sleeve, took one and offered another to Pierre. He ran and
he smoked, and it would not surprise Buckles to learn he could run
and smoke at the same time without emitting a cough, but this time
he waved the cigarette away.

She flipped her Zippo into flame. "I'd guess two miles. We can
ask at the desk."

"Sounds right. So I did four, there and back. That's about my
limit."

"You wear dress shoes when you run?"

"If I ever need to make tracks, I will not have the opportunity
to lace sneakers."

She liked her mother's boyfriend. "Is Mom coming down soon?"

"KJ waits for me to come up. I'll need a shower. I am her advance scout today, supposed to call the room when you arrive. I
go up, we return to you together. There are decisions that must be
made before the red-eye for New York takes off."

"Let me call her."

He gripped his outstretched shoe, bent his foot backward to
stretch his hamstring and calf, then held the position for a five-
count until his forehead touched his knee. "Wait, *cher*, not yet.
You're early; I'm early. Let's take the opportunity to know each
other. *Assez. Parlez en peu avec moi.*"

He flashed his room key and asked a hotel bar waiter if the
hotel served chicory. The waiter did not know what that was. Pierre
asked for a towel and ordered two carafes of American coffee that
arrived on a silvered tray. The white towel went around his shoulders and head like an old-fashioned boxer.

Buckles would never have thought to ask someone to bring her
a towel in a hotel lobby. "You are used to hotel services," she said.

"I travel some. These days, KJ travels with me. Your mother is
more my partner than a companion. We like Room Service." He
dropped a cube of sugar into his cup and stirred in a dollop of
cream. Buckles took her coffee black.

"You seem to get along. I'm glad for her. What exactly do you
do, Mr. Doucet?"

"You need to call me Pierre."

"Pierre, then. My mother said something about import and export making a lot of money, but I am unclear. Do you cheat your customers?" She grinned, thinking she was being clever.

Pierre took her question far more seriously than she had meant it. His porcelain cup rattled back onto its saucer on the silver service. They were an arm's length apart separated by the circular glass table. His eyes were golden brown and his dark hair, still damp with perspiration, tumbled limply over his eyes.

Pierre and KJ had agreed that Buckles needed to know that they planned on leaving the business and that doing so would be possible for them. She did not need to know he was getting too slow to trust himself, and that with KJ in his life, he had become more cautious. If he did nothing he would be dead in a year or less, and KJ probably with him.

"It is time. Your mother does not want to be the one who tells you, but she wants you to know. We erase people."

"I don't understand."

His eyes held her. "I kill people," he said. "For money. I have always killed people, but now your mother joins me."

Buckles laughed. "You are teasing me."

"*Non, vraiment.* It is not a crime of passion and I am not a psychopath. I take no pleasure from it. It is a simple job. Murder is my trade. There is a man in New Orleans who made the arrangements. When he contacted me, I did my work. But I no longer trust him, so your mother and I need to leave." Pierre leaned awkwardly to roll to his hip in his seat so Buckles could see the outline of the small pistol in his loose trouser pocket. "A knife is also strapped to my ankle," he said, "but I have never used it on a person. It is a last resort. Like running. It is a precaution. With correct planning, last resorts are never necessary."

He expected her to be wide-eyed, but she surprised him and stood. "I will show you something, but you cannot tell my mother."

"I cannot promise that. If she asks, I must tell her."

"But if she does not ask?"

"Then I need say nothing."

"Good enough." Buckles turned her back to him. "Lift my shirt," she said. "Not too high."

Pierre saw the 5-inch Modello 952. "*Maudit!* That's not a gun, it's a cannon."

She shrugged. "I weigh less than one-ten. I need stopping power." She turned again to face him. "And my knife is here." She patted her abdomen and sat. "If you tell KJ, she will only worry. Please keep it secret. I have caused her enough worry."

"If she does not ask whether you carry a pistol, I don't need to tell her." He said: "Be sure to police your brass, my friend. Especially I you load your own clips."

"I don't understand."

"It means picking up the cartridges after you have fired. If you do not wear plastic gloves when you load a clip, you may as well leave a calling card. Fingerprints are forever. My work is up close. A small-caliber revolver is enough. Revolvers hold their cartridges even after the bullet has been fired. Have you shot anyone?"

"Not yet. Would you shoot someone if I hired you? Have you shot many?"

He chewed his lip with uncertainty and sidestepped her question. "I will give you some advice you did not ask for, so it is worth all you pay for it."

"Which is not a cent." She saw again why her mother loved this man whose core seemed to be nothing more complicated than melancholy.

"Don't."

"That's funny advice coming from a man whose trade is to erase people. 'Erase.' That's the word you used, right?"

Pierre leaned forward to take one of her cigarettes. "I will smoke one cigarette to tell you a story." He sat back in his chair, the towel wrapped over his head and shoulders like an exhausted boxer's. "I was very close to my mother. Maman could afford nothing. When I left home, all she could give me was advice. She told me, 'Whatever you do, be the best at it.'"

"That is good advice."

"It is. Maman was never wrong. I hope to see her again at the Gates of Heaven before I am cast into Hell, not because God is merciful to me, but because God will reward her. She will ask me what I did, and all I will be able to say is that I killed people. I built nothing. I created no life. I kill very well and very cleanly with no cruelty or pain. I will never kill a woman. Maman stays with her *beau gamin*, not a ghost, but a voice in my head. A voice that comes to me in my dreams. She has said to me that, when you kill a man, it is the greatest crime because you steal all his days to come and that means you rob God because only God own days. No one may rob God without paying."

"Even if someone deserves killing?"

"Especially if someone deserves killing. God is jealous of His justice. It is our place to forgive."

"But not you. So you believe in God?"

"I pray God does not exist."

They both smiled. Pierre lowered his eyes and placed his burning cigarette on the lip of an ashtray. "Kill no one." He extinguished the cigarette as Buckles lit another for herself. "If there is someone you want dead, we can take care of it. You'd never have to know."

"I need to do it myself or not at all."

"That's vengeance, not necessity."

Buckles returned a steely gaze.

Pierre sat back. "You took all that better than KJ supposed you would."

"She thinks I am still a little girl."

"You will always be her little girl," Pierre said. "The house dick has been eyeballing you since you came in. No, don't look. He does not care if you are a hooker come to meet me in his hotel as long as we do our business upstairs and out of sight, but if he suspects you are cruising for clients in his lobby, he will need to act."

"Why would he think I am a hooker?"

"Take no offense, but this is San Francisco, I am a tourist in an Aloha shirt so loud it can be heard in Los Angeles, I am older, and, forgive me, you have a certain look some might think was commercial. Black leather and short hair. It would surprise no one if I were paying you."

Her coffee had cooled. With sudden insight, she saw how things were. "The two of you planned this little ambush. My mother wanted us to talk without her." She smiled slyly.

Pierre's thin lips allowed a faint smile. "*Formidable*. KJ is eager for you to know our plan and whether you will want to join us, and for that you needed to understand our import-export trade. It turns out you carry a larger weapon." He toweled his hair dry of the final trace of sweat. "You know, your mother is the least self-conscious woman I've ever known. Happy to be who she is. Doesn't make a fetish of how she looks. I'd call it self-confidence, but she doesn't care about labels. She just goes forward."

"That's funny. The woman who taught me to drive a car tore away the rearview mirror so I could not be distracted by what we passed."

"You are very much alike. The only blemish on her life was you disappearing. It left a hole in her." A shade of regret darkened Buckles' eyes. Pierre hastened to say: "But she made peace with that, I think. You went when you had to."

"What about my father?"

"You mean for her or for you or for me?"

Buckles shrugged.

"*Pour moi*, I never knew the man. Your mother also does not make a fetish of her past, so your father for her is not much more than a memory. Their only connection was you. But you are grown, now. She moved to Manhattan, I think even before the divorce was official. Walked away from a house and car, but has never looked back. Became involved with a theater project that failed. She told you all about that. For your mother, the only question is always 'What is next?'"

"She has not called my Dad?"

"She is leaving that to you."

"Mom is very far from the woman I knew as my mother. The same, but different. Did you do that?"

"KJ was never meant to be a suburban housewife. It is not in her, or if it was, when you vanished, it was extinguished. She'd have left Jack sooner or later. She deserved better."

Buckles smiled. "Meaning you?"

"*Mon Dieu, non.* I am not a good man, *cher*. Not at all a good man. Do you believe in Fate?" He tapped his spoon dry on the serving tray. The gesture was delicate. His nails were manicured, while hers were chewed to ragged cuticles.

"That's a funny question, but yes, I do, some." She sat back against the hard chair. "Not Fate like in old books, but in general. We are born with chances, but they are limited by who we are."

"How did one so young get so smart?" The towel hood dropped from his head and he rolled it into a rough collar.

"I read a lot."

"*Moi aussi.* We shall talk more about books another day. But now your mother expects us soon." He dabbed his lip dry on a paper napkin. "We met when we were younger than you are now. I don't think you know that. In New Orleans. A chance meeting on the street. I did not know who she was, and she did not know me, but I thought how this girl with her initials on her blouse and yellow hair could make me happy as someone I was not but wanted to become. A dream, really. But then we lost each other. That was Fate."

"The war?"

"*Non.* I never served. I was a boy loose in a big city in love with cards and the streets. A gambler. I cheated to live. I was so good at it I was hired to deal in illegal casinos. That's a long story, but also not for today."

"The same woman who taught me to drive and smashed my rearview mirror said a man who did not gamble had no blood in his veins."

"Wise again, but a gambler must know when to quit. It is possible to win, but impossible to beat the house. I learned that lesson while your mother went to school. You could say we attended different colleges. Then Fate again. I was in New York. Rain canceled my flight from LaGuardia. I stepped into an antiquarian bookstore and there was your mother. The thunderbolt struck a second time. It took us a while to realize we'd met before. After that, whenever business took me again to New York, we stayed together. Then we began to travel together." He seemed to savor the memory. "May I telephone her now?"

"Will you say I am armed?"

"Only if you want me to."

"I might, someday. But not now."

"*Bon.*"

Pierre dialed the room from a bank of house phones at the lobby's edge. Buckles asked a busboy for more coffee and a third setup, then lighted a fresh cigarette. The house detective seemed happier when Pierre rejoined Buckles. They people-watched until KJ stepped from an elevator onto the atrium floor. Her mother, once a subdued housewife, strode as if she owned the place. She had learned to swagger. As if a refugee from Scarsdale ready for a hard day of sightseeing, she wore white pumps and white pants with a crimson scarf knotted at her neck. Nothing about her was subdued; everything about her said certainty.

KJ was no Grandma Dot. Her mother had eaten the same breakfast for as long as Buckles could remember, half an English muffin, burned, with a smear of peanut butter, a half grapefruit, and, like Buckles, black coffee. Pierre ate even less, black coffee and a Danish. "You can only get a decent beignet in New Orleans," he said. Since Grandma had crossed her mind, Buckles thought to ask for a waffle with extra whipped cream, smiled to herself, and stayed with nothing more than coffee.

KJ told her they were leaving the country. "You can join us. We'd be pleased. It's a retirement of sorts. You'll need a passport, so I brought these for you." She snapped open her purse and withdrew Abigail Sinclair's birth certificate, the child of John and Kelly Jo. "Use my New York address." She scribbled it on a napkin. "I've not lived there for a while, but I still pay rent. The name 'Sinclair' is on the lease."

Buckles squinted with doubt. Pierre asked if any of the people Buckles had met in her travels knew her true name. "Only Pussy," she said. "The gay boy they put in jail for desertion."

"They have no reason to interrogate him," Pierre said, "and he has no reason to trade information for a lighter sentence. Besides, he is probably out by now."

"Do you think so?" Buckles' heart quickened.

"Don't search for him. If you found him, he might be watched. Then you would take his place in a cell." Pierre said he believed that no paper trail connected Abigail 'Buckles' Sinclair the hippie hitch-hiker to Florence Goodbody the Wisconsin student to Abigail Carpenter the knocked-up cheerleader known far and wide as the subversive Mother Abigail.

All that followed her might be Florence Goodbody's finger-prints, the fucked up kid from Wisconsin, and those prints would be filed on a card somewhere. The Feebs were creating a database of millions of prints in computers, but not yet. Her identity was open. She could choose to be herself.

"Where will you go?" Buckles asked.

"*La Gomera*," Pierre said.

"That's not in France," her mother said. "It's Spanish, an island city off the coast of Morocco. Part of the Canary Islands. An extinct volcano that sticks its head out of the Atlantic Ocean. To get there you have to fly first to Tenerife and then take a ferry or charter a private seaplane. We have arranged a villa there on a cliff over the ocean facing Tenerife itself. I've not seen it yet, but Pierre says the views are magnificent."

"It sounds out of the way."

"That's the point," Pierre said. "I never thought I'd get there, but now it seems like the right idea. If *Newsweek* had not run your picture, we'd have already been there."

Buckles thought, then extinguished her cigarette. His tone told her they had put themselves at risk, delaying their departure. What, she wondered, pursued them? "I can't go with you. Not yet, anyway. I have two bits of business I have to finish."

Pierre looked up sharply at her from under his lowered brows. "Can we help?"

"Promises must be kept. Promises to myself."

"Are you sure you have to do it at all?" he asked.

Buckles nodded.

Her mother looked worried. "But you'll visit. I can't stand losing you a second time."

"I will when I am done, Mom, I swear it. Expect a long visit someday."

Pierre put his hand over KJ's wrists to still further talk. "*Cher*, your child is a grown woman. She will do what she must." He turned to Buckles. "*Les Beauchamps*. You can always find *les Beauchamps*. They are the wealthy emigres from Quebec who live on top of the mountain in the house with walls of glass on the Tenerife side of the island. Made their fortune in the import business."

"People think that means drugs."

"*Mais bien*. That will leave people with a touch of fear." He withdrew a roll of currency from his pocket held by a red rubber band. Sure no one saw him, he casually handed the bills to Buckles. "For plane fare when you are ready. It is two thousand."

"I can't take that."

"We insist. Life is too hard without money. Money means options. It ensures your mother will see you again. Please."

Buckles chewed her lower lip. "I will trade you my sunglasses." She took hold of the beaded cord that hung at her neck.

KJ smiled. "Sunglasses?"

"They were given to me by Grandma Dot. I told you about her. The one swept away by a tornado. She was crazy, but no fool. She took me in when I needed help. Her plan for me and her grandson did not work out quite as she hoped. He was arrested. No one lives happily ever after. But look closely at the left side. You see the pockmarks that used to hold stones? I removed them as I needed. A little heat and a nail file. The two stones still in the plastic are not rhinestones." KJ took the glasses. "They will make lovely earrings. Grandma would like that you wear them and think of me. When I come to visit, please wear them." Pierre started to object, but Buckles reminded him he had offered to help and this was the only help she could accept. "You can save me the trouble of finding a fence and persuading him to buy from a stranger. It's never been terribly difficult, but it has its risks, and I am always cheated on the price."

"Is there blood on these stones?"

"I think no. Grandma said diamonds are untraceable. Like I said, she was crazy, but no fool."

Buckles fastened her leather tunic as they walked to the Hyatt's street escalator. Light filtered through the atrium's glass.

"You're going on that wild goose chase with that map, aren't you?"

"I have to."

"And the other thing?"

"I have to do that, too. Don't ask me what."

They embraced. It took a while for the two women to part. Pierre stood off to the side. KJ stroked her daughter's head with her hand as if Buckles was an infant, and then Buckles sank from view. From the escalator's bottom, she looked up to where her mother wore a brave face. She blew KJ a kiss.

"That's quite a girl," Pierre said.

"No thanks to me."

"I doubt that."

"You gave her back her diamonds?"

"*Bien sur*. She will find them in her pocket where I dropped them."

KJ kissed his cheek.

Her life in Oakland was ended. She used a dime to unscrew the plate off a newer rice burner in the lot and slipped it into her tunic pocket, where she found the sunglasses Pierre must have returned to her beside the roll of bills he'd pressed on her. She should take the time to exchange Lilith's tags someplace less public. Since Lilith had never been legally registered, Buckles periodically stole a fresh tag now and again. It was like giving sweets to her best friend, not to mention it would be the depths of stupidity to be stopped somewhere by some sharp-eyed pig who noticed an expired tag. Even if it took only a few days for the theft to be reported, and even if every pig in the Bay area did nothing but look for a stolen California motorcycle plate, Buckles and Lilith would by then be long gone.

Whether she would ever again see her mother was an open question. All she knew for certain was that everyone she ever loved became an outlaw. The crowd that opposed John Law and the Power now included her mother, her mother's very smooth, murderous boyfriend, angry Celeste, poor Pussy, mad Grandma, and, yes, herself. Outlaws all. She never found the Revolution, but had made her own.

South of Barstow, Lilith's engine purred near silent in the gathering darkness of their beloved desert, the black-clad woman and her machine slipping through gathering night. On long stretches of road, Buckles extinguished Lilith's headlight. In the slight moon's light, though the speedometer needle had them at 85, they seemed to be afloat and barely moving. Emerging stars were immobile; brooding silhouettes of faraway mountains drew no closer. Why had she delayed spending another night on her blanket roll yards beyond the edge of an asphalt road? She exchanged Lilith's license plate and used to the old one to scoop a shallow depression in the dry earth, then gathered fist-size rocks to encircle a crackling fire she crated from a few dry sticks. The desert night cooled quickly. Leaning back onto her two elbows, smoking a cigarette, Buckles felt as though she'd at last returned to where she belonged, alone beneath an open sky and a river of stars.

She'd be calling on Big Bill. Nothing else would bring her peace.

She'd not realized that her time in California had loaded so much tension into her shoulders until her back and neck muscles unknotted under the stars and she no longer needed a joint to pass the night. She'd doubled her bedroll, used her helmet as a hard pillow, stayed clear of *arroyos*, looked for snakes and spiders, and by sunup discovered endurable bug bites on her legs that itched but were not crippling. With her return to the pebbled and baked land of the desert, her shoulders dropped and became limp, and her breathing eased. California was a land of crazies.

She could have spent the rest of her life unwinding, and that would not have been a waste of her life, but there was work that had to be done. She needed a night in a room to sleep in a bed, to buy a decent meal or two, and rent enough privacy to finish what she'd started. She found a small roadside court a half mile from a very ordinary diner, wolfed down a western omelet with a side of corned beef hash that did not taste like reheated death, showered, and was asleep before sunset.

Her mind churned as she slept. By morning, her plan was clear. She would first need to overcome her fear of building an explosive more powerful than a wine bottle filled with gasoline and corked by a tampon.

Building a pipe bomb had much in common with preparing a meal for 50 people. She'd memorized the recipe after tearing the pages from a copy of *The Anarchist's Cookbook*. Like Mother Abigail's stew, the instructions were simple and basic. Assemble the ingredients, work in a properly ventilated place, avoid accidentally killing yourself. A little creativity was all right, but where straying from the best procedure for a stew might spoil the meal, a mistake with a pipe bomb could create either a dud or an accident that would blow her own ass to Kingdom Come.

She stopped for basic provisions and to fill a canteen. She had no trouble getting a CB radio mounted on Lilith's handlebar over the throttle. It did not block her left mirror. The black pigtail cord went to a headset that fit under her helmet. The guy who installed it at a dusty motorcycle shop was younger than she and seemed intimidated by her, unable to hold eye contact. "If you don't want a headset to talk to no passengers, just keep it on 19," he said. "You'll have more company than you can stand." She asked about his tools and he gave up a hardware store down the highway. She came away with a drill guide and a 5 mm drill.

As she crossed the Arizona border, she risked her first CB message. "This is Little Cherry Lollipop eastbound. Come back." Static was general, but listeners knew a woman's voice when they heard it. In two hours, she had four requests for her 20 and offers for a night of fun and relaxation. She told her suitors that Little Cherry Lollipop's truck was tight enough for a woman alone, much less a woman and a friend. The word *tight* got the hoots and coarse puns she expected. Men were so damned easy. She played the tease for a while more, grew bored with it, and decided not turn the radio back on until she was closer to Albuquerque, the place Big Bill once claimed held his little piece of heaven. Every detail of that night haunted her still, every word and gesture remained indelible.

It was time to do some erasing.

It was nothing to find black electrical tape, four six-inch lengths of two-inch lead pipe, eight pipe caps, and epoxy. "Repairs," she muttered and paid extra while the store turned the pipes in a lathe so that the caps would fit perfectly.

She picked up cheap binoculars, not much more than a toy, but good enough for what she had in mind. Obtaining cotton for wadding was as easy as walking into a drugstore, as was getting her hands on a few heavy-duty firecrackers. What town didn't look the other way on July 4th? She settled on something called ashcans, mildly illegal M80 sticks of black powder attached to three inches of fuse, presumably long enough for any idiot setting one off to get far enough away or throw it twenty feet without blowing his fool head off. That night, she scraped the ground with her boot heel and placed an ashcan firecracker in the dirt. It exploded with a sound to shake down hills. Though she was fifteen feet away she was showered by dry dirt. No wonder pipe bombs were the explosive of choice of terrorists everywhere.

Black powder proved trickiest, but since hobbyists made their own ammunition all over Arizona, the stuff could be had without petty legal forms. All she needed to do was bat her eyes, broadcast a broad smile, and touch a man's wrist. If all that failed, she'd offer a small bribe.

In a gun shop west of Winslow, no one questioned her story that she was in search of the perfect gift for her father, a collector of antique Colt revolvers. Grandma would have been proud of her, natural-born grifter. The mark recommended Hodgdon black powder. It needed careful handling, but her father the experienced gun collector could be trusted. "Try not to open the stuff and get yourself blowed up before you get this to your Daddy," the clerk said. She allowed her eyes to round with wonder and admiration as he educated her about Wyatt Earp and his brothers mixing it up at the O.K. Corral down in Tombstone, as if she cared about some dead dick-slinger. Her first time across Arizona, when she'd fled Illinois and zigzagged across the southwest, she'd seen the billboards to visit the O.K. Corral. *Stand Where They Fell!* Near Bisbee, she'd read Earp's story, a gambler and whoremaster who with his brothers straddled both sides of the law, just another American hero famous for gunning down fellow citizens.

She came away with two pounds of Hodgdon's and rolled further east on the old Route 66, a piece of America being discarded where it was not being modernized. They were calling it the interstate system, and the idea was to create roads that went coast-to-coast without a traffic light; only incidentally those broad new highways would also be designed to allow quick military deployment into every corner of America and could in a pinch serve as landing strips for all manner of aircraft, which is why electric wires so seldom crossed the interstate roads.

Buckles could not resist standing on a corner in Winslow. Damn, but she liked that song. She rolled a joint, sat on the curbstone, and took it easy.

Buckles took a room near Winslow. At midday, she drew her room's curtains and turned on every light before she invented a serviceable worktable by pulling two dresser drawers free of the motel room's furniture and flipping them face down on the bed. She grounded everything in the room, including herself, unplugged the TV, and checked the lamp cords to be sure no wiring was frayed. She then segregated her supply of black powder behind the closet door.

The first step was to set the drill guide on each of the lengths of pipe. She was nervous about running the drill itself, but that was why the black powder was resting behind a closet door where no accidental spark from the drill's coil or anywhere else in the room might find its way to the explosive. She'd need only two drilled pipes, but had obtained four lengths on the expectation she'd screw at least one up, but she worked slowly and carefully, her hands steady, and when no screw-up happened, she grew confident. When each of two pipes were drilled dead center, she spit on a few inches of black thread, looped and tied it around an ashcan fuse, and then with the point of her Piranha switchblade worked the spit-damp thread to the drilled hole, drawing the firecracker into the pipe with its fuse outside. That was easier than she thought it would be; her hands were nimble from dicing onions back in Oakland. She taped the fuses down on the outside of the pipe, set them with epoxy, carefully washed the ends of the pipe with a touch of Lilith's engine oil, and then hand-tightened one end of the threaded pipe with a threaded cap. She went for a two-hour walk to wait for the epoxy to dry solid.

The sunlight made her blink. The motel had eight rooms; if anyone else had spent the prior night at the motor court, they were gone. Buckles, at lunchtime, was the only remaining occupant. She saw no convenient diner and wanted to be sure no one entered her room, so she sat on a metal chair that must have been painted red and white a million years ago, but sun and wind had bleached the red to a vague pink, the white trim was chipped, and the chair's bolts were rust- stained. She gnawed on some beef jerky she took from Lilith's saddle bag. When a Mexican housekeeper came to the room, Buckles waved her away. "*Más tarde, gracias,*" she said. The desert sky was clear of clouds. She tilted back in the metal chair. Though she never owned a watch and did not care to, she could not say with precision how much time passed. It seemed likely that she dozed.

Buckles tested the epoxy with a finger. It was solid, the ashcan fuses seemed intact. It was time for the delicate work.

She splashed her face with cool water and prepared her switch-blade again by opening it in advance. Since she had no funnel, she poured black powder onto a creased sheet of paper and poured about an inch of the stuff into a drilled pipe. She half expected she'd blink and explode, but her hands stayed steady and her breathing stayed regular. She understood the basics: the greater the compression, the greater the explosion. Using her opened knife, she carefully tamped the layer of black powder with a narrow layer of cotton wadding, poured in more powder, tamped it flat again, and repeated the process until a pipe was filled, taking extra care when the tube of cotton and powder had to be worked around her firecracker detonator. When the pipe filled, she walked away, drew a nervous breath, steadied her breath, and then closed her eyes as she touched the metal leg of the room's bed to discharge any static electricity. When nothing happened, she wiped the pipe's open end with a rag she'd dipped in Lilith's motor oil to suppress any chance of a spark, and then hand-tightened a cap on the remaining open end. Then she washed her hands and repeated the entire process for a second pipe.

Before setting out on Lilith, she offered her remaining black powder to the wind and put both her safely sealed bombs in Lilith's left saddlebag beside the three capped wine bottles. As long as no flame invaded her saddlebag, her explosives would remain dormant, but for safety's sake, if she stopped, she would park Lilith in shade. She estimated she had enough explosives to boost a small tank into orbit. Maybe a large tank.

She decided to approach Albuquerque from the south, which meant she had to cross the last of Arizona by abandoning the main roads and travel over land not much more than clay baked solid by the sun, sterile land on which the government had settled Indian reservations. She headed north hugging the Rio Grande. At Socorro, she paid cash for room 104 at The Oasis, a whitewashed cinderblock motor court curled around a blue gem of a swimming pool and two pitiful half-dead palm trees. The pool reminded her of Tuscola where frightened teenage boys tossed plastic lounge chairs into the water as a tornado bore down on them.

Either she had lived a full life or at 24 she had grown old: Everything reminded her of something from her past. It had been a long time since she'd been in anything as soothing as a warm swimming pool, so she carefully placed Lilith's clinking saddlebags on her room's bed, remounted Lilith, and found a nearby shop that sold her an aqua-and-yellow bathing suit. Her neck and wrists were dark as a field hand's, but the rest of her was sickly pale. A mirror showed her a bony white girl made scrawny by stoop labor.

In the sun on a recliner, she forced her mind blank. Over planning could become obsessive, and she'd make more errors than if she planned nothing at all. Her past revisited her, pulling her back to her days at Dobbs when she'd swum wind-sprints a half-dozen pool lengths at a time, succeeding with creditable flip turns. She'd been pretty good if not a star, second leg in a freestyle 400-yard relay team. The great attraction of swimming had always been the total physical effort that halted all thought, the regulated breathing, the rhythms of her entire body, and the delicious isolation and utter silence that buoyed her up, face down in water. A competitive swimmer hears no cheering crowd, but only the beating of her own heart. At The Oasis pool, Buckles grabbed her knees to her chest and bobbed weightless, holding her breath as long as she was able, her eyes open wide in clear water. How had a girl on a high school swimming team arrived in New Mexico to do murder?

Wishing she had a large-brimmed straw hat, she resigned herself to a nasty sunburn. Topless at her parents' pool when she was a girl, she'd burned herself to the color of dark toast applying nothing more than baby oil mixed with iodine. She put a stem of Grandma's sunglasses between her lips.

On the pool's far side, thirty yards from the pool deck beyond a galvanized steel fence, Socorro's main street ran north-south. Whenever the sun grew too hot, she dipped again, swimming sleek as a seal. Desert air dried her in seconds. Was she ready to grow her hair to what it had been before she fled Illinois? All that brushing and all that detangling, all a girlie waste of time was perhaps not so stupid; the hundred nightly brush strokes her mother required had become a ritual that centered Buckles.

Two families joined her, their three kids with infinite energy jumping in and out of the water yelling *Marco Polo*. The fathers drank from sweating brown bottles of Dos Equis they pulled from a blue metal cooler filled with sloshing ice, more beer, and several cans of lemonade. One of the mothers fished out a bottle of Corona, and offered it to Buckles. She accepted it. It was cold as a beer could be. The woman who uncapped Buckles' Corona moved awkwardly and with some effort, smiling, as she placed her palm on her stomach and said, "She's kicking the hell out of me today. Seven months. This one will be a girl, I think. A fighter, for sure."

The pregnant woman was named Marilyn. She was no older than Buckles, probably younger. Buckles introduced herself as Abby. The third woman, less talkative, was Reina. Their husbands were Pedro and Richie, both of whom operated heavy equipment for New Mexico Potash. They were vacationing together, a half day's drive from home, returned to The Oasis because it had a pool, color TV, and they could afford it. In two days they would take in the balloon fiesta.

"Are you going?" Marilyn asked.

Buckles knew nothing about it, but she was interested to learn that just a few years ago an Albuquerque radio station had dreamed up a publicity stunt.

"It just grew and grew," Marilyn said, cracking open her can of lemonade. Dozens of hot air balloons slowly rise from the valley floor to ride updrafts up the sides of the Sandia Mountains. "They get real high. We were here last year and the kids were excited to see it again." Marilyn's eyes never strayed from the children at the pool's edge.

This was the life Buckles had skipped.

Back east, Buckles would have had more options than the two young mothers because she came from wealth, but the essentials— work, husbands, and a crowd of children—would have been the same. It had once sounded like death in life to her; right now, it did not seem at all bad.

She'd left Scarsdale a flower child in search of America, contemptuous of people who did not embrace the coming of an age of peace and love, but on her journey to make that age of peace and love come into being, she'd passed over balloon festivals, swimming pools, cold beer, noisy kids, lazy husbands, days of bright sunshine, and idle chatter with strangers. Now that Buckles was intent on blowing up Big Bill, she could not help but wonder if that life might not have been enough.

Buckles lowered herself into four feet of cooling water beside Marilyn, their elbows folded behind them on the pool deck. Then the three kids, brown, wet, and slippery, took turns leaping into their outstretched arms. Buckles wondered at the immediate trust the children had in her, a stranger drinking a bottle of their parents' beer. They splashed in the water beside her and locked their arms around her neck.

When Marilyn and Reina invited Buckles and her man to join them for dinner, they were mildly surprised that Buckles rode that motorcycle alone. No one disapproved, but Marilyn said Abby had to admit a woman traveling alone on a motorcycle was unusual. "And brave, too," Reina added, with the faintest note of jealousy.

After a time, the two wives gathered their kids and smother-wrapped them in towels. "We always go to Blake's," Marilyn said. "If you have a mind, you can join us. It's just burgers, but the kids love the place. It is where we go every year. But I guess you have a date, right?"

"Don't do anything I wouldn't," Reina said, and Marylyn playfully slapped at Reina's arm.

"There's not much Reina wouldn't," Marilyn said, their husbands ahead and safely out of earshot. The two mothers giggled like teenagers, which, Buckles realized, they practically were.

She liked them. She said she just might show up for a burger after all, but knew she would not. She skipped any evening meal to sit alone and smoke in the open air. What might two young mothers have thought to learn that their new friend into whose arms their children had trustingly leapt hid enough explosives hidden in Room 104 to turn The Oasis into a smoking crater?

In the morning, riding south she put out a her first feeler over Channel 19. Little Cherry Lollipop hoped to learn the 20 of her old buddy, Big Bill and his rig, the *Donna May*. There was plenty of chatter on the highways from El Paso to Albuquerque. Buckles turned down the squelch to make out what was what. There was a Kojak with a Kodak in the spaghetti approaching El Paso and plenty of offers to take the back door on any convoy Little Cherry Lollipop cared to join. She was asked why as a friendly lady she did not sleep late, and she explained that the Lollipop was not against good times, loved to sleep late, and with a throaty laugh Grandma Dot would have admired because it left so much unsaid, explained she was indeed a friendly working girl, but also a full-blooded licensed driver on a westbound short run in a boss man's Freightliner hauling a skateboard from Armadillo to the Sticker Patch. She hoped to join up with her old buddy, Big Bill, on the flipside.

Then she went silent, listening. Broadcasting in search of Big Bill was like casting a filament of line into a trout stream. That made her the lure. She might attract a nibble from a new wave of drivers before casting again. Claiming she was a trucker, while she rode Lilith in slow circles south, she put out two more breakers hoping to learn *Donna May*'s 20 before she illegally crossed a highway divider and came about to head north again. She passed right through Socorro and passed The Oasis, then stopped a few miles beyond NM 6 where she checked into a new place that called itself the Hacienda Motor Lodge.

Close to Albuquerque, The Hacienda's rooms were nearly filled with *touristas* and their children. Buckles was lucky to get Room 212, a second floor room at the end of a concrete walkway that overlooked an alley, a low row of what might be repair garages, and then endless desert. The day was not done, and Buckles might have hunted some more, but her eyes ached. She planned the next day to cruise a half dozen roads west of the Rio Grande, trolling for any sight of Big Bill or a Peterbilt named *Donna May*.

Lilith's saddlebags fit in the bottom drawer of her room's bureau. What she'd worn for most of a week was ripe, so she soaked her duds in a tiny bathroom sink of hot water after scrubbing them with a bar of motel soap. She changed into her spare underpants and her spare T-shirt, wrung out her clothes, and on the walkway before her room draped her laundry on the railing.

She leaned her chair back against a wall to enjoy a cigarette as evening gathered. She left the radio on and room door open, listening to Albuquerque. Her bare legs were pale and lean. When she'd been a girl back East, she'd have taken pride that her thighs did not touch. She and her mother might have planned pedicures. If anyone saw the knobby-toed young woman wearing only her ratty green T-shirt and her bare legs up to hold her feet to a bar, they would have had an eyeful. But who gave a crap what such people thought? Even her mother, whom she'd once thought hopeless, had run from that sort.

Buckles sifted through what she wanted to do and what she could genuinely make happen. Big Bill might be dead or in jail, but if that were the case she'd need to know it so she could either piss on his grave or discover a way to pour gasoline into his cell before she threw her lighted Zippo in after it.

She helicoptered her cigarette butt two stories to the ground, then unrolled her cigarette pack from her shoulder to withdraw one of the three joints she had left from Oakland. She'd smoked two in the deserts of Arizona. They were exceedingly good shit, rolled from some of Ishtar's finest weed.

Her reveries turned on how badly she needed to be up close to see the prick as he died. The closer she'd be, the riskier the plan. She ought to be satisfied with just making him dead, but that was Pierre Doucet's way, not hers.

She'd need to tape two pipe bombs to each of *Donna May*'s two diesel fuel drums located under the driver's seat. That much seemed basic to every plan that came together in her mind. Under cover of night, she's need to crawl on her belly under the truck with six five-inch lengths of tape attached to the chest of her leather tunic, roll to her back to use three lengths of tape to fasten a pipe bomb to each drum, laying their fuses to one side, not pointing to the ground, and then shimmy her ass back out. She'd do that under the cover of darkness in the smallest hours of a morning.

Then what?

She might wait for Big Bill to set out. The truck would cough thunder while it warmed up. Diesel always took a bit of time to start, which was why truckers left their engines running when they were not moving. Buckles would watch from a distance with her binoculars. She'd come down hard on Lilith's kick-starter when the truck began rolling. Lilith and she could emerge from her hiding place and pace *Donna May*. The engine still cold, the truck would be sluggish at first, with or without a trailer. She'd be in her leathers, of course, her night spent in darkness at the roadside waiting from a few hundred yards off. She'd have prepared two wine-bottle Molotov cocktails by twisting off their tin caps and then resealing the bottles with tampons that, once soaked, would flame steadily until she broke the glass or until they burned out. For easier access, she'd need to move the primed firebombs from her left saddlebag to the plastic mesh laundry bag she'd hang on her right handlebar. Pacing Big Bill, Buckles would lift her visor so he'd know the motorcyclist beside him was a girl. Counting on at least a few seconds of surprise, she'd smile, and then throw him the finger. She hoped he would grin and prayed he still had that big black beard because it would burn so well. She had no illusion Big Bill would recognize her, but the son-of-bitch would follow Little Bill, and Little Bill would be in charge from the moment Big Bill saw her smile. Then, still smiling, she'd spin the flint of her Zippo and ignite her first Molotov cocktail.

That was the moment at which her imagination divided among several alternatives. If his cab window were open, she might try for the window shot just to see his eyes go wide with disbelief and fear. But a window shot had to be tricky for two moving vehicles that would not be moving at the same speed, like playing making a basketball show from a moving train. Even if she succeeded, if the wine bottle did not immediately shatter, Big Bill might be able to toss it free of the cab. In any event, she'd have to throw a second bottle to ignite her firecracker detonators in the pipe bombs taped to the fuel tanks under *Donna May's* cab and Big Bill's ass. Whichever tank blew first would certainly blow the second. The most certain try was to launch both fire bombs at the fuel drums. Only a touch of flame was needed to ignite ashcan fuses, burn past the epoxy sealant, and blow Big Bill and *Donna May* to Hell. Fancy one-handed motorcycling would surely slow her down, so she'd need to accelerate hard and fast to get far enough away. She just might manage it.

That plan had the attraction of looking Bill in the eye, but she might be better off simply running well past *Donna May* and laying down a wall of fire across the road itself. She'd have to get lucky to have the flames find the fuses, though. *Donna May* might be slow enough through the flames, but even then the odds of a fuse instantly catching fire seemed remote. She'd be left in the middle of the road with a truck bearing down on her accelerating through a curtain of black smoke and red fire. She'd be waiting with a third firebomb ready, it was true, but head-on had to be the worst possible angle to ignite the bombs taped under the cab.

She'd need to get up close and personal to insure she could see the *Donna May* shudder and then lift from the ground on two orange fireball explosions that lifted and tipped the truck over onto its side, tires in the air, a burning iron coffin sweeping on edge toward her. If God loved her, she'd see Bill through the smoke as he caught fire before he and *Donna May* and whatever trailer he was hauling fused into a pile of molten garbage.

None of it seemed likely, though. It required too much luck.

Buckles lit another cigarette.

She should stop planning this elaborate Road Runner cartoon shit and simply place the barrel of her pistol an inch from the smug prick's eye to blow away his worthless face and empty his skull of brains. He'd be just as dead.

The sun was a palm's width above the desert horizon to the west of The Hacienda Motor Lodge. Long shadows stretched closer to her. The temperature of the New Mexico night would be dropping quickly. She would soon need more clothing than a pair of bikini cotton underwear and a sleeveless T-shirt. Gooseflesh puckered her arms and thighs.

The music from her room's radio was a mariachi band. They played *Adelita,* the song of female revolution. It put her in mind to have a meal of *chiles rellenos* and *cervezas* in some hole-in-the-wall dive where the flaking walls reeked of cooking oil and there was a jukebox with few Anglo songs, but once The Cherry Red Lollipop dressed and threw her leg over Lilith, she rebroadcast her lure on 19. Within seconds, a voice calling himself none other than the one and only Memphis Cowboy said he was kind of maybe almost certain that possibly if he wasn't wrong, and he could be mind you, while he knew nothing about no man calling hisself Big Bill, he'd once see'd a rig stenciled *Donna May* off-road in a backwater shithole called Jarales. She thanked her new good buddy and told him she owed him bigtime.

She left Lilith's motor running to sprint up the flight of concrete stairs to 212. In the yellow light of a 40-watt desk lamp she pored over her wrinkled roadmap. She checked the clip in her gun and grabbed her saddlebags. Jarales was less than fifteen minutes away, ten if she redlined Lilith's tachometer.

It did not take long to circle in on the *Donna May*. Sure it was Big Bill's, she rode past to stop more than a little more than a football field away. She cut Lilith's engine and pushed the bike off road as she'd done a thousand times before. The sky was dense with stars, but no moon would rise that night. Buckles balanced her helmet on the BMW seat and lay prone on a very slight rise to inspect the scene with her cheap binoculars. They were no more than a toy, but at this distance in the half darkness, they would do.

The *Donna May* stood cold beside a doublewide mobile home. The cab was hitched to an empty flat trailer that might haul heavy equipment lashed to it. Big Bill was probably home on an overnight stay in the middle of a short run and had stopped for his own bed. He'd be gone by morning. Indistinct silhouettes moved inside the well-lighted trailer home.

She learned Big Bill did not live alone. She could not see the details of the flower beds on each side of the prefab house, but any sort of flowers in the desert meant someone watered the ground to care for living things. That surely could not be Big Bill himself.

Buckles' knife cut several lengths of black tape that she stuck to her chest. She loosed the newspaper wrapping from the wine bottles, unscrewed their caps, checked the gasoline and Styrofoam mix, and stoppered each again with an absorbent, flammable tampon. She tenderly lay them on their sides so the tampons might soak through.

Time crept. She lay on her belly in the dirt peering through her binoculars, but eventually the mobile home's interior lights first dimmed and then went dark. It was time. Her pulse was steady; her breathing regular. She left her 952 Modello in her upturned helmet, knowing she would be scuttling on her back. It would not do to have it discharge accidentally. She also left the binoculars before she draped her saddlebags around her neck and crouched into a duck-walk, counting on the night, her black leathers, and the *Donna May* between her and the doublewide trailer to keep her invisible. She tested the rocky ground at every step to ensure she'd not stumble and that her bottles of homemade napalm did not clink.

Uninterested in her, the snake she met under the truck quickly slithered away. Her knife scored the surface of the metal fuel drums to create a firm grip for her tape. As she peeled them from her chest, the strips of black electrical tape rasped like stubborn zippers. A shower of dry dirt and accumulated road crud fell into her eyes as she attached the pipe bombs to the underside of the fuel drums. It was one of those operations that called for three hands, but Buckles struggled, took her time, and got it right, the 3-inch ashcan fuses free with no chance of being accidentally extinguished once lit. Igniting the firecracker fuses of her pipe bombs with a flaming Molotov cocktail was like horseshoes and hand grenades—close was good enough.

She was halfway back to Lilith when light and sound from Big Bill's tin can house tumbled after her. It was quiet, but to Buckles in the silent desert, it sounded like marbles clattering down a washboard. Buckles wore no watch, but it must have been near 2:30 in the morning. Could Big Bill be setting out so early? She pivoted to see the silhouette of his woman backlit in the open trailer door, a squalling baby in her arms. She might have been Mexican; more likely she was Hopi or Navajo. Bells on the woman's moccasins faintly rattled. She chanted softly, surely a lullaby for her sleepless baby.

Where did Big Bill come off having a life? Maybe he'd found God and Jesus, too. What if instead of roaming American highways sodomizing underage girls, Big Bill now went to church to pray for his children and his own worthless soul? She doubted it, but stranger things had happened. Shouldn't a man pay for sins in this life? Or could he just be granted God's pardon? As a Flower Child she'd hauled herself up into the *Donna May*, an innocent. She regretted nothing she had done since that day, though she'd lied, cheated, stolen, and injured those who pursued her, but Buckles and her Beretta and her switchblade remained otherwise clean of blood.

She had prepared for retribution, not the murder of a man with a life worth having. Fate stuck its hand in again; revenge required she make Big Bill's woman a widow, his children orphans.

She would never be able to kill the son-of-a-bitch. Pierre's sole word of advice had been *Don't*.

Big Bill's woman and her baby returned to their trailer. The door closed. The moonless night returned to total darkness.

Buckles crouched motionless a long moment to be certain she was still unseen, then rolled Lilith forward keeping the hulking shadow of the *Donna May* between her and the trailer. The air was still; the stars hard. The truck and its flatbed rested at the unpaved road's edge, at least 100 yards from Bill's metal prefab home, but only about ten feet from where Lilith waited. Desert cicadas sang. Buckles turned the flint wheel of her Zippo, hoping the distances were sufficient for the baby and its mother to remain safe, and, yes, Big Bill safe as well. She hurled a lighted firebomb under the truck, heard the glass wine bottle shatter, smelled the gasoline and Styrofoam, and saw the first blue licks of flame flicker beneath the truck cab.

She came down hard on the kick-starter. Lilith roared to life and had her 200 yards down the road when the first pipe bomb exploded. Still running, Buckles turned her head and saw the first of the two fuel drums catch. The *Donna May* shuddered and lifted from the ground, the second drum exploded, and like a great wounded beast tethered to the flatbed trailer reared vertically, impossibly balanced on end, and fell back to its side in a pyre of black smoke and orange flame.

Buckles delayed her departure from New Mexico for the balloon fiesta. On the north side of Albuquerque near the Sandias, Buckles crossed her arms over her chest and leaned her hips against Lilith. Enormous multicolored balloons, striped orange, red, green, blue, and yellow, lay deflated and flat over the ground while propane burners forced heated air to fill them. They inflated and seemed alive, rising unsteadily, then more firmly, becoming incandescent and straining for release. At a signal Buckles neither saw nor heard, they shed their last restraints and floated silent and free into the sky.

She finally understood the first advice Grandma Dot had given her: *Wash the poison out of your life. Be whole. Pain is no private treasure. It's just pain.*

She detached Lilith's rearview mirrors and discarded them. What need? She would never again look back. She discarded the CB radio and its distracting patter, then pulled on her gloves tight, flexed her hands, lowered her helmet's visor, and raised the collar of her black leather tunic. She stood to straddle Lilith, then brought her Doc Martens down hard onto the kick-starter. She twisted the throttle. The BMW's grumble coughed into a roar, and the motorcycle shot forward.

She would dare to cross the lowest place in America, Death Valley, a place that no longer held any fear, but she would then climb skyward more than a mile to Lake Tahoe, rising from the parched earth into brooding pine forests where every tree strained heavenward on mountainsides that were no less than God's own hand cupping a lake filled by ice-blue water. She might or might not uncover the promised buried lockbox that had drawn her across the continent. What matter? It had sustained her with hope when she had none. Buckles would rise to breathe sweet air beside pure water beneath the sky that had no limits.

Haverhill Massachusetts, February 2021

About the Author

Now settled in Haverhill, Massachusetts, **Perry Glasser** has roamed America, living in New York City, Fort Lee, Tucson, Des Moines, and Wichita. He was named a Fellow in Creative Nonfiction for the Commonwealth by the Massachusetts Arts Council and is the author of three collections of short fiction, *Metamemoirs* a collection of self-reflective essays, and the prize-winning novel *Riverton Noir* (Gival Press).

Books by Perry Glasser

Suspicious Origins
Singing on the Titanic
Dangerous Places
Metamemoirs
Riverton Noir
The Ghost of Amelia Parkhurst

Printed by Imprimerie Gauvin
Gatineau, Québec